PRAISE FOR REBECCA ANDERSON

'Skilfully done . . . their struggles feel believable and nuanced.'
The Irish Times

'Wildly entertaining, shame-busting . . . an empowering novel.'
Inis Magazine

'Candid, relatable and reassuring. Fans of Holly
Bourne and Netflix's *Sex Education* will adore it.'
The i Paper

'Sensitive and honest. moving and insightful.
An excellent title that deserves promotion.'
The School Librarian

'A great book for those who need it.'
Bookseller review

'This book healed my inner teenager!'
Bookseller review

GALENTINE'S DAY

Rebecca Anderson lives in Hertfordshire with her partner and beloved guinea pigs, who she is obsessed with (the guinea pigs, obviously). She is a twin, has a degree in graphic design and is a practising counsellor with too many creative hobbies to list.

Her writing explores sex, relationships, friendships and mental health, which she tackles with honesty and humour.

rebecca anderson

GALENTINE'S DAY

avon.

Published by AVON
A division of HarperCollins*Publishers* Ltd
1 London Bridge Street
London SE1 9GF

www.harpercollins.co.uk

HarperCollins*Publishers*
Macken House, 39/40 Mayor Street Upper
Dublin 1, D01 C9W8, Ireland

A Paperback Original 2026
1

A catalogue record for this book is available from the British Library.

ISBN: 9780008765736

This novel is entirely a work of fiction. The names, characters and incidents portrayed in it are the work of the author's imagination. Any resemblance to actual persons, living or dead, events or localities is entirely coincidental.

Set in Sabon LT Pro by HarperCollins*Publishers* India

Printed and bound in the UK using 100% Renewable
Electricity at CPI Group (UK) Ltd

For my gals – my ride-or-dies – who've loved me through all my chapters, character development, and questionable side quests xxx

Also Amy, Maria and Cordelia – The OG Galentine girlies.

Prologue

Hannah

Hannah was back in dreary old England, and true to form, it was absolutely pissing it down. She didn't hate being home. England was fine, her apartment was fine. But her grandparents didn't totally uproot their lives in Uganda and come to Kensal Green for Hannah to live a *fine* life. They did it so she could live her *best* life, and life never felt better than when she was travelling, seeing new places and meeting new people.

There really was no need to settle for a boring life these days. There were more opportunities than ever to live extraordinarily. Christ, you could even make a fortune selling your worn Primarni socks or, heaven forbid, your own farts in a jar. Hannah missed that particular job opening but ended up with something much better. Well, not so much ended up but worked her perfect ass off to create her swimwear business using just an iPhone, a social media account and the drive to make the most of the opportunities she'd been so luckily afforded.

Hannah blinked at Alicia's front door – sage green with a brass knocker and framed by two symmetrical hanging flower baskets that she'd no doubt chosen before even getting the keys. *Deep breath. You've got this. You're strong. You're . . . Oh God, what am I doing here?* Yes, it was tradition for the three of them to meet every Galentine's Day since they were eighteen, but this year felt different. This year *was* different. There was no Marnie – just Hannah and Alicia.

The sound of the safety chain being unlatched and the door opening caught Hannah off guard.

'Come in! How long have you been waiting out here?' Alicia was smiling, but there was a slight twitch in her right cheek as if she'd plastered the smile on a second before opening the door.

'Only a few seconds.' Hannah balanced her overnight bag on one shoulder and pulled Alicia into a clumsy hug. How long had she been watching and waiting for Hannah to arrive? She was only fifteen minutes late – not bad going for her.

Hannah followed Alicia down the hallway. It had been ages since she was last here. It was before shit hit the fan – so at least five years ago, maybe six. And yet, nothing had changed. Everything was as expected. The hallway was pristine but Alicia apologised for the mess. Her hair was washed but up. She smelt like Dior Sauvage, having upgraded from Britney Spears Fantasy in her first year of uni. She was wearing the standard millennial uniform of jeans and a nice top.

In the kitchen, Hannah dumped her bag and leaned on the breakfast bar while Alicia emptied some Doritos into a large sombrero-shaped bowl. It was unlikely that she hadn't had the time to do this beforehand; perhaps it was more about the performance, of being the hostess with the mostest, or just something to do to fill the awkward silence between them that often reared its head when Marnie wasn't there to soften its edges.

'Tea?'

'Behave. Get me a glass, I've bought some champers.' Hannah waved the Harrods bag with a grin.

'I'll stick to tea,' said Alicia as she flicked the kettle on.

Hannah caught the words before they fell out her mouth. *God, you're not pregnant are you?* She knew that wouldn't go down well.

Alicia handed Hannah a champagne flute and turned to busy herself with making tea.

In the silence, Hannah took in her surroundings. Magnolia walls, the same colour as when Alicia had moved in. Endless photos of Alicia and Hugh in white frames hanging from the dado rail – perhaps an attempt to bring some character to the bland newbuild. There were only two pictures of Hannah, Alicia and Marnie; Hannah was sure there had been more the last time she'd been here. One was at their Sixth Form prom, the three of them grinning from ear to ear, smiles off-piste from the pre-game bubbles, and the other was from Alicia's wedding, Hannah and Marnie either side of the beautiful bride in their matching dusty pink dresses. It was weird to wonder: if Alicia were to get married again, would both Hannah and Marnie make the cut?

Speaking of. 'Have you heard from Marns recently?' Hannah asked it casually, but her shoulders tensed – always the side effect of bringing the elephant into the room. Not that Marnie was an elephant.

'Not today.' Alicia sipped her tea while leaning against the counter but did not meet Hannah's eye.

Today? Hannah hadn't heard from Marnie much this

month, apart from the sparse explanation of why she wasn't joining tonight and the few fleeting messages in the group chat – aptly named the Hot Mess Express. The group chat had once been treated like a top-secret MI5 file, but these days it was mostly a space to share screenshots of people they went to school with whenever someone got divorced or announced a pregnancy, and swap hurried messages in an attempt to catch up on each other's lives as economically as possible in the snatches of time they had between this life thing and that one.

'Anything important?' Hannah took another gulp of her drink.

Alicia shook her head but offered nothing else. She put her cuppa on the side with a little more force than necessary and started poking about in the freezer.

Did Alicia know something Hannah didn't? It used to be the other way around. While Alicia was at home studying and getting into bed at 9pm, Hannah and Marnie were gaining illegal entry to the Railway Club in town using fake IDs, getting shitfaced and scoping out the most tattooed men they could find. Alicia was most often the third wheel when it came to in-jokes and you-had-to-be-there moments. It wasn't a calculated, *Mean Girls* thing. It was just how it was. Best to change the subject.

'How's Hugh?' Probably not a better topic.

'Fine,' Alica said, head now in the fridge, shuffling sauces and bottles around the shelves for apparently no reason at all. 'Why?'

Because that was the polite thing to ask and Hannah was running out of things to say? Not that there was any need for politeness. They'd seen each other at their absolute worst. Like that time Hannah had mixed antibiotics and vodka at Rosa Keech's seventeenth birthday and spent the night crying in the bathtub while Alicia caught her sick in a plastic cup. Or when Marnie's daughter, Sophie, was really poorly with bronchiolitis and Marnie burst into tears when the girls turned up at the hospital with an iced coffee and a *Heat* magazine. Oh, and you couldn't forget the time Alicia broke down a couple of years ago about her perfectly curated life. You wouldn't think it looking at her now, as she slid two pizzas into the oven below a sign that said something about coffee in an unreadable cursive that was one step away from *Live Laugh Love* or *One Prosecco, Two Prosecco, Three Prosecco, Floor*. Her wobble appeared to have been swept under the carpet and her existence reinstated as if her breakdown had never happened.

'Just asking.'

Alicia finally shut the oven door and joined Hannah at the breakfast bar. 'Hugh is Hugh,' she shrugged. 'Enough about me. How's Nala Swim going?'

The knot in Hannah's stomach loosened. A safe, fun subject. Not like uptight Hugh, or what was going on with Marnie.

'Amazing. Going from strength to strength, at risk of sounding like a complete business-wanker.' She polished off the last splash of fizz in her glass. God, she'd put that away quickly.

'I'm so pleased to hear that.'

Hannah studied Alicia's face for any sign of insincerity but couldn't find it. She poured herself a second glass of champagne. 'We're launching a new line later this year. A collab with Swymz. The first meeting was supposed to be today, but we've pushed it back to next week.'

'You rescheduled a meeting with Swymz to be here?'

'You know I'd never miss Galentine's.' Yeah, she'd been a bit shit over the years, like missing out on various birthdays, Sophie's christening and Alicia's engagement party, but she'd only missed one Galentine's Day out of fifteen. Why *was* she so committed to upholding this tradition? She didn't really know at this point. Perhaps it was because the word *failure* wasn't in her vocabulary. Or maybe there was some sentimentality in Hannah, hidden deeply below her unshakeable exterior.

Alicia sighed. 'I feel bad, now. Some oven pizzas and a bottle of bubbly you bought yourself is hardly going to make up for letting Swymz down.' She looked genuinely devastated.

'It's fine, they didn't mind.' They did, but Hannah was holding the cards. If Swymz wanted to work with her, they'd have to do it on her terms. There was no denying that it felt good to have that power and status. Although at times it felt like a rather hefty responsibility, managing everyone, deadlines, timelines, customers and partnerships. She had so many plates to spin she was at risk of dropping some, and more and more recently, she was realising that it was close to impossible to have it all.

'You okay?' Alicia's brow creased.

'Me?' *Who else would she be talking to?* 'I'm grand. You know me.' Hannah grinned but it was now her cheek that was twitching.

Why was this so painfully awkward? After all they'd been through, the highs and the lows, it was just Alicia. But what did *just Alicia* really mean to Hannah now? Could they still call themselves best friends when they only saw each other once or twice a year?

Best not to think about it too much. Nothing ever good came from that.

Chapter One

13th February, 2013

Alicia

After almost two hours of tidying, tweaking, sorting and primping her already immaculate bedroom, Alicia stepped back and surveyed her handiwork. She was especially proud of her colour-coordinated bookshelf, the idea for which she'd added to her 'Galentine's Day Sleepover' Pinterest board the night she'd told the girls of her plan. On her desk sat three wicker boxes filled with face masks, scrunchies and Haribo love hearts, each decorated with red ribbons and labelled with each girl's name written in calligraphy (another Pinterest special). Her heart-adorned Primark pyjamas were laid on her pillow, ready to be joined by Hannah and Marnie's matching sets that they'd purchased at Westfield Shopping Centre last weekend.

Everything was perfect and absolutely worth the fact that Alicia's mum was not currently speaking to her. In her mum's words, Alicia had been 'charging around the house all week like Mussolini', making 'bizarre demands' and 'upsetting her dad's blood pressure'. Was asking them to buy new duvet covers to replace the hideously dated spare ones and requesting a six-pack of Barcardi Breezers really too much to ask?

Oh my gosh, that was the doorbell. The knot in Alicia's stomach she'd initially put down to excitement turned to anxiety quicker than Hannah jumped from one love interest to the next.

Speaking of Hannah. That was definitely her talking animatedly to Alicia's mum. Damn Marnie and her crappy timekeeping. Alicia had specifically requested that Marnie do her absolute best to get there before Hannah. Yes, Hannah was one of her best friends, but being one-on-one with anyone was sometimes awkward. At least in groups Alicia could sit quietly, listen and observe rather than have to scrabble desperately for something interesting to say to keep Hannah's attention.

'Alicia, can you come down and help Hannah with her stuff, please?' her mum called, as she made her way down the hallway.

'I'm so excited for tonight, thank you so much for having us,' Hannah gushed, in true Hannah form.

Descending the stairs, Alicia felt the weight of her mum's gaze before she even looked up. The flicker of disdain in her mother's eyes was unmistakable, a continuation of her earlier grievances. Alicia could almost hear the unspoken sighs about the chaos that three giggling, overexcited teenagers were bound to bring. Her mother's quiet, tidy domain, so carefully maintained in their suburban four-bedroom semi, braced itself for an invasion of noise and sleepless rebellion.

Alicia avoided eye contact with her mum as she hurried to grab the duvet and three pillows that Hannah thrust in her direction.

'We'll go straight upstairs.'

'Take a girl for dinner first, will you?' Hannah laughed.

Alicia's mum coughed.

'Hannah!' Alicia chided, taking two steps at a time and not daring to look back.

Hannah followed behind, lugging her beautiful Ted Baker overnight bag.

In the bedroom, Alicia put Hannah's stuff in a neat pile in the corner. They'd do the blow-up mattress later, after dinner but before the film.

'Wow.' Hannah stood, hands on hips as she looked around the room as if she'd never been there before. 'It looks like Pinterest's wet dream in here.'

Pride swelled in Alicia's gut. *Yes, Hannah likes it. Thank goodness for that.*

Hannah moved to the desk and sifted through the baskets, upending everything that Alicia had spent fifteen-plus minutes neatly packing. She laughed. 'You've really gone all out, bless you.'

All of Alicia's pride over her set-up vanished. She'd tried too hard. It was cringe, too much. Alicia bit her lip. 'I just thought it's a special occasion, why not make the effort.'

'It's cute.'

Cute? *Oh God. She hates it.* Why had Alicia even suggested the sleepover in the first place? She'd only blurted out an invite in panic, a desperate attempt to quell Hannah's rising distress over being rejected by a boy in the *sacred* month of February.

Marnie and Alicia had been sitting in the common room during a free period. Marnie was reading her biology textbook and Alicia was having a mental breakdown over her Extended Project Qualification, having been unable to say no to Mr Wartly when he suggested she write about whether Angela Carter should be considered part of the literary canon. She was distracted from her rising hysteria by a message from Hannah in the group chat that said *come to the sixth form toilets. It's an emergency*. Alicia assumed that Hannah needed an emergency pad or tampon, whereas Marnie seemed certain Hannah just needed Nurofen for the hangover she was battling after the two of them went out the previous night to a gig down at the Railway Club. Alicia had been invited, but politely declined because it was a Thursday night and she knew the only reason Marnie and Hannah were going was because they'd set their sights on two of the band members. Alicia wasn't excited at the prospect of being the third wheel, again.

In the bathroom, the girls were met with a locked stall and the sound of Hannah blowing her nose.

Marnie tapped on the door. 'Babe. It's us. Can you unlock the door?'

Silence.

Marnie looked at Alicia, eyes wide as if to say *help me out here*.

'If you don't unlock the door, we're going to climb over,' Alicia offered, hoping that Hannah wouldn't make them do something quite so undignified, considering they were both in their rolled-up skirts and sheer tights.

After a minute or so, the lock clicked and the door creaked open a crack. Marnie barged her way in, grabbing Alicia by the wrist behind her.

'Move your butt, we need to close the door.' Marnie flapped at Alicia like Alicia had the superpower of vanishing into thin air. Alicia shuffled past Hannah who had not moved from her slumped position on the closed toilet lid, and using the sanitary bin as a step, climbed onto the ledge that held the cistern. It was always a good place to sit in moments like this, of which there were many. Moreso now Hannah was part of their lives.

Marnie squatted down in front of Hannah; Alicia winced at the thought of what she might kneel in if she were to topple over.

'Babe, what's happened?' Marnie reached for Hannah's hands and squeezed. Alicia patted her on the head and then immediately regretted her clumsy choice of consolation.

'It's Hugo.' Hannah sniffed. She pulled out a further metre length of toilet roll and blew her nose into it.

Ah yes, the elusive Hugo. The mythical 'perfect man' Hannah had got off with at a family Christmas party, whom neither Marnie nor Alicia had met. They'd only seen a few blurry photos of him appearing to be taken on a potato, but that were actually taken by a very drunk Hannah on her BlackBerry.

'What about him? Is he okay?' Alicia asked.

'He's fucking fine,' Hannah spluttered dramatically.

'What then?' Marnie said, firmer this time. She was the only person who could ever get away with using such a tone with Hannah. Alicia didn't even have that tone in her repertoire.

'You know I was going to ask him to Oceana for the Valentine's themed night?'

'Yeah,' Marnie and Alicia said simultaneously.

'The tosser said no. He rejected me. In February of all months. It's meant to be the month of love.' Hannah broke down again and pulled yet a further ream of paper from the roll.

Marnie shook her head. 'Oh Han. He was an ugly prick anyway. You can do so much better.'

Alicia was forever grateful for Marnie, who was far better

11

at dealing with these sorts of dramas than she was. She was always very kind and tried her best to comfort people who were sad, but she never felt like she did a good enough job. Marnie just seemed to possess the innate ability to sit with others' discomfort and hold it, without the clumsy back pats and *there theres* that were Alicia's go-to.

'He wasn't ugly. He was beautiful. He was the one. He was . . .' Hannah was now weeping again, just as the bell rang for break time. *What a performance.* Alicia hadn't cried this much when her Nanna died.

Alicia knew that any minute now, the toilets would fill with the chatter of students, and Hannah wouldn't care. She might even turn up the volume for added dramatic effect, and Alicia couldn't stand the second-hand embarrassment.

'Well, you're busy that night anyway,' Alicia blurted out, unable to stop the words from spilling out.

Marnie frowned and even Hannah spun round to look at her.

'Huh?'

'You're both busy that night because I'm having a sleepover, 13th Feb. Gals only. A celebration of female love.'

'But it's a Wednesday. You never do anything on a school night.' Marnie squinted at Alicia suspiciously.

'Celebration of female love sounds like we're going to be scissoring each other all night or something,' Hannah added. At least she was no longer crying; Alicia's words had had the desired effect.

Alicia shrugged, trying to play it off as casual. 'I was going to mention it tomorrow.'

Marnie's face lit up and even Hannah managed to smile. 'Oh my God, what an amazing idea. Galentine's Day with my gals!'

'Yay!' Marnie pulled them all into the most uncomfortable of hugs, Alicia bending down from her perch on the ledge, arm hooked around Hannah's neck like a choke hold, and Marnie crouching awkwardly with an arm looped around each of them.

And that was how their Galentine's Day sleepover was born. Now here Alicia was, bearing the weight of the inaugural sleepover, wishing she'd kept her mouth shut.

'Shut the door.' Hannah's strange request brought Alicia back into the present day.

Alicia frowned. 'Why?'

Hannah wiggled her eyebrows. 'Just shut it.'

Alicia did as she was told, as Hannah rooted around in her overnight bag. She pulled out what looked to be a rolled-up towel, and after some further faffing about, out slid a rather large bottle of tequila. 'I bribed Emmanuel to get it for us. That's what older brothers are for, right?'

Alicia's mouth dropped open. 'Hannah!'

'What? We're practically adults now, are we not?'

'Well, yeah.'

'And what do adults do?'

Taxes, mortgages, work, make sensible decisions . . .

'They fucking drink, that's what.'

Alicia shook her head, trying to work out what to say. She didn't want to upset Hannah or come across as boring, but her mum would kill her if she knew they were drinking.

'You are so . . . naughty—'

The door burst open, cutting Alicia off mid-sentence. Her heart leapt to her throat, panic flaring for a split second before she saw it was Marnie, not her mum, striding into the room.

'Marns!' squealed Hannah, balancing the tequila on the

desk carelessly, leaving Alicia to grab the wobbling bottle and shove it into her wardrobe.

'My girls,' Marns squealed back, dumping her sleeping bag, air mattress and multiple bags for life in the middle of the room.

'Love the PJs.'

'Thanks.' Marnie twirled, showing off the two-piece set that matched Alicia's – baby pink with a smattering of red hearts. 'I thought the plan was for all of us to wear them,' she laughed.

'Not in public, though, you silly cow.' Hannah grinned.

Alicia would have *died* if that was her, but Marnie was clearly unphased

'I think they look great!' To Alicia's surprise, her mum appeared at the door.

Thank goodness I hid the tequila.

Bizarrely, Mum was smiling, a proper one that was not forced, and she was sure she even caught Marnie winking at her. 'Be good now, will you girls, and have a wonderful evening! I'm just downstairs if you need anything. Unless it's past 9pm, in which case, I will be in bed.'

'We shall be as good as gold.' It appeared that Marnie had worked her irresistible charm, and Alicia's mum had genuinely begun to thaw.

Instantly, Alicia's nerves settled, despite Marnie dropping onto Alicia's bed with her shoes still on and opening a family-sized bag of Doritos on her freshly changed sheets.

Alicia's mum had always viewed Marnie as a good influence, right from the day they first met in Year Six when Marnie had moved to Alicia's primary school. Both only children, they stuck to each other like long-lost sisters, and it had been just the two of them for six years until Hannah joined them

14

in Sixth Form, barrelling her way into the friendship before Alicia could even form an opinion on whether she liked her or not. It wasn't the easiest of transitions to go from two to three; sharing Marnie wasn't something she'd had to deal with in the past – other girls (and boys) came and went but none managed to infiltrate their bond. Until Hannah.

Being a two worked well as things often came in pairs: hotel rooms with twin beds, school projects and seats on the bus. Alicia hated that awkward standoff that happened when one person had to offer to work with someone else, take up the cot bed or sit next to a stranger on the way to town if the back seats were occupied. That someone was *always* Alicia.

The first thing Hannah and Alicia did was get changed into their PJs to match Marnie. They then spent at least half an hour taking photos of them posed like the Charlie's Angels to the soundtrack of 'She Will Be Loved' by Maroon Five, 'Girl on Fire' by Alicia Keys, and 'Thrift Shop' by Macklemore. This was followed by making silly videos on Vine and then spending at least an hour on Alicia's laptop stalking their Year Six crushes, which went hideously wrong when Hannah 'accidentally' liked a photo of Jordan Dunfrey from 2012 while signed in as Alicia. The girls decided the only option was the deactivate her entire account.

Marnie then insisted on blowing up the airbed, despite it being before dinner and therefore not on Alicia's schedule, but she let it slip because she was riding high on Pepsi Max and the frenetic energy of the group. Being a threesome did have its perks.

They scoffed pizza while all lying on the double air bed watching an illegal stream of *Magic Mike*. By watching, they meant they chatted the whole way through, only giving it their undivided attention when *that* scene came on and Alicia almost choked on her pizza.

At 11:30pm, when Alicia's dad had gone to bed, Hannah unearthed the tequila from its hiding place.

'Who fancies a nightcap?' she said.

'You sound like my uncle,' Marnie groaned.

'Would your uncle also do this?' Hannah said, before wiggling her hips and singing 'da, da da da da da da, tequila,' much to Alicia and Marnie's horror and delight. They joined in, trying their best to whisper but overwhelmed by the hilarity of it all, failing miserably.

'I'm up for it if you are. Alicia, do we have your blessing?' Marnie panted, dropping onto the bed, all danced out.

Hannah joined her. 'Pretty pleeeease.'

Hmmm. Tonight's going so well. I have to keep the party going.

One shot wouldn't hurt.

Five shots later, the girls sat side by side on Alicia's bed under the covers and a mountain of blankets.

'Isn't it mad that we're here because Hannah was parred off by a guy.' Marnie rested her head in the crook of Hannah's neck. 'I'm not sad that happened. Soz, Han.'

'Oi. Don't mock my broken heart,' Hannah said as she leaned into Marnie.

Alicia felt left out, so slid her arm through Marnie's, looping it tightly. She liked the confidence that came with drinking. Maybe she'd do it more often. 'Marnie's right. If it hadn't happened, we wouldn't be here right now.'

'True. But I really thought he was The One.'

'Why?' Marnie said, curiously this time. 'You say that about all of them.'

'Ahhh, you're right.' Hannah sighed. 'He's super sexy, but honestly? He's also super boring. Very strait-laced. Wants to be a lawyer.'

'I bet his favourite position is missionary,' snorted Marnie, voice louder than Alicia preferred because her volume control was rather hit and miss at the best of times.

'Shhhh.' Alicia dug her elbow into Marnie's side gently, then burst out laughing.

'Oh, totally,' replied Hannah. 'He'll probably make good money, but who needs a rich husband when you're going to be earning six figures yourself?'

'How do you plan on doing that?' Alicia was genuinely intrigued. She didn't know anyone who earned that much. Her parents were comfortable, but six figures? Madness.

'I'll do what I have to do. Maybe I'll be a fashion designer. Or work in a costume department in Hollywood. The world is my clam.'

'I think you mean oyster.'

'Same difference.'

Marnie sat up and grabbed the tequila bottle and started topping up everyone's glasses. 'You'll smash it, Han. You always do.'

'I know,' Hannah grinned.

Gosh, how easy must life be to have such an innate sense of confidence? Alicia couldn't relate. Instead, she had a failsafe plan.

'Remember us when you're super famous. Maybe you could visit the school I'm teaching at and give an inspirational talk or something.' Alicia sipped her drink, having become accustomed to the initial burn in her throat.

'You can do all sorts with an English degree. Journalism. Author. You could be more than a teacher, you know?'

17

Hannah was right, but Alicia had already decided. 'Teaching is a recession-proof profession.'

'You sound exactly like your mum,' Hannah said, but there was a softness to her voice that was rarely there when she hadn't had a few units.

'What's wrong with that?' The alcohol made Alicia feel more confident.

'You are your own person. What do you want to do?'

'Honestly, I'm more than happy to become a teacher, get a nice house, marry and settle down.'

'Why?'

'Why not?' And Alicia really did mean it. Yes, some people liked being spontaneous, wanted to travel the world with just a backpack and a dream. But she wasn't one of them. She liked her home comforts, being with family, knowing that dinner was at 6pm on the dot, and that she and her mum would watch *X Factor* on a Saturday night. So much in life was unknown, and that was terrifying. Surely it made sense to seek out security wherever you could.

'Anyway, we don't need to worry ourselves with all that boring stuff right now. We've got so much to look forward to before having to—' Hannah pretended to retch '—settle down.'

'I'm hungry. Where are the Doritos?' Marnie leaned forward, hanging her top half off the bed, bum in the air. Hannah smacked it. 'Owwwww,' shrieked Marnie, before toppling sideways onto the floor with a thump.

Alicia, Hannah and Marnie howled with laughter, but Alicia quickly shut up remembering her parents in the next room. If that wasn't going to wake them up then she didn't know what would. Crisis-mode activated. Alicia picked up the pillow that Marnie had been lying on and shoved it in

Hannah's face. Job done. She continued to wail but this time it was muffled. She slid herself off the bed and did the same to Marnie but with her bare hands.

'Shhhhhhhhh.'

'Sorry. Sorry,' Hannah wheezed, the hilarity of the situation rendering her unable to breathe. 'I'll whisper now.' *Gasp*. 'I promise.'

Alicia raised her eyebrows at Marnie, whose face was still beneath her hands – a warning. Be quiet, or else.

'Okay, okay,' muffled Marnie, before they all settled back onto the bed, more breathless with frenzy than before.

When everyone had calmed down, Marnie spoke. 'I'm so excited for next year.'

The exhilarating carefreeness she'd just experienced deflated like air from a balloon. Excited? Alicia couldn't say the same. Scared, yes. Nervous about making new friends and keeping up with a relentless work and study schedule? Also yes. And that was all dependent on whether or not she'd get the grades needed for her course at Hertfordshire University. AAB. Of course, she'd study hard and really knuckle down when it came to revision, but you could never truly know how you'd do until you got your results in your hands. How did Hannah and Marnie not seem to worry about any of this?

'Same,' said Hannah.

'What are you both excited about?' Alicia bit her lip.

'Everything,' Hannah answered first. 'Freedom. My own place. Meeting new people.'

What was wrong with the people around Hannah currently? She probably didn't mean it offensively to Alicia and Marnie but still.

Marnie interjected. 'Can't wait to get as far away from my parents as possible. Oh, and also have sex. Lots of it.'

Marnie couldn't be moving much further away from her parents. St Andrews, Scotland, to study geography, to be exact. She was literally moving to another country. The opposite of Alicia who was going to the local uni and commuting from home.

'You have to text us the minute you lose your virginity, Marns.'

'Obviously. I'll FaceTime afterwards. When they're still in bed with me. Alicia, you have to do the same.'

'Don't hold your breath. You know I'm waiting until I meet someone special.'

'Waste of time.' Hannah shook her head. 'Better to get it over and done with in Freshers' Week. Then you can shag about without people worrying about hurting your feelings.'

'I don't want to shag about.'

'But it's so fun.' Hannah sighed as if reminiscing about a fond memory.

'Is it? You always make it sound shit.' Marnie raised her eyebrows suspiciously.

Hannah had lost her virginity in Year Ten to her boyfriend of six months, Trey. Since then she'd slept with three other people: a one-night stand who apparently smelt like bacon, then her on again, off again Year Twelve boyfriend, Stanley. Her most recent notch on the bedpost was Hugo. Apparently they'd done it at the end of his garden during the family Christmas party, and Hannah had worried about getting frostbite on her flaps (her words, not Alicia's). Marnie was right, Hannah really didn't sell it.

Time to change the subject.

'This has honestly been one of the best nights of my life. I love you girls.' The words felt strange but right in Alicia's mouth – strange because she was rarely one to be outwardly sentimental, and right because she meant it with her entire being.

'Awwww. Group hug.' Marnie threw her arms around Alicia and Hannah's shoulders from her spot in between them and squeezed. 'We love you too.'

'And we love Galentine's,' Hannah added.

'We must do it every year now,' said Marnie. 'It's a tradition. Every year, no matter what. Even when we're at uni, working career women, married, mothers—'

'No thanks,' Hannah scoffed.

'Retired old bags, then. You'll be one of those eventually, even if you don't have babies. Do you hear me? Every. Damn. Year. Got it?'

'Got it.' Alicia and Hannah nodded.

A sleepover every year, no matter what? A vow from Marnie and Hannah not to drift away in the chaos of university? A steady anchor in the terrifying unknown of the future. *Count me in*. Alicia held her glass in the air. 'To the future!'

'To Hugo,' Marnie added.

Hannah grimaced. 'Really?'

'Yes!'

'Fine. To Hugo.' Hannah raised her glass. 'And of course, to Galentine's!'

'To Galentine's!' Alicia and Marnie repeated, before the three of them downed another shot.

Hot Mess Express 🚂 😜

16th February, 2013

Marnie: I am officially going vegetarian.
Alicia: Why?
Marnie: One word: horsemeat.
Hannah: 🙊
Alicia: Is that still a thing?
Marnie: I don't know but I'm not taking any chances.

April 20th, 2013

Hannah: Alicia, a reminder to take a break from revising to wash your hair and eat something.
Alicia: Will try. So much to do, so little time.
Marnie: It's not worth getting ill over. Breathe, woman!!!
Alicia: Your lack of panic is making me panic more. Not long to go now.
Marnie: I work best under pressure.
Hannah: It's all about balance. Cheeky lil mindmap (in glittery gel pens, obv), followed by a cheeky lil reward (rest, snack, hot drink, nap). Never fails me.
Alicia: HOW ARE YOU BOTH SO CHILL?

May 14th, 2013

Marnie: Absolutely shitting myself about my biology exam. Pray for me plz!

Alicia: I thought you worked best under pressure.

Marnie: Tell that to my stomach. Too many energy drinks last night. 😵

Hannah: Did you learn nothing from Will in *The Inbetweeners*?

Marnie: WAH. Going in now, see you on the other side.

24th June, 2013

Hannah: What are you both wearing to Victoria's A Level party? I'm thinking bodycon blue dress with heeled boots x

Alicia: Jeans and a nice top.

Hannah: Marnie?

Marnie: My ripped black jeans and stripey top. Maybe my new hat.

Hannah: Alicia, can you get us some booze plz?

Alicia: Why me? Marnie's 18 too.

Marnie: You've got a car, alcohol is heavy.

Alicia: We can all go together on the way.

Hannah: Good shout. Can't waitttttt.

22nd July, 2013

Alicia: Did you see that Kate Middleton gave birth to a new kid? Prince George!! Hannah you officially share your birthday with a royal. So jealous!!

Marnie: Yes!! So cuteeeee.

Hannah: I'm trying my best to be enthusiastic for you, you little royalist 🙄 Can't wait to see you at the pub later to celebrate ME <3

1st August, 2013

Alicia: Who fancies joining me on an Ikea trip for uni bits? And meatballs obv.

Marnie: YES! Minus the meatballs for me.

Hannah: We also need to go shopping for Zante. I want a bikini for every day. And I need some tan.

Alicia: I need sun cream.

Marnie: I need flip-flops.

Alicia: Have you both checked your passports are in date?

Marnie: Yes, mum.

Hannah: Two weeks to go ahhhhhhhhhhhhhhhhhh.

14th August, 2013

Hannah: God it feels good to not have to revise. So glad it all paid off. ABB. Get in.

Marnie: Boffin. Happy with my BBC over here. Mum and Dad are disappointed I didn't get any As but I think even if I'd got As they'd then be disappointed I didn't get an A* lol. How are you feeling AAA LICIA?

Alicia: Chuffed. Relieved. Able to sleep.

17th August, 2013

Marnie: Where r u?

Alicia: Marnie and I are worried sick!!!

Hannah: On the beach.

Alicia: Alone?

Hannah: Wht do u think? 😏

Alicia: We're coming now. Don't do anything silly.

Hannah: U better hurry then coz im abt to skinny dip

Marnie: WAIT FOR ME I WANNA JOIN.

1st October, 2013

Alicia: How's uni life treating you both? One week living away from home already!!

Marnie: Not dead yet.

Hannah: Loving it. Out every night. My hallmates are a right laugh.

Alicia: Good. Herts uni is good so far. Have made a nice friend called Neelam. We seem to live in the library!!

Marnie: I've not even been to the library here yet, lol.

Hannah: Me neither. First year is for fucking about. I'll knuckle down next year.

Alicia: If you say so 😖 You both back for Christmas 21st December?

Marnie: Yep. Got a whole month off but I'm going back mid-Jan for Josh's birthday celebrations.

Hannah: Flatmate?

Marnie: Guy on my course x

Hannah: I reckon I'll head back a bit earlier too. But still plenty of time to catch up over Xmas. Red Lion Christmas Eve?

Alicia: Yeah but I want to be home by 10 to watch *Home Alone* with my family.

Marnie: I'll get a taxi home then. 10 is too early for me.

Hannah: I'll go halves on a taxi with you x

25th November, 2013

Marnie: Anyone wanna see *Hunger Games* with me at Christmas?

Hannah: I'll come!

Alicia: ABSOLUTELY!!!! DON'T YOU DARE GO WITHOUT ME.

Marnie: It's happened. I am no longer a virgin. I promised I'd tell you as soon as I did it, and that's exactly what I'm doing. He's still in my bed. Don't even know his name. Details to follow . . . I think we're going to do it again. Back soon. Ish. X

Chapter Two

13th February, 2014

Marnie

Central Saint Martins student accommodation was exactly as Marnie had pictured it. After a mammoth six-and-a-half-hour train journey (that almost didn't happen because of a leaf on the line or some bollocks like that) Marnie couldn't have been happier to see Hannah's face waiting for her at the bus stop before marching her excitedly to her new flat.

Marnie couldn't believe that it was Galentine's Day again already. The past year had whizzed by, although it was hardly a surprise when she thought of how much had happened in the past twelve months. To call it a mental year was an understatement.

A Levels, getting into uni (hurrah!), the rite-of-passage trip to Zante. Ah. Zante – an experience of wild proportions. One-night romances with charismatic Irish guys all round, making out on the beach until sunrise. Alicia even had her tits fondled for the first time ever. They never saw the lads again after that night, choosing to savour the mystery of a holiday romance.

But the biggest shift of all was starting uni.

The first term at St Andrew's was everything Marnie had wanted it to be. She was free to do whatever she wanted, and that's exactly what she did. Staying up until three in the morning watching trash TV with her flatmates Becky and Caroline, going out two, sometimes three nights a week. Wearing whatever she wanted without her mum making her usual comment: *is that what you're wearing? Where's the rest of it?*

She'd joined three societies – Geology, Marine and Amnesty International – and even signed up to the gym, though she was yet to get any further than her initial induction where a lovely man called Mo taught her how to use the equipment.

Despite falling in love with St Andrews, there was something comforting about being back *down South*. As Marnie had climbed off her train at St Pancras International and headed out into the bustling city of London, she was reminded of how it felt for the sun to touch her face. Yes, it was chilly (it was February after all), but it was nothing compared to the grey, almost arctic atmosphere of a coastal town in Scotland.

This year's Galentine's Day was going to be wildly different to last year's. No adults in sight (unless they counted themselves) and the agenda? Dancing and drinking. They should have a higher tolerance for alcohol this year, considering they'd all survived the madness of Freshers' Week. Crucially, Alicia's mum and dad would not be there to tell them off for overdoing it on the tequila. Marnie still felt bad about Hannah throwing up the next morning on their obviously very expensive Persian rug.

Eugh, tequila. The thought of it made her want to heave, although it didn't take much at the moment. She'd been suffering from a persistent low-level nausea most of the time, that increased to a stomach-churning and uncontrollable urge to vomit when she'd catch a whiff of something pungent, like when someone opened the fridge in her hall's kitchen, or when her coursemate Kai wore an insane amount of Lynx Africa. A bit of nausea wasn't going to ruin Galentine's, though. She wouldn't let it, even if she had to take it easy on the drinking.

'I'll give you *Le Grande Tour* when Alicia arrives.' Hannah strode down the hallway with her usual confidence, fluffy pink slippers and red toenails clashing with the navy carpet the texture of a scouring pad.

'That will be in nineteen minutes according to her last message.'

'Hmm.' Hannah bit her lip as if weighing up her options. 'In that case, I'll introduce you to everyone in the kitchen while we wait. They're all super nice. Not really my kind of people, but they're a laugh.'

Marnie braced herself. These people were definitely going to be what her nan would call an *eclectic mix*, probably of artsy types, private school wankers cosplaying as *artistes* and am-dram sorts given that Central Saint Martins was a *world-renowned arts and design college* (as Hannah frequently reminded her). Best to get it over with. Intros were not Marnie's favourite thing to do. She'd managed to introduce herself to everyone in her flat on her first day at St Andrews, although she only went into the kitchen to say hello to everyone after her mum threatened to go in there herself when she'd flat out refused to leave her room. Meeting Hannah's lot *should* be easier. But then again, these people were Marnie's competition for the position of Hannah's best friend, alongside Alicia, obviously. Although if there was a ranking, Marnie had a sneaking suspicion she knew who'd be number one.

In the kitchen – a standard uni kitchen affair not dissimilar to Marnie's – Hannah gestured towards a pretty girl in a beret sitting at the table. 'This is Tilly. Flat four.'

'Alright.' Tilly nodded then went back to looking at her laptop. Was that a smidge of hostility in her energy? She was *definitely* hoping to become Hannah's new bestie. Either that or she was just French. Berets were a French thing, right?

'Jonesy. Flat eight.' Hannah giggled and flapped at a blonde, floppy-haired boy who wore a red Ralph Lauren jumper and beige chinos a size tighter than necessary. Hannah had definitely shagged him.

'A pleasure,' Jonesy drooled with a slight lisp.

Marnie immediately recognised his type – the sort of person who had his Waitrose Essentials hand delivered by Mummy, who came every week with an ice cooler of Gressingham duck and Lanson champagne, the bottle dressed in a tiny branded tennis jacket. Marnie had seen a fair few at St Andrews. Uni was a mix of normal people and poshos, and she'd never met so many people who went skiing every year or had a personal trainer/horse/au pair.

Hannah yanked open the fridge before Jonesy could say anything else.

'Posh twat,' she mouthed behind the open fridge door. Suspicions confirmed.

'Pepsi?' Hannah pulled out two cans before Marnie could refuse.

'Oh, do you have anything else?'

'I have this or water.' Hannah frowned. 'You love Pepsi Max. I got it especially.'

'Just avoiding caffeine at the moment. Makes me jittery.'

'Since when did you turn into Alicia? One can't hurt.' Hannah slammed the fridge shut and pushed the can towards her.

Fuck. If this was how she was going to be over a can of Pepsi, how on earth would Hannah take it when Marnie told her she wasn't going to be drinking? Maybe she'd just hide it, pretend she was.

Time to change the subject. 'Is that everyone, then?' Marnie moved to sit at the table, the opposite end to Tilly who looked like she might growl if she got too close.

Hannah cracked open her Pepsi. 'Everyone else is in lectures. Bunch of geeks.'

Jonesy moved to lean next to Hannah who was sitting on the kitchen counter. He nudged her and grinned. 'Apart from the spectre of flat two.'

Marnie was intrigued. 'Don't tell me your flat is haunted. I swear ours is. The halls are like, over a hundred years old.'

'Isn't it more likely someone's just nicking your milk?' Tilly snorted.

Marnie scowled. Bitch.

'Na, he's not a ghost, it's definitely an actual human person,' Hannah insisted. 'But we've never seen him. We know he's in there because I hear his door opening and closing and him talking to someone on the phone through the walls. He doesn't use the fridge or his cupboards though and no one's seen him go in or out.'

'Sounds like a ghost to me.'

Jonesy pulled a chair out beside Marnie and sat a little too close to her. 'He's real. She's not lying.'

'If you say so.' Marnie crossed her arms and shifted her chair away from him. 'Where the hell is Alicia?'

Hannah pulled her phone out. 'Three minutes away. Have

you noticed she's updated the group chat every . . .' Hannah paused. 'Two minutes with her ETA. Which has stayed the same to the minute *despite* the bus driver having to stop to let a bunch of ducks cross the road.'

'Gotta love her.'

'Who are you talking about?'

Everyone in the kitchen turned. It was Alicia, standing awkwardly by the door, brown backpack over one shoulder.

'How the hell did you get in here?' Hannah hopped off the counter and grinned.

'Some guy let me in.'

'Good to know the place is secure.' Tilly slammed her laptop shut and walked past Alicia to flick on the kettle.

'You making tea? Alicia loves tea, don't you Alicia?'

'Oh no, I'm fine, thanks.'

'Tilly doesn't mind, do you, Tilly? This is Alicia, my best friend, future teacher extraordinaire. Excellent at Boggle.'

'I've only got green tea,' Tilly said, without looking up.

Marnie watched Alicia smile twitchily. If Marnie disliked small talk and meeting new people, Alicia was practically phobic of it. Apparently she'd made a couple of friends at uni, but it did seem harder seeing as she was staying at home and not in halls. There was nothing as bonding as being dumped at a new place by your parents and being expected to fend for yourself on a diet of vodka and pasta. Marnie felt sad that Alicia hadn't had the pleasure.

'I'm really okay. I had plenty to drink on the way here.'

Marnie spied Alicia's Thermos tucked into the bottle holder of the rucksack. Of course she came prepared with an actual flask of tea. Marnie really did love her.

'Come here, then. Where's my hug?' Marnie went over

and pulled her into a huge bear hug. She smelt like she had her whole life, with the subtle addition of a new perfume.

Hannah followed suit. 'Room for a small one?'

'I've missed you both so much.' God, it felt good to be back with her girls. It really hadn't been that long on paper. They'd caught up over Christmas, doing last-minute Christmas shopping on the Saturday before Christmas Day (big mistake, they'd queued in Primark for over forty-five minutes) and then went for drinks at the Red Lion for New Year's Eve. But today felt different.

Too soon, Hannah pulled away. 'Let's go to my room. You can dump your stuff off, Alicia, and we can start getting ready for later. Eeeek. Can't wait to show you girls a proper night out in London town. Just you wait.'

'Three-way, oioi. Can I come?' Jonesy continued to make himself known.

'Fuck off.' Hannah grinned at him. Marnie could tell she meant it, but with a smile like Hannah's, it probably gave Jonesy a boner.

He blew her a kiss. 'Shame I'm not around tonight, it would have been a laugh to join you.'

'Even if you were around, it's girls only I'm afraid.' With that, Hannah linked her arms through both Marnie and Alicia's, and marched them out the kitchen.

Hannah's room was, again, exactly how Marnie had expected it. Tidy, but not in an *everything needs to be super perfect* Alicia way. She had more makeup and skincare than a Mac counter on her desk instead of the standard laptop and lever-arch files, and an impressive collection of high heels, boots and shoes lined the shelves. Hannah had made the room her own by laying a pink fluffy rug on the nasty navy carpet – obviously that colour to hide the sins of spilt alcohol, sick and general antics of many students past. A lattice of fairy lights and printed photos decorated the wall nearest the bed, a mix of snapshots from Hannah's old life and new.

'So which one of your flatmates have you shagged, then?' Marnie asked as she flopped onto Hannah's bed. She landed in a mountain of pillows and a furry pink throw that matched the rug. Alicia joined her while Hannah sat on the swivel chair.

'There's a chart on the noticeboard.' Hannah nodded behind Marnie, where, true to her word a bedraggled-looking piece of A4 hung from a daisy-shaped drawing pin pierced through one corner. As expected, Jonesy's name was the first one on there.

'Didn't think Jonesy was your type.'

'Is that the dude in the kitchen?' Alicia asked, failing to conceal her horror.

'Yeah. And he's not my type really.'

'Why then? Big dick?' Marnie frowned. 'Very *generous*?'

'Couldn't tell you. I was totally obliterated on vodka at the time and it's pretty normal to start with the flatmates then attempt a more exotic location, like Hackney or Southbank when more practised. I'd rather not do the walk of shame on the tube with the morning commuters.'

'But him, really? You could do way better.' Marnie raised an eyebrow.

Hannah spun on the chair, her long brown hair bouncing with the momentum. 'Don't slut shame me.'

'I'm not!'

'It's important to be safe.' Alicia always knew what Marnie meant, even when Hannah missed it.

'You sound like a safe sex video I was forced to watch

in Year Eight. I'm still traumatised by that.' Hannah made her way to the wardrobe and started shuffling through the myriad of clothes that hung there.

Alicia glanced at Marnie. They did this often: the quickest of glimpses that had become a part of their unspoken language formed over multiple years – an expression of solidarity and understanding. 'I didn't mean it like that. I meant you don't want to be taken advantage of.'

'Or murdered,' Marnie added.

'I'm just loving single life. Leave me be.' Hannah pulled a silver bodycon dress from the wardrobe and held it up to her tiny frame. 'Have you done it yet, Ali?'

Alicia shook her head. 'Waiting for the right person, still.'

'But these are your prime shagging years.' Hannah threw the dress on the bed beside them and then started perusing her shoe shelf.

'I'm sure I'll get over it.'

Marnie loved the way that Alicia was always just . . . herself. She never did things just because everyone else did. If she didn't want to do it, there wasn't enough peer pressure in the world to get her to break. It was admirable.

'Don't get over it, get *under* it.' Hannah flung a pair of black strappy heels to join the dress on the bed. Marnie knew the next thing to follow would be jewellery. 'So, the plan for tonight. Get ready now and pre-drinks here, taxi to town at 8pm. Spoons for more prinks. Then Yates then Fabric. It's free entry before ten.'

'What about dinner?' Alicia's brow creased.

Hannah shrugged. 'Skip it?'

'I can't just skip dinner. I'm starving.'

'Same,' Marnie agreed. Despite not really feeling like eating anything, when she didn't eat she felt even worse. She reckoned she had about an hour before the nausea peaked again. The plain ham sandwich she had on the train just about did the trick, but it wouldn't last forever.

'I'll have a greasy kebab and cheesy chips after, when it doesn't matter if I look fat or not,' said Hannah, knowing full well that she'd never looked fat a day in her life.

'You'll be sick if you drink on an empty stomach.' Alicia was back in mum mode.

On the topic of stomachs . . . Marnie looked down at her own waistline which was more bloated than usual. Whoever coined the term 'Freshers' fifteen' was not wrong. She'd already planned on hiding it in a loose-fitting t-shirt dress. She wasn't one for bodycon or tight clothes anyway. That was Hannah's domain. 'I'll need to eat.'

'Fine. But I'm not cooking. You can have toast or nuggets if you do it yourself.'

Marnie reckoned she could stomach that just fine, and it would buy her another few hours of feeling slightly less queasy. 'Toast and nuggets it is.'

After their beige feast, the girls took turns to shower and blow dry their hair. Hannah put her hair in curlers and wore a sheer dressing gown with fur trim as if she was a 1940s Hollywood film star. Inevitably, out came the wine – the cheapest rosé you could get at Tesco.

To Marnie's surprise, even Alicia was drinking, though Marnie knew she'd stop at a sensible amount like she did at Christmas.

'So gals, I have some important news to share with you.' Hannah was at her desk-cum-dressing table, with a huge light-up mirror and every inch of surface area covered with bottles, brushes and palettes. Marnie and Alicia had to make do with their laps and a handheld compact.

Over the years, Marnie had learned not to take Hannah's announcements too seriously. Hannah lived for the drama and could make anything sound thrilling – even a story about her nan's swollen toe or a trip to Morrisons became worthy of a monologue at the Edinburgh Fringe. Marnie had always admired her creativity.

Alicia looked up from her mirror where she was applying dots of her concealer. 'Go on. Put us out of our misery.'

'I'm going to be an influencer!'

'How does one do that?' Alicia went back to blending in her makeup with a pristine-looking beauty blender, the opposite of Marnie's unwashed ball of bacteria.

'One works hard at it in the same way you would any job.'

'Hmmm. Okay.' Alicia clearly wasn't convinced. Hannah couldn't have been surprised. If the path was not a well-trodden one with a clear route from A to B, it wouldn't be considered feasible in Alicia's mind.

'Don't be negative, you'll bring my vibration down and then it won't happen.'

'And that will be my fault?'

'Yes.'

Marnie stepped in to change the subject. Alicia and Hannah would never see eye to eye on certain things so it was Marnie's job to redirect such conversations before they escalated. It was that or blast the hairdryer at full volume. 'What are you influencing?'

'Fashion, beauty, makeup. I have an Instagram and a YouTube channel.'

'If it makes you happy,' Marnie concluded, swiping on a bold smudge of black eyeshadow from her worn Naked Palette. If anyone could be a successful influencer, it was

Hannah. Yes, she had her flights of fancies, but she always went all in. Marnie had no doubt she'd get wherever she wanted in life, she just had to choose something and stick to it, for a change. Maybe this would be the thing to stick.

'See, Alicia, you could just be happy for me.'

Marnie gave up trying to mediate. *Oh well, I tried.*

Alicia rolled her eyes. 'It's not that I'm *not* happy for you. I want the best for you, and I'm not sure this is it.'

'Alright, Mum. Well there's no need to worry about little old me, I know what I'm doing,' and with that, Hannah turned in her swivel chair and started slathering on an expensive-looking Estée Lauder cream.

Now was the time for the hairdryer.

As Marnie dried her candy-floss pink hair – a new addition last September as part of her uni rebrand – she noticed everyone else was getting to the bottom of their glasses. Although her show of picking up her drink and putting it to her lips must have been fairly convincing, her full glass was not.

She switched off the dryer and grabbed her makeup bag. 'I'll do my eyeliner in the bathroom – the lighting's better,' she said, slipping into Hannah's en suite. She pushed the door ajar, careful not to fully close it and raise suspicions. A quick glance over her shoulder confirmed no one was watching, and she emptied her wine down the sink.

She joined the others back in the room.

'Did you do your eyeliner, babe?' Hannah studied her face with a frown.

Fuck. What an idiot. 'Errr. Yeah. Just went subtle.'

'Oh. Did you go for the shadow technique rather than the liquid? Looks nice.' Hannah went back to her own face where she was slicking on the final coat of Mac Ruby Woo. 'Taxi in five. Shoes on. Lippy on. Down your glasses, gals!'

Marnie's stomach roiled as the taxi wove its way down the side streets of London, taking the route only a taxi driver who knew the roads like the back of their hand would do. She focused her attention out of the window that she'd cracked open slightly when she hoped no one would notice. She had motion sickness at the best of times, but now she was feeling more fragile, things were choppy to say the least. They jolted over a bump, then lurched as the car braked hard to dodge a bus muscling into their lane. Marnie clenched her cheeks, eyes squeezed shut. Deep breaths. The nausea clung stubbornly. It was going to be a long night. She was silent the rest of the way, smiling and saying at most 'mhmm' in fear that if she opened her mouth to speak she would throw up. Thankfully, her quietness seemed to go unnoticed as Alicia and Hannah filled the space with the chatterings of tipsy young women. Hopefully, the more they drank, the less they would notice that Marnie wasn't.

Clubbing while feeling sick was *not* pleasant – in fact, it was like the seventh circle of hell. But Marnie plastered on a permanent smile and bobbed her head to the music whenever she felt Alicia or Hannah looking at her.

Hannah had insisted on getting Jägerbombs the minute they arrived, to which Marnie had to claim she was going to wee herself if she didn't go to the toilet that very second (in fairness, it was true). This excuse allowed her to avoid the Jäger, but she still ended up taking two sips of a vodka orange before discreetly disposing of it in the pot of a plastic Yucca plant. Thankfully, she'd eventually found a system that semi-worked: offering to buy the drinks and quickly making her escape before anyone could object. That way, she could escape the claustrophobic sweatbox that was the dancefloor, order herself a plain coke and claim it was a double Jack Daniels. She'd be broke by the end of the night, but sober.

Coming back with round number four, Marnie joined Alicia and Hannah in the throng of clumsy partygoers getting down to 'Wake Me Up' by Avicii. The constant jostling felt like her stomach contents were in a blender, but she worked out that if she stuck her nose in her drink and sniffed, it helped a bit to mask the pungent mix of aromas around her – copious amounts of Jo Malone, alcohol, body odour and aftershave.

This is fine. I can do anything for just one night. Worst comes to worst and I am sick, it wouldn't be that strange in a place full of shitfaced students who are dry humping against the DJ booth. The mental strength it took for Marnie to get through to the end of the song was more than she needed to get through her Year Eleven Duke of Edinburgh, and they'd even got lost for three hours on that trip. She'd do that again three times over than subject herself to this ever again.

And then it got worse. A tall, wide man, clearly off his tits, barged into their circle, arms flailing, grabbing onto anyone he could reach like a malfunctioning claw machine. Hannah kept dancing, unfazed by the fact she was now wedged under his armpit, while Alicia managed to dodge him but kept her awkward shuffle going. It was too much.

The stench of his sweat hit her like a punch to the face – so rancid she could practically taste it. Nausea rose in her throat, followed by the telltale rush of adrenaline and saliva. She couldn't hold it back anymore. She had to get out. Fast. She shoved her way through the crowd, slipping on a wet patch as she went.

In the bathroom, she fell into a stall, dropped to her knees and emptied the contents of her stomach into the toilet. Just as she'd finished the first heave, she caught a whiff of the overflowing sanitary bin and felt the liquid on the floor seep through her tights and off she went again, retching with such force her eyes watered and her throat burned as if someone held a lighter to it.

She sat there for what felt like an eternity, in fear that if she moved she'd go again. Finally, she pulled herself up onto her feet and shuffled on weak legs to open the stall door. Right in front of her stood Alicia, eyes full of concern.

'Oh my God, Marnie. What's wrong?'

Fuck. Shit. Fuck. How much had she heard?

'Not feeling too good. Must have been a dodgy nugget.'

'But I'm feeling fine. So is Hannah and she had one.'

'Drinking too much?'

'You've had barely anything.'

Balls. Of course Alicia had noticed. Why did she have to be so bloody observant?

'What are you both doing in here without me?' Hannah had appeared, looking more than worse for wear, pink-faced and lipstick smudged.

'Marn's not well.' Alicia looked at Marnie, brow crumpled with concern. Marnie looked away.

'Tactical chunder?' Hannah smiled, eyelids heavy and movements clumsy as she shuffled around in her bag and pulled out her lippy.

Alicia shook her head. 'Maybe we should go home.'

Yes. Home sounded like a wonderful idea.

'But it's only eleven. One more drink?'

'I can't. I'm really not feeling it.' *Take the hint, Han.*

'You can! Stop being a pussy. One little drinky and then

we can call it a night. We have to stay until at least midnight. Otherwise tonight will have been a total fail.'

'I really think we should go home.' Alicia crossed her arms, steadier than Hannah who was now leaning on the sink for stability.

'Of course you do, you'd rather we'd have gone to bed at ten!'

'Don't be out of order. I'm really not feeling it. Please.' Did Marnie really need to beg?

'Boring much.'

Fury rose in Marnie's chest. She was tired. She felt sick. She looked like shit. Was Hannah really that selfish? Really that . . . unaware. 'I'm not fucking boring, Han. I think I'm . . .'

Alicia stepped forward. 'Pregnant?'

Marnie's brow crumpled and tears she didn't know were there forced themselves out with gusto. She didn't care there were other people there. She didn't care she had a piece of toilet roll on her shoe or that her tights had a ladder from ankle to thigh.

'No. You can't be.' Hannah stared at her, mouth agape.

Marnie wiped her eyes with the back of her hand. She forced the tears to stop. She was good at that. Zipping it all back up and putting it in a box. When she was semi-composed again, she spoke. 'I very much can be.'

'How?'

'When a man loves a woman very much . . .' Marnie tried to smile but the weight of her predicament made it impossible.

Alicia bit her lip. 'Whose is it? Do you know for certain you are?'

'Don't know.' Marnie shrugged.

'How can you not know?'

'Hannah. That's not helpful,' Alicia scolded. 'Marns, what we're going to do is go to a late-night pharmacy and get a test, okay?'

'I don't want to know.'

'I don't care. It's better to know now so you can have time to . . . work out what you're going to do about it.' Marnie had never seen Alicia so decisive.

'Obviously she's getting rid of it. She can't keep it.' Hannah looked at Marnie, eyebrows raised. 'You wouldn't keep it, would you?'

Marnie threw her hands up despondently. Of course she couldn't keep it. She couldn't have a baby. How would she finish her degree? She'd never even held a baby before. She was nineteen. What would her parents think? Her mum cried when she'd got a D in her GCSEs, for Christ's sake.

But then the thought of getting rid of . . . it. Them. A part of her that, through her own calculations, must have been growing inside her for at least the last six weeks . . .

'We're going. Now.' Alicia grabbed Marnie's hand. They all looked at each other.

Without a word, Hannah nodded, grabbed Marnie's other hand, and they headed out the loos.

Back in Hannah's room, the girls sat on her bed. Marnie clutched the carrier bag they'd acquired from the only 24/7 pharmacy. Alongside two pregnancy tests (according to Alicia, you could never be sure with one), they'd also grabbed some Gaviscon, micellar water and cotton pads, to make their purchase seem less weird and more 'casual' – Hannah's idea. Not that they could have looked anywhere close to casual, considering they were dressed to the nines in heels, fake tan and falsies. They'd also stopped at the corner shop for a bag of Thai Sweet Chilli Sensations; there was no time for a greasy kebab but Hannah and Alicia needed something to combat the alcohol they'd sunk – Hannah more than Alicia.

It was now almost midnight.

Marnie pulled the tests out of the bag and looked at them.

'Do you need a wee?' Alicia asked.

'I always need a wee.'

The three of them chuckled a bit, then it was back to silence.

'Actually, I've changed my mind. I'm just being dramatic. It's super normal for your period to be late due to stress.'

'Are you stressed?' Hannah pulled the cotton pads and micellar water from the bag and started taking her makeup off.

'I didn't think so, but then again, how could I not be? Uni is a huge change to school. Moving all the way to Scotland.'

'But I thought you loved uni. Loved living away from home.' Alicia peered at Marnie as she nibbled on a single crisp.

'Maybe it's my diet, then. Greasy chips, undercooked chicken and reheated Chinese takeaway would upset anyone's stomach, right?' Saying that, Marnie had always been known for her Stomach of Steel, her claim to fame being that she'd gone her whole life without having a proper case of diarrhoea, and the last time she'd been sick had been when she was four.

'Come on. We're here with you. Better now than on your own.' Alicia grabbed one of the pregnancy test boxes and opened it, sliding out its contents and reading the instructions.

'I don't want to do it.' At least Marnie had been living in the unknown. To Alicia, the unknown was terrifying, but to Marnie right now, it was bliss. She didn't want it confirmed because then it would be real.

After a couple more minutes, Marnie snatched the test from Alicia and swung herself off the bed.

'Fine. I'll do it.'

She didn't shut the door. The girls had seen worse, although she was sure it was on no one's agenda to be watching her as she pissed in a toothbrush holder. She pulled her knickers back up and joined the girls back in the room.

'You look. I can't do it.' Marnie thrust the test to Alicia. Alicia patted the bed beside her but Marnie shook her head. She couldn't sit down. She needed to pace. What happened in the next few minutes had the power to change her entire life.

Alicia set a timer.

Every second felt twice as long as it should, her heartbeat the opposite. 'Oh my God. This is the longest three minutes of my life.'

'Is that what you said to the sperm donor who . . .' Alica elbowed Hannah hard in the ribs. 'Never mind.'

'Why's it taking so long?' Marnie was about ready to be sick again.

The alarm went off. Alicia flipped the test over in her hand.

'It's positive.'

Chapter Three

Hannah

Marnie grabbed the test and stood frozen, staring at the little white stick in her hand.

'Fuck.' Hannah didn't know what else to say. What the hell was the correct way to react? There was a baby in Marnie's womb. Or was it just cells at this point? Yes, probably.

'Are you sure?' Marnie still didn't look up.

'Yes.'

'Where are the instructions?' Marnie snatched them from Alicia's grasp. 'Where does it say that a line is positive? Are you sure there's a line? It could just be the shadow. God, why is the lighting so shit in here?'

It was Hannah's turn to snatch as she grabbed the test and went into the en suite. 'The light is better in here. I'll check.' Alicia could be wrong. It was one of the cheapo tests. They did debate getting one of the ClearBlue ones that said in black and white Pregnant or Not Pregnant, but it was fifteen quid.

Balls. The line was faint but it was definitely there. Hannah flipped the stick this way and that, squinting at it from a few centimetres distance to then arm's length.

Nope. Still two lines.

'And it's definitely two lines for pregnant?' Hannah said, joining the girls back in the bedroom. She already knew the answer.

They were back in their positions on the bed, all three sitting side by side, backs against the wall.

'What am I going to do?' Marnie whispered, dropping her head into her hands.

Alicia rubbed Marnie on the back. 'You have options. We don't need to panic.'

Hilariously ironic from Anxiety Alicia, but now wasn't the time for jokes. Now was the time for support. The panic would come later.

'Totally. This isn't the 1950s anymore, babe. Do you want a drink, to calm your mind down?'

'Really, Hannah?' Alicia's eyebrows arched in dismay.

'Oh yeah. Sorry.'

'Let's take the other test tomorrow with your first morning wee, just to confirm. Then we'll go to the clinic. They can talk you through options.'

'But what about uni? Mum and Dad? They're going to be so disappointed in me. What about my future? It's ruined. I've fucked it up.'

If Marnie had a baby, she was right. But Hannah couldn't say that.

'Everything will be okay. We've got you.' She slid both arms around Marnie's waist and rested her head near her stomach, making sure not to lean too heavily. There was a living being – or the beginnings of one – inches from Hannah's face.

'Yes. Whatever you choose, we'll be here for you.' Alicia squeezed Marnie's knee.

'But I'm scared. I can't have a baby. But the thought of having an abortion . . . but then what if I leave it too late and I have no choice?' Marnie whimpered.

'We'll cross that bridge when we come to it.'

'What would you guys do?'

Hannah knew what she'd do in this situation. She'd get rid of it, obviously. How was Marnie even questioning it? 'I couldn't have a baby. Not now. Preferably not ever.'

Alicia sighed. 'I don't know what I'd do.'

It was pointless asking Alicia. She'd never find herself in the position of an unwanted pregnancy. She'd have to be having sex, firstly, but also she'd never risk an unprotected shag.

'You say you'd get rid of it but it's not that easy.' Marnie shook her head.

'Don't you just have to take some pills and be done with it?' Hannah read somewhere it would be like a heavy period. Or was that just a myth? You couldn't believe everything you see online – she knew that. Since starting her Instagram account a few months ago, most of her posts were smoke and mirrors. A photo captioned *solo date night* of a bubble bath and candles was all for show, but no one wanted to see the reality of her eating a bowl of microwave peas while watching a *Made in Chelsea* marathon. Things were moving on from Tumblr and Pinterest, and Hannah was keen to keep up.

'If it's early enough, yeah, but some of the horror stories I've heard . . .' Marnie's voice petered out. 'And if it's too late then you have to have surgery.'

'Oh.' Hannah didn't know that. 'Still, that would be easier

than giving birth, wouldn't it? And having a baby for the rest of your life?'

'Physically, maybe. But I'd be killing it.' Marnie whispered the last part.

Then the sooner it's sorted the better.

'You wouldn't be killing it, Marns. Look, this is rubbish but you're not on your own. We're always here for you, aren't we, Han?'

'Of course,' replied Hannah. 'Everything's going to be fine.

Hot Mess Express 🚂 😃

17th February, 2014

Alicia: Marnie, have you had any more thoughts about what to do yet?

Marnie: Lots of thoughts, no conclusions 🙄

Hannah: Have you spoke to the doctor or called the clinic?

Marnie: No.

Alicia: It sounds scary but you only have to call to get some more information to help inform your decision. It doesn't mean you have to go through with anything.

Marnie: Just can't bring myself to do it.

Hannah: We will do it with you.

Marnie: Soon. Not yet. I need more time.

Alicia: The longer you leave it, the harder it will get x

Marnie: Wah.

Hannah: When are you telling your parents?

Marnie: Never? lol. I'll only tell them if I keep it. They don't need to know otherwise.

Alicia: Are you sure they won't be able to help?

Marnie: How would they help? Mum will be devastated, Dad will disown me.

Alicia: Do you really think he would?

Marnie: Hopefully not, but he won't be pleased.

Alicia: They will love you no matter what.

Marnie: I'm not so sure.

21st February, 2014

Marnie: I told Mum. It just came out, I couldn't keep lying about it.

Hannah: And?

Marnie: I haven't been kicked out but they've made it very clear what they want me to do.

Alicia: And that is . . .?

Marnie: Get rid of it.

Alicia: Is that what they said?

Marnie: Yep. That I'll fuck up my life if I keep it and how disappointed they are that their only child and the first in the family to go to university is thinking about throwing it all away. We called the clinic to discuss. I have an appointment tomorrow.

Hannah: Do you want us to come?

Marnie: I do, but Mum is insisting on coming with me.

Alicia: What about your dad?

Marnie: His usual silent resentment. He hates me.

Alicia: I'm sure he doesn't, he's probably just shocked.

Marnie: I get that, but how do they not see that I feel all of these things and more? It's so shit. I can't believe I've got myself into this.

Alicia: Life happens. They will get over it and you will be okay. Promise me you will keep talking to us and don't do anything you don't want to do? It's your choice at the end of the day.

Marnie: I'll try x

Hannah: <3

1st July, 2014

Hannah: I'm nominating you for the #icebucketchallenge, Alicia.

Alicia: I'm not doing it!

Hannah: But it's for charity.

Marnie: Have you actually donated anything to charity or are you just doing it so Jason Hill can see you in a wet t-shirt? 😏

Hannah: Dunno what you mean!

27th August, 2014

Alicia: Anyone watching GBBO?

Hannah: What do you think?

Marnie: I am! OMG poor Ian. #Bingate. Almost cried over a baked Alaska. Hormones be raging.

28th October, 2014

Marnie: She's here. Sophie Jade Grendle. 8 pounds exactly. RIP to my vagina. You'll have to meet her asap while you can still enjoy newborn snuggles and her head still smells like baby x

Hannah: OMG congrats. Was worried about you when you went AWOL for two days. Glad you aren't dead x

Alicia: She's perfect. Love her so much already.

Hannah: How was the birth?

Marnie: Will elaborate more on video call but long story short, at one point I begged Mum to shoot me in the head and end it all x

Hannah: :/

Alicia: Ouch.

Hannah: Did you poo during labour?

Marnie: Dunno. Told Mum and the midwives not to tell me if I did. They can take it to their grave.

Alicia: Will you breastfeed?

Marnie: Maybe. Bit weird for me to get my tits out in public when I'm not drunk, but hey ho. Let's get a date in asap.

17th December, 2014

Alicia: Would either of you mind if I brought Neelam to the Red Lion at Xmas? She's staying round the corner with family for Christmas x

Marnie: Of course, the more the merrier!

Hannah: Fine with me. I look forward to meeting your one friend 😭

Alicia: OI!

2nd February, 2015

Hannah: Galsssss. Galentine's is fast approaching. Can we nail down some plans plz. Shall we go out for dinner? The Lounge looks nice. Very Instagrammable! I've got a new dress I want to wear out toooooooooo. Thoughts?

Marnie: Great idea. I'll put my three-month-old in her best heels and put her two strands of hair into an elegant updo x

Hannah: I thought your mum was having her?

Marnie: She's still breastfeeding, babe.

Hannah: Give her a bottle?

Alicia: It doesn't work like that.

Hannah: And you know that how?

Marnie: She's right. Baby is coming with, I'm afraid.

Hannah: Where? Can't have a baby in my uni house.

Marnie: Can we go to your parents' place, Alicia?

Alicia: Mum and Dad said never again after tequilagate 😵

Hannah: Well it will have to be at yours then, Marnie.

Marnie: I'm so sick of mine. If I spend much more time here I'm worried I'll go crazy.

Hannah: You cannot be serious. Where will we put a baby at mine?

Marnie: I'll bring her travel cot.

Hannah: And put it where? In the bath?

Marnie: She's only small.

Marnie: Pretty plz. I'll pay for the takeaway.

Hannah: Alicia, are you sure your fam won't have us?

Alicia: I'm sure.

Hannah: FFS. Fine. But not my uni house. I'll talk to Mum and Dad about co-opting the basement.

Marnie: PERFECT. LIFE SAVER. Can't wait to see youuuuuuuuuu.

Alicia: Me too! I bet Sophie is so much bigger already.

Hannah: Love ya both. G2G.

10th February, 2015

Hannah: Follow my YouTube channel please! Also can you ask your friends and family to follow my Insta? Doesn't matter if they like lifestyle or beauty stuff, just need numbers.

Social media strategy 2014-15: @LondonGirlHan

Bio: Just a girl living in London. Personal blog, doing my thang. Come along for the ride! x

Platform	Content
YouTube	What I wear to a 9am lecture!
YouTube	Uni room tour
Instagram	Fresh hair who dis?
Instagram	The best avo on toast <3

Followers: 12

@PinkNanny: Loved your uni room tour x

@LondonGirlHan: Thanks Nan lol x

Chapter Four

13th February, 2015

Alicia

Marnie, in her true no fucks given style, appeared on Hannah's doorstep with an actual suitcase, a bag for life tied to the handle, a changing bag on her back, and baby Sophie in the crook of her elbow. She was already dressed in her pyjamas, obviously.

'You are utter chaos, you know that, right?' Hannah said with an affectionate grin.

Alicia was grateful for Marnie's whirlwind arrival – it hadn't been awkward just her and Hannah, but equilibrium was always restored when two became three.

'Me? Chaotic? Someone take my baby,' Marnie thrust a crying Sophie towards Alicia and Hannah.

Hannah expertly dodged the wailing baby. 'I'll get the suitcase. It's more my style.'

'I'll take her,' said Alicia, with Sophie being deposited in her arms before she finished her sentence. She clutched onto a writhing Sophie with a vice grip as Marnie and Hannah embraced.

'Missed you, girlies.' Marnie grinned, as she slid the changing bag off her back and pulled a dummy out of its many pockets. She popped it into Sophie's mouth.

'Oh no, why is she crying?' exclaimed Alicia, taking in Sophie's devastated face, bright red and wet with tears.

'Babies do that,' laughed Hannah. 'Shall we head to the basement?'

Marnie smiled. 'I thought you'd never ask.'

At the top of the stairs, Alicia stopped. Marnie and Hannah had already sped off, turning the corner out of sight. Was she really entrusted to carry the baby down a flight of stairs? How would that work logistically? Two hands on the baby or one hand on the bannister? Was Alicia really going to have to sit down and bum-shuffle her way down?

'You alright? Want me to take her?' Marnie appeared at the bottom of the stairs. Thank God.

'Yes please. Don't want to drop her.'

Marnie expertly grabbed Sophie from Alicia's hold and skipped down the stairs with no hesitation. 'She bounces.'

Alicia followed. 'I do not want to know how you know that.'

The next half an hour was spent sorting out the sleeping arrangements and of course, changing into their matching PJs. Gone were the fleecy pink Primark sets, to be replaced with a much more mature red satin set from Victoria's Secret, chosen, of course, by Hannah. This year, even the baby matched, with Marnie sliding her into a red baby grow with little heart snap-buttons running down the front and an embroidered heart on the front pocket. Alicia felt self-conscious wearing them. The shorts were much shorter than she was used to and she didn't have as much to fill out the strappy top as the other girls so she made sure to wear her dressing gown whenever she ventured out of the basement.

As they caught up on the general gossip of life – *Has anyone heard from Jonie McCarty since her twerking episode to Robin Thicke at the pub over Christmas? Has Marnie's nan gotten over the death of Margaret Thatcher yet? What does everyone think of Hannah's new fringe? Who's read* Fifty Shades of Grey? – Marnie expertly held, rocked and fed Sophie. It was mad to think that four months ago, she'd never done any of this motherhood stuff before, and now here she was, acting as if she'd been doing it all her life. Was this newfound skill just something that happened when your body grew and subsequently popped out a child? Alicia sure hoped so. She loved babies but interacting with them never came naturally to her.

Alicia and Marnie had met Sophie for the first time properly when she was just four weeks old.

Nanny Sheila had led them into the living room where Marnie was sitting cradling the tiny pink bundle that was her daughter.

'Oh my God, she's so cute,' was all Alicia could think to say. What words could have possibly done justice to a moment with such magnitude?

Marnie had grinned. 'Want a hold?'

Hannah had bulldozed her way in, despite Alicia dying to be the first. Hannah sat with the baby as if it was a bomb about to go off, only erasing the look of fear and mild disgust on her face for an Instagram-worthy photo using the dog-filter for added insult to injury.

'Am I holding it right?' she'd said through her dazzling smile.

The minute the photo was taken, Hannah turned to Alicia. 'Your turn. I know you're desperate for a cuddle.'

Alicia made sure she was sitting in a comfortable position

with her arms supported in the chair and an extra cushion for good measure.

Alicia stared at this tiny human, who'd only existed as a bunch of cells last Galentine's Day, with a mix of awe and overwhelming love. *I'm holding Marnie's baby. MARNIE'S BABY. One day, I'll have one. Maybe more.* In fact, according to The Plan, she'd be holding her first within five years. She better get a shift on and meet Mr Right if that was going to happen.

Maybe she'd give herself a little more time. The years were already going quickly, and if what the older adults in her life kept telling her was true, the years would only speed up. But then, Alicia had a plan, and what was the point of a plan if she wasn't going to stick to it?

Now here they were, almost three months later, staring at Sophie all over again, who this time was grinning at them all from her vantage point of the baby bouncer.

'This thing's a life-saver,' said Marnie as she tucked a blanket over Sophie's legs. 'She loves it.'

'She looks so much bigger already since the last time I saw her.' Alicia had visited two more times since that first visit, just her and Marnie, and each time Sophie was looking less and less pink blob, more actual human being.

'Yep. Nanny Sheila thinks she'll be tall, like my dad.'

Sophie's light blue eyes stared up at Alicia, framed with the most delicate wispy white-blonde lashes. God, she looked so much like Marnie. It was like Marnie had created her single-handedly. There had still been no mention of the father, even all this time later. Not even Hannah had brought it up, which meant it was seriously taboo.

'How is it living with Nanny Sheila, then?' Hannah asked.

'Great. I don't love how far it is, but she's so much more

supportive than my parents ever would be. I'll tell you that for free.'

'It is a shame you're not closer.' Though it was hardly Mordor, Aylesbury wasn't just down the road like Marnie's parents' house was. Ideally, Alicia wanted to visit every week, uni dependent, and dreamed of being that auntie who helped out often and supported Marnie as she navigated the demands of motherhood. But as it was, Marnie's parents weren't the most understanding, and their house was tiny, so it was mutually agreed that Marnie would live with Nanny Sheila until the extension was finished (and likely, the majority of the newborn phase was over, much to her parents' benefit).

Still, seeing them both every few weeks was better than not at all, and more often than Hannah had managed. It had also been nice spending that one-on-one (ish) quality time with Marnie – it was like the old days before Hannah arrived on the scene (with the addition of Marnie's mini plus one, obviously).

'What does she do, then?' said Hannah, sliding a Vaseline tub from the front pocket of her pyjamas and slicking it on her lips.

Marnie shrugged. 'Eat, smile, sleep, cry and shit.'

'Fun.' Hannah's brow raised.

'Does she have a bedtime?' asked Alicia.

'I'm hoping she'll go down at 11 ish. Might be up for a feed at three or four. Then back down. But you never know. This is very much out of her routine.'

'Get you using all your fancy mum words. She'll go down. Very much out of her routine.'

Marnie smiled. 'I know. Who do I think I am?'

'Mummy.' The word felt weird in Alicia's mouth. 'Is it weird to be called that?'

Marnie absent-mindedly stroked Sophie's chubby cheeks as she spoke. 'Yes and no. It's like she's been here my whole life. When I saw her face for the first time, I had this feeling we'd met before. But then I catch moments where I'm like, what the actual fuck? This thing came out of my vagina. How am I being trusted to know what I'm doing?'

Hannah's face lit up. 'I used to feel like that when I was first driving after passing my test.'

'Totally the same thing,' said Marnie, to which they all giggled.

Smiles quickly changed to frowns of concern as they all began to sniff the air. Uh oh.

'Either one of you has farted or the baby needs changing.' Hannah grimaced.

'Well done, Agatha Christie.' Marnie stood up and grabbed the changing bag from her pile of belongings in the corner.

'Shotgun not me.' Hannah backed away quicker than she'd swiped the first hold of baby Sophie three months ago.

'Obviously I'll do it. She's my baby after all.' Marnie unzipped the bag and pulled out an array of nappy-changing paraphernalia.

Alicia should offer. Marnie had been through so much, it's the least she could do. 'You deserve a break. I'll do it.' Was this a bad idea? She'd never changed a nappy before, what if she did it wrong? 'Well, I'll give it a go, anyway. You'll have to coach me through it.'

'Deal.' Marnie detached Sophie from the straps of the bouncer and slid her out. 'I'm not going to turn down an offer like that.' Marnie put the blanket down in front of her and placed Sophie on it.

Hannah's eyes widened. 'You're not going to do it here, are you?'

'Yeah. 'Fraid so.'

'Ewwww. Do you have to?'

'The bathroom's too small. You'll get over it.'

'Fine. Tell me when it's over. And if you get shit on the carpet, we're officially over as friends.' With that, Hannah threw the duvet over her head and the smothered sound of 'All About That Bass' by Meghan Trainor emanated from beneath the duvet.

Alicia shuffled next to Marnie. 'Sorry if I get it wrong.'

'The worst that will happen is you'll get shat on.' Marnie grinned.

'Gross, stooop.' Hannah muffled.

Marnie rolled her eyes. 'Drama queen,' she mouthed. Alicia smiled back with the thrill of someone in on the joke.

'Unpop these.' Marnie gestured to the heart snaps that Alicia had admired earlier. 'She might cry. She doesn't like being naked.'

'Can't relate.' Hannah laughed to herself.

Alicia did as she was told, fumbling like an idiot despite it being a simple task.

'Perfect. Now slide her legs out then shuffle her down so the baby grow is out of the danger zone.'

'I don't want to hurt her.'

Marnie expertly slid one of Sophie's legs out and gave her little foot a kiss for good measure. Marnie tickled her belly and Sophie giggled. 'She's more sturdy than she looks.'

'You make it look so easy. You're such a natural.'

'I've had some practice. The first time I did it I put the nappy on backwards. And super hilarious you think I know what I'm actually doing. I'm raising this child on vibes, Google searches and a prayer, babe.'

That did make Alicia feel a little better. She slid out the

remaining leg and shuffled Sophie down on the mat clumsily. *Why am I shaking? It's just a dirty nappy.*

'Perfect. Now for the fun part. Are you sure you want to do this?'

No. 'Yes?'

'Undo the sticky bits, and let's get cracking.'

Chapter Five

13th February, 2015

Marnie

They'd decided against getting an Indian takeaway, all of them being put off the idea of chicken korma in the immediate future. Instead, they'd enjoyed a pizza, Marnie's suggestion because it was the easiest thing to eat with just one hand free.

By midnight, and by some miracle, Sophie had gone down in her travel cot, wrapped in a swaddle having been rocked to high heaven for at least forty minutes beforehand. Marnie was on the camping bed beside her, and Alicia and Hannah were on the pullout couch. The basement was the perfect setting for a sleepover. Unlike Alicia's cramped bedroom, it was massive, the entire floorplan of the house, and two floors away from parents. Why hadn't Hannah offered to host before?

'Night night, girls,' whispered Marnie. 'See you tomorrow.'

'You aren't going to sleep just yet, are you?' exclaimed Hannah, palpable horror in her voice.

Marnie chuckled. 'No, course not. But I am fucking

knackered.' She now understood why sleep deprivation was a form of torture.

'You can go to bed if you want to,' Alicia said.' You probably need to sleep for one hundred years to catch up on all the sleep you've lost over the last few months, but anything is better than nothing, right?'

'You're too nice,' said Hannah, but despite her accusatory words, she shuffled herself closer to Alicia. It was nice to see them show affection towards each other. Hannah was always affectionate towards Marnie, stroking her forearm and playing with her hair, to the point where some people had speculated whether they were actually together, but Alicia wasn't as touchy-feely usually.

'Nothing wrong with being too nice.' Marnie was no longer whispering. There was no need now Sophie was asleep because she was used to noise. Marnie would often hoover the house during her naps and made sure not to tiptoe around – a tip from good old Nanny Sheila. Marnie sighed. 'I love you, girls.'

'That was a big sigh. You okay?' Alicia studied Marnie.

'Yeah. Fine.'

Alicia sat up. 'No you're not.'

Marnie shifted onto her elbow to rest her head in her hand. 'I am!' she insisted, but it was pointless to argue. Alicia could always tell when something was on Marnie's mind.

'No you're not. You can go to sleep if you want to, honestly.'

'It's not that. I'm tired but I'm used to running off fumes these days.' Even on a good night, Sophie would wake up at least twice, yet she'd somehow chug on, even if it felt like moving through treacle.

'What is it, then?' Hannah asked.

Marnie sighed again, pushing the air out her lungs as if trying to expel the heaviness that lingered there in the rare moments of quiet. Did she really want to go there right now? 'Hearing you girls talk about uni, your future, your new friends and all the amazing stuff you're doing – it really bums me out. And I don't want you to stop talking about it, I am so fucking proud of you. Just reminds me that I'm not there, you know.' Marnie bit down on her lip to stop the spew of words but the dam had broken and out they gushed. 'I'm a literal dropout. I thought I'd be able to go back next year, take a year out, but that's not going to happen.'

In hindsight, the idea of returning in September had been completely delusional. She hadn't even managed to text back Becky and Caroline – her old flatmates – so how had she expected to keep up with university work? She just hadn't realised how much life would change once she became a mum. Obviously, she didn't think it would be easy, she knew it would be hard. Everyone told her it would be, especially Mum. But there was this part of her that thought, *yes it will be hard, but after the first few months I'll get into the swing of it and life will resume as before, just with the slight addition of a baby.*

Oh how wrong she had been.

'You could make it work. Bring her with you if you have to.' Now Hannah was the one being delusional.

'In September, I'll still have a baby and no childcare, and are you joking about bringing her with me? She needs me 24/7. My brain has rewired to be more attuned to her needs. There is literal scientific proof that a women's grey matter changes when they have a baby.' Marnie had read it somewhere online, and she could well believe it. Her brain fog had been utterly crippling at times, and the tunnel vision

66

she had on Sophie's wellbeing felt hard-wired, beyond a choice. 'I could do stuff when she's napping, but that's much less these days, and when she's asleep I have a million other things I need to do before I can think about myself.' Sterilising bottles, washing, cleaning, resting, replying to messages, more washing.

'Can't your mum and dad have her?'

'Ha. Hilarious,' Marnie scoffed. 'Not going to happen.' Her parents hadn't disowned her, but they were insistent that she took responsibility for her choices and they made it clear they weren't going to put their own lives on hold to take care of Marnie's child.

Marnie also didn't want to give them the satisfaction of her reliance. Mum had said so many times how ridiculous it was for her to do it alone – that with no father in the picture, she doubted Marnie could cope, which only made her want to do it more, to prove that she could. Thank God for Nanny Sheila, who made her feel supported when she needed it but not totally inadequate. And she was doing an okay job. It never felt good enough, but she kept swimming. She hadn't drowned yet.

Alicia shook her head solemnly. 'You know what her parents are like.'

At least she got it.

'It won't be like this forever, she'll be at school.' Hannah just wouldn't give up.

'And then I'll have to find a job that will work around school pickups or pay an arm and a leg in childcare. Trust me, I've looked into it. Even if I get some semblance of my old life back, I can never have the life I thought I'd have.' Marnie sat up now, peering into Sophie's cot as she spoke, taking in her delicately pale face, cherubic lips and the way her little chest rose and fell with each breath. She was worth it, but that didn't negate all the bad stuff. She sighed again, a long weary sigh that hung between defeat and tenderness. 'I love her so much, more than I ever thought possible. But I do miss my old life. Mostly, though I miss the life I thought I was going to have, you know.'

'That must be so hard. If it's any consolation, it's not that great.' Alicia picked at the edge of the duvet that she and Hannah were tucked below. 'I often feel like I'm doing uni "wrong". I haven't moved out of home, or made loads of new friends or joined loads of societies or partied lots or taken drugs. So maybe you're not missing out as much as you think?' Alicia's voice wavered, seeming totally unconvinced even by her own words.

'Yeah,' Hannah agreed, equally unconvincingly. 'You're just doing things differently to us.'

'Hannah's right,' said Alicia. 'Think about it, when we're having babies—'

'Count me out,' Hannah snorted.

'Okay, when I'm having babies at like, thirty—'

'Thought it was twenty-five?'

'Twenty-five, thirty, whatever. Sophie will be at secondary school. You'll have more of your life back.'

That was true, but she'd still be behind and it still wouldn't be as she'd always pictured her life. 'But I won't have a degree, or my twenties to get started climbing the career ladder. I'll have to do a job that will let me take days off when Sophie's sick. And I'll have to work in something like . . . admin.'

'My aunt's in admin,' Alicia protested. 'Nothing wrong with admin.'

'Sorry, I don't mean it in a rude way. I just always thought I'd do something more. Or at least something different.

Something that would make a massive difference in society. Who's going to solve global warming now?' It was half a joke, but the dull ache of sadness flickered.

'Na, I'm not having it. Who says you can't still do that?' Hannah sat up now, flinging the covers off with such drama it made Alicia jump.

'Society? Reality?' Marnie moved to lie on her stomach, head at the closest end to Alicia and Hannah.

'Fuck them! You can do whatever you want and be a mum. You shouldn't have to choose.'

'How? This is my life, Han. As much as I would love to believe the whole "follow your dreams, life's too short" thing, I can't escape the fact that I have rent to pay, a child to dress and feed for a minimum of another eighteen years.' It was a long time.

'You could make it work.'

'It can't be easy though,' Alicia said, reaching forward to grab the duvet. 'My feet are cold! Could you show your passion without tossing the duvet off me next time?'

Marnie shook her head. 'I love it in theory. But I promise you it's so much harder in practice.'

Hannah moved to lie on her stomach, mirroring Marnie. She was finally standing down. 'That sucks.' Her eyes met Marnie's with such warmth they spoke a thousand words. *She understands.*

'Yeah. It's really crap.' Marnie had to look away. 'Thanks for listening to me moaning. I promise you it's not that bad, it's just when I really think about it, it gets a bit heavy, you know?'

'Of course!' enthused Alicia. 'We'll always listen to you. You've done such an amazing job. I'm in awe of you and how you've adapted.'

'Me too. You're in your New Mummy Era right now, but your planet-saving, career-smashing chapter is still to come.' Hannah punched the pillow, emphasising her point.

Marnie nodded with conviction. 'Yes, I love that! This is a chapter, not my whole book. My time is coming.' She looked between all three of her girls – Soph included – and in that moment, the weight of responsibility and disappointment felt a little lighter because she wasn't carrying it alone.

Hot Mess Express 🚂 😵

27th February, 2015

Marnie: GIRLS. Have you seen The Dress?

Hannah: YES!! It's deffo gold and white.

Alicia: No it's not. It's blue and black. You need to get your eyes tested. Marnie?

Marnie: I'm with Alicia. Soz Han.

Hannah: You two are mad. Anyway, it's an ugly dress so who cares? Wouldn't be seen dead in it whatever colour it is lol

Marnie: My bodycon days are over. I still can't shift the baby weight 😵

Alicia: You look great!

Hannah: You do. And also when have you ever worn bodycon anyway?!

Marnie: True. But now I never can. RIP

Hannah: 🙄

4th March, 2015

Marnie: Sophie's really poorly :(We're in hospital now x

Hannah: WHAT? OMG IS SHE OKAY?

Alicia: Poor baby :'(

71

Marnie: She's got bronchiolitis. She's on oxygen to help her breathe. Horrible seeing her so sad. Haven't showered in two days and am running out of nappies and milk.

Alicia: I'll bring you some!! What size is she? And what milk? Send a pic.

Hannah: You should have said sooner. I'll come too. When are visiting hours?

Marnie: You don't have to.

Alicia: I am.

Hannah: Same. Not up for debate.

Marnie: Visiting hours 3pm to 8pm. Starfish ward. Love you xx

12th May, 2015

Hannah: I'm so sorry I can't make it to Soph's christening.

Marnie: I'll try and forgive you. What did you say you were doing again?

Hannah: Going to Amsterdam for the weekend with the uni lot.

Marnie: Lucky you. Alicia, you aren't ditching, are you?

Alicia: Of course not!

Hannah: I'm not ditching, I had it planned already.

Marnie: Just joking.

1st July, 2015

Marnie: Guess who landed themselves a job? Moi!

Alicia: Yay! Care to elaborate?

Marnie: GP receptionist. Three days a week. Wage shit but between Mum, Dad and Nan, childcare is free.

Alicia: Congrats to you, babe. You are Supermum.

Marnie: Wouldn't go that far, but will be nice to have something to do that's not baby-related. If I have to watch *Peppa Pig* one more time, I might jump out the window.

Hannah: Soz for the slow reply. Happy for you.

Hannah: Can you both like my new Insta post and share it around? Plz.

Marnie: I have made a new friend at work. Her name is Andrea and she's old but fab. I'll try not to replace you both teehee.

Alicia: YAY! Age is but a number.

Hannah: You weren't saying that when Marnie was crushing on your uncle.

Marnie: Oi!!!

Alicia: Happy Birthday Soph! Can't wait to see you all for cake and a catch-up xx

Hannah: Happy Birthday. I might be a tiny bit late, please don't do the cake before I get there I don't want to miss it.

Marnie: We'll try not to. I can't believe my baby is one. HOW DID THAT HAPPEN?

Social media strategy 2015-16: @LondonGirlHan

Bio: Lifestyle, fashion, makeup and beauty 💅 ✨
Central Saint Martin's 🎓 Starbucks Lover ☕

Platform	Content
YouTube	Massive Superdrug haul
YouTube	Get to know me tag <3
Instagram	New nails for spring
YouTube	Everyday makeup routine

Followers: 45

@Marns: Love that nail colour

@Lissy: Love it x

Chapter Six

13th February, 2016

Hannah

Hannah was walking down Oxford Street, arms laden with shopping bags, stomach filled with avocado on toast from her brunch this morning. She needed a new outfit for Galentine's tonight and also to replace the pack of cards her uni lot used for drinking games as they'd somehow ended up in the toilet. Hannah didn't mind. A pack of playing cards ending up in the toilet was such a uni thing to happen. It was up there with bringing a traffic cone home on a night out, or ending up at a random house party at 3am and leaving the next morning with five new best friends. Uni was everything she'd hoped it would be and more. Freshers and second year, she'd partied hard. She'd tried everything she should have tried as a student – sleeping with men, sleeping with women (well, one; it wasn't for her but she'd satiated her curiosity with a drunken fumble). She'd pulled all-nighters for both parties and last-minute assignments, and she'd even tried magic mushrooms. Never again.

Third year was still fun, but she was having to knuckle

down. The partying was limited to twice a week – a mid-week trip to bars after a Wetherspoons dinner and a Friday club night. It was nice to have more chilled nights in with her flatmates and best uni friends Lara, Nikita and Jo, watching *Big Brother* and sipping hot chocolates with marshmallows, but Hannah missed the madness of Freshers. There was also the sickening feeling that the end of uni was creeping closer.

Hannah pushed the thought away. She couldn't be miserable when she was in the bustling hub of Central London. She loved it here; it was so lively, exciting, so . . . her. Hopefully she could stay living here next year – money depending. It was amazing to be able to jump on the tube and be within throwing distance of incredible bars, shops, clubs and parks.

Hannah's phone rang. Mum. Best to see what she wanted now rather than later when she'd have to start setting the house up and getting herself ready.

'Hi, Mum.' Hannah settled onto a bus stop bench just opposite Selfridges.

'Hello honey, how's my baby doing?'

'Your adult child is doing marvellously, thank you. How's my lovely mummy?'

'Wonderful. And I'm not too bad. Dad's driving me barmy doing his usual farting about. Today he's decided we *must* sort out the shed. I've asked why this is suddenly so urgent considering we've not been in the shed since we moved in twenty years ago, but he's insistent it must be done today. I suppose that's what happens when you marry for love, not money.' She laughed. 'Have you spoken to your brother?'

'Not since the last message in the WhatsApp group. Why?' Whenever Mum brought up Emmanuel it was because she had some sort of news.

Despite being only three years older than her, he seemed to have lived his life in fast forward. In the first three years after leaving university, he'd checked off all the typical 'twenty-something success' milestones: landing a job at a swanky law firm with a starting salary of 40k, getting promoted every year, meeting his girlfriend, moving in together, and then proposing to her. What more could he possibly want to achieve before his thirties? Oh, God . . .

'He better not be having a fucking baby.' Hannah was sick of everyone having babies. Why was having babies the default for most people? She didn't get it.

'Wash your mouth out with soap, young lady. And no. What makes you say that? He hasn't said anything, has he? He's doing so well at work, it's not a great time to put it on pause.'

'What do you mean "put it on pause"? Lucy would be the one bearing the brunt of the child-rearing while he continues on his merry way up the corporate ladder, "providing" for the family.'

'Stop being so dramatic. Your dad wasn't that useless.'

'I'm not saying he was, but that's just what happens.'

'I won't hold my breath for any grandchildren from you anytime soon, then.'

Don't hold your breath, full stop.

Hannah's mum continued in the silence. 'No, what I was going to say was that he's made *partner*.'

'Sounds posh.'

'Very posh. He's years ahead of his peers.'

'Good for him.'

More silence.

'Is that why you called? To tell me this wonderful news?'

'Yes.'

And?

'And also to see how you are. Have you thought any more about next year?'

Next year. Yes, Hannah had thought about it. She'd have graduated. She'd be living in London, ideally in her own studio flat, but more likely in a shared house just until she got her finances in order. She would continue with her social media channels. She wasn't yet a raging success, more micro-influencer than Zoella, but Rome wasn't built in a day. She had plans to move from general lifestyle content to something more niche – apparently finding your niche was the most important part of becoming an online success, but that was the tricky part.

Beyond that, everything was . . . up in the air.

'Still the same as when you asked me at Christmas. I've been looking at internships, but they're so competitive and the pay is shit. I was also thinking about doing a master's in knitwear. Or a short course in fashion photography. I'm just going to see what doors the universe presents to me.'

'You don't even knit.' Mum huffed. 'Don't you think you need more of a solid plan? Emmanuel didn't get to where he is today by waiting for doors to magically appear and open for him. He knocked on them. No, actually he crafted them *from scratch*. He cut the trees down with his own bare hands and—'

'Deforestation is bad for the environment.' Mum wasn't getting the metaphor. She never did. And that was okay because Hannah knew what she was doing. Sort of. She'd humour her. 'What does a solid plan look like?'

'An actual job lined up that pays well and has good career progression. I'm sure Emmanuel could talk to—'

'Absolutely not. I am not a corporate girly, I'm afraid.'

'What does that even mean?'

'I don't want to work in an office. I want to be creative.'

The absolute goal was to own her own business – whether that be in photography, interior design, fashion. Something that would put her natural creative flair to good use, make decent money and give her total control over her timetable and life. Again, working out how to get there was the hard part, but she had time. Maybe she'd rethink it if she got to thirty and it still hadn't happened.

'There's no money in creativity, my dear. I've indulged your creative whimsies by allowing you to study at that place, I rather thought you'd grow out of it.' Mum's voice was heavy with disappointment and Hannah's stomach tensed with irritation. She knew what was coming.

Mum continued. 'Your grandparents risked their lives and gave up everything they worked hard for to give you the opportunity to do something worthwhile with your life, not fanny around with paints.'

'Oh really? You never said.' The guilt trip. Her mum's speciality.

'Stop it with the sarcasm, we didn't raise you to be so . . . boisterous.'

Boisterous? Really?

She didn't have time for this. Marnie and Alicia were due to arrive within the hour and her room and the kitchen were a total dive.

'I have to go. I'll text you later. Bye.'

She wouldn't, but it felt like the right thing to say. Hannah loved her mum so freaking much, but bloody hell was it annoying when she went on and on. She wasn't even twenty-one, for God's sake. The world was still very much at her immaculately pedicured feet.

And it wasn't like she lacked drive. Yes okay, Alicia had her forty-year plan or whatever it was, but anyone could be a teacher. And Marnie was just doing Marnie. Hannah could have a baby and be a mum if she really wanted to, but . . . well, fuck that. Just because she wasn't going for the easy option, the option expected of her by everyone else, didn't mean that she wasn't going to succeed. They just needed to be patient and then she'd show them. *I told you I'd nail it*, she'd say. *Bet you wish you'd believed it when I said it the first time.* Everything would fall into place. She'd bloody make it so.

Hannah had taken Alicia and Marnie to the Ask Italian on Park Street to start their Galentine's celebrations. They could have stayed in and had a takeaway in their PJs, but Hannah always liked an excuse to get dressed up. Her outfit of the day videos were getting popular, and she really needed to post about her new Kurt Geigers. A few glasses of bubbly might also help butter the girls up for when she suggested her plans for later on.

'To the gals!' Marnie held her glass of prosecco in a toast. She looked really pretty tonight in a well-fitting tailored pair of pink tartan trousers and a flattering peplum top. It was a change from her usual no fucks given approach. She wouldn't think twice about going shopping in a pair of leggings with a gusset clinging on for dear life and a band t-shirt she'd slept in the night before. She'd always been that way, even before becoming a mum. Hannah would never risk a trip out looking like Adam Sandler in case that was the day she'd meet a fan of her channel, her soulmate or a future business partner.

'To the gals,' Hannah and Alicia added, and they all clinked their glasses with a self-conscious giggle. Alicia looked like a total knockout too, in a red satin blouse and black skinny jeans. Alicia always looked presentable, but even on nights out to Watford town centre when they were teens she'd play it safe in a pair of ballet flats. It must be a special occasion if she was whacking out the kitten heels.

Hannah took a sip of her drink. 'So how's work then, Marns?' she said, relishing the sharp fizz hitting the back of her throat. Just what the doctor ordered.

Marnie shrugged. 'It's fine. Nothing to write home about but it's nice to have something for myself. At work I'm not just Mummy. I can use my brain for other things and actually have a lunch break. Everyone I work with is super nice, too.'

'Why did you apply for something so far away from home?' Alicia placed the paper napkin on her lap as if she was taking dinner with the queen.

She'd taken the words right out of Hannah's mouth. It really didn't make sense that Marnie had exclusively applied to jobs that were a minimum of forty minutes away from home when there were plenty of opportunities closer for that sort of thing; it was hardly specialist.

'It's not that far. Forty minutes on a good day, an hour on a bad one. But again, I quite like the drive. Put my tunes or podcast on or just relish the silence.'

How depressing that an hour-long commute was respite when you were a parent. Hannah added that to her ever-growing list of *reasons not to have kids*. 'What do you actually do when you're there?' Hannah was genuinely curious. Surely Marnie didn't just sit behind the desk all day answering the phone.

'I keep people on hold from eight until nine and then tell them we're out of appointments and to call at 8am the following day.' Marnie grinned.

'And you're happy doing that?' Hannah caught Alicia's eye. She could tell she felt uncomfortable because she was doing her biting lip, wringing her hands thing. Hannah didn't want to be a bitch, but she was genuinely concerned for Marnie. Marnie could do so much more than just answer phones. Someone needed to make sure she didn't forget it.

Marnie sighed. 'Sometimes a job is just a job, babe. Doesn't mean I'm going to be doing it forever.' She downed the rest of her prosecco.

'Do you not worry you might be stuck there?'

'Nope.' Marnie rolled her eyes. 'I'm bored of this conversation now. Alicia, can we toast to your teacher training? That's all booked in now, right? Mrs Murphy has a nice ring to it.'

Time to retreat. Hannah knew how far she could push Marnie and she'd reached the limit. Hannah grabbed the freshly opened bottle of wine from the centre of the table and filled Marnie's empty glass. 'She'll need a husband to be a Mrs!' Hannah laughed.

'Miss Murphy still sounds cute. Better, even. Lovely bit of alliteration.' Marnie smiled at Alicia.

'I can't think of anything worse than going back to school, though. You're braver than I am.' Hannah had never really thought of Alicia as brave before, but this was the exception. You had to be brave to willingly spend six hours a day with teenagers. Brave or completely mad. 'We were shits.'

'Speak for yourself,' Marnie teased.

'Okay, maybe not us specifically, but our year group. Do you remember that time everyone in Mr O'Donall's maths class turned their chairs to face the back and the only person he shouted at was Alicia even though she didn't want to do it in the first place?'

'Oh my God, yes! I'll never forget that. I almost cried.' Alicia swirled her prosecco around in her glass with a coy smile. She'd probably make that one splash of fizz last at least two courses.

'I'd have cried, too,' Marnie said. 'He properly went in on you.'

'Perhaps he was having a bad day.'

'And perhaps he was just a massive c—'

'Garlic bread?' The waiter cut Marnie off – just as well because Alicia looked like she was going to have a heart attack.

'Mmmmm.' Marnie had a slice of bread in her mouth before the waiter had even let go of the plate. 'I fucking *love* cheesy garlic bread. I'd die for cheesy garlic bread.'

A comfortable silence settled over the table, the kind that naturally followed the arrival of good food as Hannah and Alicia also tucked in.

After a few moments, Alicia was back to her half frown, half smile. 'It will be nice to make a difference, educate the youth of today.'

Hannah giggled but quickly realised Alicia was being serious. 'You'll be great at it.'

'Amazing, even,' Marnie added. 'If you had to pick just one teacher who really made a difference for you, who would it be?'

That was a good question. 'Hmmm,' Hannah pondered. 'I'm not sure I could name one teacher at school that I'd say *really* made a difference to my life.'

'Bollocks,' Marnie scoffed. 'You loved Miss Angel. You were her favourite.'

Ah, Miss Angel. Hannah's love for textiles and sewing had been born in her classroom – 2B, in the Design and

Technology block. Sitting at a sewing machine for the first time, she discovered an innate ability to use it. The thrill of choosing three fabrics for their washbag project had felt electric, almost like the high she'd experienced that one time she'd tried MDMA.

'I was only her favourite because I was the only one in the class who knew how to wind a bobbin.' Hannah paused. 'Oh my God. I'll tell you who I *did* love.'

'Mr Hanover?' Alicia and Marnie said simultaneously.

'How did you guess?'

'Because you never stopped talking about how fit he was during PE.' Marnie shook her head.

'I wasn't wrong though, was I?'

Alicia smiled coyly. 'Nope.'

'See! Even Alicia gets it.' Hannah cackled. 'Wonder what he's doing these days.'

'He's probably old and wrinkly by now, or maybe he'd be a silver fox.' Marnie was now onto the bruschetta after demolishing two slices of garlic bread. 'It's weird talking about school. It feels like yesterday and a whole lifetime ago already. Are we old now?'

'It is mad that Han and I are graduating this year and when we do this next year, we'll be well into the swing of jobs and adulthood.' The furrow between Alicia's brows was back in full force. She'd wrinkle there permanently if she wasn't careful.

Marnie sighed. 'I'm already there, just minus the graduation and all the fun anecdotes about being pushed home from a night out in a shopping trolley or having to study by candlelight because someone forgot to put money on the electric fob.'

'That wasn't me! My housemates in second year were total

84

idiots!' Hannah protested. 'Also, what are you on about? In what world is twenty-one old? We're still young! Stop being so depressing.'

This was exactly why Hannah's Galentine's plan for tonight was necessary. The girls clearly needed reminding that they weren't old or dead yet. She was determined for a very different vibe this year's Galentine's than the previous two. This time Marnie was not with child – neither in the womb nor out of it. They could have a *proper* night of fun: carefree and much more age-appropriate. This year she'd rather be wiping up her own sick than being within three feet of Alicia wiping someone else's arse (even if that someone was barely four months old) and the only sleepless night she wanted was the partying kind, not because a crying baby was keeping her awake. Hannah had taken herself off to the spare room last year after Sophie's second wakeup, despite Alicia's veiled comments that it was rude – a gal needed her beauty sleep.

Hannah cleared her throat. 'On that note, are you ready to hear what I have planned for tonight?'

'Oh God, what have you got planned?' Marnie eyed Hannah suspiciously.

'Drinking games, music, dancing. I've invited a few people over. Not loads, maybe like . . . ten? It's a good size group.'

Alicia, just about to wipe her mouth with her napkin, paused. 'So you're having a house party?'

'It's not a house party, it's a gathering.' It would have to be fifteen people or more to be considered a house party; everyone knew that.

'That's what Molly Yoland used to tell her mum every year before her big fuckoff house party.'

Marnie wasn't wrong about Molly, but she was wrong about tonight.

'It's *not* a house party. Just some drinks and some games.'
Marnie and Alicia looked at each other.

'What?'

'Isn't it nicer just the three of us? Enjoying each other's company. PJs. Face masks, like the OG Galentine's.' Alicia raised her eyebrows in an irritating, *I know better* way.

'A few of the rugby lads are stopping by about nine, so there will be plenty of time for just the three of us.'

'Rugby lads!' Marnie cried so loudly that the couple who were clearly on a first date on the table beside them looked over.

'They're super hot, I promise. Come on, you're both single.' The promise of hot guys would usually swing it for Marnie, and if Hannah could get Marnie on board, Alicia would soon follow.

'I'm looking for a husband, not a child. Rugby lads drink from boots and think mullets are cool,' Alicia mumbled, her attention fixed on the napkin she was folding and unfolding in her lap.

'They aren't all like that. Stop being so judgy.' Why were they both being so dramatic? If Alicia was to meet her forty-year-plan deadlines, she'd need to stick her head above the parapet at some point in the near future.

'Look, Han. Galentine's Day is for gals, it says it in the name. You've seriously gone and invited some guys?' Marnie dropped her cutlery down on her empty plate with a clang. 'Not cool.'

'Feels like you're being a bit . . . ungrateful. I thought it would be fun. You know, Mum's night out. I genuinely thought you'd appreciate an opportunity to let your hair down. I wanted to give you the proper uni experience you'd never had. Sorry I got it so wrong.' Why were they both acting like she'd conspired to make the night as horrendous as possible? All she wanted was to have one last hurrah with them before they were forced to join the adult world and its oppressive expectations.

A prickle of hot tears surfaced out of nowhere. Oh God, what was happening? She blinked rapidly, fumbling with her false lash in a desperate attempt to disguise the sudden wave of emotion.

'Are you okay?' Marnie's face crumpled with concern, and once again, her gaze flicked to Alicia. Why did they always do that?

'I'm fine, just something in my eye.' Hannah cringed internally. She was dangerously close to pulling a Tracey Beaker and blaming it on 'hayfever'.

Marnie's face softened and she sat back in her chair. 'When you put it like that, it makes more sense. I wish you'd asked us rather than sprung it on us, but I do get it now.'

'Maybe we can compromise and say everyone has to be gone by eleven so we can get into our matching jammies with a hot chocolate and watch *Trainwreck*?' Alicia said, her napkin now torn to shreds on the table in front of her.

Hannah smiled. 'Deal.' The tears had retreated. Thank God for that. 'It's going to be an amazing night.' She was sure of it. So sure, in fact, she reckoned she could even push it to midnight.

Chapter Seven

14th February, 2016

Alicia

This was not what Alicia had signed up for. This was *not* Galentine's Day.

It was now midnight, way past when Hannah agreed to chuck everyone out, and yet her uni house was still packed with randomers, most of them men. The sanctity of Galentine's had been well and truly ruined.

The music and chatter of bantering people meant that you couldn't have a proper conversation, and Alicia found herself at the dining table, squashed between Marnie and a rugby lad with massive shoulders who took the idea of manspreading to an entirely new level. The table was sticky, and in the centre was a washing-up bowl filled with a cocktail the colour of dirty dishwasher. There was no way she was going to drink that, even if she did lose whatever stupid game they were playing next.

'Let's play Never Have I Ever,' shrieked Hannah over the loud music and drunken voices. She was well on her way to being totally shitfaced.

'I'll go first,' another lad, the shape of a fridge, said in a thick Scottish accent that made Alicia think of Shrek. 'Never have I ever been arrested.' He chugged like he was dehydrated, slamming his beer can on the table after downing it.

The crowd jeered.

'Oh my God, Mike!'

'No you haven't!'

'Whaaaattttttt?!'

Alicia couldn't care less. Of course, she didn't drink to that one.

'Me next,' said a girl with purple hair and a heavy fringe – Kathleen, she said her name was. Or Kathy. Not that it mattered; Alicia didn't care. 'Never have I ever had sex with two people at once.' Kathleen took a deliberately drawn-out sip, her face smug as the men around the table erupted into hoots and hollers, mimicking the grating enthusiasm of a pub when someone drops a pint.

To Alicia's surprise, Hannah didn't drink. Hannah would have told her and Marnie if she'd done something like that, but it would also be the sort of thing she would stretch the truth on if it made her appear more fun to the people around her.

'Never have I ever got off with someone the same sex as me,' Lara, Hannah's housemate shouted over the continual jeers of the Fridge Lads.

'How about now? That's what girls do at sleepovers, right?' Mike scoffed.

'Obviously Jo's drinking,' yelled someone else.

'I'm a fucking lesbian, Chris,' Jo shouted.

Hannah pushed her chair back and stood, waving her drink in the air so it was dangerously close to sloshing onto the glum-looking girl beside her. 'My turn,' she slurred.

'Everyone BE QUIET. I'm talking!' No one appeared to listen but she carried on anyway. 'Never have I ever had sex,' she said, before falling back into her chair.

'That's a boring one.'

'Everyone's had sex! We're not fifteen.'

Most people around the table laughed and took a sip or a swig. Marnie's eyes bore into Alicia, but she avoided meeting her gaze.

Alicia could take a sip – it would be easier than enduring the inevitable comments, the horrified gasps and the shock that anyone would dare still be a *virgin* at the matronly age of twenty-one.

'Oh my God, you didn't drink!' someone called, snapping Alicia back into the room.

It was too late. Great.

'You can't *still* be a virgin?'

'You're beautiful. I'll help you fix that. Right now? Hannah, can we borrow your room?' This Mike guy needed a swift kick in the balls.

Everyone laughed, and Hannah joined in, keeping up with the rowdy crowd.

Alicia's cheeks flushed hot, and the prickle of panic, anxiety and humiliation crept up the back of her neck. She needed to get away but she couldn't move.

'Oh fuck off. If she wants to have sex with a sweaty man-child, she'll keep you in mind.' Marnie shoved her chair back, the legs scraping on the sticky vinyl floor. She turned to Alicia. 'I'm sick of this. Do you want to go upstairs?'

'Ooooo, upstairs. Fine, you can do the honours if you want,' Mike sneered.

Marnie sucked her cheeks in and held her drink above Mike's prematurely balding head. 'Watch it.'

He held his hands up in surrender.

'Thought so,' Marnie said, as she grabbed Alicia's hand, and pulled her to safety.

In Hannah's bedroom, Marnie shut the door and turned the lock. She slid down the doorframe and sat back against it as if she was afraid that someone might barge their way in.

'Are you okay?' she asked.

'Fine.'

'Sure?'

No. But what else could Alicia say? She wasn't ashamed of her choice to wait, but it was the public humiliation that got her. Hannah knew that Alicia's answer would be no, and that everyone there would find it a ridiculous idea that a woman her age had yet to put out. So why did she ask it? She could have said something like *never have I ever had sex outside* or something, just to make it that bit less obvious.

Alicia perched on the edge of Hannah's bed.

'She was totally out of order. Do you want me to say something?'

'No point. She's drunk now anyway. It would only end in an argument.' Alicia picked her fingernails.

'I'll say something tomorrow.'

'Please don't.' It was best to sweep it under the rug and just move on.

Marnie sighed. 'Okay. I would though. She needs to be told sometimes.'

'I know you would.'

They both jumped as someone banged hard on the bedroom door.

'Oi. Who the fuck is in my bedroom?' It was Hannah, and she was slurring even more than before. 'Get out! You better not be having sex in my bed—'

Marnie rolled her eyes and then turned to open the door.

'Oh, what are you two doing in here? Come downstairs. Everyone's playing strip poker.' Hannah wiggled her shoulders and pretended to lift the hem of her top up.

'Absolutely not.' Alicia wasn't going downstairs while everyone else was still here, clothes or no clothes. Was Hannah really that oblivious to what had just happened?

'Marnie?' Hannah reached for Marnie's hands but she snatched them away.

'You know how I feel about my body now. There's no way in hell.'

'You've got a lovely mum-bod. Nothing wrong with a little belly.'

Marnie's face dropped. 'Really?'

This was about to get ugly. Alicia had to do something. 'Can you just tell everyone to go, now? It's past twelve. You agreed eleven. We can watch the film and sober up a bit and pretend this never happened.'

'It's a bit rude to tell everyone to leave now.' Hannah swayed sideways and then staggered, grabbing the doorframe. She giggled. 'Ooopsy.'

'And it's not rude for you to tell me I have a mum-bod?' Marnie snapped.

'I didn't mean it like that. Come on, everyone just needs to lighten up.' Hannah now reached for the light switch and flicked it on and off. She howled with laughter.

Marnie's hand shot up to cover the switch. 'Lighten up? It's past midnight, Alicia and I have made the effort to be here, which with childcare is not an easy thing for me. We came here to see you, not be the butt of everyone's jokes or dick about like we're sixteen.'

Hannah scowled. 'God, what happened to the Marnie

that used to go clubbing with me on a school night? You're acting like Alicia.' Hannah turned to Alicia, eyes trying and failing to focus on her. 'No offence.'

Offence taken.

Marnie shook her head, a total look of disdain in her eyes. 'I grew up, that's what happened.'

It was Hannah's turn to roll her eyes. 'Stop being so high and mighty. You're twenty-one.'

'And I have bigger things to think about now than what dress to wear on a night out or what would be the best way to totally humiliate someone who's meant to be my best mate.'

Alicia's stomach tensed. What would Hannah say to that?

'Just because you're a mum doesn't mean you have to totally give up on everything. You used to have dreams. You used to be fun. We're not old farts just yet. Why can't you just let your hair down?'

So she was just going to totally ignore Marnie calling her out?

Alicia stepped forward, fueled by adrenaline and frustration. 'We aren't against letting our hair down or having fun, but why is your version of fun getting wasted in a room full of gropey men taking the piss out of people for making different choices to you?' Did she really just say that? Perhaps she'd drunk more than she thought.

Hannah's eyes were wide before her eyebrows lowered. She lifted a finger up and waggled it in Alicia's direction.

'Ohhhhh, I see what this is actually about.'

Alicia crossed her arms. 'And what's that?'

'You're jealous because three years into uni, you still haven't met someone *worthy* of you.'

'There's nothing wrong with a girl who has standards.' Marnie practically spat the words.

'There's a difference between high standards and someone who's using high standards as an excuse to keep people away.'

'You're chatting bollocks, babe. You've had too much to drink,' Marnie said, cheeks now pink.

'Yes, you're talking absolute *shit*.' Alicia's voice quivered, but God, did it feel good to say it. 'You're projecting. It's *you* that's jealous. Jealous that I know what I'm doing with my life and you don't have the foggiest.'

'"Have the foggiest",' Hannah mimicked. 'I'd rather not have the foggiest than waste my life being a housewife or working a boring nine-to-fucking-five.'

Marnie's mouth was agape. 'Is that what you really think of my life? That I'm wasting it?' Her voice cracked and she wiped away her tears fiercely. 'I'm going before I do something I regret.'

Oh God, she'd never hit Hannah, would she?

'Fine. See if I care. Where are you even going?'

'Hotel? Home? I don't know. Just away from you and your twatty little rugby lads.' Marnie snapped, spinning on her heel to storm past Hannah.

'Me too,' Alicia said, her voice firm. There was no way she was staying here. Without another word, she ran to grab Marnie's hand and the two of them stormed down the hallway, not looking back.

Chapter Eight

14th February, 2016

Marnie

The only place they could find that was still open and not a club was a 24/7 McDonald's. They decided they'd probably miss the last train back from Euston so didn't even bother trying to bust their arses to get there and opted instead for a twenty-box of chicken nuggets to sober them up. Either they'd find a shitty hotel or pay for a taxi all the way back home – it would probably cost the same either way. They weren't going back to Hannah's unless it was to pick up their overnight bags.

'I can't believe her sometimes.' Marnie dunked a nugget in a massive tub of BBQ sauce. She wasn't being over-sensitive. Commenting on anyone's 'mum-bod' was not okay. She might not make it obvious and didn't bang on about her weight or body anywhere near as much as Hannah, but she wasn't blind. She knew her body looked different now than it did before Sophie. It felt different too, her clothes hung at unfamiliar angles and clung in spots she hadn't been aware of before, and she had to cross her legs now before she sneezed in case she pissed herself. 'How dare she comment on my body.'

'Horrible.' Alicia shook her head. 'And making out like it's only a problem to invite guys to Galentine's because I'm jealous? I'd rather shit in my hands and clap than get with one of those boys.'

Marnie grinned for the first time since they arrived. 'I'm liking this new fiery side of Alicia. And honestly? Same, and I'm known for having terribly low standards.'

They both chuckled.

'I do wonder what's going on in her head sometimes. She's so . . . elusive.'

'I feel that too. I don't know why she's so against letting us in.'

Hannah was more than happy to divulge the surface-level stuff – who she was shagging, how amazing uni was, the size and shape of her most recent conquest's penis – but when it came to knowing how she was actually feeling beyond all that, Marnie felt held at arm's length.

'God knows.' Alicia took a sip from her hot chocolate – Marnie had to go for Coke because otherwise she'd fall asleep. 'I do wonder if she's alright.'

'Yeah.' Now her anger had thawed a little, it had also crossed Marnie's mind. Yes, Hannah could be super stubborn when she wanted to be, but tonight she seemed different. They'd never had a row as blazing as this one. 'But if that is the case then she needs to talk to us, not take it out on us.'

'Totally, I—'

'Can I join you?'

Marnie looked up and blinked multiple times. God, she was tired, but there was no mistaking Hannah. 'How did you find us?'

'I have your location on Snapchat.'

'Oh.'

In the following silence, Marnie slurped her drink and Alicia cleared her throat then started faffing about with her fries. It wasn't up to either of them to break the ice. Marnie refused to be the one to back down this time.

Hannah slotted herself into the seat beside her and sighed. 'I'm sorry.'

'For what?' Marnie said, without looking up.

'Are you really going to make me beg?'

'Maybe.' Marnie dropped her empty drink on the table.

'I'm sorry for saying all that shitty stuff I didn't mean.'

'You did mean it though.' Marnie finally looked at her. Hannah's mascara was smudged all over and she had lipstick on her teeth. She'd be horrified if she knew she was out in public looking like that, although the harsh lights of McDonald's were never flattering at this time of night. *Note to self: never come to McDonald's for a date.*

'Maybe I meant it a bit?'

'At least you're being honest now,' Alicia broke her silence, face softening.

'I just really wanted tonight to be a success. I really wanted you both to have an amazing night. You'd made so much effort to get dressed up, and now I've royally fucked it up.' Hannah rested her head in her hands. 'Can I have a nugget?' she mumbled.

'Fine.' Marnie pushed the box towards her.

Hannah took one and nibbled at it absentmindedly. Her eyes closed for a moment, as though trying to shake off a heavy thought.

Marnie caught Alicia's eye, whose face mirrored her concern. 'Are you okay?'

Hannah blinked. 'Me? Yeah. Why?'

'We were just talking . . . you don't seem yourself.' Alicia said.

'Just Mum being annoying. Everything's fine. In fact, it's better than fine.'

'For fuck's sake, Han. Just give it a rest, will you?' Marnie raised her voice. 'We're your friends. Talk to us.' She didn't mean to sound angry.

'Fine.' Hannah dropped the nugget she was holding onto the sticky table. 'I'm scared.'

'Of what?' Alicia asked softly.

'The future? Next year? You two are all sorted. I feel like I'm heading to the edge of a cliff blindfolded and I don't know if the drop is a few centimetres or a few hundred metres.'

'Great metaphor,' Alicia smiled. 'You'll land on your feet, whatever the drop. Or maybe you have wings?'

'Alicia's right, you will! You always do.' Marnie had resigned herself to this fact a long time ago, no longer feeling jealous. It was Hannah's brand: everything just . . . worked out.

'Thanks.' Hannah picked the nugget back up and took a bite. Best not to think about all the germs that were now in her mouth – hopefully the alcohol would kill them all before they did too much damage. 'I always thought everything would be fine, but I'm wobbling.'

'Might be the copious amount of alcohol you've had tonight,' Marnie nudged her shoulder into Hannah gently.

'Yeah, and that.' Hannah groaned. 'I don't want to grow up. Do I have to?' At least now she had a smile on her face.

'Unfortunately so. But don't worry, we're here, stepping into the abyss of the unknown with you. Chip?' Alicia pushed her extra large portion of fries into the middle of the table.

Hannah took a handful and crammed them into her mouth. 'How very poetic,' she said with her mouth full.

'I'm an English student.'

Marnie wrapped her arm around Hannah's. Her bony and narrow shoulders made her, for once in her life, seem small and vulnerable. Marnie squeezed her hard, but it didn't feel hard enough. Gosh, she loved her. 'Life is scary, but as long as we have each other we'll be just fine,' she said, and she meant every word of it.

Hot Mess Express 🚂 😜

16th April, 2016

Marnie: Thoughts on this guy? He's proposing a date at Nandos.

Hannah: No. Absolutely not.

Marnie: Why?

Hannah: He's wearing a hat in all his photos.

Marnie: And?

Hannah: He's bald.

Marnie: So? Some of the sexiest men are bald.

30th April, 2016

Marnie: Okay, think this one is a goer. He's also got a kid. He likes bitcoin.

Alicia: He looks nice.

Hannah: No!

Marnie: What's wrong with this one?

Hannah: Everything?

Marnie: I might still go, ngl. I need a good shag. I'm closing up.

22nd June, 2016

Hannah: Anyone want to come to London this weekend?

Hannah: ??

Hannah: Hellooooo?

24th June, 2016

Marnie: Sorry!! I'm really not keen on travelling to London with Sophie. Makes me anxious. I could ask Mum and Dad but I'm pretty sure they're out doing God knows what this weekend so can't babysit. Sorry xxxxx

Hannah: Alicia?

Alicia: Meeting up with Neelam this weekend :(sorry. PS Soz for the slow reply, Mum and Dad were devastated at Brexit. Had to go round and make sure they were okay x

Hannah: No worries X

16th September, 2016

Hannah: Anyone around for a video call? Bored and need to vent about this new temp job!! You'll never guess what happened on Friday!!

18th September, 2016

Hannah: ??????

Hannah: Are you both dead?

Hannah: Hi.

Marnie: Soz, been a shit friend. Keep starting a reply then getting sidetracked. Hope you're okay xx

15th November, 2016

Marnie: Girls, I need some reassurance plz. Ive been offered extra hours at work and I could do with the money, but it would mean Sophie going to nursery two mornings a week. Mum and Dad have flat out refused to take her, which I suppose fair enough but also FFS they are her grandparents, I'd have thought they'd want to keep spending time with her.

Alicia: Nursery sounds like a good plan. What's up?

Marnie: Mum guilt. She's only two :(But what else can I do? Andrea said she'd come with me to check it out and see if the vibes feel right.

Alicia: I bet she'll love nursery. She can make little friends and play all day.

Marnie: I hope so. But what if she hates it?

Hannah: Kids are resilient, she'll get used to it and you're an amazing mummy!

Marnie: Thanks girls xx I think I will go for it but I'll deffo cry on her first day.

15th December, 2016

Hannah: Is anyone going to the Red Lion this Christmas?

Marnie: I can't. Obvious reasons. I think a few people are, only like three or four though.

Hannah: Alicia?

Alicia: I'd rather not.

Hannah: Please?! It's tradition.

Alicia: I'll go for one x

30th January, 2017

Marnie: Hey, sorry for the radio silence. Sophie is being quite challenging atm (read: a little bitch). Still love her, but omgggg they weren't lying about the Terrible Twos. Still would love to do Galentine's Day, but I'm not sure I can make it work. I feel bad leaving Sophie with anyone else at the moment. Not for my sake, but for theirs 🤭

Alicia: While we're on the subject, I'm a bit worried about doing a sleepover on a Monday night.

Hannah: Noooooooo!!! Marnie, you can't miss it. And Alicia, it has to be on the thirteenth. Always. You said you had an inset day?

Alicia: On the Monday I do, but I have to be in school on Tuesday.

Hannah: Pull a sickie?

Alicia: No! I'll lose my job!

Hannah: We can do it at my parents again and you can bring Sophie? Mum and Dad are on holiday that week anyway so they wouldn't be a problem.

Marnie: Doubtful. The thought of trying to get her to sleep anywhere that's not home is awful. It takes over an hour as it is. She'll be a nightmare out of her routine.

Alicia: Oh no :(Are we really going to have to cancel?

Hannah: No! We're not cancelling. Can we do it at yours then, @Marns? Then Sophie will be at home in her own space. Your parents can help out, can't they? It's the least they can do!

Marnie: I want to say don't talk about my parents like that, but you have a point.

Hannah: So ask them!

Marnie: Fine. But don't hold your breath.

Social media strategy 2016-17: @LondonGirlHan

Bio: Lifestyle, fashion, makeup and beauty 💅 ✨
Central Saint Martin's 🎓 Starbucks Lover ☕

Platform	Content
YouTube	Everyday makeup routine for a coffee date
YouTube	I'm moving! Flatshare in London
Instagram	Graduation makeup and outfit
Instagram	New shoes <3

Followers: 120

@Grlpwr: LOVE THE SHOES

@Lissy: How high are those heels?!

@HamTheMan: Welcome to the 12 West Mews gang.

@Lola_69: My bedroom neighbour <3

@BarneyBoi: Stop nicking my milk 😵

Chapter Nine

13th February, 2017

Hannah

As always, Hannah was running fashionably late. Marnie was expecting them at hers at 2pm – a weird time but it meant that they had some of the day to hang out – but it was now 1pm and Hannah was in the shower.

Thank God she'd managed to save Galentine's Day. Messaging in the group had been sporadic at best and everyone seemed to be perpetually busy. It was a miracle she managed to get Alicia out at Christmas, and they'd had a good time, even if they had been home by ten.

She squeezed out the last of the shampoo and speed-washed her hair, using the dregs as body wash. It wasn't ideal but she was getting paid tomorrow so she could treat herself to a new one then; probably more likely Alberto Balsam as it was only a quid, rather than Herbal Essences or Tresemmé, but it would do for now.

Despite her determination to save Galentine's, Hannah had no idea how it was going to work this year with a two-year-old in tow. At least when Sophie was tiny, she'd stay where they put her and she wasn't running about causing total mayhem. Would Marnie's parents take her for the whole time? Unlikely. More realistically, they'd be on hand at bedtime and overnight if she kicked off. There was nothing worse than the ear-piercing shriek of a tantrumming toddler. For Hannah, the question of whether she wanted kids had never been up for debate, but the primal urge to launch a screaming child out of her vicinity spoke volumes. Obviously, she loved Sophie, but that was only because she was Marnie's.

Speaking of, Hannah could hear the shrill cries of a child through the thin wall of the bathroom. It really wasn't the glam life she pictured when she imagined herself living in London. She was sharing with three others, similar to uni but without the endorsement to drink every night because they were 'adults'.

Not one of her uni friends wanted to stay in London. Lara chose to go back up north; Jo had started renting a place in Essex to be near her girlfriend's family; and Nikita decided to travel the world before settling down wherever life took her. So Hannah had to find a place with a spare room that was larger than a cupboard and roommates who weren't serial killers, nudists or passive-aggressive note-writers.

Lola, Hamish and Barney, in their four-bedroom townhouse, ticked most of the boxes. It had a corner shop three minutes down the road that sold raspberry Hershey chocolate bars, was within fifteen minutess walk to a tube station, and crucially, had two toilets. Hannah did, however, have to mentally block out the obnoxious cheering that came from Barney's room on the day Trump was elected as president, and the black mould on the backs of the wardrobes. The family with seven children next door were not ideal either, but beggars couldn't be choosers and there was something about the grittiness of it all that helped Hannah convince herself she was living the authentic London Dream.

Hannah made it to Marnie's by 2:45pm, which wasn't bad going. For once, the Euston train had been kind to her, and by travelling off-peak, she'd avoided the dreaded rush from concourse to platform when the departure was announced. There was no place more suitable for the phrase *survival of the fittest* than Euston station at 6:27pm on a weekday.

Marnie was back living with her parents, moving into the new annexe extension just before Christmas. It meant she was ten minutes away from Alicia, and Hannah knew they'd been spending time together while she was in London. It didn't bother her, not really. Well, a little. They were allowed to hang out without her of course, but it was more of a practical issue than anything else. Hannah was feeling increasingly left out of all the gossip, and looping her back in meant Marnie and Alicia had to relay all the information twice over whenever the three of them were together. Inevitably, things slipped through the cracks.

When Hannah arrived, Alicia was already there, sipping a cup of coffee and answering the door for Marnie with the familiarity of someone who spent plenty of time there. She led her into the annexe where Marnie was sitting on the floor playing with dolls beside a pink-cheeked, scruffy-haired smiling Sophie.

'She finally arrives,' Marnie grinned, as Hannah followed Alicia through the door.

'Now the party can really get started.' Hannah settled onto the sofa next to Alicia and took in her surroundings. So this was Marnie's new place.

It was more glorified lean-to than annexe, in Hannah's opinion. Yes, it was plastered, heated and made of brick, but it was long and narrow with a double bed at one end and a tiny living area at the other. Hannah would be happy living here on her own if it was a studio flat in London, but Marnie shared this tiny footprint of space with Sophie, too. Of course they were allowed in the rest of the house – it wasn't a prison – but Marnie's parents were insistent that she was as independent as possible. Hannah thought they were just lazy.

'Say hello to Auntie Hannah,' Marnie said to Sophie, who totally blanked her, too invested in her dolls to break focus.

'Hello Sophie, I like your dolls,' Hannah said anyway. She never knew what to say to small children, but she always made sure to use her normal voice – it seemed much more respectful to them and less humiliating for her. Alicia was much better at this stuff than her, proven by the fact that she slid herself off the sofa and slotted seamlessly into the role of mummy doll in Sophie's game of mummy and baby.

'How are you then, Han? You still working for Mr Prick?'

'Yep. And he continues to be one.' Hopefully Sophie wasn't at the age where she could copy what they were saying. 'Better than working in hospitality, though.'

Getting a decent job was continuing to be elusive, but Hannah was able to cover her disgustingly high rent by taking whatever she could through the temping agency she'd signed up for in November. Temping felt okay because it was just that – temporary. There was no chance she'd get stuck in a dead-end job for the rest of her life because the opportunity to do so wasn't there even if she'd wanted to. It worked for her in many ways – it wasn't great for making friends as she was never anywhere long enough to form lasting bonds, but she had her housemates to keep her company most of the time, so she couldn't complain. Between the four of them, they had a decent social life, there was always someone around for a drink at the pub, or a friend of a friend who Hannah would bump into out and about.

She'd so far been a waitress and a marketing assistant. Currently, it was three mornings a week maternity cover working as an executive assistant for Tony Price – a twat with too much money and judging by his attitude to women, a small penis.

'I miss working three days a week.' Marnie sighed. She'd increased her contract to five mornings a week, nine till one.

'It's lush.' When she wasn't working, Hannah spent her time mooching about London, working on her social media, and going to bars and pubs with Lola. Nights out weren't as frequent as they had been since Lola had started a full-time position as a graphic designer in early December, but the social media stuff kept Hannah occupied. 'Gives me time to do my content.'

'How's that going?'

'I'm enjoying it.' It wasn't getting the traction she hoped for, not yet anyway, despite working hard on it. How was it fair that a man online could sprinkle salt in a mildly seductive way and become an overnight sensation when Hannah was sat here with a degree and a social media content strategy and getting no more than twenty likes per post?

'Excellent stuff. Alicia was just telling me how great the teaching's going, weren't you, Alicia?' Marnie's eyes flicked towards her, a brief spark of something passing through them, but in a split second, it was gone.

'Yeah. Really good.' Despite what she was saying, Alicia looked stern, panicked even.

'What?' Hannah frowned.

'Nothing. Just a mad Christmas party.' Alicia shrugged.

'Who knew that teachers don't actually live under their desks?' Marnie grinned. 'Affairs, drugs and did you say someone showed up to the morning briefing the next day with only one shoe?'

'Yep.' Alicia nodded, her face softening.

'No way! God, now it makes sense why all the teachers just put a DVD on for the last day of term.' Hannah laughed. 'Sounds like most of them were hanging out of their arses. Did you have a Christmas do, Marns?'

'Yeah. Not quite as raucous as Alicia's. The most exciting thing that happened on ours was that Joyce accidentally flashed her tits to the whole staff roster.'

'How do you accidentally do that?' Alicia's eyes widened.

'Wardrobe malfunction and too much wine. We've all been there.'

'Sounds like a laugh.' It did sound nice, to have that camaraderie of a permanent workplace, friends, socials. The content creation could be quite lonely. Still, if she knew anything about herself it was that she was independent. If she just kept pushing, something would click, and soon she'd be the one getting invited to parties. All of the schlepping across London on a packed bus to spend her mornings buying extra hot Americanos with seven granules of sugar for a bellend with too much money would all be worth it.

It had better be, anyway, because otherwise what the hell was she doing?

Hannah was snapped out of her existential crisis by the shrill pierce of Sophie's scream.

'What?' Marnie's eyes were wide, her face a mix of surprise and confusion.

Alicia held her hands up in the air. 'I didn't do anything.'

Sophie continued to shout and scream, kicking her legs and saying words that Hannah couldn't understand.

Marnie picked her up, a rogue flailing foot almost smacking Alicia on the chin.

'Do you need a minute?' Marnie said, repeating herself four times to no avail. She turned to Hannah and Alicia. 'This gentle parenting thing is a con, I swear.' She turned back to Sophie. 'Do you want an ice cream?'

The screams ceased, replaced by gentle sobs.

'What was that about?'

'Beats me. Think she's over-tired. That's what happens when you wake up at 4am and refuse to go to bed until eleven.' Marnie threw Sophie on her hip and went over to the mini freezer. 'There you go. Hopefully a Mini Milk will help ease the trauma of Alicia holding the baby wrong.'

Alicia looked affronted. 'I just held it normally.'

'How very dare you.' Marnie kneeled back down with Sophie on the rug beside a rather wary-looking Alicia. Sophie licked her ice lolly as if nothing had happened, despite her face being wet with tears and the colour of a tomato. Marnie took a deep, audible breath and sucked her lips into a thin line, donning the expression of a naughty child. 'So, don't hate me,' she said, without looking up.

Hannah sat forward in her seat. 'Why are you saying that? What have you done?'

'I've not done anything.'

'Then what is it?' Alicia frowned. At least this wasn't something that only Hannah was in the dark about.

'So I've sort of promised Sophie we'd go to soft play

today. She kicked off at mini Tesco this morning and I was embarrassed and a bit scared and it just slipped out.'

'She's two, Marnie.'

'Yeah, and she's fucking scary. You just saw it first-hand.'

Soft play? As in a giant warehouse full of screaming kids, surfaces sprinkled with norovirus and grubby floors that you're forced to walk on with no shoes? 'Absolutely not,' Hannah said incredulously. 'You don't know what's under all those balls – there could be a turd for all you know.'

'Why are you so scared of germs now all of a sudden. You've put worse in your mouth.'

'I don't know what you're talking about,' Hannah said. 'It was only one time—'

'Please, it will only be for an hour. And if I tire her out today she'll be in a better mood and more likely to sleep tonight.' Marnie was on her knees, channelling her inner Oliver Twist. 'Alicia?'

Alicia smiled and shrugged. 'Happy to go with the flow.'

Of course she was. So happy to go with the flow that one day she might drown.

It was futile, but Hannah would give it one more go. 'Do we have to? I can't think of anything worse. Can't she just play here—'

'No.' Marnie stood up, eyes switching from pleading to over it in a millisecond. 'Can you just, for once in your life, stop being so dramatic? Help me out, will you? I told you it was going to be hard to make this work but I begged my parents to help out by having Sophie tonight so we can do this. The least you can do is compromise.'

The room fell silent.

Bloody hell, that went from zero to one hundred real

quick. Hannah crossed her arms. 'Fine, but I can't think of anything I want to do less,' she grumbled to her feet.

'You'll get over it.' Marnie grabbed a *Peppa Pig* backpack from the footstool and began chucking a selection of toys, wipes and nappies in it.

Hannah looked at Alicia, waiting for her acknowledgement that Marnie was overreacting, but she was back to playing silently with the dolls, despite Sophie now sitting on the floor staring at Marnie, mouth agape.

'I said fine, okay.' Pause. 'Sorry.'

'Good.' Marnie zipped up the bag and threw it on her shoulder.

'Good,' Hannah said quietly.

Soft play it was.

Bounce and Giggles was just as hellish as expected. Hannah was far from giggling and the only thing she wanted to bounce was her head off a hard surface, which was impossible in a place made entirely of sponge.

They'd paid an eye-watering ten pounds each, despite them all either being an 'accompanying adult' or under three feet tall.

Hannah had borrowed Marnie's Crocs in fear of leaving her new Nikes in an unmanned cubby hole and risking getting them swapped for a pair of Skechers by a tired or malevolent parent. They'd not even stopped for a coffee in the designated coffee area, where exhausted-looking parents sat sipping watery-looking instant coffee and chowing down on ready salted Pom-Bears. Despite the uninspiring cuisine, Hannah was wrought with jealousy as they were led straight to the ballpit by an overexcited, bouncing Sophie.

Marnie sat waist-high in the ballpit and Alicia was getting

stuck in too, holding Sophie's hand as she climbed the soft foam steps and encouraging her to slide in a rather irritating baby voice to slide in. Hannah perched on the edge, feet dangerously close, but not touching the balls; there was no amount of money you could pay her to go in any further.

'So I did see that guy in the end.' Marnie picked up a faded red ball and threw it in the air.

'Which one?' Hannah had lost track of the amount of dating profiles Marnie had dropped in the group chat. Was she talking about the one who always wore hats, or was it the one who was in between jobs because he was focused on writing his screenplay?

'Screenplay guy?' Alicia asked.

'No, Chris.'

'Who's Chris?' Since when did they ever refer to any of the guys by their proper names?

'You know Chris. The one I sent you.'

'You sent us loads.'

'The fit one.'

None of them were Hannah's type.

'Oh,' Alicia said. 'The one who did that silent retreat in Peru?'

'Yeah!'

Ah, that one. The one who declared himself a free spirit, which Hannah took to mean he did magic mushrooms on the reg and needed a fat spliff to get to sleep every night. Marnie was worth more than that, but after her outburst earlier, Hannah was going to keep her mouth shut. 'How was it?'

'Fine. Seen him a few times now.'

'Glowing review.'

'It's not serious. I rarely have time to go out these days so it's just the odd occasion when Mum will have Sophie and we go for some drinks and cinema. He took me to see *Sausage Party* on our first date.'

'Romantic.' Alicia laughed, as Sophie flung herself headfirst into the balls.

'I know, right? But it's nice to have someone to go out with. Get dressed up. Reminds me I'm more than just mum. I've still got it.' Marnie wiggled her chest.

'And you don't want anything more serious?' Hannah couldn't help herself. Why was Alicia happy to collude with Marnie and her shitty dates?

Thankfully, Marnie didn't take offence and continued to run her hands through the balls as if she was treading water. 'I don't know. It's a big ask expecting someone at our age to settle down with someone who has a kid that's not theirs.'

'How about an older guy?'

'There is this guy at work.' Marnie and Alicia looked at each other and shared a knowing smile. Hannah's heart sank.

'Ooooo. Is this the dishy doctor?' Alicia said.

'Maybe,' Marnie replied coyly.

Dishy doctor? This was the first time Hannah had heard of him. Also, who under the age of fifty-five ever described someone as dishy? 'Care to explain?'

'Just this guy at my work. He's older. Very sexy. We've been flirting a bit over email.'

'How very Bridget Jones!'

'Indeed.'

'He sounds nice.' Hannah could get behind a doctor. A doctor sounded more worthy of Marnie than a pothead or someone who bought NFTs.

'Shame he's married.' Marnie lay back in the ballpit, now mimicking a child making a snow angel.

'Oh,' she said. Hannah hadn't pegged Marnie as a homewrecker. *Would I sleep with a married man?*

'Oh indeed. Unhappily might I add, and that has nothing to do with me.' Marnie sat up. 'Are you having fun, Sophie?'

'Yeh,' Sophie panted, climbing up the foam steps again with Alicia's assistance, wobbling at the top on unsteady legs.

'Alicia?'

'Having a blast,' Alicia said, also panting and red-faced. 'This is hard work.'

'Welcome to my life.' Marnie smiled smugly. 'Alicia?'

Alicia's eyes narrowed. 'What?'

'Might you have some exciting news you want to share?'

Alicia's eyes widened. 'I—'

Alicia was cut off by a menacing cackle, as Sophie let go of her hand and slid down the ramp away from the ballpit. 'Bye Mummy,' she shouted, charging off at an astonishing speed for someone with such short legs.

'Shit!' Marnie thrust herself forward in a clumsy attempt to relieve herself from the clutches of the ballpit, but momentum failed her and she remained stuck, flailing around like one of those blow-up tube men.

'I'm on it,' Alicia shouted, sliding down the ramp and sprinting awkwardly after Sophie, dodging small children as she went.

'Give me a hand, will you?' Marnie said, still flailing.

Hannah did as she was told, trying not to think about her bare ankle as she dipped it in to steady herself as if navigating piranha-infested waters. Once free, Marnie charged after Alicia and Sophie, and against her will, Hannah did the same, trying to channel a brisk yet casual trot rather than anything more humiliating.

'What did you want to tell me?' shouted Hannah, as she dodged a swinging punch bag in Sophie's wake.

'Now's not a good time,' Alicia yelled, as she threw herself through a set of foam rollers that Sophie had just disappeared through.

'Marnie!' Hannah begged to Marnie's feet as she too disappeared head-first through the rollers.

What the hell was going on?

'Tell me! It's not fair for you two to be in on some little secret that I'm not.'

'In a second!' Marnie called from somewhere above her.

They continued to dodge and climb for what felt like ages, with Hannah desperately trying to navigate the spongy hurdles in a mini skirt without flashing the dads or indecently exposing herself to small children.

Finally, they stopped. Alicia and Hannah dropped to their knees, breathless and now three storeys up. Hannah hadn't realised they'd covered quite so much ground, and the height was dizzying even for a fully grown adult. She eyed the netting that enclosed them, hoping it was secure.

Marnie was on her back, panting like a dog without water, clinging onto the hem of Sophie's shirt. 'Fine . . . Shall I . . . tell her?'

'Tell me what?' Hannah was close to shouting. Sophie looked up from the giant shapes she was playing with and frowned. Hannah lowered her voice. 'Tell me,' she said, urgency still palpable.

'I've got a boyfriend.' Alicia said it so quickly it took Hannah a few seconds to process.

What? 'Since when?'

'Just after Christmas? I can't remember exactly.'

Like Alicia wouldn't know the exact date she'd met her first-ever boyfriend.

'Why does Marnie know but I don't?'

'It just came out when I saw her at the weekend.' Alicia bit her lip and stared at the floor.

'Didn't fancy telling me?' Hannah tried to keep her voice cool but it was a struggle, especially as her adrenaline was still pumping so loudly she could feel her heartbeat in her ears.

'I wanted to say it in person,' Alicia said, still to the floor. Guilty conscience much?

'Sounds like an excuse to me.' Hannah crossed her arms. 'What are you rolling your eyes for, Marnie?'

'This is meant to be a happy moment for Alicia and you're making it all about you!'

'You left me out!' Hannah was shouting now.

'You two always left me out,' Alicia squeaked.

Marnie shot daggers at her. 'Really, Alicia? I'm on your side.'

'There shouldn't be sides.' Alicia rolled onto her bum and pinched her brow. 'Look. I'm sorry I didn't tell you. It's all really new to me. Can we all just calm down for a second? I think we're overstimulated.'

Hannah took a deep breath, and put on her most calm voice. 'I still don't understand why you didn't tell me. Just seems weird. We've always shared everything with each other.'

'And I will. I'll tell you everything!' Alicia's eyes were desperate. 'I just wanted to wait until tonight because it felt more special. I don't know. Maybe that's stupid. I should have thought about how it would make you feel. I didn't mean to make you feel left out.'

'It's fine.' Hannah spoke over her, no longer wanting her pity.

Alicia bit down on her lip. 'Are you sure?'

Hannah did a half nod, half shrug. 'I need some air. I'm going to get myself a coffee. Anyone want anything?'

Marnie and Alicia looked at each other.

'I'll get a Fruit Shoot or something later,' Marnie said.

Alicia picked at a loose thread at edge of her sock. 'Nothing for me, thanks.'

'Okay, back in a bit.' Hannah turned and retraced her steps, the descent much harder without the adrenaline that had propelled her up in the first place. She made it down safely, albeit narrowly avoiding an arse-to-face collision with an embarrassed-looking father.

In the café, Hannah sipped her coffee – or more accurately, scalding hot water with the slightest attempt at being coffee. *Well, this is shit.* She had so been looking forward to Galentine's, seeing the girls and finally catching up, all three of them together. Yet here she was, white socks now the colour of her dad's old pants, likely having ingested norovirus, and finding out that Alicia and Marnie had been sitting on this massive secret that she was left out of.

Was Hannah being unreasonable? Or was it Alicia being out of order? Surely best friends told each other straight away whenever anything life-changing occurred. She'd told Marnie.

Maybe Hannah just wasn't Alicia's best friend anymore.

Hannah didn't want to make a scene, not like last year. Their friendship couldn't withstand many more dramatic storm-offs and misunderstandings, and right now, Hannah needed her friends more than ever. She could go home, make a statement, but to what? Her house would still be empty, mouldy, lonely. And it would only be to prove a point. If she did leave then Marnie and Alicia would get even closer and she'd get even further away.

She downed the rest of the bitter coffee and took a deep breath. Back to the ballpit it was; at least she could sit down there.

Marnie and Alicia went silent on Hannah's arrival, with the only sound being the conversation happening between Sophie and her new friend – a giant squashy banana.

'You okay?' Marnie finally said, back on her throne of balls.

Hannah didn't look up. 'Mmm.'

'Coffee shit?'

'Yep.'

Silence. And then . . .

'Owww!' A plastic ball smacked Hannah square in the right eye.

Marnie and Alicia looked totally horrified as Hannah rubbed at her eye and squinted. It didn't actually hurt but it had made her jump.

'Oh my God, Soph! Say sorry to Auntie Hannah.'

Sophie stood in the centre of the ballpit, the balls coming all the way up to her waist. Her eyes were wide and she bit her lip. She waddled over to the steps where Hannah was sitting and held her pudgy little hand out. Hannah reached for it, and Sophie gripped with all her might to climb next to Hannah.

'Sowwy Aun-nie na na.' Sophie reached out and patted Hannah's eyebrow. Hannah braced for a miscalculated pat and a grubby fingernail to the eyeball but it didn't come. Sophie's face morphed from concerned to a smile. 'Love you.'

'Awwwww,' Marnie and Alicia cooed in unison.

Hannah took in Sophie's face – her damp hair clinging to her forehead, her small peg-like teeth peeking through a shy smile, eyes wide with pure innocence. A little Marnie, through and through.

'That was quite cute.' Perhaps Hannah just needed to relax a bit. Yes, this wasn't part of the Galentine's plan, but it didn't have to be that bad. The girls could still chat – they could catch up anywhere really – and on the bright side, the ballpit could be a decent place to take some aesthetic videos and pictures for Insta. 'Budge over. Room for a small one?'

With that, Hannah took a deep breath and dived head-first into the pit.

Chapter Ten

13th February, 2017

Alicia

After the excitement of soft play, Sophie was much easier to put to bed. It was a quick twenty minutes and two bedtime stories, a welcome change from the drawn-out struggles Alicia had witnessed previously. Marnie's parents were now on shift, so if Sophie were to wake up, Marnie, Alicia and Hannah wouldn't be disturbed – in theory, anyway.

They too were all completely knackered after running around all day, and since Alicia and Marnie had work tomorrow, they were already tucked in bed, lights off except for a set of fairy lights strung along the curtain pole; it was only ten-thirty.

'So are you going to tell me all the juicy goss about the wonderfully handsome *Hugh*? I want all the details,' Hannah said, from her spot next to Marnie in the double bed.

Alicia had the sofa, which worked just fine for her as she much preferred her own space.

'Of course, what do you want to know?' She was happy to share the details with Hannah now, it felt like the right time.

Although what she'd said about wanting to tell her in person was partly true, she had purposely held back from telling her sooner. There was some power in knowing something that Hannah didn't, for a change.

Hannah was so experienced and opinionated with everything. What if she'd made a comment that would make Alicia see Hugh differently? Make her question whether what she had with Hugh was as good as she thought it was? She didn't want it to be spoiled by anyone. She was even hesitant to tell Marnie. She only did because she was incapable of lying and Marnie had asked her outright one Saturday morning when they'd taken Sophie to Cassiobury Park.

'How did you meet? What's he like? What does he do? How's the sex?' Hannah didn't stop to take a breath.

'We met on placement during my teacher training. He's a geography teacher at Langley Oak.' She'd always hoped to meet a teacher – someone who got what it was like to be on the frontline of education and who shared the same time off as her. It also meant they couldn't be angry at her for having to pay peak prices for holidays because they were stuck with term times too. He couldn't be more perfect.

'Are you going to tell me the story? Set the scene, describe it in great detail. Come on, Alicia, everyone knows the best part about a new boyfriend or girlfriend is telling the story. The meet cute!' Hannah's eyes glinted and a smile tugged at the corner of her mouth.

'It's really nothing special.' Alicia felt the weight of Hannah's expectation bear down on her. She didn't have a magical movie moment to talk about.

'Nothing special? Bollocks! This is the moment you met your future husband.'

'It's still early days.' Alicia's cheeks flushed, although it was nice for Hannah to take such an interest in her life, for her to be the one with exciting news for a change.

'Yeah but we all know that you'd only go out with someone you were serious about.'

'She's right,' Marnie added.

'True,' Alicia said. 'Okay, I'll tell the story, but it really isn't that interesting.' She moved herself into a more upright position, and took a deep breath, channelling her teacher mode. 'So I'd just started my new placement at Langley Oak. One Friday, I got stuck in the most horrendous traffic, despite leaving an hour for what should have been a twenty-minute journey, and so I slid into the all-staff meeting by the skin of my teeth.'

'That's very unlike you!' Marnie chuckled.

'Yep. And so there I was, out of breath, sweaty, probably bright red trying to be as inconspicuous as possible and fell into the only spare chair left, and there he was, frowning intently at a pristine copy of *The Alchemist* by Paulo Coelho.'

'What's that?' Hannah asked, to which Alicia had to stifle her dismay at both the comment and the disruption.

'Only one of my favourite books ever. How have you not heard of it?'

'I'm more of a romcom kind of girl.' Hannah shrugged. 'Back to your romcom moment!'

Alicia shook her head fondly, but she was getting more into the storytelling now. 'He must have felt me staring because he glanced up and our eyes met. His frown of concentration – which was super sexy by the way – turned into a smile. One of those where his eyes creased at the corners like he was really happy to see me despite not knowing who I was.' Alicia's stomach flipped at the memory. It really was one of those moments where time slowed down and everything and everyone in the room faded away. Like two souls had connected again after years – or lifetimes – apart. There was a familiarity to him that felt both comfortable and thrilling. She wasn't going to say that out loud because it was horribly clichéd, but, much to her delight and embarrassment, it was true.

'I'm getting fanny flutters!' Marnie fanned herself. 'Let me guess, your eyes kept meeting across the room.'

'Yep. Throughout the whole meeting, I couldn't stop myself from snatching glimpses of him, and he did the same to me. I could sense it.'

'So how did you go from staring at each other over briefing notes to boyfriend and girlfriend?' Hannah's eyes still sparkled with intrigue. Alicia hadn't lost her interest yet, it seemed.

'Well, fast forward two weeks of swapped smiles and holding doors open for each other with polite good mornings, I found myself close to a nervous breakdown at the photocopier when it was chugging out blank paper instead of copies of *Before You Were Mine* by Carol Ann Duffy. Who was there in my moment of need but Mr Hugh Brown? He offered to help, but, and I quote, he said "I'm going to offer to help because it's the right thing to do, but honestly I haven't the foggiest how to get it to work when it's on one of its benders."'

'He did not say *the foggiest*?!' Hannah yelped, drawing Alicia from her story with gusto.

Her gut flipped at the recollection. 'He did. That's when I knew we'd be a good match. It still took me a few more weeks before I built up the courage to ask him if he wanted to grab a coffee at lunch. Thankfully, he said yes, otherwise I'd have to move schools.'

'You did not ask *him*?' It was Marnie's turn to yelp. She smacked her pillow three times with such glee Alicia was worried it might burst and they'd all be covered in feathers.

'I did.' It had turned into a ten-minute coffee in the staffroom at lunchtime because teaching didn't allow a full lunch break, Alicia soon realised. But it was the most magical ten minutes of her life.

'Oh my God, you dark horse! So proud of you. You never told me that part,' Marnie said, shaking her head with the frenetic buzz of excitement.

Their energy was contagious, and now Alicia felt herself buzzing with the thrill of it all. She'd done it. She'd met her future husband.

'That's such a beautiful story.'

Hannah's words took Alicia aback. 'Is it?' Of course, to her it was, but on paper it was nothing special.

'Yes! It's just so . . . Alicia.' Hannah chuckled.

Hannah was right. It was so . . . *her*. Understated. Sensible. Ordinary. But oh-so amazing. And the girls could see that, too.

'So you asked him out and then what?' Marnie prompted, rubbing her hands together, still smiling

'He took me to the British Library.'

Hannah kicked her legs under the covers with a squeal. 'Oh my God, this just keeps getting better! Of course he took you to a library.'

'Not just any library, the British Library.'

'And then what? Please tell me you shagged him in the toilets.'

'What do you think?' The thought of it did cross Alicia's mind, however fleeting. It was very unlike her, but Hugh just *did* something to her no one else had ever managed to. 'We went for a wander around Camden and then home.'

'So when did you shag him?'

'I don't know. Maybe a month in?'

'I bet you were frothing by that time!' Hannah looked suitably horrified. 'A month?!'

'Not sure I'd go as far as to say frothing but I was definitely ready.'

'I should hope so, you did wait for twenty-two years. Was it amazing?'

'Yes and no.' Alicia couldn't pretend it was one hundred per cent perfect. It had been full of fumbles, polite chat and at one point, an accidental headbutt. But it was also full of love and gentleness. Hugh knew he was her first and treated her with care. 'It felt alright but nothing mind-blowing.'

'Love the honesty,' Hannah said.

'First times rarely are mind-blowing. I'd take mind-blowing over accidentally falling pregnant though.' Marnie snorted.

There was a beat of silence.

Would this be the moment she divulged further details about her one-night stand that resulted in her forever baby?

More silence.

No, she would not.

'Marnie's right. No one's bouncing up and down on it like a spacehopper on their first rodeo.'

'I thought that's what your first time was like, Han?' Marnie took the words out of Alicia's mouth.

'Baby Han had no idea what she was talking about.'

Now it was Alicia's turn to appreciate Hannah's honesty.

'I'm pleased to report that the sex is much better now.' She smiled to herself, her mind drifting off to the previous Saturday night. They had ordered a Chinese takeaway and started the evening curled up on the sofa before making love there and then. She'd had her first-ever partnered orgasm with the help of her new and trusty bullet vibrator. Now that *was* mind-blowing.

'You dark horse. I love it. Has he gone down on you?'

'Hannah!'

'What? This is important information.'

'Stop! You're making her blush,' Marnie giggled. 'But has he?'

Alicia threw the duvet cover over her head. 'I'm embarrassed,' she muffled.

'Why? We're all friends here.'

She wasn't sure why, it just felt . . . exposing. Hugh was a private person, and perhaps he wouldn't want Alicia divulging all of the details of their sex life like both Hannah and Marnie did. They often shared such detail Alicia felt like she was there, for better and for worse.

Alicia emerged from her duvet cave, face hot. 'Yes, he has. Can we talk about you two now?' Alicia could only handle being the centre of attention for so long, especially when it concerned *that*.

'Has he met your parents?' Hannah asked.

Alicia's cheeks cooled. Safer territory. 'Yes. We all went out for lunch in the New Year.' It had been wonderful. Alicia was worried her parents would be awkward or too serious, but they did her proud, and by the end of the starters, everyone had warmed up and it felt like old friends meeting for a hearty lunch. Alicia had sat there admiring the scene, basking in the thrilling glow of her new and old life converging in the most perfect way. All of a sudden, she had an entirely new set of family and friends within her reach, a world far removed from the close-knit group she was used to: Hannah, Marnie, Mum, Dad and Neelam.

'That's so grown up.' Marnie nodded, face full of approval.

Alicia grinned. She couldn't help it. 'I *am* grown up.'

'Yes you are,' Hannah laughed. 'You've had your pussy licked. That's very grown up of you.'

Alicia cringed but giggled. 'You're disgusting.'

'That's why you love me.' Hannah shifted up in the bed and propped herself against the headboard. 'How often do you see him? Does he have his own place?'

'Yes he has a flat. I'm there two or three times a week. I'm at a new school for my placement now.' Eugh, school. Alicia glanced at the time on her watch. Almost eleven. She could talk about Hugh all night but she really did need to get some sleep soon.

'Booooo,' Marnie said. 'No banging in the stationery cupboard. Probably for the best.'

'Unfortunately not.' The words sat heavy in Alicia's chest. Of course Alicia might not have done something as wild as having sex in a cupboard, but sharing breakfast, sneaking out of Hugh's flat in the morning, and then staggering their entry times had felt thrilling, exciting, naughty – words she'd never imagined herself being.

Long term, though, this was for the best. Seeing him every day wasn't healthy. With distance, she could focus – on training, on teaching – without the distraction of his knowing glances or stolen touches. Still, she'd miss the rush of it all.

Marnie rolled over to face her. 'Proud of you.'

'Me too,' Hannah added. 'You've done it. Your future husband, the wonderful, sexy Hugh Brown.'

Alicia swallowed, warmth rising in her throat. 'Thanks, guys. I really am happy.'

She'd taken the first step. The plan was officially in motion and life could finally begin.

Hot Mess Express 🚂 😜

28th March, 2017

Alicia: I am pooping my pants! Meeting loads of Hugh's school friends tonight at a wedding.

Hannah: Not sure that would be the best first impression.

Marnie: I'm sure it will be fine. People's friends are an extension of them so chances are they're a decent bunch and you'll all get on well. If not, you'll have to dump him x JK

Hannah: Just be yourself.

Alicia: That's terrible advice for someone who is boring.

Marnie: You aren't boring!

Alicia: All I do is teach and sleep.

Hannah: And you like to read!

Alicia: I am just THRILLING 😑

Marnie: I'm sure you have a million funny stories about the students. Maybe have a glass of wine or two to loosen up.

Alicia: Wish me luck xx

29th March, 2017

Marnie: Did it go okay with Hugh's friends?

Alicia: Yes!! It went fab. Had a lovely time, don't know what I was worrying about. They are all super nice and two of them are teachers too. I have officially been added to the WhatsApp group.

Hannah: You have been indoctrinated. Don't forget about us with your newfound popularity xx

2nd April, 2017

Hannah: I have finally stopped working for Tony the Twat. Should be starting another admin role in a couple of weeks (send help) but it will give me time to apply for a few internships I've seen. Will send them over.

Hannah: This one is for a design internship at Jennifer Clair helping design their garments. Fashun, darlin.

Hannah: This is less up my alley but still looks fun – social media assistant. Could learn some good marketing skills for my social stuff there.

Marnie: Both look amazing!!! How are you possibly supposed to have two years' experience in the industry when it's supposed to be an entry level opportunity though?!

Alicia: Ridiculous. I'm sure you'll smash it though, they'd be lucky to have you.

Hannah: Fingers crossed!!

4th May, 2017

Hannah: Didn't get the internships. Annoying but it wasn't meant to be. I'm trusting the universe that it will present me the right thing at the right time. In the meantime, I suppose I better get myself some more power suits if I'm going to be office-based for the foreseeable.

Marnie: That sucks. You'd have been perfect for both! You rock a powersuit though. Keep going.

Alicia: Ever thought about teaching?

Hannah: LOL NO.

4th June, 2017

Marnie: OMG Hannah, are you okay? I saw the terror attacks on the news.

Hannah: I'm okay xx Stayed in today for once in my life. Lola was thinking about heading to the market sometime this week, too. So scary and so close to home! Thinking about all the people who lost their lives and who have to live with the trauma of it all :(What is wrong with people?

Alicia: 🙉 So horrendous. No words. Glad you're okay. 🖤

Marnie: Love you both xx

24th July, 2017

Hannah: Get in Kem and Amber!!!!!

Marnie: Camilla and Jamie WERE ROBBED.

Alicia: Who are you talking about?

Hannah: *Love Island*, babe.

Alicia: 😵

Hannah: You're the only person in the UK not watching it!

Alicia: If you say so,

8th August, 2017

Marnie: Have you both seen GOT?!

Hannah: No and don't plan to.

Alicia: Not yet!! No spoilers.

Marnie: Hurry up and watch it!!! I need to talk to someone about it. It was EPIC,

29th August, 2017

Marnie: Who's fucking idea was it to move GBBO onto Channel Four?! These adverts can fuck right off.

Alicia: That was the most British thing I've heard in a while lol.

Marnie: FUMING,

27th November, 2017

Alicia: ROYAL WEDDING HERE WE COME!!!

Marnie: Meghan will look amazing <3

Hannah: Damnit. There goes my lifelong dream of marrying the only ginger I've ever considered shagging.

Marnie: 😵

23rd December, 2017

Hannah: Where did you disappear off to at Christmas?

Alicia: Yeah! You were gone by 9. Very unlike you to leave before me.

Marnie: I was tired and had an early morning the next day.

Hannah: Never bothered you before . . .

Marnie: What are you insinuating?

Hannah: Nothing. Clearly you are just a changed woman!

Marnie: 😑

Hannah: 👊

31st January, 2018

Marnie: Sophie's started a new playgroup and she loves it there, but fuck me, the other mums there are so . . . awful.

Alicia: Oh no, why?

Marnie: Just feel they look down on me because I am younger. Might just be in my head but I didn't get good vibes.

Hannah: Bitches. Fuck em.

Alicia: Why did you move playgroups? Thought you loved the last one?

Marnie: I did. Just felt like time for a change. Wanted one more local.

Alicia: I thought it was local?

Marnie: Na,

Marnie: I'm hosting Galentine's this year

Hannah: Mum and dad okay with that?

Marnie: Actually, I've moved . . .

Hannah: WTF?

Marnie: It was spontaneous.

Alicia: Where? Details?

Marnie: Sophie kicking off. You'll see it when you come. It's not far – just in Ricky.

Hannah: You're living in Rickmansworth? You posh little bitch!!!!

Alicia: So you're no longer living at home?

Hannah: ????????

Marnie: Address is 29 Red Apple Orchard.

Alicia and Hannah

Alicia: WTF is going on?

Hannah: I'm as confused as you. She not said anything to you?

Alicia: Nope. I saw her two weeks ago!

Hannah: Hmmmmm.

<u>Social media strategy 2017-18: @LondonGirlHan</u>

Bio: Just a girl living in London.
Lifestyle, fashion, makeup, beauty and flatshare life
in Le Big Smoke. Central Saint Martin's Graduate.

Platform	Content
YouTube	Swimwear haul for larger busts x
Instagram	Quick matcha before I apply for an internship . . . eeeek
Instagram	OOTD – Business casual but make it sexy
Instagram	Out Out with my housemates

Followers: 201

@Mac_addict: Where's your lipstick from x

@Steffi_In_Style: That dress 😍

@Marns: Good luck with the internship!

@BarneyBoi: Same again 2nite?

@Lola_69: YOU SLAYED LAST NIGHT

Chapter Eleven

13th February, 2018

Marnie

Marnie was in the bedroom, attacking her hair with Sophie's Barbie brush in a manic attempt to make herself look presentable. As always, her energy and time had been spent on seeing to Sophie, making sure she was washed, dressed, fed and entertained. She'd also spent the morning dashing around the house, making sure the mess from breakfast had been tidied away, and that Steven hadn't left any skid marks in the downstairs toilet, despite having spent most of the previous week on her knees – scrubbing, of course.

It had paid off. The house was immaculate. She'd even wiped the walls and skirting boards down for Christ's sake. It was important that the girls saw how well she was doing for herself this time. Goodbye chaotic Marnie, who was still living at home with her parents and shagging bottom-feeder men for a morsel of validation, hello grown-up, adult Marnie who had a doctor as a boyfriend and who lived in a four-bed detached house in the expensive town of Rickmansworth. She told herself that because Rickmansworth still had a

Wetherspoons, she wouldn't completely forget where she came from, but that was a hard thing to do in a place where house prices were miles above the national average.

Their relationship had been intense and things had moved quickly, much to the dismay of Marnie's family and work friends. Nanny Sheila had made her thoughts known as she often did – *I don't like him, he reminds me of Jeffrey Dahmer* – and her dad offered her the helpful advice of: *don't shit on your own doorstep.* Marnie's friend at work – Andrea – had tentatively advised her against pursuing him purely because he was her boss. Marnie was inclined to listen to her because she was a wise woman, especially when it came to motherhood (the stuff that Alicia and Hannah didn't get), but when something felt right to Marnie, nothing anyone would say would stop her doing what she wanted.

Marnie had been aware of Steven for over a year, but it wasn't until December that they'd hooked up for the first time – the result of a very boozy Christmas party and a freshly divorced Steven. Since then, he'd wooed her with expensive dinners, stolen moments during lunch breaks, and the most amazing sex Marnie had ever had. When Steven suggested a day trip to the zoo, she even introduced him to Sophie. It was the family fantasy Marnie had always dreamed of.

'I think they're here. I heard a car door outside.' Steven appeared at the door and wandered to the window to peer out. His dark blonde hair was floppy, thinning just the slightest bit at the crown and he was wearing his jeans and his best fleece. He looked sexy, but Marnie would brace herself for the inevitable comments from Hannah that she was dating someone who wore Regatta unironically. At least it wasn't a gilet.

'Don't do that! You'll look creepy.'

'This is my house, I'm allowed to live here,' Steven chuckled, bemusement visible on his face.

'This is *our* house.' It felt good to say.

Things at home had gotten increasingly tense over the previous year. Sharing a kitchen with her mum, who had very particular ways of doing everything, was a constant source of conflict. If Marnie wasn't stacking the dishwasher wrong, she was using the wrong clip to seal the grated cheese bag – or God forbid, leaving it open. To top it off, her mum had recently suggested increasing her rent to cover the 'rising cost of living'. Marnie was already paying out of her arse to live there, and it wasn't as if her parents had a large mortgage to pay off. She bought her and Sophie's groceries separately and didn't have the time to use much hot water in a lavish bath or long, indulgent shower. She was in and out, and Sophie was often dunked in the leftover hot water from Marnie's mum's hour-long soaks.

Marnie had shared her thoughts with Steven mid-January. He was slower to warm to the idea, but she saw his wariness for what it really was: an understandable fear, but not worth letting it get in the way of the amazing thing they had together. She'd managed to persuade him it was the right move from a financial and practical point of view – she knew how to speak his language – and now here they were.

He came up behind her and wrapped his arms around her waist, nuzzling into the crook of her neck. She leaned back into his tall, sturdy frame and took a deep breath. He smelt like vanilla and sweat. In the chaos of getting everything ready, she'd not realised how nervous she was, and his presence was just the grounding elixir she needed.

The doorbell rang.

'Mummy, they're here!' Sophie squealed up the stairs.

Shit.

Today Alicia and Hannah were finally going to meet him, though they didn't know it yet. Marnie wanted it to be a relaxed, casual affair so was going for the element of surprise. Steven was under strict instructions that he stay no longer than ten minutes before heading out with Sophie to his parents, and it would be played off that he was running late having meant to leave before their arrival – a totally believable story seeing as he was a doctor and it wasn't unheard of for his practice to run up to forty minutes behind schedule.

'I'm nervous,' Marnie whimpered, feeling herself revert to her child-self and wanting nothing more than to be rolled up into a duvet burrito and told everything was going to be taken care of. How would they react? Hopefully they'd be happy and not mad at her for keeping things close to her chest. In Marnie's defence, it had been such a whirlwind that she hadn't had much time to process it all herself.

Steven kissed her neck and her legs went weak at the knees. 'There's really no need to worry. I'll be my usual charming self, and you just be you.'

She took a deep breath. 'Okay. Let's do this.'

Chapter Twelve

13th February, 2018

Marnie

'Since when were you living in a fucking mansion—'

Hannah was halfway through her greeting when she stopped abruptly. Marnie was hiding in the snug, tucked just out of sight with Sophie ready for their grand reveal. She'd give anything to see the girls' faces right now, likely a picture of utter confusion as Steven answered the door. Better put them out of their misery.

Three, two, one.

'Surprise!' They jumped out, Marnie waving her hands manically, beaming at the shock on her best friends' faces.

Hannah blinked. 'What's going on?' she said, face a picture of total bemusement.

Alicia said nothing, her knitted eyebrows and forced smile doing all the talking necessary.

'Auntie Lissy,' Sophie giggled, charging down the hallway and flinging herself at Alicia. Once she'd given her a greeting that wouldn't have been out of place in *Love Actually*, Sophie ran back to Marnie and now decided she was shy. She clung to Marnie's legs, hiding her face against her thigh and looking at the floor coyly. Hopefully Hannah wouldn't take it personally.

'Nice pyjamas,' Steven grinned.

Alicia grimaced. 'Oh. Er—'

'Bloody hell. I'd forgotten what we looked like.' Hannah looked down at herself and shook her head.

Both she and Alicia were wearing their matching PJs, this year a red polka-dot set with white lace trim that Alicia had chosen from Oliver Bonas (*on sale, she wasn't made of money*).

'Come in then!' Marnie beamed. 'Welcome to Casa Del Loveshack. Oh, and can you take your shoes off, please?'

'What is this? Buckingham Palace?' Hannah laughed, but she did as she was told, sliding off her Chelsea boots and eyeing Marnie suspiciously. 'You know I'm a shoes off girly anyway.'

'I'm Steven.' He reached for Hannah's hand and pulled her into a formal hug, air kissing both cheeks. How European. How cosmopolitan. *Look at us! Proper grown-ups!*

Over his shoulder, Hannah mouthed 'what the fuck?' to Marnie who flashed her most guilty smile. Was she mad or just shocked?

'I'll be out of your hair very soon. I'm so sorry, I'm running a little late.' Steven shook his head apologetically, word-perfect to their script. 'But what a pleasure to meet you both! Marnie never stops talking about you.'

It was funny to see him with her friends like this, two parts of her life colliding. Old and new. She could imagine Alicia liking him because he was more on the serious side, but Hannah? It could go either way.

Alicia stepped forward tentatively. 'I'm Alicia. Lovely to

meet you! What a lovely surprise,' she said, her voice high and the sort that she only ever used on the phone.

Sophie now started to paw at Marnie's thigh, tugging her shirt. 'Mumma, up. Up. Mumma, UP!'

'Shall we go to the snug?' Marnie huffed as she slung Sophie onto her hip. God, she was getting heavy. One of these days she wouldn't be able to pick her up. Where was her little girl going?

'The snug?' Alicia and Hannah's eyes met, and Marnie tried to work out if they were impressed or taking the piss. Also, what a strange shift in dynamics – Alicia and Hannah sharing covert glances? What alternative reality was this?

Still, she led them into the snug, gesturing for them to sit down on one of the plush sofas. She loved this room. The olive-green hue of the walls wasn't something she'd have chosen, but it really worked in here, and the multiple editions of anatomy books on the alcove shelves either side of the fireplace were very sophisticated. If it was up to Marnie, she'd maybe have a few more trinkets and knick-knacks about, but as Steven rightly said, it was just more stuff to dust.

Hannah sat next to Alicia, who was acting as a throne for Sophie who'd climbed onto her lap. Steven and Marnie sat on the sofa opposite, his warm hand resting on her knee. She was hyperaware of the way both Hannah and Alicia were staring at her, seemingly taking in every interaction between them both.

'What a lovely house,' Alicia said politely, leaning around Sophie. 'Beautiful snug. I've always wanted a snug.'

'Is it a snug or just a sitting room? What exactly are the determining factors?' Hannah laughed, pearly whites bared, head thrown back. A bit much.

'It's nice to have a room away from the rest of the living area.' Steven shifted in his seat and squeezed Marnie's knee.

Silence. Even Sophie wasn't her usual distraction because she was now busy playing with Alicia's hair.

Hannah coughed. 'So, Steven. What is it you do for a living?'

'Steven's a doctor,' Marnie interjected.

'Ah, so this is the sexy doctor.' Hannah wiggled her perfectly plucked and pencilled eyebrows.

'It is indeed.' Marnie chuckled, although she sensed Steven tense and it was now his turn to clear his throat.

'Thank you, my love. Yes, I'm a doctor. How about you two? One of you is a teacher?'

'Yes, that's me. I teach English at Berryfields,' said Alicia, as Sophie hopped off her lap to start rummaging around in her small toybox in the corner of the room.

'You enjoy it?' Steven said, raising his voice slightly over the noise Sophie was making. Hopefully he wouldn't get irritated.

'Yes. It's something I've always wanted to do. Have you always wanted to be a doctor?'

'When I was younger I wanted to be an astronaut, but I get terrible motion sickness.'

Marnie laughed loudly, doing a stellar job of covering up Hannah and Alicia's polite but awkward chuckles. He wasn't the funniest guy, bless him, but she really appreciated that he was making an effort.

Steven turned to Hannah. 'How about you? I hear you're in the creative industries?'

'Yes, that's me.' Hannah was interrupted by Sophie who, now arms laden with toys, proceeded to dump them all in a pile in the middle of the room. Steven winced. He was a sensitive soul, bless him.

'And where did you study?'

'Central Saint Martins.'

'Lovely part of town. What do you do, then?'

'Yeah, remind me again. I lose track.' Marnie frowned at her. It was hard to keep up with all her various projects and temp jobs.

'I'm dabbling. Trying to find my place in the industry, you know?'

'Dabbling in what?'

Hannah appeared to bristle but then smiled. 'Oh, all sorts. I'm looking at art gallery assistant jobs, opportunities in theatre sets and costuming, that sort of stuff. I don't want to commit to something I'm not sure of and I'm keen to leave plenty of time and creative energy for the influencing stuff.'

Marnie continued to frown. As far as she knew, Hannah had been struggling to get her foot in the door of anything mildly creative, and was still with her temping agency doing admin or office work. Still, she wouldn't call her out on it right now. 'How's the influencing stuff going?'

'What is this? The Spanish Inquisition?' Hannah's laugh was shrill and forced. 'Fine, thanks. Consistency is key when it comes to social media. I post every day, at least once. Ditched YouTube because it took too much time and had barely any reach. I'm just throwing everything at it and seeing what sticks. Still yet to have my viral moment, but numbers are up a fraction since last year at least.'

'It takes a certain type of person to do that online stuff,' Steven said, leaning back and resting his arm behind Marnie.

Hannah's smile dropped.

'Sorry.' Steven quickly sat forward again. 'What I meant was that not everyone is comfortable on camera and wants to share so much of themselves on the internet.'

Good save.

'It doesn't bother me.' Hannah sat back and crossed her legs, the picture of orchestrated nonchalance. 'You could say the same for any job, I guess. It takes a certain type of person to be a doctor. Being that close to the general public and all their gross health issues isn't for everyone.'

'Touché.' Steven slapped his hands on his thighs and stood. 'Right, better be off. Sophie, how does a KFC sound?'

'KFC!' Plastic Peppa Pig clattered to the floor. 'Yum.'

'Thought so.' Steven ruffled Sophie's hair and then looked up. It was so nice to see them bonding. It had taken a while for Steven to warm to Sophie – he wasn't a naturally paternal person – but they were getting there. 'It was lovely to finally meet you both. Have a wonderful night and I'll see you tomorrow at breakfast. We'll be sure to keep out of your hair.'

'Bye, love.' Marnie stood to peck him on the cheek. His gaze lingered on her and in that moment, everything finally started to feel like it was clicking into place.

Chapter Thirteen

13th February, 2018

Hannah

'What the fuck just happened?'

'You just met my lovely doctor boyfriend. That's what happened.' Marnie wiggled her eyebrows and smiled mischievously. She was clearly loving this.

'I realised that much. Why didn't you warn us?' Hannah gestured to her nocturnal get-up. 'Did you purposely want us to look like complete tits?'

'You look like the cutest, most fashion-forward tits I've seen. And I didn't warn you because I didn't want it to be a big thing.' Marnie shrugged but Hannah could see in her eyes a glimmer of awkwardness.

'It is a big thing,' Alicia exclaimed. At least it wasn't just Hannah thinking it.

'I knew you'd say that, which is exactly why I wanted to keep it casual.'

'There's nothing casual about this whole set-up, babe.' Hannah still couldn't wrap her head around it. 'He seemed nice, from the fleeting five minutes we've known him, anyway.'

'He is nice.' Marnie smiled softly but didn't offer up any more information.

That was okay because Hannah didn't need permission to ask the important questions.

'Whose idea was it to move in?'

'Mine. Well, both of ours really.'

'And how is he with Sophie?'

'He's great! He loves kids.'

Unlikely.

'Not got any of his own?'

'Na.'

'Is he divorced now, then?'

'Yeah. Nothing happened between us until him and his ex were well and truly over.'

Again, unlikely.

'Do you know why they split?'

'They wanted different things. She wanted kids – well, that's not the only reason. Like I said, he loves kids.'

'Loves them but doesn't want them?' Alicia squinted.

'Yeah, that is a possibility, you know.' Marnie crossed her legs and tucked a cushion beneath her chin, hugging it like a koala. She looked like Marnie again, more relaxed and less upright and proper.

'That's fair.' Steven was certainly not Marnie's usual type, but that wasn't necessarily a bad thing. Hannah wouldn't make her mind up about him just yet. She needed to give the guy a chance.

Marnie's face lit up. 'Do you want the grand tour?'

Alicia was already on her feet. 'I'd never say no to a tour. Hugh and I have been talking about getting our own place, selling his flat and getting a house. We won't be able to afford something like this, but it's always nice to see what's about.'

'Amazing! That's so exciting.' Marnie chucked the cushion onto the corner of the sofa and stood too.

Life was all moving forward for both of them, it seemed. 'I don't know how people afford to get on the property market at all these days. We definitely missed a trick by not investing in property when we were still in the womb.' By the time Hannah would be ready to settle down, she wouldn't even be able to afford a garage let alone a proper house. Although saying that, in a few years she'd be making a lot more than she was now. It was only a matter of time before something fell into place, she could feel it.

'Hugh's family will help,' Alicia said with a hint of self-consciousness.

'It's the only way, really,' said Marnie. 'That or get yourself a man with a house already.'

'Ah, so you're playing the long game with Steven, then?' Hannah wiggled her eyebrows.

'Maybe? Na, I'm joking of course. It's certainly a perk, though.' Marnie bowed. 'Now please, follow me to the drawing room.'

There was no drawing room, but the house was impressive, and Hannah and Alicia made all the right oohs and ahhs as Marnie led them round upstairs, despite the decor not being to Hannah's taste. It was too plain, very minimalistic, bordering on stark.

Sophie's room was especially bare. There was a painting of poppy fields on the wall and cream bed sheets matching cream curtains which matched a cream rug on the wooden floor. If there was anywhere in the house that should have felt a bit more relaxed, had a bit more personality and soft edges, it should be Sophie's room. It felt more like a spare room than a little girl's room, surely Marnie could see that?

Back in the kitchen – the standard middle-class renovation: a large, open-plan kitchen-diner with sliding doors leading onto the massive, mature garden – Marnie flicked on the kettle.

'Tea? Or I can make you a proper coffee if you want? I have decaf,' she said, patting a large, shiny monster of a machine.

'Fancy. Go on, then.' Hannah slid herself into a matte black bar stool tucked under the granite kitchen island.

Alicia leaned against the island also, eyes wide as she took in the sizeable garden. 'I bet Sophie loves the garden. Plenty of space for a Wendy house or trampoline.'

Marnie lined up three matching grey mugs on the counter. Had she chucked her mismatched charity-shop collection before moving in? 'Yeah, we're working on Steven to let us get a trampoline. He's precious about the grass going yellow underneath it.'

'Oh.' Hannah frowned and looked at Alicia, but Alicia seemed less concerned with the garden and was now stroking the kitchen island in apparent awe.

'This kitchen space is to *die* for. Can I take a picture to show Hugh?' Alicia slid her phone from her pocket and started snapping.

'Isn't it? I haven't shown you the best bit yet.' Marnie walked over to a door along the far wall and pushed it open. 'Tada!'

'A utility room! You lucky bitch.' Alicia was practically shouting, clapping her hands like a toddler who'd just spied their birthday cake.

Hannah had never seen her so passionate. 'Have we really reached the age where we're getting wet for a utility room?'

'I think so.' Marnie laughed.

'God help me.'

Marnie passed Hannah her latte – proper froth and everything – and handed Alicia her tea.

'So, what do you think?' Marnie slid herself into the stool beside Hannah and looked at her expectantly.

'It's lovely,' Alicia said enthusiastically.

'Mmm.' Hannah didn't know what to say and had never been a good liar. She followed it up with a cough for good measure. 'Nice.' It *was* nice. But there was almost no indication that a child lived there, nor Marnie. In Marnie's annexe, they were always tripping over dolls, accidentally sitting on Barbies or 'admiring' Sophie's new artwork from nursery, displayed part proudly, part ironically on the fridge. Here, everything was very neat, in its place and grown up.

Marnie frowned at her. 'Why are you being weird?'

'I'm not.'

'Yes you are. What's wrong with it?'

'Nothing's wrong with it. It's just very . . . tidy.'

'Shock horror I'm actually living like an actual adult and not a goblin.'

Hannah didn't mean it as a compliment, nor did she appreciate the comment about living like an *actual adult*. What did that even mean, and what must Marnie think about Hannah still living in her houseshare? Yes, the house was a shithole, but Hannah was allowed to say that because she lived there.

'Where's all of Sophie's stuff? Where's all of your stuff?'

'Sophie's stuff is in the ottoman in her room and the box in the snug. You saw her playing with her toys earlier!' Marnie took a loud, obnoxious sip of her drink. 'And as for my stuff, I had a huge clearout before moving in. I Marie-Kondo'd the shit out of everything.'

150

So that's where her mugs have gone . . . 'Hmm.'

'Stop saying that!'

'It's a lovely house! It just feels a bit weird. I'm sure you'll add your touches soon and it will feel more like your home, not just Steven's.'

'You're right. I just need time to settle in. Work on Steven about Sophie's bedroom—'

'And the trampoline,' Alicia added, having been her usual self by staying at a safe distance, merely observing and piping up only when the conflict had started to fizzle out.

'Yep, and that.' Marnie looked from Hannah to Alicia. 'Anything else you'd like to criticise before we move on?'

Well, if she was asking . . . 'There aren't any pictures of Sophie around.'

Marnie rolled her eyes. 'And?'

'Just an observation. Why are you being so defensive?'

'I'm not being defensive!'

Alicia and Hannah swapped a look.

Marnie stood up from her stool and crossed her arms. 'Why can't you just let me have something nice for a change?'

'It's not that we don't want you to have anything nice,' Hannah said. 'It's just—'

'Jealousy? That messy old Marnie has, by some miracle, landed on her feet despite having made horrendous choices and not deserving for it to work out?' Marnie headed to the patio doors, head shaking. 'I need some fresh air.'

'Marns—' Hannah said to the back of her as she disappeared down the long winding path before being swallowed up by the dark, looming trees.

151

Chapter Fourteen

13th February, 2018

Alicia

'Do you think we're being a bit unfair?' Alicia wasn't sure 'we' was quite right as it had been mainly Hannah who'd done the talking, but Alicia hadn't exactly helped matters. She was unsure about how to feel about all of this, either.

Steven did seem quite serious, but serious wasn't necessarily a bad thing. Hugh was serious, earnest and sincere. It just seemed like an odd choice for Marnie, who'd always talked about how important a sense of humour was in a guy and who'd once put happy-go-lucky like Jack Black at the top of a Perfect Man List when they were sixteen.

Hannah didn't do more than shrug.

'Shall we follow her?' Alicia busied herself collecting up the used mugs that lay on the side from their drinks. Half of Alicia's tea was left in hers but she didn't fancy it anymore.

'Give it five.' Hannah ran her hands through her hair. She was rattled, Alicia could tell.

'We've really upset her.' She chucked the dregs down the sink.

'I didn't mean to.'

'I see it comes from a good place, I guess sometimes you do get quite . . . passionate about some stuff.'

'And?'

'I'm not saying you shouldn't, but maybe it could be said a bit more . . . tactfully.' Alicia held her breath, half expecting Hannah to fight it but hoping she could see where she was coming from.

Hannah closed her eyes and drew a slow, laboured breath. 'That's a fair observation,' she said. 'I forget that not everyone thinks in the same way as me. The intention is never to hurt her, always to protect her.' Hannah's face softened.

'I know,' Alicia said, surprised by this rare show of vulnerability. *She can do it when she wants to.* 'Perhaps she needs to hear that from you, though. Shall we go find her?'

'Yeah.' Hannah took one more deep breath and stood. 'Whack out your phone torch, or we might get lost. Who knows how many acres she has here.' A flicker of a smile crossed her lips.

After cautiously following the path Marnie had taken into the garden, they finally discovered her hiding place.

'A garden room, of course,' Alicia muttered, taking in a cabin that stretched the entire width of the plot. She followed Hannah through the door, fingers crossed for a peaceful resolution.

Marnie was laying on a sofa, sprawled out looking very sorry for herself and like the subject of a Renaissance painting. She heaved herself into a more upright position when she clocked Alicia and Hannah.

An uncertain look passed between her and Hannah. Who would break the standoff?

'I'm sorry for what I said,' Hannah chewed on her lip. 'It didn't come out as I meant it to.'

Marnie didn't look up. She tapped her foot on the laminate flooring, seemingly lost in thought.

'Say something please?' Hannah inched closer.

'Okay.' Marnie said slowly. 'It feels like you always find something to criticise about me and how I live my life. It makes me feel shit. Better?'

Alicia wasn't sure that was totally true, but she wasn't going to fight it. If that's how Marnie felt, that's how she felt.

Hannah took another cautious step towards Marnie and sat precariously on the sofa next to her. Neither of them looked at each other.

'I just feel very fiercely protective of you,' Hannah said to the floor.

'Doesn't feel like that and I don't need protecting. I'm doing just fine. So what, the house is a bit more him than me right now?' Marnie crossed her arms, gaze also fixed to her feet. 'I didn't want to barge into Steven's house, guns blazing, as if I owned the place. I know he's not perfect but I really love him and he takes good care of Sophie and me. It's so much better for her to grow up somewhere like here than where we were. Ricky's got great schools and despite the house not being perfectly decorated, she has her own bedroom. It's more than we have at my parents.'

Hannah nodded slowly, finally turning to Marnie. 'I'm happy for you. Really, I am. And I'm sorry for what I said in there.' She tentatively slid her arm to link with Marnie's. 'Forgive me? Pretty please. You deserve the best and I always want to make sure that's what you're getting. I promise it's not just because I'm a huge jealous bitch.'

Marnie leaned her head on Hannah's shoulder. 'And that is why I love you. But like I said, trust me. I'm not stupid. I may have made questionable decisions in the past, but I'm not a total moron.'

'You are the opposite of a moron.' Alicia joined them on the sofa, linking her arm through Marnie's other one and squeezing.

'Sorry for being a drama queen,' Marnie sighed. 'I didn't realise how stressed I was about you meeting Steven. I hope you like him.'

'We do,' said Alicia. 'As long as you're happy, that's what's important.' And she meant it.

'I am.' After a few more seconds, Marnie shook them off. 'Right, let's park that and get back to the celebrations. Have you clocked tonight's activity?'

Alicia and Hannah glanced at each other and then around the room. Three easels, three red berets and a brand new box of paints decorated the little dining table in the far corner.

'I'm intrigued.' Alicia squinted at her.

'I see paint brushes so I am instantly sold.' Hannah rubbed her hands together.

'Excellent.' Marnie wiggled her eyebrows. 'Get your berets on, girls. Let's get stuck in.'

An hour later, the fun was in full swing. One end of Marnie's garden cabin was sleepover-ready, with the futon pulled out, the air mattress inflated, and enough pillows, duvets and throws to drown in. At the other end, Alicia, Hannah and Marnie sat at their easels, berets on, and paintbrushes in hand. The task? To paint a portrait of each other, to the best of their abilities. It was a 'date idea' that Marnie had seen doing the rounds online and thought it would be a laugh for them to give it a go, especially if wine was involved.

Alicia studied her masterpiece of Hannah. She was not a creative person but she was giving it her all. She'd preferred to have got Marnie because Marnie would likely take less offence than Hannah at a misplaced brushstroke creating the accidental illusion of a moustache or a few extra pounds, but alas, she was stuck with her fate.

'Alicia, anything to update us on?' Hannah didn't take her eyes off her canvas as she dipped her brush in a bright pink blob of acrylic – Marnie's hair, no doubt. She'd mentioned earlier that she was thinking of dying it back to blonde, but she'd insisted it wasn't anything to do with the fact that Steven's ex was blonde. She just wanted to look a bit more mature. 'Anything new in your world?'

'Not really. My life's pretty boring.' She'd started her permanent teaching job in September, which was going well. She'd had a few wobbles in the first term when it came to behaviour management; Berrywood was a rougher school than her previous two placement schools, so she'd had to get used to that. But with the support of her mentor and now friend Mrs Logan – and a shoulder to cry on after the challenging class that was 9C – she was finding her rhythm.

'Things must be going really well with Hugh if you're seriously considering moving in.' Hannah still didn't look up, now swishing her brush in very theatrical swooshes. Her painting would be perfect, no doubt.

'Yeah. I'm staying at his flat most nights. I have a toothbrush there and a drawer. I've basically moved in, but it still feels like his place, not ours. It will be nice to have somewhere that we've both chosen together.'

'Totally.' Marnie nodded. 'But like you said earlier, that will come with time. I hope.'

Alicia hoped so too.

'Is Hugh the one then, d'ya reckon?' Marnie said over the flatulent sound of a bright green acrylic bottle.

'I'm not sure I believe in The One.' Alicia paused, mid-brushstroke. It sounded very unromantic, but it didn't mean she didn't love Hugh. She'd never felt about anyone the way she'd felt with him. He was absolutely worth the two-decade wait.

Hannah dipped her paintbrush in the glass of water in the middle of the table that was now the colour of swamp water. 'Are you saying he's not The One, then?'

'Not at all. I'm saying that it would be very unrealistic to think that there's only one person out there for all of us.'

'Okay, so is he the one for right now?'

'Yes, and hopefully forever!'

Marnie got it – she always did. It was Hannah who bought into the idea of soulmates and perfect matches. Knowing Hannah, though, she'd get what she wanted and more: the perfect love story, the happy ending. 'I can't imagine my life without him. Is Steven the one for right now?'

Marnie scrunched her nose. 'I want him to be. I don't want to be introducing Sophie to lots of different people. I want her to have stability.'

'That's fair enough.' Alicia never wanted to say it but she did worry about Marnie's . . . impulses when it came to men. Not that Alicia ever doubted that Marnie always had Sophie's best interests at heart.

A few minutes passed as they all focused on their paintings, umming and ahhing and at one point an *oops* from Marnie.

'I need more wine.' Marnie downed tools and stood, wandering over to the fridge to retrieve a fresh bottle of wine. 'Anything new in Hannah's world?' she said, unscrewing the cap of a crisp-looking bottle of white.

Alicia braced for potential impact. This could go one of two ways.

Hannah leaned in close to the canvas, tongue sticking out in concentration. 'I'm playing the field. I'm sampling all the platters I can before I decide on anything serious. They need to be able to keep up with my lifestyle, for one.'

What lifestyle? Drinking and partying? Alicia was sure she'd find plenty of men who'd keep up with her on that front. Alicia could see Hannah with a Finance Guy, the sort that would do coke on the Friday night and Park Run in Richmond Park on the Saturday.

'Any more details?' Marnie asked as she filled Hannah's glass.

Unlikely. She was always coy about her love life. All Alicia and Marnie got from her was the occasional voicenote about a passionate tryst she'd had the night before and the odd screenshot of a profile pic saying *mine for one night only*. Hannah did casual well, but there was always a reason, a red flag as to why they never extended beyond date three. At least Hannah wasn't going to settle for just anyone, although Alicia was doubtful if anybody would ever make the cut.

'Na. Nothing of note.' Hannah gestured to her now empty wine glass. 'Fill me up, would you kindly?'

'Is your mum still on your case?' Marnie said as she filled Hannah's glass dangerously close to the rim.

'Think she's given up.'

'That makes two of us. Just waiting for Alicia to disappoint her parents and then bam, the hat-trick.'

'Well, that's never going to happen.' Alicia didn't have it in her.

'Stranger things have happened. Look at Marnie, the Golden Child. Pregnant at nineteen!' Hannah took a sip of her wine.

'I can't argue with that. It's been years now and I still don't feel like Mum and Dad are fully over it,' said Marnie. 'Right, are we ready for the grand reveal? Hannah, you go first.'

'Drumroll please.' Hannah smacked her hands on the table in a crescendoing beat. She flipped her canvas round and held it up like she was a gameshow host holding up the grand prize. 'Voilà.'

'Oh my God! It's amazing!' Marnie squealed.

'You've really caught her likeness, wow.' Of course Hannah's was fab. It was super stylised, painted in vibrant colours with an artsy black outline that could give Andy Warhol a run for his money.

'I'm going to frame it, maybe it can be the first piece of my choice of decor for the house,' Marnie teased. 'Now my turn.' Marnie flipped over her canvas. 'Sorry, Lissy. I did my best.'

What was *that*? It didn't even look like a person. It looked like a—

'Did you wipe your arse on it?' Hannah howled.

'It's not that bad . . .' Alicia mumbled, entirely unconvincingly.

'Stop lying!'

'Sorry, I wanted to be polite. Is my nose really that big? You're going to give me a complex now.' *Surely, I don't look like that?*

'No! I'm just a shit artist. You literally look like a skid mark.'

'Don't say that.'

'The Skid!' Hannah was now crying with laughter, gasping for air and smacking the table with such vigour the water in the pot sloshed. 'Fantastic.'

'I refuse to be The Skid!' Alicia contested, but now Marnie was laughing too, and her laughter was contagious – she was a snorter.

Once the giggles died down, Marnie turned to Alicia. 'Last but not least,' she said, as she wiped a tear from her eye and shook her head.

'Errm.' In all the excitement, Alicia forgot that she had to show Hannah her painting, which, despite her best efforts, was pretty shocking. She'd purposely gone as glamorous as possible and made Hannah's already perfect nose even smaller just to be sure. But still her stomach tensed. Perhaps the hairline was a bit high, or the angle of the chin was too square. Or—

'On three, two, one . . .'

Alicia spun it around before she could change her mind.

'Yours is good!' Marnie enthused. Why did she sound so surprised? Alicia had got a B at GCSE art.

'Thanks.' Alicia looked at Hannah, who was biting her lip and frowning. 'Thoughts?'

Hannah studied Alicia's canvas for an uncomfortable amount of time.

She hated it. She was offended. Alicia should have insisted on doing Marnie. She—

'I *love* it.' Hannah squealed. 'You've really got my nose perfect!'

Hot Mess Express 🚂 🤪

15th February, 2018

Marnie: OMG have you seen the news? KFC has run out of chicken.

Alicia: How does that even happen?

Marnie: Sophie is devastated x I'm secretly pleased because I can try and get her into Quorn.

Hannah: You're her mum, if you wanted her to be veggie can't you just do that anyway?

Marnie: I don't want to force it on her, it's her choice.

22nd March, 2018

Hannah: I have a job. Like a proper permanent one. Sick of all the temping stuff and feels like a waste of time trying to get into anything mildly creative. I'd rather use the time I was spending applying for stuff on my own socials.

Alicia: Aw, well done!! What are you doing?

Marnie: You've joined the rest of the world. Welcome to the dark side.

Hannah: Working for a catering company in a project manager/admin role. Sounds more important than it is. But

161

it's fine. Just temporary. Not sure the people who work there are my type of people, but oh well. It is what it is.

Marnie and Alicia
18th April, 2018

Marnie: It was so nice to meet Hugh! Lovely guy. Wouldn't expect anything less for you <3 Can't believe it took us this long.

Alicia: That's okay, life's busy and we were away at Christmas. But yay. So glad you like him. He said you were lovely and he knew you'd get along the minute you asked if anyone wanted to share the Camembert starter with you 😂

Marnie: Cheese often brings people together x

Alicia: Shame Hannah couldn't make it. I swear she's always busy. Doing what, who knows?

Marnie: I always think that. Oh well, maybe if you suggest a date sometime next year she'll be able to commit 😅

Alicia: Yeah. Speaking of, I have news. I better put it in the group chat or Hannah will think we're leaving her out.

Marnie: Ooooooooooooooooo.

Hot Mess Express 🚂 🤪

18th April, 2018

Alicia: So it's official. Hugh and I have exchanged on our first ever house!!

Marnie: OOOOMMMMGGGGGGGGGGG.

Marnie: Pics? When are you moving in?

Marnie: I AM SO PROUD OF YOU.

Alicia: www.zoopla1234532/property27.com This is the one.

Three bedrooms. One for Hugh and me, one spare and one that would make a decent nursery. Good school catchment area. Nice garden. It doesn't have a driveway so I need to brush up on my parallel parking, but it's worth the compromise!

Marnie: Soz, I can't come and visit if I have to parallel park. Been nice knowing you.

Hannah: How the fuck are you affording that? Omg congrats. I love it!!!! Soz for slow reply.

Alicia: No worries. Thanks! Obv don't want to get too carried away until we've got the keys, but we are hoping to have a housewarming party in the summer holidays, so let me know when you're both going away and I'll work around that. You need to meet him Hannah!!!! No holiday for us this year! Can't afford it lol.

19th May, 2018

Marnie: As expected, Meghan looks beautiful.
I LOVED the dress.

Alicia: It was lovely, preferred Kate's though. Timeless and elegant. I'd like my wedding dress to look like that.

Marnie: Is there something you aren't telling us?!

Alicia: Haha, no. I wish.

Hannah: Didn't watch it.

Marnie: What do you mean YOU DIDN'T WATCH IT?! It's a historical moment.

Hannah: I'll get over it. Fuming we don't get the day off though lol.

15th June, 2018

Alicia: We're in! Eating pizza while sitting on the floor is a rite of passage for any new homeowner, right?

Marnie: OF COURSE! Send us a tour.

Alicia: It's such a mess though!

Marnie: That's the point. I want to see its raw potential.

Alicia: Fine, will send one tomorrow morning. Bed soon. Knackered.

Hannah: Let me guess, mattress on the floor?

Alicia: How did you know?

Marnie: Will you christen it tonight ;)

Alicia: Too tired! Again, tomorrow morning.

Marnie: Don't send the wrong video 😵

Alicia: No chance of that.

7th July, 2018

Marnie: If I hear 'It's Coming Home' one more time, I'm going to move to the US or something.

Hannah: Not sure that would be any less insufferable, babe.

Alicia: Understatement of the century . . .

Marnie: Is it awful a part of me wants England to lose?

Alicia: I hate football but even I want them to win.

Marnie: Why?

Alicia: Just feels like a special moment in history.

Marnie: You are full of surprises x

Alicia: Can't tell if that's a joke or not ha.

27th September, 2018

Alicia: I have been invited to one of Hugh's school friend's Hen dos on the 13th Feb . . .

Marnie: Don't you dare.

Hannah: NO!

Alicia: Of course I've said I can't go. Who do you think I am?

3rd December, 2018

Marnie: STOP WHATEVER YOU ARE DOING AND WATCH THIS VIDEO. Sir David Attenborough ON Climate Change at COP24. So fucking powerful I was crying.

Alicia: Will do.

Hannah: I'll watch it for you.

Marnie: Don't watch it for me, watch it for the planet!!

Hannah: Okay x Your passion is inspiring.

3rd January, 2019

Alicia: Can someone please tell Piers Morgan to get back in his box?! Out of all the things to get mad about in the world, a vegan sausage roll is not it!

Marnie: I'm actually well looking forward to trying it! I miss sausage rolls.

Hannah: I really should try and be a veggie but I just can't give up nuggets.

Marnie: The Quorn ones are nice.

Hannah: They aren't the same though.

Alicia: I could give up meat quite easily but could never be vegan because cheese.

Marnie: OMG CHEESE. YUM.

31st January, 2019

Marnie: STEVEN IS A FUCKING TWAT I SWEAR IF HE LIES TO ME ONE MORE TIME I WILL LEAVE

Alicia: Are you okay? What's happened?

Marnie: He told me he hadn't contacted his ex-wife AT ALL since the divorce was finalised but then I saw a message he'd sent her saying 'Goodbye, I wish you well.' LIKE WTH? Why lie?

Hannah: BELLEND. NEXT.

Alicia: Seems innocent enough? The message I mean. Obv the lying isn't ideal.

Marnie: He knows how important honesty is to me.

Hannah: I wouldn't put up with it.

Alicia: You don't put up with anything. No one is perfect.

Hannah: But where is the line?

Alicia: Fair point.

Social media strategy 2018-19: @LondonGirlHan

Bio: Fashion | Beauty | Lifestyle ✦
Creative soul in London ♀
Studying Law 🎓
Girl of many hats – rocking them all! #bossbitch

Platform	Content
Instagram	OOTD First day as a Law student
Instagram	New stationery haul ✏️
TikTok	🎓 Day in my life as a Law student 🎓
TikTok	Study with me 📚

Followers: 265

@Mumma_Bear: So proud of you x

@Jett: Sxy Bby: You got snap?x

@Hackney_Bish: Living the London dream!

@Marns: Good luck for your first day

@BigManNigel: What are the laws around lking so sxc?

@Emanuel92: Good luck baby sis

Chapter Fifteen

13th February, 2019

Alicia

Alicia was hosting this year's Galentine's. Hannah was still in her London houseshare, so that was a no-go, and Marnie and Steven were going through a rough patch (again), making her place a bad idea. Alicia would have insisted anyway – she was eager to show the girls around now that she'd finally sorted out all the rooms and made the house feel like home.

She and Hugh had gotten the keys to their new place last June, courtesy of Hugh's grandma's inheritance, their astute savings and the government's Help to Buy scheme. Marnie had visited a few times, watching it transform from a maze of boxes into something more liveable, but Hannah had yet to see it. The housewarming party they'd envisaged hadn't yet happened; Alicia had really underestimated how long it would take to get everything in order.

She settled onto the green velvet sofa and opened up her email. Alongside wanting to show off her house, Alicia had, of course, a schedule of things to do. First up was a Paint 'n' Sip session at Pottery Palace starting at 5pm. The portrait painting last year had been a raging success, so she was confident it would go down well. She navigated to the booking email to double (triple) check she'd got the right time and day and screenshotted it for added measure. She dropped the screenshot in the WhatsApp group alongside a reminder that it was important they were on time (Alicia didn't want to have to rush and two hours went by really quickly).

It was also important to make sure no one (Hannah) was bored or, God forbid, suggested a spontaneous night out. After pottery painting, they'd return home, change into their matching pyjamas and Alicia would cook her speciality: vegetarian lasagne. They'd eat in the conservatory, which she'd decorated with red napkins, a heart-patterned table runner, and fairy lights. Then, she'd present her carefully curated photo slideshow. To end the night, they'd watch *To All the Boys I've Loved Before*, snacking on popcorn from the Valentine's-themed boxes she had bought especially for the occasion. It was going to be perfect.

'It looks wonderful. Do you always make such a big effort for Valentine's Day?' Hugh joined her on the sofa, lifting her feet up and placing them across his thighs.

'It's Galentine's. And not really, but it's the first one at our house so I want to make it special.' Alicia's mind flashed back to the first-ever Galentine's Day at her parents', six years ago. She'd made a real effort back then, too. It was mad that now, here she was in her own house, as an adult and homeowner, preparing for their sleepover once more.

'Well, you've done an excellent job.' Hugh massaged her feet. 'Will you be doing the same for me tomorrow?'

'Depends if you've been a good boy.' Eugh, why did she say that? 'I mean, I might have something special for you. You'll have to wait and see.'

'I can't wait.' Hugh smiled his gorgeous smile, seemingly not having noticed her awkward attempt at flirting. 'Carluccios is booked for 7pm. Then home for a nice early night.'

'You're speaking my language.' Alicia shuffled herself closer to him and nuzzled her head in the warm crook of his neck. He smelt like their favourite mango shower gel and the sandalwood aftershave she got him for Christmas.

Alicia wasn't sure if an early night was a euphemism or whether he actually meant it. Their sex life had been different since they'd moved in. They were both knackered during term time, often in bed by 9pm and asleep as soon as their heads hit the pillow. Half terms and holidays were a different story, and they'd always find the time and energy to reconnect physically and emotionally with each other then. Quality over quantity. Nothing to worry about.

Alicia stood up quickly. 'Bums. I've forgotten to take the pasta sheets out of the freezer.'

'Bums indeed.' Hugh stood too, gently reaching for her wrist before she could turn away. He turned her palm over in his hand and stroked her ring finger, tracing the white gold band with its two-carat diamond. 'Are you going to tell them?'

'Of course,' Alicia said, a little too forcefully. 'Sorry. Yes, I am.'

'I'm surprised you didn't text them the minute it happened. Marnie, anyway.'

'Yeah, I know.' She'd learned her lesson that she couldn't just tell Marnie at risk of upsetting Hannah. 'I wanted to enjoy it just the two of us for a bit. I'd also like to see their faces when I show them.' Alicia added the last bit because it made her feel better. She slipped the ring off her left hand and onto her right. She wanted to choose the right moment and not have it spotted before she was ready to share.

She was engaged. What a crazy thought, even now, three weeks later.

'I hope you're going to put that back on,' Hugh grinned.

'Tomorrow morning when I've hit the clubs tonight, yeah?' Alicia joked, reaching her arms around his neck.

'Because my soon-to-be wife is such a party animal.' He snaked his arms around her waist and pulled her close so they were nose to nose.

'I can't wait to share my life with you.' It sounded cheesy, but she meant every part of it.

'And I you, my love. There's no one else I'd rather spend forever with than you.' He kissed her on the lips gently.

Gosh, how had she got so lucky?

Pottery Palace was a completely different affair to its usual chaos. This was all due to one crucial difference: no children. After 5pm, gone were the kids' birthday parties and overexcited chatter of children painting overpriced piggy banks a beautiful brown sludge colour, and out came the plastic wine glasses, mood lighting and Smooth Radio playing in the background.

'It's nice here. Quiet and chill.' Hannah had chosen a large pasta bowl because her favourite one had been mysteriously broken and none of her flatmates had yet owned up to the crime.

Pride swelled in Alicia's stomach. Hannah's approval was always nice to have, even now. 'Hugh and I often come here to go to the grocers and butchers on a Sunday.' Alongside Pottery Palace, the shopping village was home to many other little independent shops, each housed in a mini stable conversion. It was still surreal that this was Alicia's life now – the comfortable familiarity of shared routines and the beginning of family traditions. She was living the domestic dream, or was it the domestic plan? After all, this was exactly how she had always pictured it.

'I can't believe I still haven't met him.' Hannah shook her head.

'Soon.' Alicia smiled. It wasn't like they hadn't tried to find a date that worked for all four of them to meet, but it never quite happened, and neither Hannah nor Alicia had reached out to make separate plans.

'Get us being all creative again,' said Marnie, going gung ho with the pink paint on a unicorn figure for Sophie.

'I'm going to cover my bowl in lots of little red hearts. An ode to Galentine's.' Hannah beamed. 'Let's hope our creations are better than the portraits last year.'

'God, yeah.' Alicia had just about forgiven Marnie for The Skid atrocity.

'Thanks for organising it.' Marnie smiled. 'You better get a shift on though, we've only got a two-hour slot, haven't we?'

'I'm just working out what design I want to do.' Alicia stared at her still blank spoon rest. 'I was thinking sunflower?'

'Yes! Perfect. Now stop faffing and get stuck in.' Marnie thrust a paintbrush in her direction.

'Is there a pencil anywhere?'

'Just wing it.' Hannah laughed.

'I've never wang anything in my life.' Alicia frowned. 'Wang? Wung?'

'Winged?' Marnie shook her head. 'It doesn't matter. Just get on with it.'

Alicia did as she was told, and both Marnie and Hannah cheered as she applied her first swipe of yellow.

'She's off!' Hannah grinned. She turned to Marnie. 'How's things going with Steven, then?'

Alicia held her breath – she never knew whether that question was worth the risk. One day, she could be greeted with tears, the next, Marnie would be back to waxing lyrical about how wonderful things were.

Marnie bit her lip. 'Alright, I think. I never really know how long it will last though before we're back to Jeremy Kyle.'

'Why do you think it's like that?' Hannah's brow creased.

Marnie sighed. 'I don't know. Age difference maybe? He's just so . . . stubborn. Everything has to be done his way. There's no compromise.'

'That's tough.' Alicia couldn't say much more out loud. She wanted to say *for Christ's sake, girl, leave him. You're miserable, he's miserable, what the hell are you doing?* But of course she couldn't be quite so upfront about it.

'I really want to make it work. I can't move Sophie again. She's settled at school. She likes Steven and his family. I'm not giving up on it just yet.'

'You know it's better to be in a single-parent family than it is to be with the wrong person, arguing all the time.' Hannah must have taken Alicia's comments on board last year about being more tactful with her words, and appeared to be able to strike a better balance between honesty, kindness and authority. Alicia admired the effort. It also helped if Alicia wasn't on its receiving end.

Marnie sighed. 'You're right. You always are. Eugh. I'll see how it goes this time, but if there's any more fucking about, I'm done.'

'That's the attitude.' Hannah nodded assertively, without looking up from the very delicate little heart she was painting.

Marnie looked at Alicia. 'How do you do it? Find the good ones?'

'Errrm.' God, how did she do it? 'Fate?'

'So you've changed your tune on the whole soulmates slash The One thing?' Hannah chuckled.

'No? Maybe? It just feels more like luck than any skill on my part.'

'Oh behave!' Marnie scrunched her nose affectionately. 'You held out for the right person. You dated him for ages before having sex so you knew it wasn't just lust. You knew what you wanted and didn't settle for anything less. Don't do yourself a disservice.'

Alicia focused on her sunflower leaf, her hand moving slowly as heat spread to her cheeks. 'I'm not sure about that.'

'I am.' Marnie dropped her paintbrush in the water with a plop. 'Maybe I'll never get there.' She crossed her arms.

'You will!' Hannah put her paintbrush down too and squeezed Marnie's elbow. 'Sometimes we have to wade through the shite to get there. Alicia's the lucky exception.'

'Absolutely,' Alicia agreed. Could she really be the exception, not the rule for a change? She absentmindedly felt for the ring on her left finger and did her usual millisecond panic whenever it wasn't where she expected it. It would be back on her left hand soon – she was almost ready to tell the girls. Her stomach churned with a mix of anxiety and excitement.

Marnie shook her head and slid her arm away from Hannah's grip, like a dog shaking off muddy river water. 'I'll be okay. I just can't even think about going through a breakup.'

'Well, you don't need to think about it now. You're here with us, painting and sipping. Life couldn't be better.'

Hannah smiled gently, picking her paintbrush back up and holding it to her chin in thought. 'Do I have your blessing to change the subject?'

'Please do.' Marnie picked her paintbrush back up, this time loading it with a sparkly lilac colour.

'I'm going to be a lawyer.' Hannah beamed, hazel eyes sparkling.

'A lawyer? Since when?'

'I've not started it yet, but I've enrolled in a law degree starting in September.'

'Why law?'

'Why not?'

There were lots of reasons Alicia could think for why not. For a start, it was a corporate job, which Hannah had never wanted.

'It's not pressure from your mum, is it?' she asked.

'No. I wouldn't do something I didn't want to do. Especially not a degree that costs money.'

'So why the sudden U-turn, then?'

'You know me, I like to step out of my comfort zone. When you step out of your comfort zone—'

'Amazing things happen. Yeah, we know. It just seems so left-field. Not bad, just a surprise.' Marnie sipped the dregs of her wine and reached for the bottle.

'I like to keep you on your toes.' Hannah said. 'Top me up.'

Marnie did as she was told, topping up everyone's glasses, despite the fact that Alicia had barely drunk any of hers. 'Well, that's super exciting. Where are you studying?'

'The Open University.'

'I didn't even know you could study law that way.' It was mad how much could be done online these days. Alicia could have studied to become a teacher through the OU if she wanted to.

'Yep. Figure that way I can keep a foot in the door at my current job working part-time and still work on my social stuff. Did you see that an egg got more likes on Insta than Kylie Jenner? What am I doing wrong?' Hannah laughed but it didn't reach her eyes.

'I hear law can be quite intense,' said Alicia as she did the final brushstroke on her first layer of sunflower. Two more layers to go. Did Hannah really think she was going to juggle a degree, a part-time job and her social channels?

'It will be okay.' Hannah shrugged. 'Anyone for a coffee? I'm enjoying the wine but I fear if I have any more right now I'll totally ruin my beautiful masterpiece of a bowl, and I do actually want to use it.'

'Decaf latte, please. No caffeine after 2pm for me.' If Alicia had coffee in the afternoon, she knew she wouldn't sleep that night.

'I thought you were a no caffeine girly full stop?' Hannah said.

'That's changed since becoming a teacher. And I have the audacity to wonder why I'm anxious all the time.' She laughed a little as she said it but her anxiety had seemed to be getting worse recently, even when she was on the decaf. It was most likely due to stress at work and the whole moving house thing. She'd booked in a doctor's appointment in hopes they'd be able to help with it.

'I'll have an espresso, por favor.' Marnie fluttered her lashes.

'Got it.' Hannah zipped off to the counter and Marnie pushed her chair back. 'In fact, I better go for a wee, I feel a sneeze coming on and my pelvic floor ain't what it used to be.'

Alicia glanced at the clock on the menu board above the counter. They only had half an hour left of their slot. She had to tell them about her engagement before they went back to hers, otherwise they'd see the engagement cards on the mantelpiece. Alicia's palms began to sweat and her heartbeat quickened as Hannah headed back, followed closely by Marnie.

Below the table, Alicia slipped the ring off her right hand and replaced it on her left. It was now or never. 'Do you think this ring goes with my eyes?' She held her hand up and displayed the glistening diamond in all its glory. *Well that was cringe.*

Marnie frowned. 'Erm, yeah I guess— omg, what?' Her eyes widened.

'No way. Is that an engagement ring? Alicia, please tell me that's not an engagement ring.' Hannah's mouth fell open.

Alicia waggled her fingers, still holding them at eye level. 'It is! I'm engaged.'

'Since when?' Marnie dropped into her chair, shaking her head.

'Oh, only a few weeks ago.'

'A few weeks ago?!' Hannah cried.

'Yeah. When we were in the Lake District'

Alicia looked to Hannah and then to Marnie. Marnie chewed on her lip. What was she thinking?

'You're only telling us this now?'

Alicia continued to smile but it quivered at the corners. Marnie was upset, of course she was. 'I wanted to tell you in person.' There it was: a reason they couldn't be angry at. She'd already used it with Hannah a couple of years ago when it came to telling her about Hugh in the first place, but it hadn't failed her then so surely it wouldn't fail her now?

Both Marnie and Hannah said nothing, so Alicia babbled on.

'I've been so looking forward to telling you all about it. I did write out a message but it didn't feel right and then I thought I could call you and do it over video chat but I really wanted to see your faces in the flesh.' Still nothing from either Marnie or Hannah. 'I've even done a slideshow with photos for after dinner.' Alicia's voice was desperate now.

'A slideshow? You can tell you're a teacher.' Hannah emptied a sweetener packet into her mug. Her face didn't quite form a smile but her eyes were soft.

Marnie on the other hand – Alicia still couldn't read her. It was hardly a big deal, was it?

Finally, her face pulled into something that resembled a smile. 'Congratulations,' she said. 'Roll on the slideshow.'

Chapter Sixteen

13th February, 2019

Marnie

Over dinner, conversation carried on as normal as they tucked into lasagna and homemade garlic bread. Marnie did her best not to think about why it had taken weeks for Alicia to tell her she was engaged. Other people had been told – this was evident from the rows of cards lining the fireplace – so why not Marnie? Baffled was the word. And hurt. She got that maybe Alicia would be hesitant to tell Hannah, but not her. Never her. What had changed?

Am I not a priority now she has Hugh and all of his friends in her life?

Have I slipped down the list of important people to tell because Alicia is a We now and not an I?

Am I jealous of the engagement?

Even with the house and the older, more mature (debatable) partner, Marnie still lacked that sense of security that Alicia clearly had with Hugh, the commitment to a shared future together.

Push it away. Now's not the time. Stop being so self-centred.

Maybe she was overthinking it. She'd expressed her genuine shock at the announcement but beyond that, what more could she do? She didn't want to spoil the night, Alicia had gone to such an effort, so Marnie came to the conclusion she just needed to get over it.

After dinner, the three of them headed to the living room, where Alicia had laid out heart-covered popcorn boxes and red fluffy blankets. Alicia connected her laptop to the TV screen, balanced it on the coffee table and navigated to her PowerPoint doc. Even her desktop was organised and totally spotless, unlike the chaotic energy of Marnie's screenshots-everywhere-free-for-all.

'Alexa, play Slideshow Playlist,' Alicia said, with not a dot of irony, and Jason Mraz began to serenade them all with his classic 'I'm Yours'. 'Ready?'

'Ready as I'll ever be,' said Hannah from her spot on the sofa beside Marnie.

'Can't wait.' Marnie threw her blanket over her knees and tucked into her popcorn.

Alicia stood next to the TV, clicker in hand, teacher through and through.

'So it all began in the Lake District, in a little cottage called The Bothy.' A photo of an old, white pebbledash cottage appeared on screen with a hand-painted, twee sign.

'Sounds like a euphemism.' Marnie sniggered.

Hannah giggled. 'Did you do it in The Bothy?'

Alicia ignored them. 'We went for a lovely walk around Lake Windermere, and went to see *Mary Poppins Returns* at a vintage cinema that had paper tickets and everything.' She flicked through the next few slides showing what Marnie assumed to be Lake Windermere, the red velvet interior of the cinema, and the paper ticket.

'Then we went home and ordered Chinese and went to bed.'

'DID YOU DO IT IN THE BOTHY?' Hannah giggled again.

'Yes. We did. In front of the fireplace.' Alicia smiled in the way she always did when she was chuffed but embarrassed. 'The next morning, Hugh told me he'd booked us tickets to visit Beatrix Potter's house, Hill Top. You know she's my favourite author, and so we headed there. We even went on a tiny passenger ferry across the lake to get there.'

Alicia clicked through more photos, all very artsy shots of the landscape, old bookcases and mahogany interiors.

'It was lovely there, and the garden was beautiful. I was bent over to look at a particularly interesting miniature scene from Peter Rabbit depicted in a flower bed, and when I turned around, Hugh was on one knee.' Alicia's voice broke.

Marnie felt it too, the rush of emotion shooting up from nowhere and pricking the backs of her eyes. *I want that.* 'That's perfect.'

'It really is.' Hannah said, bottom lip out.

Alicia cleared her throat. 'I said yes, of course.'

The obligatory shot of a well-manicured hand and the ring – understated yet beautiful – filled the screen. It certainly looked expensive. Marnie would guess it was at least two grand, maybe even three. A ridiculous amount of expendable cash to have just for a ring. Steven had enough to do that, sure, but by the way he spoke about his first marriage, it seemed he was happy to not do it again. Was Marnie really okay with never getting married?

Push it away.

Alicia continued after wiping away a stray tear. 'And the happy couple.' Click.

181

A photo of a beaming Alicia and Hugh filled the screen, Alicia holding her hand up again for good measure – another classic composition.

'Oh my God,' Hannah whispered, hand over her mouth.

'It's beautiful, isn't it?' Alicia gushed.

'No—' Hannah's stammered, her face drained of colour.

'What do you mean, no?' blurted Alicia.

'This can't be happening.' Hannah shook her head, blinking like a maniac. 'Is that Hugh?'

'Who else would it be?' Alicia frowned, her previous smile replaced with an overwhelming look of concern. 'Hannah, you're scaring me.'

'No, no, no. Hugh can't be . . .'

Chapter Seventeen

13th February, 2019

Hannah

'. . . Hugo?' No, Hugh – Alicia's long-term partner and now fiancé – could not be Hugo. The guy who'd broken Hannah's heart in Sixth Form after they'd had sex at a family party, Hugo. The person who'd set this whole Galentine's thing in motion and, in a weird way, was the reason they were all sitting here now.

Alicia stared, open-mouthed as her playlist continued in their stunned silence. Marnie looked from Hannah to Alicia, eyes wide in horror.

Hannah glanced back at the photo. Maybe she'd got it wrong.

She hadn't. God, he looked good. Not her type anymore, but he'd grown into his face. The angular jaw and sharp Roman nose looked more harmonious now that he was a fully fledged man. Alicia's man.

Say something. Anything. 'But your Hugh is a teacher? Hugo wanted to be a lawyer. He'd started his first year of training when we met.' Hannah wasn't quite sure about the point she was trying to make but babbled it frantically hoping it would somehow change reality. Whether he was a teacher or a lawyer, it was still Hugo.

'Hugh studied law but switched in first year. It wasn't for him.'

Alicia hadn't told her that. Hannah would've remembered. But then, would she? It's not like there was any reason to suspect that Hugh and Hugo were the same person.

Oh God. That meant . . .

'You're telling me that you've both had sex with the same guy?' Marnie grimaced.

Really, Marnie?

'No,' Hannah said quickly. 'I don't even count it.' It was a drunken fumble; a quick in and out. But she counted it at the time because it meant she could claim to have Done It with three people. Three felt like a decent number.

'I feel dizzy.' Alicia's face was pale and her eyes were wide yet distant.

'Sit down,' Marnie ordered.

Alicia stepped slowly towards the armchair and sat, frowning and blinking. 'No. How?' Alicia pinched her brow. 'What the hell am I supposed to do with this information?'

'Nothing. It doesn't have to change anything. It was a long time ago.' Should Hannah say sorry? Even though she hadn't actually done anything? This was supposed to be Alicia's special moment, and now . . . this.

Alicia shook her head continuously. 'So I'm just supposed to move on like nothing has changed knowing that . . . that . . .'

'It was one time that we . . . and like I said, I don't count it. It didn't last long . . .'

'He was the one you . . . at the bottom of the garden . . .?'

Marnie really wasn't helping, yet Hannah nodded. She could've lied but what good would that do now?

'Hugh wouldn't do that. He's never been that adventurous. Unless it's just me—' Alicia's face crumpled.

'God no! It was years ago! We were kids! You're adults now, both in respectable teaching jobs, imagine if one of your students saw you.' Hannah made a conscious effort to remove any hysteria from her voice and then continued. 'This doesn't have to be a big deal. I'm fine about it. Just surprised.'

'How can you be fine about it?' Alicia was crying now, wiping her tears aggressively with the back of her sleeve. 'How can I be fine about it?'

'How did we not notice?' Marnie shook her head also, covering her mouth with her hand.

'Neither of you are on socials.' Hannah always thought that was weird, but Alicia had never been into social media – she didn't even have Myspace or Bebo back in the day. It was no surprise that her partner was equally offline.

'But I must've showed you pictures.' Alicia looked at her desperately.

Had she? Probably. But men weren't great at taking flattering pictures of themselves. Whenever girlfriends showed photos of guys they liked, the conversation always turned to convincing each other that *he looked better in person*. 'I didn't recognise him in the pics you sent?'

'How? Did you even look at them?'

'Yes!' *Did I? Now I'm thinking about it, I'm not entirely sure . . .*

'You clearly didn't. Is my life that boring to you that you don't even bother to look at the stuff I send?'

'No! I'm a busy person.'

'Doing what, exactly? You say you're too busy to look

at what I send but somehow find the time to give detailed feedback on every dating profile Marnie sends?' Alicia's voice trembled.

'This can't all be on me. Has he never seen any photos of us three? You've never shown him any of us hanging out?'

'I have.' Alicia slid her phone from her pocket and began frantically scrolling. 'So either he doesn't recognise you or . . .' Her eyes widened.

'Or what?' Marnie asked slowly, the sofa below them shunting as she shifted in the seat beside Hannah.

'He's lied to me!' Alicia's voice was shrill despite an obvious attempt to clip it.

'He wouldn't lie to you,' Hannah said, voice trembling.

'How do you know? You don't know him— oh.'

God, this was bad. This was *so* bad. *And I thought I'd hit rock bottom last week*. Dinner had been frozen peas on toast and she'd even briefly considered becoming a stripper after a painfully humiliating meeting at work where she'd been called out in front of the whole team for having the lowest performance of that week.

That was nothing compared to this. Turns out, she still had further to fall.

She moved to crouch down in front of Alicia, taking in her crumpled face. She grabbed her hands and squeezed but Alicia avoided looking at her. She was shaking, hands cold and clammy.

'Look, he's with you. He loves you,' Hannah said as gently yet firmly as she could. 'If anything, *I'm* jealous of *you*. You've got your life together. You're engaged for Christ's sake! You own a house. You have the career you've always wanted. You have Hugh.'

'You said it wasn't about Hugh.'

Hannah dropped Alicia's hands and stood up in frustration. What more could she do? 'It's not! I mean you have a stable partner, someone who wants to spend the rest of their life with you. We all need a Hugh.' She needed to stop talking. It wasn't coming out as she wanted but she needed Alicia to understand. 'I've never had any of that. No man ever sticks around longer than a couple of weeks for me. I don't know what I'm doing with my life and I'm living like I'm still a student.' Hannah was crying now. 'I'm sorry, okay? I didn't know!'

'I'm not saying you did. It's not your fault. I just . . . I don't know . . .' Alicia's eyes were desperate as they met Hannah's, but there were no words Hannah could say that would make this better.

She'd had sex with her best friend's soon-to-be husband. How could she ever come back from that?

You are cordially invited to the matrimony of
Alicia May Murphy and Hugo Patrick Brown.
12th December, 2019.
Pendley Manor, Tring.
Children welcome – love, laughter, and a happily ever after!
Please RSVP promptly.

Bridesmaidsssss 🏛

14th April, 2019

Alicia: What do you think of this colour? Or do you prefer the dusty pink over the mauve?

Alicia: Do you think it matters if Hugh's tie is navy even though the colour scheme is pink?

Alicia: And you're both sure you're happy with the dress? I wanted to go for something that flattered everyone and that you both feel comfortable in.

Alicia: Sorry, last question. I want live music but Hugh says a DJ is better. Thoughts?

Hot Mess Express 🚂 😀

30th April, 2019

Alicia: Can you both RSVP to the wedding please?

Marnie: Obviously we're coming.

Hannah: Lol duh.

Alicia: It just helps for numbers. Also, we're having an engagement party 19th June. Put it in the diary!

Marnie: It's in! Can't wait.

Hannah: I can't do that day!! It's Lola's 30th.

Marnie: Alicia's engagement is more important.

Hannah: I know but I said yes to Lola first.

Marnie: Not gonna argue with you. I'll be there A, no matter what.

Hannah: Sorry :(

20th May, 2019

Marnie: Me and Steven have split. I couldn't do it anymore. I'm moving out next weekend.

Hannah: Where to?!

Alicia: Do you want help moving? Or Hugh and I can watch Sophie for you on Saturday? Can't do Sunday as we're visiting his sister and new baby.

Marnie: Might take you up on that offer. Back in with Nan for a month to save up a deposit then I'm looking to rent a flat in Dunstable. Cheaper there.

Hannah: For a reason . . .

Marnie: There are some nice parts.

Hannah: Have you left work?

Marnie: Yeah, but it's fine. I'm working my notice and already have an interview elsewhere on Friday.

Alicia: Not fair that you have to move jobs!

Marnie: I know. But he was there first plus I'm ready for a change. Hannah, are you around on Sunday at all?

Hannah: Ah, so sorry, I'm not.

Marnie: Bums. Anytime that week?

Hannah: That week's tricky for me.

Marnie: Ok.

29th May, 2019

Marnie: I got the new job btw. It's in Hitchin so not too far. Another receptionist job, this time in a primary school. I'll miss Andrea, but looking forward to being part of a bigger team.

Alicia: CONGRATS XX

Hannah: Well done x

1st July, 2019

Alicia: I want to do a thing us three and Hugh before the wedding. Just dinner or something. Feel like it would be weird for the first (ish) time Hannah meets him to be at the wedding. When are you both free in the next few weeks?

Hannah: Sounds good. Will send over some dates when I'm home.

Marnie: I'm free most of the time, just give me plenty of warning for childcare.

Hannah and Marnie
15th July, 2019

Hannah: I'm here, where are you? I'd rather not go in on my own.

Marnie: I'm running late. Be there in fifteen! You'll be fine. Since when were you scared of Alicia?

Hannah: It's weird!

Marnie: I'm sure Hugh feels just as awkward. Just get it over with. Rip the plaster off.

Hannah: FINE. Going in.

15th July, 2019

Hannah: Well I'm glad that's over now.

Marnie: I bet. Probs weirder for Alicia though. Her best friend and fiancé meeting for the first time but not really the first time 😵 You did great. Polite but not awkward. I think you did the right thing being upfront with it all.

Hannah: Thanks, yeah it doesn't need to be weird. Glad we've done it before the wedding too.

Marnie: Yeah deffo. I have to ask . . . any other feelings there?

Hannah: No! Has Alicia asked you to ask that?

Marnie: No! I'm just curious.

Hannah: No. No feelings at all.

Marnie: Thank fuck for that.

Hannah: Even if I did, I wouldn't act on them! You know that, right? Are you sure you're not with Alicia?

Marnie: Yes!!

Hannah: Good. I hope we can all move on now.

Hot Mess Express 🚂 🤪

24th July, 2019

Alicia: God help us all. Bojo is officially in charge.

Hannah: I don't mind him, I think he's quirky.

Marnie: You baffle me. It deffo could be worse though. Our blonde idiot isn't half as horrendous as the US version.

Hannah: That's true.

29th October, 2019

Hannah: FYI I'm not doing law anymore.

Alicia: You dropped out?

Hannah: No, I've consciously decided it's not something I want to do.

Alicia: Okay. Are you alright about it?

Hannah: Couldn't be better! I don't know what I was thinking. Mum must have been sending me some weird subliminal messages or something.

Marnie: Subliminal? She'd have it tattooed on her forehead given half the chance.

Alicia: Lol.

14th December, 2019

Marnie: Hope married life is treating you well, Ali. It was a beautiful ceremony for the most perfect couple. Thank you for letting us be a part of your special day.

Hannah: You looked incredible and the first dance song was perfect. 'At Last' by Etta James. I couldn't think of a more fitting tune xx

Alicia: Pleasure is all mine xx Speaking of, which one of you slept with Hugh's cousin?

Marnie: Guilty. I was going to tell you, I promise.

Alicia: It's fine, he told Hugh who told me. He's a good-looking guy but I wouldn't expect anything serious from him. He's a bit of a man-child.

Marnie: Ah really? He seemed like a nice guy.

Hannah: They all are if they want to get in your pants.

Marnie: I felt a bit lonely going to bed on my own that night.

Hannah: I'd have gone to bed with you <3

Marnie: You looked busy with the best man.

Hannah: You are mistaken. I'm sort of seeing this guy called Joe so I thought I better not.

8th January, 2020

Marnie: Have you seen the Megxit announcement? Harry and Megz are heading back to the US and stepping down from royal life, whatever that means.
Alicia: Devastated.
Marnie: It's the best for them.
Alicia: Yeah, still sad though.
Hannah: No comment.

1st February, 2020

Marnie: The whole Coronavirus thing is a bit scary.
Alicia: I hope it doesn't affect my honeymoon. It's nowhere near China so should be fine, right?
Marnie: Yeah, no point stressing about it. We're fine here, the Atlantic will protect us!

Social media strategy 2019-20: @LondonGirlHan

Bio: Daily outfits & fashion finds 👗 ✨
OOTD addict 📷 London Life 💂

Platform	Content
Instagram	Wedding ready for the most beautiful bride 👰
TikTok	Come to afternoon tea with me and my uni girls x
TikTok	Charity shop haul
Instagram	OOTD – Yoga and life admin day 🧘

Followers: 302

@Caz777: The workout set is beaut.

@PilatesGirl: Where do you do yoga? I'm looking for somewhere in central x

@JoJo: Best finger sandwiches I've ever had!

@EllieP: Who did the bridal makeup? X

@CakeyB: You always find such hidden gems. Can you tell us your fave charity shops?

Chapter Eighteen

13th February, 2020

Alicia

Roll on 3:15pm. Today, yet again, Alicia had reached her limit. *This is it. Teaching is not for me. I tried, and I failed.* It hadn't helped that she'd forgotten to take her anxiety meds this morning, but her alarm hadn't gone off so she'd had to prioritise getting dressed and looking semi-presentable over anything as luxurious as taking her tablet or brushing her teeth.

It was only now, when there were fifteen minutes left of the school day, that Alicia had managed to sit down, though there was still no respite. She could barely see the classroom beyond the tower of marking stacked in front of her.

It had been one of those days. Teachers and students needing something from her at every turn, a fight in the canteen where she'd almost had her glasses knocked off, no time to take more than a bite of her sandwich at lunchtime, and a moment where she'd had to go into the stationery cupboard in order to take some deep breaths and stop herself from crying. Why, oh why, had 11C decided to play up the exact minute the headmaster was doing a one of his informal observations?

Couldn't she catch a bloody break? And she couldn't even let herself think too much about this whole coronavirus thing.

At least tonight was Galentine's: something to look forward to, even if it was at Marnie's new place. It wasn't ideal – it was tiny and Alicia had no idea where they were all going to sleep – but Marnie insisted they'd make it work, and at this rate, Alicia could fall asleep anywhere. The idea of hiring out an Airbnb for the night was also floated in the group chat, but they were all skint – Hannah because she was still on minimum wage, Marnie because she'd had to put down a huge deposit and one month's rent upfront to secure her new flat, and Alicia because of the wedding.

Ah, the wedding. It was mad to think that she was now a married woman. A wife with a husband.

To avoid any dramas, neither Marnie nor Hannah were maid of honour, both bridesmaids alongside Neelam and Hugh's little niece Zara. Alicia would've liked it to have been Marnie, but she'd never admit it out loud, let alone follow through with it. Despite people telling her it was her day, and everything was up to her, everyone knew that was a load of toot. Weddings were rarely about the couple, more about the guests and their politics; should they put Hugh's warring, divorced aunt and uncle on the same table? No. Were children and babies welcome, even if a very vocal one cried the whole time Alicia and Hugh were saying their vows? Yes. Was Hugh's school friend Jason allowed to bring his new girlfriend as a day guest even though neither of them had met her before? Yes, because otherwise that was rude.

Gosh, she was being cynical. It was a lovely day really. Despite being exhausting, and her and Hugh barely saying a word to each other outside of the church because they were so busy working the room, the band had been good and everyone seemed to have a good time. Also, crucially, it had actually happened.

Things had been dicey after Hannah's bombshell, to say the least. Hugh had managed to convince her that he hadn't recognised Hannah in the photos – *she looks different now. It was years ago* – but Alicia still hadn't been able to look at him in the same way now she knew he'd had sex with her best friend. Yes, it was before their time. Yes, she knew that, aside from being psychic or being a time-traveller, eighteen-year-old Hugh wouldn't have known it was a bad idea to have sex with this beautiful, confident girl in his parents' garden. But still he'd shifted in her eyes, changed form. She wouldn't go as far as to say things were tainted, but things were changed.

In the first few weeks, whenever they'd had sex, a voice in Alicia's head would chime in. *He did this with Hannah before you. Perhaps she was better at it than you.* Alicia would push it away but it always came back. Even on their wedding day, she'd scrutinised Hannah and Hugh's interactions more closely than anyone else's, and she hated just how good Hannah looked in the dusty pink empire dress Alicia herself had picked out.

Obviously things were better now. They were married, and life was ticking on as it should. They also had the honeymoon to look forward to – a two-week jaunt to Barbados in July. Time was healing and Hugh had chosen her. He had the option to choose Hannah all those years ago and he didn't. This was what Alicia always came back to, and it tended to work. Most of the time.

At last, the bell signalling the end of the school day rang. Alicia stood instantly and glanced again at the pile of marking on her desk. She should stay until at least four-thirty to make headway, but if she was going to make it past 9pm, she'd need to go home and have a nap before heading to Marnie's.

She could take one pile with her – she might find some time or energy to do it.

Lol. Who are you kidding?

She grabbed her handbag and zipped as fast as she could out of the classroom.

Alicia, Marnie and Hannah were doing what they did best – eating and chilling. Thank God they were past the days where they went out out, and Alicia was incredibly relieved that the only thing expected of her tonight was to polish off a tikka masala in the comfort of an elasticated waistband.

Better still, seeing as Marnie's place didn't have enough space for a dining table, they were set up on the sofa, balancing their plates on their laps and serving themselves from the coffee table.

'It's nice here,' Hannah said, scooping a large dollop of mint sauce onto her poppadom and carefully guiding it into her mouth. 'Cosy.'

She hadn't been here before, unlike Alicia who'd visited multiple times, including to help Marnie move her stuff out of Steven's place.

'Yeah, I'm happy. I can do things my way, and the only person I have to think about is Sophie. I hadn't realised how much energy I spent arguing with Steven. Even small things like what to have for dinner turned into some sort of debate.'

'And I see there's a trampoline out the back.' Alicia had spied this new addition when she'd parked up.

'There is indeed. Soph shares it with the other kids in the block, but she loves it and she has so many friends here.' Marnie grabbed the remaining pilau rice and upturned the entire carton onto her plate. 'Also, the Indian takeaway down the road is banging.'

'Who knew you'd be happier here than in your mansion

in posh Rickmansworth,' Hannah grinned. 'I assume Sophie's at Nanna's right now?'

'She is. She's treated like a total queen there.' Marnie smiled to herself and shook her head. 'She's a sassy little cow, now. Love her to bits. You'll have to come and hang out with us both soon, Han.'

'Absolutely. A plus side of me dropping out of law is that I'll have more free time so I can see you more and help out with Soph.'

Unlikely, Alicia thought. Hannah had only spent a month on the course and left over three months ago. It hadn't seemed to make any difference to her availability, so she could hardly blame her lack of helping Marnie on that. Also, what about the previous years when she was only working part-time? Or the multiple times Marnie invited them both over so Hannah could see the flat and on one occasion Hannah had been *too busy with life* but had then posted to Instagram that she'd been out for an afternoon tea with her uni lot. Alicia was half surprised that Hannah didn't cancel on her wedding day.

'That would be nice.' Marnie smiled, but Alicia recognised her facial expression. She didn't buy it either. 'Soph had a lovely time with Auntie Alicia and Uncle Hugh when I moved in the last of my stuff.'

Alicia was sure Marnie didn't mean it as a slight to Hannah, but the timing was such that it made her feel proud of her own role in Sophie's life.

'Aw, I'm so glad to hear that. We had a lovely time.'

They'd gone to Whipsnade Zoo. They'd got there for opening time at 10am sharp, with their pre-booked tickets and eighty-one pounds lighter than they had been previously – turns out that children were more expensive than either of them had realised.

They stayed there all day in an attempt to get their money's worth, and by 5pm, everyone was exhausted and grumpy. Hugh was doing his grunting instead of talking thing, Sophie was close to tears when Alicia said she couldn't buy the extra large monkey toy at an eye-watering price of seventy-five pounds, and Alicia had come close to breaking point herself when she couldn't locate her car keys in her handbag. They were in her pocket.

It was a relief to hand Sophie back to Marnie, and it was only then that Alicia realised her nervous system had been permanently stuck in fight-or-flight mode for the entire duration they had her. That night, when Alicia lay on the sofa watching *Call the Midwife* under her heated blanket in total, utter, blissful silence, she relished her current lack of responsibility.

'Any thoughts on when you and Hugh are going to have one?' Hannah tore off a piece of naan and dunked it into her sauce. 'Someone once said to me – and I can't remember who – that the people who thought most about whether or not to bring a life into the world would probably make really good parents.' Hannah popped the bread in her mouth and looked at Alicia with a genuinely kind smile that took her off guard.

Marnie's face scrunched up and she looked at Hannah in mock offence. 'I see how it is,' she laughed.

'Oh my God, sorry!' Hannah was laughing now too, her plate of tikka masala wobbling, dangerously close to spilling on Marnie's cream sofa. 'That's not me saying that people who it just happens to by accident don't make good parents. But it must be true that many people don't know what they're getting themselves into until they're knee-deep in nappies or postnatal depression and wondering what the hell they've done to their lives.'

'Preach. Don't say sorry. I had no idea what I was getting myself into.' Marnie shook her head. 'You can do all the research you want and be told how hard it will be at every turn, but nothing prepares you for how hard it *actually* is. And that's not me saying there's not amazing parts of it, too. But it's so conflicting. The highs are euphoric, but the lows are sometimes in the depths of hell.' Marnie chuckled and then placed her hand on Alicia's leg. 'Sorry, Alicia, I didn't mean to make that about me.'

Alicia was more than happy to continue talking about Marnie, but both she and Hannah turned to Alicia expectantly.

'Hmmm. Not now. One day, though.' Alicia busied herself with spooning out way more tarka daal than she needed on her plate. 'Hugh wants to start trying soon. I've said I'll do another year in teaching first, then we'll look at it.'

'That's exciting,' said Marnie. Hannah stayed quiet.

'Yeah. Scary too.' An understatement of massive proportions.

'It's normal to have second thoughts. It's a huge thing.'

'I'm not having second thoughts,' Alicia said quickly. 'It's definitely happening. Just not yet.'

She'd never questioned whether she'd one day be a mum. That's what little girls did when they became women. They'd buy a house, get married and then have babies. It was always part of the plan. But *one day* was quickly becoming now, and the closer to that moment she got, the scarier it felt. These things didn't just happen, most of the time anyway. It needed to be an active choice. How did one go from saying 'when we have kids' to 'let's have unprotected sex while I'm ovulating.' It was an incredible leap, but one that she appeared to have signed up for within the next twelve months.

Best not to think about it.

Chapter Nineteen

13th February, 2020

Hannah

It was 10pm and Alicia had gone to bed. She was hanging on for dear life by nine-thirty, so Marnie and Hannah gave her their blessing to have an early night, and she was now fast asleep next door in Marnie's room. They chose to stay up and were now settled under blankets on Marnie's battered yet disgustingly comfortable sofa. Hannah allowed herself to be hugged by the squidgy pillows as she sipped her hot chocolate with whipped cream, marshmallows and a shot of Baileys. It was nice to finally be here. She'd been a bit crap this last year with making time to hang out. Of course she'd seen them both at the wedding, but that was the last time and before that it was a fair few months.

'So are you feeling okay about dropping out of law? You're now an official dropout like me.'

Hannah bristled at the phrase but didn't show it. 'More than alright. Relieved. Free. It wasn't for me. I gave it a go, and I hated it. At least I made my mum proud for all of a month.' Hannah laughed but her stomach tensed.

'God, I wouldn't have wanted to be you when you told her.' Marnie said. 'I think I'd rather tell my mum I was pregnant again.'

'Fair.' Breaking the news had been agonising. Mum had been ecstatic when Hannah first told her about studying law. For the first time, she saw that same gleam in her eyes that she always had when talking about Emmanuel, and they'd celebrated with a home-cooked meal of chilli garlic mogo and matoki chips.

Hannah had thought so much about how she would phrase the news that she practically had a script ready in her head by the time she was semi-ready to make the call, but the minute Mum picked up the phone, Hannah drew a blank.

'Err, hi Mum,' she'd stuttered as she fiddled with the drawstring on her hoody. 'I, uh. You okay?'

'I'm fine, my dear. Now's not a great time. Your father—'

'I'm not doing law anymore.' The words had tumbled from her mouth, unpolished and far from the script she had rehearsed. The silence at the other end of the phone hung painfully in space between them and Hannah felt the desperate urge to retreat. 'I'll leave you to whatever you were doing. See you soo—'

'Hold on a second, young lady.' Her mum took a sharp breath.

Hannah braced for impact. 'Mmmm?'

'Why on Earth would you drop out?' Drop out. Like she couldn't hack it. Like she'd failed.

'I hated it.' It was the simple truth. Learning about criminal offences, negligence, the justice system. It was just so . . . depressing. And not only that, it was boring.

'What will you do for money?' Her mum's clipped tone was equal parts hurtful and irritating.

'I'm back full-time at my job.'

'The silly catering company? You could do so much better than that! You're not a student anymore Hannah. When will you understand that?'

'I'm well aware.' *Painfully aware in fact.* She was always the biggest advocate for others when it came to reminding them they were destined for good things, so it was never far from Hannah's mind that she was not practising what she preached.

The weight of her mum's displeasure was too much to bear. 'I'm sorry, I just couldn't do it. I have to go. There's someone at the door—' She'd hung up before her mum could hear her cry.

Back on Marnie's sofa, Hannah took a comforting sip of her hot chocolate. 'So anyway, I'm back to the role of Disappointment Child. It was nice while it lasted.' Hannah forced a smile, squashing the embers of emotion that had flickered as she recalled the moment.

'So, hows full-time employment going? Any better than it was at the wedding?' Marnie reached for the tube of whipped cream on the coffee table and squirted a generous dollop into her mug. She offered it to Hannah, who decided she could do with the extra sugar, and chose not to think about the extra calories.

'Same shit, different day. It's close to soul-destroying, but at least I'm earning money rather than getting myself further into debt.' Hannah wiped a stray blob of cream from her nose.

'You're supposed to drink it, not snort it,' Marnie teased.

'My bad.' Hannah's spoon tinkled against the side of her vat-sized Sports Direct mug as she stirred the cream into a swirl that resembled the eye of a tornado. She nodded towards the direction of the bedroom. 'Do you think she's alright?'

Marnie's brow creased. 'Yeah? As alright as she usually is. She's worried about this Covid thing.

'God, yeah. It's scary. I knew as soon as it hit France we were fucked.' Hannah tried not to watch the news too much usually but this whole Covid-19 palaver made that difficult. At first it felt far enough away being the other side of the world, but as each day passed it crept closer and closer.

'Hopefully it won't get any worse.'

'Let's hope so. God, I don't even want to think about it.' The best option was to push it to the back of her mind. She had bigger fish to fry. 'So you don't think there's anything else bothering Alicia apart from that, then?'

Marnie leaned forward and put her mug on the table – no coaster but the watermarks already on the surface told Hannah that wasn't a priority. 'What makes you say that?'

How honest could Hannah be? Alicia and Marnie were super close, arguably closer than Hannah was to either of them. Would what she said now be repeated back to Alicia or would Marnie be able to keep her mouth shut and help Hannah work out if her feelings were valid or whether she was just imagining stuff? 'Please don't repeat this to Alicia.'

'I won't. Unless you're sleeping with Hugh—'

Hannah grabbed a cushion from under her and swung it at Marnie. 'Cheeky bitch.'

'Oii! Watch your hot choc,' Marnie giggled, shouting at first but then switching speedily to a fervent whisper.

'This sofa's seen way worse, I bet.' Hannah shifted to place her almost empty mug on the coffee table beside Marnie's. 'Don't joke about that sort of thing.'

'Sorry. I couldn't help myself.' Marnie's expression became more earnest. 'Of course you can talk to me.'

Hmm. Hannah would have to trust her. 'Do you think she still feels weird about the whole Hugh thing?'

'It's been, like, a year now? Why do you think that? She was totally normal with you tonight. And at the wedding.'

'You think she was normal at the wedding?'

'Yes, why, do you not?'

'I genuinely don't know whether I'm just being paranoid.' Hannah bit her lip as she recalled the wedding. 'Every time I spoke to Hugh I noticed she was watching us. It made me feel really uncomfortable, to the point where I tried my best to avoid him completely, especially later into the night when I was drunk.' Hannah knew she could be a bit handsy and over-friendly when she was drinking – but that wasn't just with men, it was with everyone: women, men, old people. 'I didn't even want to smile when I was near him in case she got the wrong idea.'

'Well, I don't think you have anything to worry about. She's not said anything to me. If I thought there was something up, I would say. Trust my judgement on this.' Marnie looked at Hannah without so much as a flicker. She seemed pretty certain.

Hannah nodded. 'Okay, thanks.' Marnie's judgement wasn't always the most accurate, but then again, it wasn't as if her own intuition had a great track record either.

She'd take Marnie's word for it. Alicia was often worrying about something, perhaps Hannah was just being paranoid or even narcissistic to think she had anything to do with it. Still, as she pulled the duvet up to her chin and sank deeper into the sofa, she couldn't quite shake the whisper in her gut saying otherwise.

Hot Mess Express 🚂 😵

23rd March, 2020

Marnie: What the actual fuck just happened? We aren't allowed to LEAVE THE HOUSE? HOLY SHIT.
Hannah: Bit scary.
Alicia: Terrifying.

26th March, 2020

Marnie: I've been put on furlough, which is a good job really. There's no one else to look after Sophie and I can't even imagine trying to work and home-school her. Mum and Dad are terrified they'll catch something so don't want to mix with anyone, not even their own child or grandchild.
Alicia: God that sounds tough. Call me if you ever need and I'll try to support you from afar!
Marnie: Thanks. I'll be alright, don't worry about me, you've got more important things going on like teaching a bunch of teenagers online. GOOD LUCK WITH THAT ONE!! AHHH.
Hannah: Also been put on furlough. Fine by me. Getting paid to do fuck all? Yes please.

28th March, 2020

Marnie: I hear there's a black market for bog roll now.

30th March, 2020

Hannah: You still up for the Zoom on Friday?

Alicia: Yes!! I have some games we can play.

Marnie: Of course you have. Always so prepared!!

Alicia: That's me.

Hannah: Are you clapping for the NHS?

Alicia: Yes! You?

Marnie: Yep, Sophie loves banging the pots and pans together. Neighbours must love us.

Hannah: Would be better if they got paid a proper wage. But I am clapping.

Hannah: Dare I ask. How's online teaching?

Marnie: You asking me or Alicia?

Hannah: Both.

Marnie: As you can imagine, it's chaos. Sophie doesn't listen to me like she does her teacher, and getting her to sit still and pay attention to the computer is a nightmare. Can't imagine how anyone is doing this and working!!!!

Hannah: Alicia?

Alicia: Utter hell.

Marnie: Care to expand?

Alicia: Today, someone in my year ten class worked out how to draw on the virtual board. You can guess what happened.

Marnie: Dick and balls?

Alicia: Yep.

Hannah: That's hilarious.

Alicia: Yesterday, someone in my year eight class thought it would be funny to unmute themselves and fart.

Marnie: Lol. How do you keep a straight face?
Alicia: It's hard to smile when you're losing the will to live.

18th April, 2020

Hannah: I'm going on a date tonight.
Alicia: That's against the law!!!
Hannah: It's on Zoom.
Alicia: Oh.
Marnie: How does that work?
Hannah: Just a video call. Will be nice because my housemates are driving me mad.
Marnie: Who is he?
Hannah: Guy called Marcus. Seems sweet. He's a paramedic so really on the frontline.
Marnie: God, sounds like a goodun already.
Hannah: Yeah. Looking forward to it.
Alicia: Let us know how it goes. Good luck!!
Hannah: Will do.

4th May, 2020

Marnie: Do you want to see something funny?
Hannah: Always.
Marnie: Look at this pic . . .
Hannah: OMG WHAT HAPPENED?
Marnie: I thought I'd try and cut Sophie's hair.
Alicia: Never a good idea.
Hannah: She looks like Lord Farquad.
Marnie: I know. And that's not all.
Alicia: What . . .?
Marnie: Tadaaaaa.
Hannah: NO YOU DIDN'T.

Marnie: Yeah. I've always wanted to see what I looked like with a fringe. I should have stayed wondering . . . lol

Alicia: It's not that bad

Hannah: Alicia stop lying.

Alicia: It's not!

Marnie: It's fine, I don't care. It will grow back. Not seeing anyone much anyway so screw it. Might even shave it off.

Alicia: Really?

Marnie: If I keep having to do this home-school shit I might end up doing a Britney.

Hannah: Leave Britney alone!

Alicia: 😂

1st June, 2020

Marnie: If you think 2020 couldn't get any worse, have you seen *Cats*?

Hannah: Not seen it but seen enough memes online to know exactly what you're talking about 😂

Marnie: Apparently they had to hire someone specifically to edit out the arseholes post-production.

Alicia: WHAT?

Hannah: STOP IT!

Marnie: I'm not joking.

Hannah: Amazing. I'll be seeing James Corden Cat in my nightmares.

Alicia: Speaking of nightmares – I have been signed off work with stress. I'm fine but just needed a week to get my head above water. It's been a lot!

Marnie: Oh no :(I hear you. This year has been so tough for many. I hope the time off gives you what you need. I wish I could have time off from just life.

Alicia: If only. Hang in there.

Alicia: I'm doing a BBQ for my birthday this year. Just a small thing with you girls, Neelam and Hugh. Please do a Covid test first just in case.

Marnie: Are you doing it on your actual birthday?

Alicia: Yeah x Unless either of you can't make it, in which case I'll do another day?

Marnie: I'm free

Hannah: By some miracle, so am I!

Alicia: Fab x

25th September, 2020

Marnie: Han, your last TikTok got 900k views!!! WTH?

Hannah: I KNOW!!!!!!! Don't even know what was so special about that one. The algorithm baffles me.

Alicia: Well whatever you're doing is clearly working.

Hannah: Thanks :D About bloody time! Ha

To: LondonGirlHan@gmail.com
From: Moana@TheBeautyBox.co.uk
Subject: Hannah X BeautyBox
Hi Hannah,

I hope you're doing well! My name is Moana, and I'm reaching out on behalf of The Beauty Box, an online makeup store that curates the best in beauty, from must-have essentials to the latest trends.

We've been following your content and absolutely love your style and influence in the fashion and beauty space. We think you'd be a perfect fit for an exciting collaboration with us. We'd love to work together to showcase our latest makeup collections and share them with your audience.

Here's what we have in mind:

✤ A gifted selection of our top beauty products

✤ A paid collaboration for an Instagram Reel, TikTok video, YouTube short, and a Blog post

✤ Exclusive discount codes or giveaways for your followers

We'd love to discuss the details further and tailor this opportunity to fit your content style. Let us know if you're interested, and we can set up a quick chat!

Looking forward to hearing your thoughts. 💕

Best,

Moana Bryant, Social Media Manager, The Beauty Box

31st October, 2020

Marnie: Did you see they announced another lockdown? I can't do it again!! SEND HELP.

Hannah: They're taking the piss.

Alicia: Not happy. Are you both okay?

Marnie: Still alive.

Alicia: The bare minimum. You sure you're okay?

Marnie: Fine. Just sick of this now x

21st December, 2020

Marnie: Are you fucking joking? Christmas lockdown? Fuck that. I'm still going to my nan's, she's in my bubble. They can't stop me. I will literally go insane otherwise.

Hannah: I think that's fair enough. I'm pissed but I think Christmas with Hamish, Lola and Barney will be a laugh. If I was on my own with my kid though I'd also fuck off the rules.

Alicia: Don't get into trouble though.

Marnie: Who's going to check?
Hannah: Exactly. Do what you need to do babe x

To: LondonGirlHan@gmail.com
From: info@BloomBeautyHouse.co.uk
Subject: 🕯 You're Invited: The Bloom Beauty House
Exclusive Influencer Event
Hi Han,
   We're thrilled to invite you to an exclusive evening
of beauty, connection, and curated experiences at
The Bloom Beauty House – a celebration of
self-expression and standout style.
Join us for a night of:
🌸 VIP product previews & live demos
💅 Personalised glam sessions with top MUAs
📷 Content-ready spaces to capture your looks
and style
🍸 Luxe cocktails, treats, and surprises
🛍 A gift bag blooming with must-haves
(worth £300+)
Date: Thursday, May 16th
Time: 6:30PM – 10PM
Location: Sushi Samba, Covent Garden
Dress Code: Bloom-core chic 🌷 (Think floral, glowy,
glam. Picnic, but make it bouji.)
Space is limited, and this is an invite-only experience –
no plus ones.
👉 RSVP by May 5th to secure your spot
We can't wait to see your beauty bloom.
With love and glam,
Team Bloom
@bloombeautyhouse | #BloomWithUs

29th December, 2020

Hannah: I'm moving out of this shithole woooooooooo,
Alicia: Since when?
Hannah: Everything's popping off with the social stuff now so handed my notice in on the houseshare early December.
Marnie: You kept that quiet.
Hannah: Wanted to wait till it was all confirmed before telling anyone.
Alicia: Where are you moving to?
Hannah: Still London, just be nice to have my own space x
Marnie: Send us the info then you tease.
Hannah: I want to keep it a surprise x
Marnie: You annoy me 😑
Hannah: Thanks, babes 😊 Patience is a virtue.

Social media strategy 2020-21: @LondonGirlHan

Bio: Lockdown realness ✂️ 👗
Restyling from my closet
Fashion creativity from home 🏠 ✨

Platform	Content
Instagram	Me and my prince charming 💗 💕
TikTok	Designing an outfit for the beach using only thrifted items 😼
TikTok	Turning an old tablecloth into something wearable!
Instagram	GRWM to go to Mini Tesco

Followers: 29.6k

@PixelRaccoon: You two are the cutest! 💕

@EchoNebula_: Couple goals much? 🥺

@ToastQuantum: You are so talented!

@VibeCactus: You always find the best stuff in charity shops!

@LunaZebra95: LOVE THE TABLECLOTH PATTERN 😍 😍 😍 😍 😍

@CrypticNoodle: Imagine being able to look this amazing in a tablecloth?! SLAY 💧 💧 💧 💧

@GlitterPeach: Can you do a tutorial on how you get your ideas?

@LilacDaydreamz: I love watching your content. It's such a lovely distraction from the shitshow of the world atm

@VelvetMuffin: DM for collab

@crybaby.exe: Mini Tescos is the highlight of my miserable existence!

@saturns.ring: You even slay in joggers and a mask bbe

@NovaPetal: PLZ MAKE A BIKINI NEXT!! 😺

@bittersweet.pea: What foundation do you wear?

@ghostinlipgloss: Vinted is the only thing keeping me sane. And this page <3

@minty.on.mars: DM for collab

Chapter Twenty

13th February, 2021

Hannah

Hannah stood in the kitchen of her rented flat watching Joe (topless) as he made her a skinny flat white with the shiny new Ninja Luxe Café she'd purchased last week. Thank God for Klarna. Saying that, even with Klarna this time last year she was barely able to afford the luxury of a daily £4 Costa latte, let alone her own machine.

It felt bad to admit it considering the state of the world, but this past year had been a damn good one for Hannah. Being locked down in her houseshare had drawn her as close to insanity as she'd ever gotten. If it wasn't for the government mandated one hour a day of exercise and essential shopping trips – chocolate and wine were essential, yes – she would have likely been locked up for causing grievous bodily harm to Hamish for his obnoxiously loud Zoom calls at three o'clock in the morning.

Overnight, Hannah had swapped evenings surrounded by friends, alcohol and music, with nights in, alone. She wasn't used to her own company, not properly. She'd always been surrounded by people, and truth be told, she didn't know what to do with herself. She needed to keep busy, so she threw herself into filling her ample spare time by making content for her social media. One day it was learning the newest TikTok dance, another it was jumping on a trending sound or doing her ironic 'Get Ready With Me For My Night Out At The 24-Hour Tesco' videos.

She'd also accidentally found another more niche corner of the internet – upcycling thrifted or second-hand clothing pieces and transforming them into something completely new – an old tablecloth into a skimpy two-piece set, or an oversized t-shirt into a sexy black mini dress. This was partly inspired by her new financial situation: poor. She was never rolling in it before, but when lockdown hit and she went on furlough, she was living off handouts from her parents and the even stingier government. So she scoured her wardrobe for pieces to sacrifice, and begged her flatmates to give her any fabrics or old items of clothing they no longer wanted – old boxers not included.

It snowballed, starting with a few comments here and there to thousands of likes and followers from all over the world. It was a nice way to connect with people when physical connection was off limits, and it turned out Hannah was pretty good at what she was doing.

It was a long time coming, but here it was. She was living her dream. And part of that dream was to finally host Galentine's at her place, and not her scruffy uni digs or her parents' basement. Hannah had spent the past few years watching Alicia and Marnie move out of home and into places that were theirs, whether rented or owned, and it felt so good that Hannah had finally caught up. In fact, she'd not just caught up, she'd totally smoked them. She knew all along that she'd do it, but she'd be lying if she didn't admit there were wobbly moments along the way.

Technically, the UK was in another lockdown, but both she and Marnie had had enough of following the rules, and so decided Galentine's would go ahead. Alicia wouldn't miss out, so agreed on the promise that everyone would test first. If the government could have a party, so could they.

'Voilà.' Joe pushed the steaming glass mug towards Hannah on the counter.

'Thanks.' She smiled, taking in the glorious sight of her current beau: dark-skinned, in good shape but not obnoxiously so, the most gorgeous eyes. They looked great together. They were a real IT couple. Real #couplegoals.

Joe squinted at her. 'What?' He smiled coyly. He knew what. 'Nothing.'

'Oh yeah?' Joe moved himself around the kitchen island and positioned his hands either side of Hannah's hips.

She turned, placing her hands in the crooks of his elbows and drawing circles gently on his skin. She knew this drove him wild, although she really should be getting ready for the girls' arrival. Thankfully it was a Saturday and they weren't due until four, but Hannah had had a lazy morning in bed with Joe (if you could consider what they were doing 'lazy') and it was already gone midday. She still needed to shower, put her hair in rollers and lay out the sleepover gift package she'd sorted for each of them.

'You're cheeky. You know what that does to me,' Joe shifted his body even closer to hers. He nuzzled his lips in the crook of her neck and planted a delicate kiss there.

'And you know what that does to me,' Hannah replied, thankful for the support of the breakfast bar behind her and Joe's sturdy frame as her legs went weak.

Once more couldn't hurt . . .

She took Joe's hand and led him to the bedroom. Everything else could wait.

'What the actual fuck, Han?' Marnie's eyes were wide and her mouth agape as Hannah led her and Alicia down the hallway and into the main living area of the flat. It wasn't exactly huge – one bed, one bath, an open-plan kitchen and living area – but for London standards it wasn't to be sniffed at. It was the floor-to-ceiling windows and the view of the Shard and London Bridge that were the real wow-factor. Hannah had had the same reaction when she first came to view the place.

'How long have you been here now?' Alicia said, her face looking as if it was battling to hide its shock.

'Just over a month. I took New Year, New Me to the extreme by moving in the first week of January.'

'Just a bit,' Marnie grinned. 'How much is it?'

'Enough.' She'd almost keeled over when the estate agent told her the rent (that's per week, not per month?!) but after a thorough check through her finances, she realised that she could just about manage it.

'It's rude to talk about money,' Alicia said. Hannah wasn't sure if she was joking or not, but appreciated the sentiment. She wanted to keep her finances vague at this stage. She was happy to show off to a degree, but no one needed to know the ins and outs of it all.

'Sorry, Miss. Will you put me in detention?' Marnie said, offering her best puppy dog face.

'I will if you call me Miss ever again.' Alicia smiled cheekily.

'So is this where we're sleeping?' Marnie dropped onto the sofa. 'Ouch, that wasn't as squishy as I was expecting.'

'It's a Denelli,' Hannah said, not that she expected either of them to understand what that meant. She didn't herself, really. She just knew it was modern and expensive and came with the apartment. She balanced herself precariously on the modern accent chair in the corner – it was pleasing to the eye but not to the glutes. 'Yep, we'll set up in here. The skyline is so beautiful at night with all the lights reflecting off the water.'

'Amazing. I can't wait to see that.' Marnie's feet – along with her grubby-looking socks – were now on the pouffe in front of her, another designer brand that Hannah couldn't remember the name of. *I can't tell her to put her feet down, can I? Pouffes are for feet, after all.*

'Ooo. I have a little thing for both of you.' Hannah headed towards the cupboard in the hallway. 'Back in a sec.'

She returned swinging three red metallic giftbags 'One for Marnie, one for Alicia and one for moi.'

Marnie upended the whole bag enthusiastically while Alicia went for the more demure strategy of fumbling one thing out at a time, finally sitting on the sofa after hovering awkwardly as if she wasn't planning on staying longer than five minutes.

'What the hell? LilySilk!' Marnie cried, holding up the one hundred per cent silk pair of pyjamas that Hannah had bought them all. She'd gone totally rogue this year, with no red or pink in sight, instead opting for white with an ornate navy-blue pattern on. 'And these socks are adorable,' Marnie continued, grabbing at the luxurious bamboo socks Hannah had also picked out.

'Aren't they!' Hannah was proud of that find.

'I'm putting them on right now. Is that okay? We're not going out anywhere, are we?' Marnie started to strip off, unbuttoning her jeans and flinging her red vest top off with a flourish, clearly not fussed that she was now sitting in front of the curtainless window in her greying bra and large pants.

'Go for it,' Hannah chuckled. 'I'll put mine on in a sec.' Hannah looked to Alicia. 'Alicia, do you like it?' She'd been strangely quiet, even by her standards.

'I love it. It's like being at a fashion show.' Alicia offered a small smile.

'But . . .?'

'No but. It's just . . . I feel bad. This must have been really expensive.'

'It's fine. It's nothing compared to the personal chef I've booked for later.'

'Personal chef?' Marnie hooted, giving Hannah a quick flash of boob as she pulled on the PJ top and slipped her bra off at the same time.

'Yep. Her menu is just to die for.'

'I can't tell if you're joking or not.' Alicia still didn't look impressed.

God, what more did Hannah have to do? 'I promise you I'm not joking.'

Alicia clutched the pyjamas in her hands, stroking the silk with her fingers. 'Now I feel even more guilty.'

Guilty or jealous? Hannah knew Alicia had been struggling with work recently, and had even taken some unpaid leave due to stress, although she didn't give any detail about why. Perhaps she was also worrying about money; she was always worrying about something.

'Don't be guilty, be grateful.' Hannah said, but it didn't come out as friendly as she'd hoped. 'Really no need to stress about it.'

Alicia put down the pyjamas after folding them carefully

and smiled. 'I am grateful. So grateful. Thank you. Just promise me you're sure you can afford it, and then I'll shut up.'

Alicia sounded exactly like Hannah's mum. *This money won't last forever. You can't rely on this as a proper income stream. Blah blah blah.*

'I can assure you I can afford this.' Her financial status was only going to get better. She was receiving multiple emails a day asking about collabs and sponsorship opportunities, she was officially part of the creator funds on her various social media apps, and she was even in talks with an agent. 'I'm not stupid, I know that the social stuff can be transient, which is why I'm starting my own business, too.'

'Starting a business?' Alicia's brow furrowed.

Here we go again. 'Yeah.' Hannah sat down on the accent chair and fiddled with the tag on the top of her giftbag.

'Doing what? It's not one of those coaching courses or MLMs, is it?' said Marnie, sliding into her new bamboo socks. At least Hannah could relax now knowing that the only socks touching the pouffe would be clean ones.

'I'm offended you think I'd do either of those things,' she replied, picking up Marnie's discarded socks and dropping them into her empty giftbag. 'It's a swimwear brand.'

'Oh my God, that's amazing!' Marnie squealed. 'What's inspired you to go down the swimwear route?'

'Good question.' Out of everything she could have done, why swimwear? She'd had other ideas – a makeup or hair care brand for example, but that had all sorts of legal hoops you needed to jump through. 'Well, it's super popular at the moment with influencers all over the world – we'll always need swimwear, right? And I'd like to make it environmentally friendly as well as super inclusive to promote body positivity, because both of those things are super en vogue.'

'And also super important,' Marnie added with a fond shake of her head.

'Of course. Do you want the mission statement?' Hannah knew it off by heart in case she ever got stuck in a lift with someone of influence and she needed to pitch it in thirty seconds or less.

'Er, absolutely!' Marnie wiggled her bamboo adorned toes gleefully. Alicia nodded.

Hannah stood up, her back and bum already stiff from the chair despite only sitting on it for five minutes. She crossed her arms and positioned her limbs in a casual yet powerful stance. 'Our mission is to create swimwear that empowers every body – blending comfort, style, and sustainability to celebrate confidence at every size, shape, and shade. Inspired by real people and real moments, we design pieces that move with you, wherever the water takes you.' She threw in a bow for good measure.

'Incredible,' Marnie nodded gleefully. 'Cannot fault it.'

'Alicia?' Her silence was bugging Hannah. How hard was it to show some enthusiasm, even if it was fake?

Alicia pulled her face into a closed-mouth smile. 'No notes. It's great.'

Hannah knew that was as much as she'd get, and actually, really didn't care. She believed in her business and herself, and that's all that mattered.

'Let me take you to my business headquarters – where the magic happens.' Hannah's chest swelled with pride. She couldn't wait to show off her plans. 'Follow me.'

Chapter Twenty-One

13th February, 2021

Alicia

Hannah led the girls to her bedroom, where she'd partitioned off one corner with an ornate screen.

'Ta da. My study and business HQ.'

She'd done a nice job. Swanky-looking swivel chair, a shelf above a white desk with an aesthetic spider plant and two books – *How to Win Friends and Influence People* and *The Secret*. Alicia recognised the set-up from some of Hannah's videos, although the pink neon sign that said Nala Swim was a new addition.

There was also a whiteboard on the wall where Hannah had scribbled a 'name ideas' mindmap and a 'social media schedule' with one column for @NalaSwim and another for @LondonGirlHan.

Alicia was well acquainted with @LondonGirlHan. More often than she'd care to admit she would find herself viewing Hannah's Instagram stories under an anonymous account and sometimes scrolling back on her grid as far as 2016. She took care not to accidentally double tap, as if each square of Hannah's curated life had the ability to explode and give away Alicia's shameful habit.

Yesterday, Hannah had posted seven stories. While Alicia was shoving a sandwich in her mouth, sat on the toilet at 1:57pm after lunchtime detention ran over, Hannah had been walking along the Southbank, sipping a matcha latte and heading to the Tate Modern. At 5:45pm, just after Alicia accidentally went into the bathroom while Hugh was wiping his arse, phone in one hand, bog roll in the other (he hadn't even asked how her day was), Hannah was getting ready for an influencer event for Revlon.

How Hannah had gone from temping and living in a house not too far off a squat, to this total overnight success baffled Alicia. It didn't seem fair that she had no plan, just went with the flow and now here they were standing in her expensive flat in London Bridge, talking about how she was going to start her own business.

Maybe that made Alicia a horrible friend – why couldn't she just be happy for her?

'So you chose Nala Swim?' Marnie said, nodding at the neon sign.

'Yeah. Just felt right.'

'Shame, because I rather like BeachBum Babe.'

'Not the right vibes.' Hannah spun the swivel chair around and pushed it past the screen. She sat and gestured for Alicia and Marnie to sit opposite her on the bed.

Who did she think she was? Lord Sugar?

'There's something I want to ask Marnie.'

Alicia frowned. 'Just Marnie?'

'Yeah. You'll see why in a minute.'

'Go on . . .' Marnie squinted and smiled simultaneously.

'Would you like to go into business with me?'

Bloody hell, she really did think she was Lord Sugar.

'What is this? *The Apprentice*?' Alicia said, although she still hadn't mastered jokey sarcasm in the same way as the other two. She just sounded mean.

They ignored her comment. 'Me? Why me? I have fuck all to offer.'

'This could be the opportunity you need to do something more with your life. You're super creative, you're always thinking outside of the box. You're always honest and you keep me grounded. I can't think of anyone I'd rather do it with. Please?'

It was like Alicia wasn't in the room. Should she just leave them to it?

'God. I don't know what to say.' Marnie chewed her lip and frowned, her eyes shifting as if she was trying to sift through a thousand thoughts in fast forward.

'Say yes.'

'I'd need to think about it. I can't just say yes. It's a huge thing.'

'No more huge than having a baby.' Hannah spun in her chair as she spoke, grabbing a whiteboard pen and adding what looked like a scribble to her board.

'True,' said Marnie. 'But still. I'm finally at a point in my life where I have my own place, work's good. I'm saving what I can, when I can to get out of my credit card debt. I'm not sure it's the right time. Plus there's a lot going on for me at the moment.'

'Oh.' Hannah put her pen down and pursed her lips. Was Marnie actually going to reject her offer? Hannah was not used to rejection. The last time she was rejected was probably . . . *No. Don't think about Hannah and Hugh together.* 'Is it ever going to be the right time, though?' Hannah continued.

227

Marnie shrugged. 'Maybe not. But I can't commit to that right now. Sorry.'

The room went silent. *Ha.* Alicia thought. *You can't always get what you want. Life doesn't work that way. Oh God, why am I being such a cow?*

Hannah plastered a big smile on her face. 'It's fine. I'll ask Lola instead.' She turned away from them again and reached for her phone.

Alicia was still failing to see why it was so obvious that Hannah would ask Marnie, and now Lola but not her. She and Hannah wouldn't work particularly well together and the thought of Hannah being her boss was horrendous, but it would've been nice to have been asked.

After a couple of glasses of wine – which seemed to be a weekend night staple for Alicia at the moment – she'd loosened up. The private chef, a lovely lady called Helena, had arrived with her negative Covid test and Le Creuset crock pot and was cooking up a storm in the kitchen, and the girls had moved into the bedroom to give her some space.

Hannah was sitting on the blush-pink velvet accent chair in the corner of her bedroom, scrolling on her phone. 'I'm going to put on some music. Any requests?'

'Nineties,' said Marnie from her horizontal position on Hannah's king-size bed beside Alicia. 'Or Y2K.'

'*Nostalgia Overload: 90s Edition*? Or *TLC, Britney & Beyond*?' Hannah pursed her lips together. 'Ooooo, *That's So 2000s.*'

'Yessss!'

A few moments later, Nelly Furtado's 'I'm Like a Bird' was playing through Hannah's speaker system.

'OMG this is a classic.' Marnie shifted to sit up and

started singing – totally tuneless but you had to admire her enthusiasm. Alicia smiled fondly.

Hannah joined in next, putting her all into the lyrics. She stood theatrically, pulling Marnie to her feet as they both hit the chorus.

They belted it out at the top of their lungs. They were skipping in circles around the room, flapping their arms like madwomen, the bed no obstacle as they jumped on it as if it was a stage, narrowly missing stepping on Alicia.

Alicia laughed self-consciously and moved out of their way, hovering next to the bed not quite knowing what to do with herself. Despite wanting to, she couldn't bring herself to join in. *You'll look silly.*

'Come on, Al.' Marnie grabbed Alicia's hands and pulled her onto the bed.

'I can't sing!' Alicia protested, stepping onto the mattress with a hesitant wobble.

'Neither can we!'

'Speak for yourself,' giggled Hannah. 'Join us! Join us!'

Shall I? Alicia downed the rest of her wine. *Screw it. It's about time I blow off some steam.* And away she went, joining Marnie and Hannah in their gallops around the room, flailing her arms and spinning and twirling. God it felt good to let her hair down. *I should do this more often—*

'Er, the starter is served.'

Everyone stopped, just as Nelly sang the remaining lyrics and the music petered out. Oh God, how long had Helena been standing there?

'Thanks,' Hannah said with a straight face, crumbling into laughter alongside Marnie and Alicia when Helena had retreated back into the kitchen. 'God, she must think we're all off our tits.'

'I'm sure she's seen worse.' Marnie panted, out of breath from her performance. She fell back onto the bed and fanned herself. 'I'm bloody starving.'

'So I'm actually in therapy,' said Marnie as she sliced her knife through the smoked salmon parcel on her plate.

It felt weird to go about their normal business, chatting away as if Helena wasn't standing only a few feet from them. She must have heard some really juicy stuff at various debauched dinner parties of the rich. *Maybe I could be a personal chef*, Alicia thought. Despite not being a particularly good cook, she could learn. She was good at learning. It was only then that she realised what Marnie had said.

'Therapy?' she said. 'How come?'

Marnie shrugged, now pushing the salmon around her plate with her fork. 'Nothing dramatic, just wanting some space to talk through some shit and find myself again. No biggie.' She didn't look up.

Alicia could tell she was playing things down – she was a dab hand at making a proverbial molehill out of a mountain. How had Alicia not noticed sooner? Had she missed the signs, or was Marnie just very good at hiding it? It felt odd that she was struggling to the point of choosing therapy, but hadn't said anything until now. But then, Alicia was the same, choosing instead to vent to Hugh, Miss Logan, or opting for the favoured bottle it up and just carry on.

'Just finding yourself, no biggie.' Hannah chuckled. 'But seriously, what's made you decide to do it now?'

'Timing, for a start. I've got a bit more time to myself now Sophie's at school.' Marnie paused. 'Lockdown was tough, too. I know a lot of people felt it so I don't want to have a pity party, and I know it could have been so much worse, but

I did feel really fucking lonely. It was the first time in forever, probably since I gave birth to Soph, that I had to sit with my own thoughts. I didn't like what they were saying.' Sadness settled in her eyes and her face shadowed.

'Shit,' Hannah said, putting her cutlery down and shifting her chair closer to Marnie's. 'I didn't realise you'd been going through so much. You can always message us, you know.'

'I know, but you've got your own lives, I don't want to be needy.'

Alicia could sense Marnie's defences going back up as she sat more upright and started shovelling food in her mouth.

'It's not needy.' Alicia smiled gently at her. 'It's just what friends do.'

'Thanks.' Marnie returned her smile. 'I'm okay. Don't worry about me.'

Alicia didn't want the conversation to be shut down just yet, a trick Marnie would pull if things got too serious. She needed to play it carefully, not be too confrontational in case it pushed Marnie further into her default *I'm fine, everything is fine* performance. 'What do you talk about?' she asked. 'You don't have to answer if you don't want to.'

'Mum, Dad. They fuck you up, your mum and dad . . . you know the saying! I know they weren't the worst, but they put a lot of pressure on me growing up. Dunno if it was because I'm an only child, but I'm starting to unpick all that now.' Marnie's shoulders lowered. 'I also talk about other stuff – Sophie, my life, my relationship with myself. Men. I'm actually on a man ban for the foreseeable.'

'God, really?' Hannah couldn't hide her horror. 'How's that going?'

'Hit and miss,' said Marnie through a mouthful of pastry. 'It's fine until I'm lying in bed on a Friday night and Sophie's asleep. The flat is so quiet and all I want to do is go on Tinder and swipe swipe swipe, even if it's just for the dopamine hit of a match. I've only caved once. The rest of the time I just end up buying stuff I don't need on Vinted.'

'I love Vinted,' said Hannah. 'One of my favourite places for thrifting.'

Alicia was curious. 'Is it any good? Therapy, not Vinted.' She'd been offered therapy by the doctor who prescribed her anxiety meds, but the NHS waiting list was long, she wasn't able to afford to go private, and even if she did, when would she have the time to do it around the endless demands of her job?

'I love it. Which is a weird thing to say about something that makes me cry every week, but it's a good cry. A healing cry. Joan is big on the benefits of crying.'

If crying was that healing, I should be more peaceful than the Dalai Lama by now. Maybe it didn't work the same for stress or frustration tears. Alicia knew what would work, but karate chopping students and telling them to just fuck off was frowned upon.

Hannah picked up her wine glass and swirled it artfully. 'Have you had any lightbulb moments?'

Marnie smiled hesitantly. 'I don't want to bore you with the details.'

'You could never bore us, Marns.'

'Challenge accepted. Well, it's become apparent that I don't know who the fuck I am outside of being Sophie's mum, which is obvious now, but I've been so busy just surviving that I haven't stopped to really think what that means. Also, the more obvious one: I have shit taste in men.' Marnie raised her glass ironically. 'Quelle surprise.'

'Is that what she said?!' Alicia almost choked on some flaky pastry. 'Aren't therapists supposed to be nice and gentle?'

'She's lovely!' said Marnie zealously. 'She put it much more politely than that – that I need the validation of a relationship, however shitty, to show me I'm worthy. I do like that she challenges me though, and sometimes calls me out on my bullshit.'

Perhaps therapy wasn't for Alicia. It sounded a bit too intense.

'Sounds like it's really working for you, I'm so pleased.' Alicia put her knife and fork together on her plate. 'You were right, Hannah, this food is amazing.'

'It really is. And that's just the starter! Roll on the other two courses.' Marnie rubbed her hands together. 'Anyway, I really am okay, so don't worry about me. I'm not planning on driving into oncoming traffic, I can assure you.'

They all laughed but Alicia was keen to make sure Marnie had felt heard, even if she didn't want to talk more about it now. 'Okay well if you ever do get to that point, talk to us,' she said. 'Or I'll kill you myself, okay?'

'Promise,' Marnie said with a nod, looking a little lighter than she had done ten minutes ago. 'Anyway, how are things with you, A?'

'Oh, fine.' The classic fine. The irony wasn't lost on Alicia. But it was always easier to say things were fine than to open up any further. She didn't want to spend her precious time off thinking about it nor did she want to look like she was competing with Marnie about who was struggling the most. 'Now OFSTED is done, I'm feeling better.'

This was true, though better than before was hardly worth much. She'd got herself so worked up about it that she'd ended up being signed off for a week by her doctor after the visit. The doctor also doubled her dosage of Sertraline.

The funny thing was that the visit went well. They'd got

a Good mark (no one was expecting Outstanding) and the English department had been highly commended. This didn't stop Alicia from feeling the need to stay up late most nights, either marking or lesson planning. The week off had been helpful and she was now feeling slightly less like she was drowning, though it was quickly dawning on her that *this* was just teaching.

'That's good.' Hannah sipped her wine. 'How's Hugh?'

Alicia bristled. They'd had a blazing row just last week when she'd realised he'd started following Hannah on Instagram (he didn't even have Facebook, since when did he decide to get Instagram?) and she'd finally brought up that she'd caught him looking at Hannah's arse at her birthday BBQ in September. The voice in Alicia's head liked to frequently remind her of their past – sometimes it was just a whisper, other times it shouted crudely *they've fucked! They've fucked!* It was exhausting.

'He's fine.' Alicia picked up her own glass and downed it.

'Sounds like everything is fine,' said Marnie.

Sarcasm? Alicia couldn't be bothered to question it. 'Mmmm. That's because it is.'

Helena appeared at the table, reaching around Alicia to fill up her glass.

'Any more thoughts on the baby thing?' Marnie said, peering around Helena's arm.

Ah yes, the baby thing. Alicia shook her head, despite it being an outright lie. In fact, she'd had plenty of thoughts. It was yet another thing that Alicia was sick of thinking about; the list just kept getting longer: her relationship, work, *the baby thing*.

She was twenty-six years old. She was married with her own place. She had a career that allowed for fairly decent maternity leave. Of course having a baby was next on the agenda, and no one would let her forget it. Least of all, Hugh's family.

Last Sunday, she and Hugh had gone round his parents' for their monthly Sunday lunch. They'd retired to the lounge after their meal, Hugh's dad, Brendan, reading his paper and his nan Beryl back on her armchair in the corner, going on about how her neighbour had her TV too loud. Alicia was on the sofa next to Hugh trying to look interested, although three glasses of wine and a full stomach made that increasingly difficult.

Beryl was cut short by Trish, Hugh's mum, who appeared at the living room door with a cardboard box overflowing with stuff.

'I've been up in the loft again,' she said, placing the box down at Hugh's feet. Every time they visited his parents, they always ended up coming home with a bootful of old shite (Hugh's words, not Alicia's), but he was too polite to do anything other than offer his deepest thanks.

Hugh, being the dutiful son he was, sifted through the plastic toys and musty-smelling bits and bobs, and after a moment of making all the right nostalgic noises, he pulled out a battered-looking toy train and accompanying rail tracks. 'God, this is a blast from the past. I can't believe you still have it. Why didn't you get rid of it? I'm happy for you to donate it to charity.'

'We thought we'd keep it for you, you know, in case.' Trish raised her eyebrows and Alicia's stomach tensed.

Oh God, here we go. I really don't want to get into this again. But she sat there with a smile and nodded.

'You aren't pregnant, are you?' Beryl interjected, voice accusatory.

'No!' Alicia couldn't keep the horror from her voice. She was immediately mortified by her reaction. 'Sorry, no. Not yet.'

'Oh, just your stomach looks—'

'Nan,' Hugh said, mirroring Alicia's look of total horror.

Alicia didn't know why people felt it was okay to comment on a couple's choice to have or not have kids. For all they knew, Alicia and Hugh had been trying, or they'd been pregnant but miscarried. People just needed to shut up.

Beryl sipped her tea. 'What? Your eggs won't last forever, you know.'

'I know.' Alicia had forced a laugh before exiting swiftly to the bathroom to compose herself.

As much as Alicia had tried to not let it get to her, Nanny Beryl's words often rang in her ears. *Am I running out of time?* Hugh had tried to talk to her on the way home about how sorry he was for what his nan had said, but also used it as an opportunity to try and talk about *timelines* and when to *start trying*.

Hugh, for once in his life, didn't seem to overthink it. For someone who read every receipt after a big food shop and who used a colour-coded spreadsheet to plan every holiday, he was very chilled about bringing a new life into the world. It made sense in lots of ways – he wasn't the one who had to grow it, birth it, breastfeed it. He'd be back at work after two weeks of paternity leave and have some semblance of his pre-baby life to remind him who he was. He also seemed to have an incredibly optimistic outlook on the whole thing – again, the total opposite to his usual realistic (pessimistic) point of view. He didn't worry about the potential traumas of infertility, baby loss or a traumatic labour. He didn't show any awareness of the long-term toll it could take on Alicia's body, her identity and mental health. The opportunity for postpartum depression, life-long anxiety, having a child with additional needs – the list could go on and on. And yes, she was focusing on all the negatives, but they were all possibilities, and she felt strongly that if they were to ever throw their hat into the parenthood ring, they'd need to be prepared for all eventualities. Truth be told, she wasn't.

'Alicia?' Marnie pulled her back into the room. 'You okay?'

'Yeah, just thinking.'

'It's not an easy decision. I'm sort of grateful in a weird way that it just happened for me. I didn't have to make such a hard call.'

Alicia often thought how much easier it would be if it were to just happen, at least then she wouldn't have to feel responsible for making the wrong choice either way. But there was no way it would ever *just happen* when she and Hugh rarely had sex, and when they did they were always very careful.

Marnie continued. 'If I have any advice to give at all, it would be to only do it if you're sure it's what you want.'

'How on earth can you be sure on something when you have no understanding of what it might actually be like for you?'

'That's what I've always thought,' added Hannah. 'You could have a baby and, despite it being hard, think *ah yes, this is right, this is my purpose* and all will be fine. But what if that didn't happen? What if you regretted it?'

'Exactly!' said Alicia, rather too enthusiastically, splashing red wine onto her empty plate.

'True.' Marnie nodded thoughtfully. 'You'd be good at it though. You're always so good with Sophie.'

That wasn't untrue. Alicia and Hugh, on the now much rarer occasion they looked after her, were always focused on her wellbeing and safety. Back when she was smaller, they stopped at every roadside even if there was nothing coming and made sure to teach her to look both ways and only cross when the green man appeared. Alicia always cut the grapes and cherry tomatoes in Sophie's lunch and always refreshed her understanding of the Heimlich manoeuvre for children in case anything went wrong. Last time they had her, Hugh had encouraged Sophie to climb the rock wall at the park while standing behind her but not close enough in Alicia's opinion. Alicia flinched with every slip and had to bite her tongue every time she wanted to say *be careful* every five seconds.

Alicia could see them as parents, and good ones at that, even if Hugh would be the sort of dad to run around the house switching off the lights complaining of electricity bills and likening the spectacle to Blackpool Illuminations.

They did a decent job. It was nice to do for one day, the odd evening here and there. But did Alicia want to do it every day, day in and day out? The relentlessness of the school run, the constant mum guilt, the having to be on duty twenty-four hours a day, seven days a week. It didn't appeal. In fact, it sounded like hell. And just because you were good at something didn't mean you should do it.

Hot Mess Express 🚂 😜

25th May, 2021

Hannah: I broke up with Joe.
Alicia: Sorry to hear that.
Marnie: Are you okay?
Hannah: Absolutely fine. It was mutual.
Marnie: What happened?
Hannah: Just drifted apart x

Marnie and Alicia
19th July, 2021

Alicia: Do you think Hannah was being weird on Saturday?
Marnie: Weird how?
Alicia: Dunno. Feel like she barely chatted to me all night.
Marnie: It was her birthday party, she probs just didn't have time to chat loads to anyone because she had to do the rounds. Like you at your wedding.
Alicia: She seemed to find plenty of time to talk to other people.
Marnie: Who?
Alicia: You. Hugh.

Marnie: I spoke to her for less than fifteen minutes all night, and I barely even saw her with Hugh!

Alicia: I did.

Marnie: I don't want to sound harsh, but you are deffo making it worse in your head. If she spoke to anyone loads, it was her new iNfLuEnCeR buddies. PLEASE DON'T WORRY. Xxx PS Still seeing you on Sat?

Alicia: Yeah x

Hot Mess Express 🚂 😵

1st August, 2021

Hannah: It's official, we have a launch date for Nala Swim!!!! Put it in your calendars and remember to share the shit out of all of my posts lol

Alicia: Well done x

Marnie: Hope we get some free stuff.

Hannah: Maybe ;) I also have something to tell you . . .

Marnie: I'm intrigued.

Alicia: ?

Hannah: I can't do Galentine's Day next year :(

Marnie: NOOOOOOOOOOOO. That will be the first time in 10 years we aren't spending it together 😵 You better have a good excuse lol.

Hannah: I do, to be fair. I'm going to be in Bali.

Alicia: Wow! What for?

Hannah: A brand photoshoot.

Marnie: Of course, I sometimes forget you're a jet setting minor celeb these days. It's fine, you've clearly got a better offer than to come and spend the night

in my living room eating frozen pizzas, although this
year I was thinking of stretching to a Domino's.
Push the boat out. 😬
Hannah: Well, I have a proposal.
Alicia: Go on . . .
Hannah: How do you fancy joining me?
Marnie: OMG.
Alicia: Wow. Errrrm.
Hannah: I will pay, obviously.
Marnie: REALLY?
Alicia: That's a lot of money! I couldn't.
Hannah: Stop being so polite. It's in half term next year,
right?
Alicia: I think so.
Hannah: Then you have no reason to say no!
Marnie: I'd like to tentatively say yes. Need to talk to my
folks first about childcare and make sure Sophie is alright.
Hannah: Of course, can you let me know by the end of next
week so I can book the flights? It won't be business class I'm
afraid.
Marnie: I'm sure we'll cope. Thank you so much!!!!!!!
Alicia: Yes really. That is amazing. X

Marnie and Alicia
4th August, 2021

Alicia: Can you make sure we've booked our seats next to
each other? I don't want to sit on my own.
Marnie: Yep. Might I suggest going to the doctor and asking
for some valium? I hear it's good for nervous flyers.
Alicia: Debated it but I'd feel more nervous taking it than
not, you know? I don't want to end up being that person
who goes doolally and gets the plane diverted.

Marnie: Can't be worse than the person who got a plane diverted because of their stinky shit.

Alicia: I think I'd just die if that happened to me.

Marnie: I'd own it. My claim to fame, ya know? Jokes aside, I'll just ply you with lots of gin. It will be fine.

Marnie: Actually, it will be more than fine, it will be fun! Bali here we come wooooooooo.

Social media strategy 2021-22: @LondonGirlHan

Bio: Fashion designer in LDN 🐱
Creating swimwear & living the dream 😊 ✨
DM for collabs | NO CREEPS!

Platform	Content
Instagram	Top-secret announcement coming soon! 🫢
TikTok	Come to Paris with me on a Top-Secret trip
TikTok	✨ Introducing Nala Swim ✨
Instagram	✨ Nala Swim is here! ✨

Followers: 425k

@cloudsnatcher: YOU TEASE

@roses.are.rad: Please tell me you're
coming out with a makeup line.

@fizzberryy: PARIS???? LUCKY COW

@sleepycyber: Eeeeeeeeeeee 😍 🤩

@opalvenom: OMG I KNEW IT!!! 🫠

243

@tinyriotclub: When can we buy???

@pixelgrit: Will they be available in XS?

@lavacat.studio: 😎😎😎😎😎😎😎 😎😎

@moss.vault: 💧💧💧💧💧💧💧

Social media strategy 2021-22: @NalaSwim

Bio: 🌸 Swimwear that loves every body & the Earth 🌍
♻️ Sustainable 🌈 Inclusive 💕 Always cute
✨ Made to make you feel amazing
☁️ Shop your fave look

Platform	Content
Instagram	✨ 🐱 Introducing Nala Swim 🐱 ✨
TikTok	Giveaway competition!!!!!
TikTok	Day in the life of a small business owner – Bali edition
Instagram	From sketch to product

Followers: 102k

@sugarnoir: I NEED ALL OF THESE! 😍

@byte.milk: Will they be available in the US?

@cosmiccrumpet: THESE COLOURS

@plasmapeach: Do you have the option for larger cup sizes?

@ghostsnapper: NEPO BABY MUCH?

@crystal09: Please think of your carbon footprint, all these trips you're doing.

@shyhowl: U lk so sxy bby

@cryingincouture: @baddieballet WE NEED THEM ALL.

@slaybellsclub: Will you be restocking the pink one? I was too late 🙄

Chapter Twenty-Two

13th February, 2022

Alicia

They were three days into their trip to Bali and Alicia couldn't quite believe she'd made it. It was a kind gesture for Hannah to offer to pay for their flights, but Alicia had insisted that she contribute towards it as much as she could afford. It just didn't feel right to allow Hannah to foot the whole bill, despite it being her idea and that she was clearly not short of cash. There was also a part of Alicia that couldn't help but think this whole thing was less about a commitment to their friendship and more about showing off. But she was in no rush to turn down a semi-free holiday and to escape the clutches of her increasingly mundane life.

Anxiety and last-minute panic almost thwarted this newfound spontaneity – she and Hugh had been going through another rough patch, so leaving him for a week might not have been the best idea – however, a deeply hidden part of her felt awakened for the first time in forever as she lay on the beach bed (beneath a canopy, slathered in factor fifty) sipping a rather risky Sex on the Beach.

At this point, Alicia was bored out of her skull with the arguments she and Hugh were having. It was like Groundhog Day. It would start off with him making a comment about expanding their family, a phrase that wound Alicia up more than necessary. It would escalate when she'd push back, trying to talk to him honestly about her fears and how she wasn't ready.

Somehow, tempers fraying, it would then morph from a conversation about babies to Alicia convincing herself that Hugh was going off her. More and more, he was taking himself off to the spare bedroom to sleep, and the little sex they had was always initiated by Alicia. This paranoia had been worse since Hannah had broken up with Joe – that lasted all of a few months – and now she was single again she was posting more thirst traps to her socials than ever before. Alicia decided it wasn't a coincidence that it was exactly now that Hugh had decided to finally join the rest of the world on TikTok.

Their last argument had been even worse because Alicia swore blind that she'd seen Hannah's name pop up on his phone, but he'd flat out denied it and refused to pass it over for Alicia to check.

I'm not going to be one of those mad couples who check each other's phones and who don't trust each other.

Are you calling me mad?

No, but you're acting crazy.

Don't you dare call me crazy.

God, she needed another Sex on the Beach.

'She's killing it, isn't she?' Marnie said, sipping her own overpriced cocktail while looking towards the water where

Hannah stood with a cameraperson, model and a few assistants looking very much the Art Director Extraordinaire as she orchestrated each shot with the ease of someone who'd been doing it their entire life.

'Absolutely.'

'If you'd have told eighteen-year-old us that in nearly ten years, we'd be doing Galentine's in Bali, Hannah with her own business, me with a seven-year-old child, and you having ticked everything off your life-plan, I wonder what we would have said.'

'Mmmm, yeah.' Alicia had ticked most of the plan. Go to uni, study to be a teacher, meet a nice man, get a job teaching, buy a house and marry the nice man. And yet, as Alicia watched Hannah, she couldn't help but think maybe she'd done it all wrong.

'Is it weird that I don't even feel jealous? Like yeah, I wouldn't mind a bit more money to take Sophie on more nice holidays, but all I feel is really damn proud of her.'

Alicia downed the rest of her drink, the liquid burning the back of her throat. 'Yeah?' Despite sounding unsure, Alicia wasn't jealous of Hannah. This lifestyle had never appealed – she was not into fashion, luxurious holidays and celeb-status – but there was something to be said about how Hannah had pushed against all expectations set for her and followed her heart. But she was the exception, not the rule. If everyone followed their heart, the world would implode, surely?

Alicia looked back towards the sea. Hannah was making her way towards them now, having just shouted something that sounded like that's a wrap, or a phrase equally as clichéd. Her hair was bouncy and voluptuous, the perfect beach wave. Her body was Bond-girl-esque, deep golden brown skin shimmering in the sun. It was laughable that she was the face and owner of an 'inclusive' brand when she herself looked like she'd stepped out of the pages of *Sports Illustrated*. Alicia was glad that Hugh wasn't here; the thought of him seeing Hannah looking so smoking hot made her stomach roil. How could any man who'd ever rejected her look at her now and think anything other than *shit, I made a huge mistake*.

'We were just saying, can you imagine what our eighteen-year-old selves would think if they saw us now? Madness.' Marnie said as she passed Hannah her drink.

'Is it? I always knew I'd do something like this,' Hannah said, as she sipped with one hand and twirled the mini umbrella with the other.

'Really?' How could someone be so confident?

'Yes, really.'

'So there's never been a time where you wavered?' Alicia needed to hear that it hadn't all been rainbows and sunshine. Some jot of humility or vulnerability.

'Nope.' Hannah shrugged, while looking directly at Alicia.

Bull. Alicia had seen how Hannah was in the years after university, flailing around, lonely and directionless. It wasn't worth saying aloud because she didn't want to ruin the trip, but why did Hannah feel the need to pretend everything was always so perfect?

Hannah waved her drink at them. 'Scooch over, I need a sit-down.'

'Yes, your highness.' Marnie grinned, shuffling over and patting the bed between her and Alicia.

Hannah joined them, sitting so close to Alicia that her warm sticky skin touched her thigh. She smelt like coconut.

The three of them lay side by side. The sound of waves

and the distant beat of music hummed in the air, rhythmic and lulling but Alicia's muscles were tense.

Hannah slurped the last of her drink obnoxiously and leaned over Alicia to balance her empty glass on the sand. 'Don't take this the wrong way, but I'm surprised you both made it,' she said, settling herself back into her horizontal position.

'How so?' Marnie asked.

'Sophie, for one.'

'And me?' Alicia shifted up onto her elbows.

'I know you can be very anxious,' said Hannah, without sitting up. 'I wasn't sure if flying long haul to a country you've never been to before would be too far out of your comfort zone. I know you struggle with change.'

'What gives you that impression?' Alicia meant it as a joke but it came out more deadpan than she'd hoped.

'Well, the biggest giveaway is that you've still got the same email address you had when you were fourteen.'

'AliciaMurphy1994@hotmail.com,' she said. 'Timeless and sensible. Unlike someone.'

'Bbygrlmarns69@yahoo.co.uk? Dunno what you're on about. Nothing wrong with that. Shows my personality.' Marnie chuckled. She sat up now and prodded Hannah gently in the hip. 'You're looking very in shape. I mean, you've always looked in shape, but even more so now. You're not on Ozempic, are you? Loads of the women at work are on it, and one of the blokes. It's all they talk about.'

'Nope, and I'm really not that in shape! I've got a lil belly.' Hannah patted her flat stomach. 'I've debated it, but I don't want to risk losing my tits or arse. Important assets for the business.'

Alicia had always envied Hannah's figure. There was

251

nothing wrong with hers; she took care of herself with fairly healthy eating, although she didn't have time to go to the gym every week, let alone every day like Hannah did. But she wasn't curvy in the slightest. It had never bothered her until someone had asked Hugh at her last birthday meal if he was a tits or arse man, and he (drunkenly) replied 'both', which would have been reassuring had Alicia had either. She didn't have enough cake to fill a plate let alone a bakery and she'd always felt a bit hard done by with her paltry A cups.

'You don't need it! There's nothing of you.' Marnie prodded Hannah's hips again and she squealed. 'Also, I'm not sure only people with big tits and arses need swimwear, either. I thought you were a feminist.'

'I am. I am,' Hannah said, finally shifting to sit up alongside them. 'I take it back. In fact, we're looking at bringing out more sizes next season. We want Nala Swim to be as inclusive as possible.'

'Perfect. Knew you had it all covered.' Marnie stuck her tongue out playfully.

Hannah grinned and then looked towards the sea with a frown, where her team were waving and beckoning her over. 'Ah shit, looks like they want to talk to me about something. Back in a sec.' She slid her body from the bed, her perfect arse just inches from Alicia's face – flawless, without a single blemish in sight.

Alicia leaned back and tried to breathe away the tension in her chest, inhaling for seven seconds and out for eleven. The scent of Hannah's coconut oil lingered, mingling with the saltiness of the sea and sand. *This is lovely, just relax* . . .

The ping of an iPhone drew Alicia from her attempt at

mindfulness. She sat herself up, glancing down at the space where Hannah had just been. Her eyes took a second to work out what she was seeing.

Hugh: Do you think she's cottoned on? I can't wait to see . . .

What the . . . Alicia's heart hammered as she read it again and again, as if doing so would change what was there on the screen, in black and white.

'Oh my God,' she whispered, swallowing the sick that was rising in her throat. 'Bitch. I fucking knew it.'

Marnie sat up. 'What?' she frowned, looking between Alicia and the phone.

'It's Hugh. Hannah's texting Hugh. Look!' Alicia grabbed the phone and thrust it towards Marnie.

Marnie's hands shot into the air as if touching the phone would scald her. 'How do you know it's your Hugh?' she said. 'And even if it was, you can't see the rest of the message.'

Why was she so blind to it? Alicia couldn't be the only one who saw how Hugh and Hannah interacted, their lingering looks and drunken hands. She wasn't going crazy. It wasn't all in her head. 'Do you know her password?'

'No!' Marnie said, alarm palpable in her voice. 'And even if I did, I wouldn't look at her phone without her consent.'

'You're really defending her?' Alicia's whole body was vibrating now, her heart fluttering and legs quivering.

'Don't be silly.'

'I'm sick of people telling me I'm silly. It's there in black and white, how can you take her side? He's my husband.' There it was again, the dizzying wave of nausea that lurched from Alicia's stomach into her throat. How could Hannah just be standing there on the beach, laughing and joking with the model as if nothing was going on?

The bitch. She's not going to get away with this. Not this time.

Alicia squeezed the phone in her clenched fist as she leapt up from the bed and stomped across the sand towards Hannah, barely registering the heat that tickled her bare soles. She didn't know what she'd do when she reached her, but right now the only thing that mattered was to make her pay.

Chapter Twenty-Three

13th February, 2022

Marnie

Shit. This was bad.

'Alicia, wait!' Marnie threw off her beach towel and scrabbled after Alicia. She needed to do something to stop this escalating, but what? Alicia was already mere metres from Hannah, who was now striding, hands on hips, towards her.

Marnie caught up with them, breathless and legs shaking with adrenaline. 'I'm sure it's not what it looks like,' she panted. *God, that sounds unconvincing. But it must be true. Alicia must have got it all wrong.*

'What's not?' Hannah stared blankly.

'You're texting Hugh! I knew it. I knew he was going off me! Of course he'd choose you over me! Who wouldn't?' Alicia turned and started pacing, three steps away, three steps back like a caged zoo animal. 'You're fucking, aren't you? Don't you dare try and deny it. God, I'm so stupid.'

Hannah's mouth dropped open. 'Are you joking? Is that really what you think of me? That I'd sleep with your husband behind your back?' She shook her head slowly, her face now contorted in horror.

'Hardly that ridiculous given the circumstances.' Alicia had lowered her voice, but now it trembled. In fact, Marnie noticed that her whole body was shaking – the hand that gripped the phone, the fingers that pinched the bridge of her nose.

'What circumstances? You're being crazy.'

'You already have everything. The job. The figure. The confidence. Why can't you just leave me the one thing I have that you don't? What are you trying to prove?'

'Where are you getting this from? Are you having a psychotic break or something.' Hannah glanced at Marnie who shook her head and shrugged.

'I saw the text! He *can't wait to see you. Do you think poor Alicia has cottoned on?*' Alicia's eyes were manic as she mimicked the message in a high-pitched voice.

Hannah's eyes darted towards the phone in Alicia's hand. 'Give me my phone back.' She lurched to snatch it at the same time Alicia thrust it at her. Hannah looked at the screen, tapped and scrolled for a second. 'That's not what it says.' She rolled her eyes and her expression hardened.

Alicia snapped her fingers and held her hand out. 'Prove it. Show me your conversation.'

'No,' Hannah said firmly.

'Why don't you just show her the conversation and we can all calm the fuck down.' Marnie tried her best to keep her voice level. *Breathe. Stay calm. Say the right thing and this can all be salvageable.*

Hannah scowled, now directing her furious gaze to Marnie. 'Why should I?'

Why wouldn't Hannah just show her the bloody messages?

Unless . . . Oh God, had Marnie got this all wrong? 'Why not?'

'I shouldn't have to prove myself to either of you. You should just believe me. It's out of principle.'

'That's fair enough, but clearly Alicia needs some more reassurance right now.' Perhaps channelling counsellor Joan would have more success, though Joan's voice would never betray her with the undertones of desperation that now tinged Marnie's.

'Only someone who's guilty wouldn't prove their innocence.' Alicia spat the words as if they were poison.

Hannah shook her head and her eyes rolled again. 'Are you fucking kidding me? The only thing I'm guilty of is arranging for Hugh to come here,' she said. 'It was meant to be a surprise for your honeymoon. I know you were devastated when Covid cancelled it.' Hannah clenched her jaw. 'But obviously, I'm just a cheating bitch.'

There was a beat of silence as both Marnie and Alicia processed what she'd just said. Of course, a grand gesture like that was far more in Hannah's nature than sleeping with her best friend's husband.

God, I'm a horrendous friend to have suspected her, even if it was only for a second.

Marnie looked between Alicia and Hannah. Would Alicia take what Hannah was handing to her or throw it back? Her eyes flickered. Remorse? Guilt?

'I don't believe you! You're just saying that because you've been caught. Just show me the messages.' Alicia's voice was less charged now, but clearly she wasn't going to let it go. Marnie had never thought of her as stubborn, but this whole escapade was totally out of character. Maybe she *was* having a breakdown of some sort?

'Are you joking?' Hannah threw her hands in the air and turned back towards the beach bed. 'I'm not doing this. Come back to me when you've calmed down.'

'Don't walk away from me!' Alicia stormed after her, slipping clumsily in the sand as it morphed from damp and firm to powdery and uneven. 'Where is he, then?' she shouted.

Marnie joined them too, kicking off her flip-flops to keep up.

Hannah stopped again and span. She tapped her foot, up, down, up, down. 'He's not here yet. He's on the plane.'

'On the plane? No, he's at a golf retreat in the New Forest. He—'

Alicia was interrupted by the shrill ring of the phone in Hannah's hand.

Hannah swiped and held the phone to her ear. 'Hello. Okay. Cool. Two secs.' She pushed the phone towards Alicia. 'It's your husband,' she said. 'He's just landed.'

Alicia and Hannah
18th February, 2022

Alicia: Han, I know you don't want to talk to me right now and I understand that. I'm not expecting you to reply and I'll leave you alone after this but I need to say it for my own peace of mind. I am SO sorry. I know just saying the word isn't enough but please know I mean it with every fibre of my being. I was in a bad place – not an excuse I know. My anxiety was really bad and I just got it into my head that you and Hugh . . . which is ridiculous. You'd never do that to me, and nor would he. But you're so beautiful and confident and successful and I'm none of those things and I couldn't let it go. I'm in therapy now.

Hannah: I've been thinking about it a lot and I need to put me first for a change. It's important I have boundaries and I need to protect my energy rn. I need space so please don't message me.

Marnie and Hannah
1st February, 2023

Marnie: Change of plan this year. I've got a deal on a caravan at a place called Sandy Balls – yes really. It's half term so Alicia and I have booked two nights, the Sunday and the Monday. You're invited to both nights, obviously. Check-in at 3pm. Will send further details closer to the time. Would be lovely to see you, we've probs got so much to catch up on. I know it's been weird this last year but it wouldn't be the same without you. X PS There is a hot tub. **Hannah:** Deffo can't do the Sunday night. Will let you know about Monday x

Chapter Twenty-Four

13th February, 2023

Marnie

Marnie and Alicia were into the second day of their stay and the sun was setting as they sipped prosecco in the fiercely bubbling hot tub. Yesterday, they'd arrived at 4pm, Marnie loaded with snacks and drinks, Alicia with the essentials like bread, milk, teabags and spare bog roll. The hope was to also have a nightcap in the hot tub; however, they had massively underestimated the palaver of having to heat it up themselves (it was a log-fired, fancy Swiss one). They'd spent close to four hours zipping in and out to check on it, peering into the fire chamber, chucking in logs and using almost an entire packet of firelighters in their desperate plight to keep it alight. Marnie had to give it to arsonists – they must be a committed set of folks despite their flaws.

In the end they gave up and settled in for the night in front Netflix's *Squid Games* vowing to email reception and ask for help first thing in the morning. Lovely Alexus turned up at 11am, lighting it for them and letting them know that the tub would be ready to use after about three-thirty.

Thankfully, Alexus was right, and at 3:30pm on the dot, they slid themselves into the hot clutches of the bubbling water and hadn't moved, apart from quick trips to go for a wee or fill up their glasses.

Despite the hot tub drama, the caravan was a good idea – Marnie would pat herself on the back for booking it. She needed a break from life, for a start. Life really was fine and the therapy was helping a hell of a lot – a fifty-minute pause every fortnight in a life that was as hectic as always.

After the loneliness of Covid, life had gone speedily back to manic. It was a constant juggle to keep all the plates spinning – the school run, Sophie's gymnastics, drama club, parent's evenings, school plays, life admin, work, Marnie's own social life which was busier now with her job at the school. She'd become especially close to three of the women at work, Paola, Lucy and Millie, and it was a godsend that she finally had local friends who were around for a quick coffee or a walk in the snapshots of time she wasn't running around in Mum Mode.

It was also a good shout to have Galentine's on neutral ground after the whole Bali Incident. Saying that, it was looking more and more like Hannah was going to be a no-show.

Marnie had only seen her a couple of times this past year, once for a speedy Costa when she was in London for some training, and the other time when Hannah needed someone to try on some of the larger sizes in her new plus-size range (in what world was a size 14–16 plus size?). Hannah and Alicia had not seen each other at all. Despite Alicia's attempts to apologise, Hannah was having none of it.

Marnie lay back, resting her neck on the edge of the tub and staring at the tree towering above them, its silhouette standing proudly against the setting sun. 'How are you feeling about seeing Han?' she asked Alicia, who was doing the same, floating opposite her.

'Anxious,' Alicia replied. No surprise there.

'She might not even turn up,' Marnie offered.

'That's what's making it worse. At least if I knew, I could prepare for it.'

'True.'

'I bet she's enjoying the fact that I'm sitting here worrying about it. She could have just said either way. But you know, *boundaries* and all that.' Alicia leaned over the edge to swap her empty glass for the bowl of Doritos resting on the step.

'Yeah? Maybe.' Marnie didn't want to say too much. The whole boundaries thing felt partly fair – Alicia had been totally out of order – and partly like a bullshit excuse for Hannah to distance herself from the group now she had better things to do. Hannah and Alicia had never been on the same wavelength, and Marnie was well aware that the only reason they were ever friends in the first place was because Alicia and Marnie came as a package deal.

'How are you and Hugh doing now?'

'Better. Way better than before.' Alicia offered the bowl to Marnie and she grabbed a handful, despite having wet hands.

Marnie threw the crisps into her mouth and nodded thoughtfully. 'It's a hard thing to come back from. Sounds like you're getting there, especially with the help of the therapist. I'm so pleased for you.' She could only trust that Alicia was telling her the truth this time around.

'Yeah.' Alicia sank a little deeper into the bubbles, her arms resting on the rim. She stared at the water, somewhere else in her mind. Then her eyes flicked up and she smiled, like she'd tossed the thought away and let it pop along with the fizzing bubbles. 'Speaking of, how's your therapy going?'

'Well! I'm still seeing lovely Joan, although we've transitioned to fortnightly sessions now as I'm feeling much sturdier in myself and need to balance the books with Sophie starting ballet and swimming.'

'Are you still on your man ban?'

'Yep! It's been almost eighteen months now. Didn't think I had it in me.'

'I'm proud of you. How have you managed it?'

'A mix of being busy and owning a very good Rampant Rabbit. I'll never need a man again.'

Alicia giggled, and her eyes locked on Marnie, her gaze both gentle and intense at the same time. 'Don't do yourself a disservice. You've done a hell of a lot of work on yourself over the past couple of years.'

'I'm blushing.' It was as close to accepting a compliment as Marnie would get. She still needed to work on feeling proud of herself and *owning it*, in Joan's words. However, she could acknowledge that what Alicia said was true in many ways. She'd worked through an awful lot, to the point where it felt like she'd totally undone herself, stripping everything back to its wobbly foundations. She'd grieved the life she thought she'd have, accepted and fell in love with the life she had and little by little started building herself back up. She started prioritising her own needs in small, doable ways, such as starting swimming two times a week when Sophie was at after-school club, and signing up to the Sustainability Society in the village hall where she would volunteer one Saturday morning a month. There was even talk of starting an evening class next September – either climate change or gender studies, she wasn't sure yet. Marnie didn't have it all like Hannah, but she was in a good place.

She closed her eyes and listened to the chirp of the crickets coming from the bushes and long grass behind them.

The sound of a car pulling up next to the caravan pulled Marnie from her peaceful moment of reflection.

Alicia sat up quickly, eyes widening. There was only one person that could be.

'Oh my God,' she said. 'She's here.'

Chapter Twenty-Five

13th February, 2023

Alicia

'What do I do?' Alicia said, panic obvious in her voice.

'What do you mean, *what do you do?* Act normal.'

'Shall I get out?'

There was a knock at the door.

'No, you stay here.' Marnie climbed out of the hot tub and hurriedly wrapped herself in a towel. 'I'll be back, don't do a runner.'

'I won't,' replied Alicia, eyeing up the height of the garden fence.

Her heart was pounding. The last time she'd seen Hannah she'd . . . Alicia couldn't even bring herself to remember the exact words she'd said to her. How would she act? Would she pretend everything was fine and dandy, or would she want to talk about it? Which was worse? Would she only talk to Marnie and totally blank Alicia? Did she only turn up because she wanted to make a scene or did she actually want to be here and make their friendship work? Did she—

'Hi.' Hannah appeared at the back door, followed closely

266

by Marnie. She met Alicia's eyes and smiled tentatively. 'Long time no see.' She pulled at the sleeve of her skintight top.

'Hi.' Alicia wanted to say something a bit more interesting but words failed her.

'I'm getting back in, it's fucking freezing.' Marnie threw off her towel and climbed back in beside Alicia.

'I'll join you. Let me get into my bikini.'

'Nala Swim, I hope.' Marnie grinned.

'I wouldn't wear the competition! Who do you think I am?' Hannah turned and went back inside.

'She seems okay,' Alicia whispered. 'Did she say anything about me when you answered the door?'

'No. Hoping we can just put this all behind us. Be back to us three again.'

'Mmm, yeah.' It would be the easiest thing. Maybe her and Hannah's friendship was beyond repair, but it was worth at least pretending for Marnie's sake. It must be horrible to be in the middle of all this.

A few minutes later, Hannah appeared again at the edge of the hot tub, hair now tied back into an effortless messy bun. 'Oh my God, it's arctic out here!' She tugged the towel around her. 'It better be super hot in there.'

'It's lush.' Marnie said. 'Now get it off!'

Hannah threw off her towel. 'Okay. I'm coming in.'

She looked amazing, as always. Alicia hated how she still felt a twist in her stomach as she took in her figure and she was even more tanned and glowing than usual.

'You've been on holiday.' Marnie noticed also. 'Where to this time?'

'Croatia. Arrived home late last night.'

So that's why she couldn't join them yesterday. Why didn't she just say that?

'Wow, and you still made it.'

Thank God for Marnie doing all the talking. It wasn't that Alicia didn't want to say anything – she *couldn't* say anything.

'I didn't want to say I'd be here and then not be able to make it due to a delayed flight or jet lag.'

Perhaps Alicia was being harsh thinking that Hannah had just been playing hard to get.

They sat in silence, the only sound being the fierce bubbling of the hot tub jets and the gentle tweets of the birds at dusk. Alicia really needed to say something. She took a deep breath.

'How are—'

'You okay—'

Both Alicia and Hannah spoke at once. They laughed nervously.

'You go,' Alicia offered.

'I was just going to ask how you both are.' Hannah smiled tentatively, glancing quickly at Alicia then eyes settling on Marnie.

'Same old for me. Sophie's started all sorts of after-school classes and she's getting on well in Year Three.'

'Can't believe she's that old already, you'll be thinking about secondary schools soon.'

'Don't.' Marnie raised her eyebrows as if trying to comprehend the madness of it all. 'I know.'

How many times had Marnie and Hannah met up without Alicia this year? Alicia hadn't asked. It seemed inevitable that when they did, Alicia and Hugh would have been a topic of conversation. She'd prefer not to know, although judging by this conversation, it sounded like it had been a while since they'd last caught up properly.

'How about you?' Marnie asked before Alicia had found the nerve to speak again.

'Yeah, same old for me too.'

'Bollocks. Tell us what you've really been up to. Croatia, for a start!' Marnie twisted to lean herself over the edge of the hot tub, dangerously close to toppling. 'Almost went arse over tit then!' she cackled. 'Drink?'

'Go on, then. Went to Croatia for a photoshoot for the new plus-size range. And before that it was Amsterdam for a few collabs.'

'I saw on Insta you'd collabed with Siren & Soleil. Mad!'

'Oh yeah.' Hannah took the glass that Marnie held to her and sipped. 'That was fun.'

'Looked good.' Is that all Alicia could think to say? *Looked good.*

More silence.

'How are you, Alicia?' Hannah was finally looking at her properly, eyes no longer flicking to Marnie or to the water. Still, she held the glass of bubbly to her lips as if to hide behind it.

'I'm okay. Things are actually pretty good.' Alicia mumbled, almost guilty to admit it. Things had really not been good this time last year following the Galentine's fallout.

Hugh had barely spoken to her for the three days in Bali after her moment of madness, and nor had Hannah. Marnie had split her time between them, helping Hannah out with the shoots and checking in on Alicia and Hugh, trying her best to play peacekeeper. The entire flight home was just as torturous. Marnie had insisted she swap seats with Hugh so Alicia and Hugh could 'work it out'. However, they were hardly going to argue so publicly in front of everyone on the plane, so the whole flight was spent in painful silence, with a million and one different things Alicia wanted to say going round and round in her head, driving her to the brink of insanity. How Hugh had managed to sleep was beyond her, and it made her all the more infuriated.

When they'd got home, Alicia was ready to explode. However, due to lack of sleep and the mad amounts of anxiety coursing through her body, the only thing she could do was burst into hysterical tears, and so Hugh put her to bed swiftly. He didn't join her, citing jet lag, but when she came downstairs at 11pm for a glass of water, he was fast asleep on the couch.

So began a long few weeks of jolting from argument to passive-aggressive silences, as back and forth as a Wimbledon match ball. Their attempts to talk it out always ended in shouting, with Hugh unable to see Alicia's point of view, and Alicia being told that she was being completely delusional. Maybe she was, but she needed something from Hugh she knew he couldn't give her.

Thankfully, with the help of a therapist (Alicia's idea), things got better, slowly and steadily. Perhaps they weren't back to how they were before, but Alicia truly felt that what hadn't killed them, made them stronger. They were more able to communicate their feelings with each other, sharing their vulnerabilities and worries, catching them before they spiralled out of control. They were having fun, trying new things like a date night every month and more weekends away. They'd found each other again.

'That's good.' Hannah nodded thoughtfully. 'I'm so pleased to hear that.'

'Yeah.' The knot in Alicia's stomach loosened. It seemed Hannah, for once in her life, wasn't going to acknowledge the elephant in the room.

'I'm starving. Is anyone else starving?' Marnie's timing was borderline comical, but Alicia appreciated the fact that she brought a semi-normality back into their threesome.

'I could always eat.' Hannah shrugged, also seeming to relax more, tipping her head back and kicking her feet up, shiny red polished toenails peeking above the water.

'Shall I put the pizzas on?' Marnie propelled herself forward towards the steps.

'I'll do it,' Alicia offered, also making a move to stand. The thought of being stuck in the hot tub just her and Hannah brought the tension in her stomach back in full force.

'No, stay. I need to call Soph to say goodnight anyway.'

'Okay,' Alicia said in her most calm and casual voice, despite now being able to hear her heartbeat in her ears. What would they talk about when Marnie wasn't there to break the ice?

Both Hannah and Alicia watched Marnie heave herself out of the hot tub, narrowly missing knocking the empty glass off the side. She chuckled. 'Oops. Be back in a min.'

And then she was gone.

271

Chapter Twenty-Six

13th February, 2023

Hannah

God, this was painful. Not that Hannah had expected anything else.

Of course, Hannah was curious as to the fallout of #BaliGate, in particular how things between Hugh and Alicia had been. She'd tried to do some gentle foraging for information via Marnie, but Marnie was cagey and so Hannah had retreated. Even between the two of them, things felt awkward. They'd seen each other twice, maybe three times this year. Her schedule had been fit to burst, so fitting in anything other than collab meetings, on-location shoots and brand events was near-on impossible.

It wasn't just Marnie that Hannah had to sideline. The girls from uni were also on a strict once or twice a year schedule – she saw them all in one go at Lara's wedding last June and needed to book in a Saturday morning sometime in the next month to meet Nikita's new baby. Shit, she had meant to reply to their group chat in the Uber on the way here.

In all the madness of life, some of Hannah's 'friends' had fallen by the wayside. When she'd moved out of her houseshare in Hackney, she wasn't expecting to see Barney or Hamish again, but it had been a surprise that Lola hadn't reached out at all. But Hannah was over that now – she had moved on to bigger and better things.

Well, mostly better. It was both a blessing and a curse to be surrounded by so many people like her. Influencers. Other women who understood Hannah's love for fashion, business ownership, and the need to carry around a tripod in her bag. People Who Got It. But the flipside was that Hannah didn't always know whether someone wanted to be her friend because they liked her or because it would further their career. Some of the girls she met were downright bitches, and they were the sort of people who'd sell their first-born for a brand deal before letting anyone else get there first.

'Marnie tells me you're an auntie now. I mean officially, by blood. You've always been an auntie to Soph.' Alicia followed up her words with a cough.

Hannah wondered what else Marnie had told Alicia. Not that there was anything that Hannah wouldn't want her knowing; if anything it felt good to know that they were talking about her.

'Yep. Gaia's four months now. Or maybe five?' Emannuel and Lucy had fallen victim to the next step in the Plan of Being an Adult: to have children. They'd gotten married eighteen months ago, a beautiful, big, ostentatious affair at a country house in Hampshire. They'd spent over thirty-five grand, which Hannah thought totally mad; even with her comfortable earnings she wouldn't be caught dead spending so much on just one day. Not even Elysian Beauty had spent that much on their launch party.

Alicia cleared her throat again. 'How are they finding it?'

'Alright? I haven't spoken to either of them much.' Again, it was one of those things that was on Hannah's to-do list. She'd met Gaia when she was a month old, and since then, she'd only been updated via photos in the group chat. Usually, the only thing she had time to do was react with a love heart emoji, which seemed insufficient but better than nothing.

'How's the rest of the family?'

'Mum and Dad are well.' She'd bought them an all-inclusive trip to Barbados for Christmas. Mum had been very grateful but almost refused to accept it, until Hannah had insisted. 'I've not seen them for a few months, but we talk on the phone often.' Mum was the one person who hadn't let Hannah off the hook with the excuse that she was busy. She'd call at least once a week to check in, making sure she was eating well, not taking drugs and didn't forget where she came from. She also told her frequently how proud she was, and how proud her grandparents would have been of her too. That felt good. Finally, she was not a failure in the eyes of her family, and she'd even go as far as to say she was outpacing Golden Boy Emmanuel – not that it was a competition. If it was, though, she'd win. Hannah went to take a sip of her prosecco but realised it was already empty. 'How's work?'

'Better?' Alicia frowned.

She didn't sound sure but Hannah wouldn't probe. 'Good.'

More silence. Hannah balanced her glass on the step, keen to do something, anything, that distracted from the heavy air between them. When she turned back, Alicia was looking at her, eyes watery yet focused.

She let out a big sigh. 'I really am sorry about last year. I don't want to stir the pot by bringing it up, but I've honestly felt like the absolute worst person for doing what I did. Please, I beg you, forgive me?' Alicia's gaze didn't leave Hannah – she didn't even seem to blink.

Hannah was taken aback, but then she glanced at Alicia's glass, which was now totally empty. *How much has she drunk?* 'Err . . . It's fine.'

Alicia shook her head and dropped her hands into the water, splashing them both with a spray of water. 'It's not fine. I know that things aren't going to go back to how they were, but I need you to know again that I'm so incredibly sorry.'

Hannah held her hands flat on the surface of the water, caressing the soft foam with her palms. 'Thank you. I appreciate it.' She wasn't going to make a scene. She didn't have to be here, she chose to come after all. She could have just gone home, using her flight back from Croatia as an excuse. But there was a reason Hannah had come to this perfectly fine but pretty bog-standard caravan park with a very strange name. *Sandy Balls, really?* Yes, things had been rocky this past year between her, Marnie and Alicia, and she still struggled to forgive Alicia for what she did, but at least in the two of them Hannah had authentic, loyal, proper friends. They'd been there for her when she was using bodywash as shampoo and eating pot noodles for dinner, way before being friends with her came with the perks of having your meal paid for or a free digital shoutout to gain online exposure. This past year had shown her the difference, and shown her that their friendship was worth saving.

The back door flew open, drawing their attention, and thankfully sparing Hannah another second in the overly sentimental, almost uncomfortable vulnerability she teetered on.

'Ten-minute call for pizza! Wooooooo!' Marnie hollered. She was wearing her pyjamas and her hair was wrapped in a towel. God, Hannah had missed her.

'Yum.' Alicia started wading towards the hot tub steps. 'We better get out and into our PJs.'

'Ahh, I don't have a set to match.' All Hannah had was whatever was left in her suitcase from Croatia – no pyjamas in sight, especially since she was a nude sleeper these days.

'You do. Marnie and I got three pairs, just in case. Size eight for you, yeah?' Alicia offered her a tentative smile before she heaved herself out of the tub with a groan.

Hannah's heart warmed. 'Yeah, perfect.'

I made the right choice coming. She'd take the friendship with Alicia one day at a time. She wasn't expecting things to go back to how they were before, but it was nice to know that things could still move forward. This wasn't yet the end of their story.

Hot Mess Express 🚂 😆

5th September, 2023

Hannah: Happy Birthday!!! So sorry I couldn't come to your bday meal Ali xxx

Marnie: Me too :(Sophie's now feeling a bit better but now we've been struck by the sickness bug! Shit and sick everywhere x

Alicia: No worries, I know how life can be. Hope you feel better soon, sounds horrendous! Sorry I've been MIA recently. Work continues to be hell. Are either of you doing anything for Xmas this year?

Hannah: Guy is taking me to New York. Sort of a working holiday.

Marnie: Guy?

Hannah: Model. Been seeing each other for 6 weeks.

Alicia: Is he the one in your posts?

Hannah: Yeah. Soft-launching the relationship lol

Marnie: He's fit. I hope he's also nice.

Hannah: He is. Very low-maintenance. Doesn't need too much attention which is good because I don't have time to be texting someone all the time.

Marnie: Just spending all my money on crap that Sophie will use once and living in my overdraft for the foreseeable lol. JK, Christmas is always nice with kids, feels more magical (and expensive).

Alicia: We're going to Hugh's parents. Hope I won't miss anything when we're away.

Marnie: I don't think anyone will go to The Red Lion this year for Christmas anyway. Numbers were thin on the ground last year and no one seems that arsed anymore.

Hannah: I thought the school chat had been a bit quiet!

Marnie: Galentine's still happening though!

Hannah: Always!

Alicia: Of course x

Making Waves:
The Swimwear Brand Everyone's Talking About

By JoJo Mcain

I meet Hannah at Sushi Samba in Covent Garden, one of her frequent haunts. She's the perfect picture of a modern businesswoman and influencer extraordinaire, dressed in a scarlet-red blazer and black leather trousers. Her glossy hair is waved to perfection and her signature smile lights up the room.

You've probably come across her online – and if you haven't, where have you been? Known to her many followers as ThatLondonGirlHan, the Hertfordshire native has carved out a niche that balances aspirational luxury with relatable girl-next-door charm. But behind the curated feeds and polished campaigns is a story of grit, ambition and a drive to break the mould.

Pushing against the boundaries often set for her – and overcoming the generational trauma familiar to many second-generation immigrants – Hannah has forged her own path. She's silenced her doubters and turned her passion into profit by launching Nala Swim, an inclusive, eco-friendly swimwear brand that has already found its way into the wardrobes of celebrities and influencers alike.

Over spicy tuna rolls and iced matcha (her favourite), Hannah opens up about business, family and the legacy she's building.

Have you always wanted to be a business owner?
"Honestly, no! After uni, I applied for countless apprenticeships and jobs in the fashion and creative industries, but nothing

worked out. I felt stuck for a long time, jumping from one temp job to another, but throughout it all, social media was a constant for me. I started creating content in my teens and over time realised I had the creativity and drive to build something of my own. It was scary but exciting. It took a while to find my place, but I did – and I've never looked back."

Who are your biggest cheerleaders?
"My close friends (you know who you are!). They've seen the highs and lows, and they've been there for me every step of the way. Even though I'm so busy and don't have as much free time as I used to, we still meet every year on Galentine's Day and I hope they feel I'm a cheerleader for them as much as they are for me. And of course, my followers need a shout out. They've grown with me and they're the best hype squad a girl could have."

What does your family think?
"At first, my parents were sceptical, especially my mum. But seeing me happy and thriving has changed their minds. Now they're so proud – my mum shows my Instagram to literally everyone she meets!"

How has being a second-generation Ugandan Asian impacted your view on the world/life?
"It's made me resilient. Our grandparents came here and sacrificed so much to give us better opportunities, and I carry that with me every day. It can feel quite heavy sometimes, but it's a constant reminder that I can't waste what they gave me. It pushes me to keep going, even when it's hard. I hope I have done them proud!"

Do you have any tips for others who want to follow a similar path?

"Don't follow a safely trodden path just because you feel you 'should' – you can do the hard thing! Life is too short to live a boring life, so follow your heart, work hard and achieve your dreams. Also, ignore the haters, they're often just jealous. I believe in you!"

What's next for ThatLondonGirlHan and Nala Swim?

"So much! We're expanding the size range even further because inclusivity has to be more than just a buzzword. I'm also working on more big collaborations and hopefully branching into beachwear and resort collections."

As the afternoon sun dips behind the Covent Garden rooftops, it's clear Hannah is just getting started. With her vision, hustle, amazing support network and unapologetic authenticity, ThatLondonGirlHan is a name – and a brand – we'll be seeing for a long time to come.

Chapter Twenty-Seven

13th February, 2024

Marnie

'It's a bit expensive,' Marnie said, spotting the price tag on the bottle of cleanser Sophie was clutching in her hand. *I'm not going to spend twenty quid on something with such a ridiculous name as Drunk Elephant for my nine-year-old daughter.*

'But Mum! This is the one that everyone's got.'

'Who's everyone?'

'Everyone on TikTok.'

God, it was still hard work being a parent. It was true what they said about each stage of parenting having its own challenges. The newborn stage with its sleep deprivation, brain fog and colic – fucking colic. The terrible twos and the horrendous tantrums. The early primary school years and Sophie's struggles to make friends. Now, on the cusp of being a tween, she had plenty of friends (which came with its own dramas) and she also now had her own phone. It didn't have any data but connected to wifi so she could talk to her pals on Snapchat while at home, as well as scroll endlessly on bloody TikTok. Marnie did her best to limit time spent on the phone, and it was good leverage when it came to behaviour management; however, the thought of Sophie being online at such a young age still made her feel uneasy.

This new obsession with skincare was rather annoying (and expensive); however, the most worrying thing of all was Sophie's comments on gaining weight and being 'fat'. It was a hard time to grow up in, and Marnie was forever grateful that she'd grown up in a relatively prehistoric age of technology, so her awkward teen years weren't forever preserved for all to see. However, the social isolation and vilification of *not* being online also had their impacts. Often, she had Andrea to turn to when she needed parenting advice, but with Andrea being that much older, her kids grew up in an entirely different generation, so Marnie just had to wing it and came to the conclusion that it was a damned if you do, damned if you don't kind of thing – a predicament that pretty much summed up Marnie's entire experience of parenting.

'Please, Mum, you said you'd get me something.' Sophie widened her eyes and stuck out her bottom lip. It wouldn't work on Marnie but she knew who would fall for it.

'Go on, then.' Daniel shook his head and grinned at her. 'I'll treat you for being so helpful sorting the loft out at my mum and dad's.'

Sophie threw her arms around him and squealed. 'Thank youuuuuuu.'

'You're very welcome. But that's it now. Okay?'

'Okay, I promise.'

'Right, let's pay for this and then head to Nando's. I don't know about you two but I'm starving.' Daniel patted his stomach.

'I just heard it rumble!' Sophie laughed. 'It sounded like a whale.'

'It did, didn't it!' Daniel turned to Marnie. 'Sure you don't want or need anything?'

'I'm good, thanks.' She smiled at him. 'I'm good with my Simple face wipes and Revlon ColourStay.'

'I have no idea what any of that means, but I'll take your word for it,' he said, as he followed Sophie to the tills.

Marnie watched them laughing and smiling together as if they'd been a part of each other's lives for much longer than just three months and her chest warmed with pride. She knew he wasn't Sophie's dad and she'd never force that, but it was lovely to see how their bond had grown slowly and steadily since she'd first introduced them.

Marnie had waited before allowing him to meet her, insisting things started slow – by her standards, anyway. And the initial tentative start had already started picking up momentum, like a snowball rolling down a hill. They were already discussing moving in together. It felt right and exciting, but after all of the work she'd done in therapy, she was hyperaware of every choice she made, trying to step back and check her motives, patterns and blind spots. Was she rushing into things again because she craved stability, or was he a worthy candidate? Was she so desperate to be loved she was blind to any potential red flags? She didn't want to become so wary of life that she stopped living it, but where was the line? It was great to be so self-aware, but also exhausting.

Daniel was the first date she'd had after unofficially lifting her man ban. Unofficially because, after discussing it in therapy, she was in no rush to redownload all of the dating apps and had the mentality of *if it happens, it happens*.

And it happened. She'd turned up to her college evening class late, looking a right mess, hair in a scruffy unwashed bun and dressed in leggings and a sweatshirt. On a coffee break, she'd headed to the canteen to grab herself a much-needed espresso from the machine and there he was. He was just about to head off, coffee in hand, when he saw her approaching.

'Ah, shit. Are you wanting a coffee?'

'Yeah . . . why?' Marnie had asked suspiciously.

'It's just run out.'

'Run out?'

'Says it needs re-filling. I'll go and find someone.'

Marnie looked at the clock. She only had three minutes until class started back up and she couldn't be late back again. 'It's fine, I'll manage. Thanks.' She went to turn away but he spoke.

'Here,' he said, thrusting his paper cup towards her. 'Have mine. I've not drunk from it yet.'

'That's kind, but I won't deprive you.'

'I insist.' He continued to hold it towards her, face kind and genuine. She hadn't thought much of him initially, but now she was properly looking at him she noticed how understatedly handsome he was, someone you could miss if you hadn't properly slowed down and taken in his features. His eyes sparkled with a cheeky glint as his smile lit up his whole face, framed by black, curly hair that gleamed like it belonged in a Tresemmé ad.

Marnie was suddenly more self-conscious of her scruffy get-up. 'I'd feel bad taking it from you.'

'Don't. I've already had three today, if I have another I'll be awake till three in the morning and I have the breakfast shift tomorrow. You'll be doing me a favour.'

'Breakfast shift sounds . . . ominous.'

'Chef. Doing a hospitality management class here.'

'Ah. Cool. I'm doing Understanding Climate Change and its Impact on the World,' Marnie tried to say it casually but instantly felt silly.

'Impressive.' Daniel smiled coyly, and Marnie noticed the hint of a dimple etched in his left cheek.

They looked at each other and a moment of something passed between them that felt so intense Marnie had to break it. 'Well, if I'm doing you a favour.' She took the cup from him and held it up. 'Thanks. I appreciate it. I'm Marnie, by the way.' It sounded weird, but she hadn't really done this before – introducing herself like a cold caller, without the familiar 'in' of a dating app.

'Daniel. Here every Wednesday.'

'Exactly here?' Marnie arched her brow.

'I can be. Same time next week?'

'It's a date.' Marnie grinned.

And the rest was history.

Daniel and Sophie were making their way back now, a pink paper bag swinging from Sophie's arm and a permanent smile on her face.

'Are you excited to get your nails done, Soph?' Marnie asked as they headed out the store. That was the agenda for this afternoon's Galentine's, and this time, Soph was joining them. She'd hoped Daniel could babysit, but he was out for dinner with his mum and two sisters celebrating Olivia's birthday. Marnie was invited, but couldn't bail on Galentine's, despite being tempted. She loved Daniel's family, but she'd made a promise to her girls all those years ago, and she wasn't one to break promises.

Sophie nodded, grin being replaced with a more reserved, forced smile.

Marnie frowned. 'What's up?'

'I'm nervous.' Sophie still didn't look at her.

'What for?'

'Seeing Auntie Lissy and Hannah.'

It didn't go unnoticed that Alicia still held the title of Auntie and Hannah did not. Saying that, it had even been a while since Alicia had been round. Marnie got it – teaching was busy, life was busy and Dunstable, although not the other side of the world, was too far away to just pop over for a coffee.

'How come?'

Sophie shrugged, now hiding her reddening face behind her fine, fair hair – the spit of Marnie.

'It will be okay. I can do the talking at first, no pressure. You can talk to Auntie Lissy about what it's like to be a teacher.'

Daniel caught her eye and pulled a face. On second thoughts, perhaps that wasn't the best idea. Marnie trusted that Alicia would give her the censored version (though she rather hoped she'd put her off in the process).

Sophie's face lit up. 'Yeah.'

'What colour do you want your nails done?' Daniel asked, wiggling his fingers like a magician about to pull a coin from behind her ear.

Sophie giggled. It was a novelty for her to have a male figure in her life, let alone one that talked about nails and understood the importance of skincare. 'Baby blue and lilac with stars and glitter,' she stated with confidence.

'Very specific. A girl who knows what she wants.' Daniel caught Marnie's eye again.

'Like her mother.' Marnie beamed.

Daniel's eyes sparkled. 'Like her mother indeed.'

Chapter Twenty-Eight

13th February, 2024

Hannah

Hannah hadn't seen Sophie since, gosh she couldn't remember. Since the pandemic? Wow, had it really been that long? Even then, it was just a doorstep drop-off of some belated birthday and Christmas presents.

Sophie was shy at first, just nodding and looking at Marnie to answer for her, but she'd warmed up, and now all four of them – Marnie, Sophie, Hannah and Alicia – were sitting side by side as they got their feet massaged and their nails buffed, trimmed and polished.

'So there's this thing called Saturn Returns. It happens when you're twenty-nine, thirty-ish and it's a time of transformation and significant life transitions. Career shifts, breakups, marriages, new relationships.' Ever since Hannah had heard about this concept on an Instagram reel, she'd added it to her *must tell the girls next time I see them* list.

Marnie's face lit up. 'Interesting,' she said. 'I can totally get that.'

'Really?' Alicia looked as suspicious and baffled as usual.

'Right? I knew it wasn't bollocks – I mean, rubbish.' Hannah glanced at Sophie, who was sitting with a magazine in her lap channelling Elle Woods from *Legally Blonde*. Hannah kept forgetting there were younger ears listening in on their conversation. She turned to Marnie, who was lying back in her seat, eyes half-closed looking every bit a pampered goddess. 'Go on, what's your Saturn Returns Stuff?'

'Is that an official term?' She opened one eye.

'It is now.'

'Hmmm.' Marnie pursed her lips thoughtfully. 'So my Saturn Returns Stuff is going back to college, as you know. But I've also met someone.'

Hannah was caught between wanting to squeal in excitement and also thinking *here we go again*. Instead, she landed on jokey sarcasm – a failsafe when one doesn't quite know how to react. 'Not one of the tutors, is it?'

'Who do you think I am?' Marnie playfully swatted at Hannah. 'But I did meet him at college.'

'Daniel,' Sophie said matter-of-factly. 'I like him because he gets us Chinese every Friday.'

'Sounds like a keeper.' Hannah couldn't help but laugh. Sophie had the same deadpan wit as her mother already. 'How long have you been seeing each other?'

'Officially since November, but we've been hanging out since September. Firstly as friends.'

It was funny to think that, when Marnie had sex for the first time, she'd notified them both before the guy had even left her bed, and yet here they were hearing about Daniel close to six months after they'd first met. Life was weird. Hannah wasn't sure how she felt about it.

'No . . .' Hannah made sure to mouth the next bit. 'S-E-X?'

Marnie shook her head.

'Wow.'

'I know, I'm as shocked as you.'

'Assume you've made up for it now?'

'You assume correctly.'

Alicia, having been silent for the last few minutes, spoke. 'You must tell us more about Daniel later, when,' she gestured towards Sophie and mouthed *we're alone,* 'but most importantly, how's college going?'

Hannah couldn't tell if Daniel was a surprise to Alicia, if she disapproved of him, or if she was simply eager to emphasise to Sophie the importance of studying over romance.

'Oh my God, I love it,' Marnie gushed. 'So far, we've learned about the history of climate change, anthropogenic climate change, impacts on wildlife and nature, pollution, politics and policies.' Marnie was so enthusiastic, the nail tech had to clamp down on her foot like Hannah white-knuckling the salon bed during her last wax. Marnie continued, 'The tutor is an amazing environmental scientist and I've learned so much. It might not be a degree, but it's a step closer to where I want to be.'

It sounded incredibly boring, but different strokes for different folks. Hannah was so pleased to see Marnie finally putting herself first. It was about time. 'Proud of you.'

'Me too,' Alicia added.

'Aww thanks, guys.' Marnie reached a hand over to each of their thighs and squeezed. 'How about you two? What's your Saturn Returns Stuff? I feel like you've both had yours already from the amount your lives have changed in the past couple of years.'

That was the understatement of the century. Hannah still frequently had to pinch herself to prove she wasn't living in a fantasy. She'd had more than her fair share of luck and dreams come true, and yet the universe just kept on giving.

'Well, there is one new thing . . .' she said, unsure of whether she was making the right choice to share or not.

'What? I can never guess with you.' Marnie was smiling and squinting at the same time.

'I've met someone too.' It felt weird to say it. Hannah was always meeting someone, always soft-launching various men on her Instagram, whether they were just friends, part of a collab or someone she was sleeping with. It helped increase engagement with people speculating in the comments if they were an item or not. But Marcus was different. For a start, she was keeping him totally offline, wanting to keep what they had away from the public eye. He wasn't into social media anyway, which had taken some getting used to, but it had helped Hannah to become more selective with what she shared and what she didn't. 'We've been seeing each other for four weeks, so it's very early days, but it feels different with him than any of the others. We're taking things slowly too.'

'Well, this is exciting.' Marnie squinted at her. 'So does that mean you've not slept with him yet?' Marnie didn't lower her voice, causing an embarrassed look from Sophie who lifted her magazine up to cover her face.

'Nosy cow,' Hannah joked, though she felt her cheeks heat. Was it that obvious?

Alicia sat forward in her seat. 'You must really be serious about him!'

'I don't want to put too much pressure on it. I'm super busy and I don't even know if I have time for a proper partner, but we're just seeing what happens.'

Had she made the wrong decision to say anything? She was forever doing that embarrassing backtracking thing where she'd have to be like *Ooop never mind*, two days after introducing someone as a potential love interest. And if she'd learned anything from her breakup with Guy (and Joe, and the rest), it was that if you shared your relationship, online or otherwise, that included the end of it, too. She'd not announced that she and Guy had broken up; however, her eagle-eyed followers started noticing she hadn't posted a photo of him in a while, and after some further sleuthing realised that he was now going out with @CaliCarly. This was news to Hannah seeing as he'd blocked her the night they called it off. It was humiliating, and it hurt, more than she'd expected it to.

'Are you going to tell us about him, then?' Alicia's lips curved upwards as she looked down at her nails – she'd gone for a classic French tip, the antithesis to Hannah's scarlet red.

Despite her still blushed cheeks and the doubting voice in her head, Hannah wanted to talk about him. She couldn't help herself. 'He's certainly different to my usual type. Remember that Zoom date I did in lockdown? The paramedic. It's him. He's got four sisters so he's super sensitive, and er, he's ginger. Totally hot ginger. But still. My own Prince Harry, as Alicia would say.' Butterflies assaulted her stomach. Despite not caring much for Royals, it felt good to be able to show Marcus off.

Hannah had liked him back in 2020, he'd made her laugh more than she had in months and at risk of sounding like a hippy, there was something about his energy that calmed her. But for some reason, after only three dates, she'd pulled away. His magnetic draw was too strong at a time when everything for Hannah – and the world – was in flux. But she'd slid back into his messages one night after watching *24 Hours in A&E* and finding herself unable to stop thinking about him.

'Sounds promising.' Marnie nodded approvingly.

'I don't want to jinx it. But yeah. If I'm still with him for my birthday in July, I'll introduce you then. I think you'd love him.' Hannah could imagine Marcus seamlessly fitting into the friendship group – he was the sort of person who got on with everyone – but whenever her thoughts drifted too far into the future, she reeled herself back in. *Don't get carried away. Your track record with relationships isn't exactly stellar.*

Marnie rubbed her hands together mischievously and wiggled her eyebrows at Hannah. 'I really want to meet this dude. Hang in there, Marcus. You can do it. You can go the distance!'

Hannah laughed. 'We'll see,' she said, but inside she hoped desperately for the same.

Chapter Twenty-Nine

13th February, 2024

Alicia

Alicia snuggled herself down in her sleeping bag on the camp bed on the floor. Marnie was next to her on a bed made of duvets and pillows, and Hannah, the lucky cow, had the sofa. Sophie was in the only bedroom next door, not having to share the double bed with Marnie for a change.

They'd done it. Another year, another Galentine's. They'd left the caravan park last year with the usual pleasantries: *It's been nice, we'll see each other soon, yeah? Let's not leave it so long next time.* Alicia had even said *Take care*, like she was signing off an email to a parent at school (at least she hadn't said *kind regards* or *best wishes*). But, despite their best intentions, aligning all three of their schedules had been difficult, and in-person meet-ups had been few and far between, so the fact that they'd managed to, yet again, make Galentine's happen wasn't far off a miracle.

'It was nice to see you both with Sophie today. It's been a while since all four of us have hung out,' said Marnie, admiring her silver polished nails. She'd probably still find a way to bite them – a habit she'd had since primary school.

'It's been too long,' Alicia agreed. She didn't want to work out just how long it was.

It had been a lovely day, especially needed after the row she'd had with Hugh last night. Gosh, Sophie was so grown up now, talking about her crush and plans for the future. How did Marnie have an almost secondary schooler?

'She was really anxious this morning about seeing you both again, but that didn't last long, did it?' Marnie laughed fondly. 'You're both naturals, you know.'

Alicia's stomach knotted in the way it always did when the conversation danced too closely to motherhood.

Hannah snorted. 'You think? Are you forgetting how I held Sophie for the first time like she was a hot potato?'

'We were young. It's always scary holding such a tiny baby, especially if it's not yours.' Marnie magicked a bag of popcorn from seemingly nowhere and chucked a couple of kernels in her mouth. 'You're great with Sophie.'

Hannah flashed her gleaming, whitened smile. 'Aww thanks. She's a good egg. You've not done a bad job with that one.'

'I'll take that. So you think you'll have one or na? I know you've always said no.'

'It's still a no. It might change, it might not. But Marcus is on the same wavelength which is such a relief.'

Something about the way her gaze met Alicia's made her tense. She clenched her fists slightly, her freshly shaped nails pressing into her palms.

Time to change the subject.

'So tell us more about Daniel, Marns,' Alicia said. 'How soon did you introduce him to Sophie?'

Marnie's face scrunched in thought. 'Maybe a month or two in? It was a hard decision because I didn't want to introduce him too soon like I did with Steven, but equally I needed to see how they got on before I knew for definite whether he was a keeper. It's such a hard balance. I hope I've gone about it the right way. He loves her and the feelings mutual. We're talking about him moving in next month.'

'Already?' The words tumbled out of Alicia's mouth before she could stop them.

'Yeah, no need to sound so shocked.'

'Isn't it a bit soon?' Hannah said. At least it wasn't just Alicia thinking it. She never knew these days if she was being fair or overly dramatic. It often felt like she saw the world in a different way to most people. Hannah, Hugh, the general population.

'When you know, you know.' Marnie shrugged, upending the popcorn bag directly in her mouth and crunching loudly.

'What if he's like Steven?' Alicia couldn't help it. Had Marnie not learned anything since then?

Marnie rolled her eyes. 'I can't live my life on the assumption that every man I ever date will be a prick, can I?'

'Well no, but—'

'But what?'

'There's no rush, is there?' Hannah added, and then her brow crumpled. 'God, you're not pregnant again, are you?'

'No! But why would that be the worst thing in the world? I've done it before – you were just saying I did a decent job the first time around.'

Alicia's heart was beating faster now. How could she be so flippant about something so huge?

Marnie continued. 'Also, I'm not rushing anything. You and Hugh hardly moved slowly. Why do I have to be judged by a separate set of standards?'

'No one's judging. We're just looking out for you.' Hannah's tone was calm and measured, totally the opposite to the agitation building inside Alicia.

'Well, there's no need. I'm a big girl. I'm not a nineteen-year-old idiot anymore.'

Hannah sighed. 'No one said you were an idiot, Marns.'

'Well, that's what it feels like. I've only ever celebrated your choices. Why can't you do the same for me?'

Because Marnie's choices weren't really choices – more like impulsive accidents or acts of desperation. *Gosh, why am I being so harsh?*

'We do celebrate you!' Hannah was sounding more irritated now.

'Look, he's met the whole family, including Nanny Sheila, and she approves. If she approves, then I don't think any of us need to worry. She's got a sixth sense for these things. She hated Steven the minute she met him. Made her mind up there and then he was a See You Next Tuesday, and that was that. I promise you, Daniel is different.'

'Do you think you'll have a baby with him, then?' After wanting to steer the conversation away from motherhood and babies, why was Alicia bringing it back? But something in her needed to know.

'He wants one,' Marnie shrugged.

Of course that's why she was changing her mind. Marnie had never talked of wanting another one. If anything, she always sounded like she couldn't think of anything worse than doing it all over again. But then along comes a man saying *I want to have a mini me* without any idea what it actually entails to be a parent, and everything else just gets thrown out the window.

Marnie continued, 'It's such a hard one. I want to be with him and the thought of stopping him from being a dad makes me feel awful. I'm not *against* having another one. It could be different this time. Easier. Not easy, I'm not deluded. But I would have someone to help with the night feeds—'

'To be in the suffering with you,' Hannah added.

'I want to say that's too dramatic but honestly I don't think you're far off.'

Alicia needed to say something. She couldn't just sit and watch Marnie throw away everything she'd worked so hard for up until now. 'But you've just started to rebuild your life and live it for you, not someone else. Sophie isn't far off secondary school, you're doing your course. You're in a relationship that you're happy in. Don't you want to enjoy all that for a bit?' *And put the whole turning your life upside-down thing on pause?* Alicia wanted to add.

'But if we're going to do it, it might make sense to get it over with. I don't mean that in a horrible way. In an ideal world, I don't really want Sophie to be an only child and we're not getting any younger.'

'Why? I'm an only child.' What was so wrong about being an only child? Alicia had never gone without. Always been the apple of her parents' eye. And there it was again – the near-constant reminder that women were on a deadline, with time ticking away as if the minute they hit thirty-five their eggs would instantly turn rotten. *That fucking biological clock.*

'Yes, and I'm also an only child.' Alicia couldn't tell if Marnie was getting pissed off again or whether she was just reading into her slightly clipped tone. 'But I did feel quite lonely when I was younger. Always envious of people who had siblings, especially sisters. That's why when we met, you became the sister I never had.'

All of Alicia's emotions that had been simmering beneath the surface threatened to break free. This time, she didn't fight them. She let the wave of anger, sadness and anxiety crash over her, surrendering to the tears that pushed their way out She wiped her eyes on the duvet but not before Marnie saw.

'Aw bless you. I didn't mean to make you cry!' Marnie stuck her bottom lip out.

'It's not you.' On top of everything, Alicia now felt horrendously guilty for being such a monumental cow.

'What is it, then?' Marnie's face was full of concern, brows furrowed, lips sucked in.

'I don't want to talk about it.' *I'm sick of talking about it.*

'Is it work?' Hannah offered.

Alicia shook her head. She wished it was, then maybe there would be a simpler solution.

'Hugh?' Marnie said tentatively.

Alicia nodded. Should she say it out loud?

'Hugh wants a baby, and I don't.' The words fell out, too heavy to hold back. It sounded awful spoken aloud, but Hugh wasn't denying it anymore, so why should she?

His words from last night echoed in her mind.

They'd just sat down on the sofa in their usual spots, Alicia on one end with her feet up on Hugh and him on the other. They'd finished their dinner, eaten on the sofa rather than the dining table because they were knackered, and Alicia had just pressed play on the next episode of their newest obsession – *One Day* on Netflix. Usually, they'd sit in comfortable silence, neither able to muster up enough energy for conversation beyond the bare minimum. But then Hugh started talking and Alicia's comfortable, routine and predictable existence was shattered.

'Juliette is pregnant.'

'And you're telling me this because?' She hated to sound bitter, but after the day she'd had at work, it was all she could offer. Why did he need to tell her that his long-term university ex-girlfriend was pregnant? What relevance did it have to them?

Hugh sighed, his features shadowing.

'What? I'm tired. I don't have the energy for this conversation right now.' Alicia kicked her feet off his lap and shunted herself away from him.

'You never do.'

'What does that mean?'

'Whenever I mention it you get snappy. We never seem to be able to have a normal, adult conversation about it.'

Alicia took a deep breath. She couldn't be bothered to argue. 'Okay. What do you need from me from this conversation?' It was something that their couple's therapist, Brenda, had taught them, and despite it sounding straight out of a couple's therapy 101 textbook, it often worked.

'I need you to listen to me and to hear what I'm saying. Without getting upset. Without making it about you.' Hugh's eyes bored into Alicia, his expression flat and serious.

'I won't make it about me but I'm allowed to be upset. My feelings are valid.' Another phrase spouted directly from Brenda.

She could tell Hugh was on the cusp of rolling his eyes, but he didn't say anything. Instead he took yet another deep breath, as if preparing for a speech. Alicia braced herself.

'When I heard that Julie was pregnant it felt like a punch

to the gut. I felt jealous. I felt, still feel, like I'm falling behind everyone else in my life, watching them live the life I want. The life you promised me.' His gaze stayed on Alicia for a second longer before flicking to the floor.

Her stomach plummeted. Was he really saying it out loud? Up until now they'd mastered the art of dancing around the subject, talking in code, sweeping it under the rug. What possessed him to bring it from unspoken concept to uncomfortable reality?

'The life I *promised* you?' Although she whispered it, Alicia's words were sharp.

'You always said you wanted children.' Hugh shifted forward in his seat, nudging the footstool away from him and resting his head in his hands.

'I'm allowed to change my mind.'

'Yes, but think about how that feels to me. You changed your mind after we married. I feel like you . . . like you tricked me.'

Alicia's heart was pounding so hard she could hear it in her ears. 'You think I *tricked* you?' She'd promised she wouldn't make it about her, but this *was* about her. Everything he expected from her. Her failings as a woman and a wife who couldn't – or didn't want to – give him what he wanted.

Hugh's fingers drummed against his thighs, frenetic and full of angst. 'Maybe that came out wrong, but the sentiment still stands.'

Fury surged in Alicia's chest, and adrenaline flooded her body like venom. *How dare he.* 'I'm not saying I don't want one, I'm not sure. I'm scared! I'm confused! You can say all you want about being there for me every step of the way, but you never could be, not properly. I'd be the one who has to be pregnant. I'd be the one birthing it, feeding it. No doubt I'd also be the one who'd have to give up my job and my identity.' Alicia was shouting now but she couldn't stop. 'Having a baby could ruin us, too. You don't even think about all that. You see everyone else around us having babies, listen to your fucking nan making snide comments and think *yeah 'spose we should*. I bet you don't even know why you want one, other than just because everyone else is doing it.'

Alicia stood up with such force she felt dizzy, she staggered forward on quivering legs. *I need to get out. Away from him.*

She slammed the door behind her, a physical boundary between her and Hugh's agonising disappointment. They hadn't spoken properly since.

'That's tough.' Marnie's face were full of sorrow following Alicia's admission. As much as she didn't want sympathy, it felt good that someone understood just how . . . shit the situation was. 'I thought things had been good between you both.'

'They are. Were.' Sadness sat heavy in Alicia's chest as she realised how much had changed in such a short time. Just a couple of months ago they'd started saving for yet another attempt at a honeymoon – third time lucky. And now they were back in a deep, dark pit with no idea how to get out.

Hannah frowned as she stroked the duvet she was buried beneath, following its swirly patterns with her newly manicured nail. 'You've always said you wanted to be a mum. What's changed?'

'I never questioned it before. But now I am and I'm not sure it's for me. There's a difference between fantasy and reality.'

Perhaps Hannah was trying to being empathetic, but Alicia was sick of having to justify her choice. Imagine if she'd turned to someone who *had* a child and asked them why they bothered? In fact, it was a good a time as any.

She turned to Marnie, who was now lying back down and half disappearing into her throne of cushions.

'Truthfully, why do you think people do it? On paper, the cons seem to outweigh the pros. No sleep, no downtime, tantrums, teenage years, poo, sick, noise, expense, loss of identity—'

'Are you done?' Marnie laughed and then she bit her lip, deep in thought. 'No, you're absolutely right. But I guess it's not always about what something looks like on paper, but how it feels in here.' Marnie patted her chest.

There it was again, the head versus the heart conundrum. Why did some people find it so easy to follow their heart without the evidence or logic to back it up? 'You and I are so different. You're super chilled out and confident and even you found it hard. I'd have no hope with all my anxieties, overthinking and high standards. I can see it now, feeling like I'm failing at every hurdle, drowning in washing and responsibility.'

Marnie rolled to face her, tucking her fleece blanket beneath her chin. For a brief moment, she looked like teenage Marnie all over again. 'I can't even offer a counter-argument to that because so much of what you describe *is* motherhood. I totally understand why someone wouldn't want to do it. But for me it's worth it. It's the hardest thing I've ever done but also the best.'

Alicia shuffled to sit up in her sleeping bag, the camp bed groaning beneath her. 'It just doesn't make sense,' she said, throwing her hands up in surrender. 'How can it be the hardest thing you'll ever do but also the best? How can it be ninety per cent slog and feeling unappreciated and ten per cent love and *still* be worth it?'

303

Marnie laughed and shook her head. 'You're totally right. I don't know. I guess all I can do is parrot Joan when she says that you can feel two opposing things at once. Two very different things can exist at the same time. Both can be true. Etcetera, etcetera.'

'If you don't want to have a child, then you shouldn't,' Hannah said bluntly, sitting up and plumping the cushion behind her with a few vigorous pats. 'No one should force you. It's your life, you'll only resent it. I know if I did it, I would resent the child and my partner, and ultimately myself for everything I'd have to give up.'

'But that's easy for you to say because Marcus doesn't want one. What would you do if Marcus did want one?' Oh how much easier life would be if Hugh was indifferent to the idea. How much less inadequate Alicia would feel.

Hannah sighed, leaning back into her freshly plumped cushions. 'I honestly don't know.'

Alicia's eyes filled up yet again with ferocious tears. What were they going to do? Not even know-everything, worldly Hannah had the answer.

'I've done everything "right",' she sniffed. 'Followed the plan. And yet it feels so empty.' She buried her face in her pillow and wiped her cheeks against it. 'Where do we go from here? I have a child I might resent to make him happy? Or he gives up his dream of becoming a dad? Both feel impossible. But the thought of divorce . . .' The word felt sharp and painful in her mouth. 'I can't even go there.'

Divorce was never part of the plan. Marriage wasn't supposed to be this hard. But Alicia was quickly coming to the realisation that life didn't always follow the carefully curated blueprint she'd hoped it would.

'You don't need to go there right now. Does she, Han?'

'Not now,' Hannah said gently. 'But it doesn't sound like it's going to go away.'

Another sob threatened to erupt from deep in Alicia's soul, helplessness engulfing her and erasing the hope she was clinging onto that this would blow over. How could there not be a solution? There was always a way out. Work harder. Take the pills. Go to therapy.

Therapy.

Brenda had helped before. She could help again. Alicia latched onto the thought, gripping it like a lifeline. It had to work. It would work. Because if it didn't it would mean her failsafe plan had failed, and that just wasn't an option.

Where would she live? Back with her parents? And the thought of starting all over again terrified her: the early days of dating, meeting the family and friends, going back to the beginning with sharing herself, both emotionally and physically with someone new. Someone that wasn't Hugh. She was hardly in her prime now, what did she have to offer in the dating pool? A woman who didn't want to have kids, who'd only slept with one man and who was perpetually stressed and anxious? Hardly a catch. And all the good ones would be taken by now, surely, and have their own baggage also.

And that wasn't even taking into account the loss she'd have to face. Her and Hugh's lives were entwined, as one. His friends were hers. She loved his family as if they were hers, she was an auntie to Zara. She couldn't lose all that. Everything in her life would look different – there was hardly any part of it that wasn't linked to Hugh in some way.

And Hugh.

How could she live in a world without Hugh? Her first and only love. The man who had stuck by her when she was at her worst. The one who knew just the right thing to say to pull her out of one of her anxious spirals. Who understood what she was feeling just by the look in her eyes. They'd made a promise to love each other, for better and for worse, in front of all their friends and family. Alicia was loyal, she was dependable, she was predictable. She was never one to break a promise.

'I'll call Brenda in the morning,' she said with a firm nod of her head. 'We're going to be okay. We have to be.'

Hot Mess Express 🚂 🤪

4th March, 2024

Marnie: How did the chat go with Hugh? Did you call the therapist? You've just dropped off the face of the earth.

Alicia: We're good.

Hannah: You've worked it out?

Alicia: Sort of? He's not mentioned it again. If it comes back up, we'll go to therapy x

Hannah: If or when . . .?

Hannah has deleted this message

Hannah: Okay x

4th September, 2024

Alicia: Everyone alright?

Hannah: Yar.

Marnie: Yep.

Alicia: Good good. Did you see that Kelly Bagley in the year above got divorced?

Hannah: I know!!! Divorced at 30! I'd divorce someone with that second name tbh.

Marnie: I knew something was up when she started posting selfies.

Hannah: And she deleted all the photos from their wedding.

Marnie: OMG! Was that the one in Santorini?

Hannah: Yep.

Alicia: What a waste of money.

11th February, 2025

Marnie: Airbnb booked for Galentine's Day. Link below.

Hannah: Bouji!

Alicia: Aw thanks for sorting it, you didn't have to!

Marnie: No worries. I've sorted the PJs for this year too!

Hannah: You do spoil us.

Hannah: Feel like we've got loads to catch up on. It's been ages!!

Marnie: Just a bit 🤭

Chapter Thirty

13th February, 2025

Alicia

'Text me when you get there safely, yeah?' Hugh said as he chucked the whites into the washing machine. He groaned as he heaved himself up to standing. Alicia had noticed that this was now a thing that they both did after any sort of exertion. One day you were young and agile, and the next you were thirty and unable to stand without your knees popping or throwing your back out with a strong fart, sneeze, or laugh.

'I will do.' Alicia put the final plate she was rinsing into the dishwasher. 'The Airbnb is only about an hour away so we should be there before five-thirty, six latest.'

'You excited to see them?'

'Yeah.' It had been a few months since she'd seen Marnie, and more than six since the three of them had hung out together. 'It's long overdue.'

'I bet.' Hugh closed up the gap between them and slid his arms around Alicia's waist.

His touch felt both warm and alien at the same time. On

instinct, Alicia pulled away. 'I've got to go, I don't want to be late.'

'It's a five-minute drive to the station.' Hugh stepped away and stooped to look in the cupboard below the sink. If Alicia had hurt his feelings, he didn't show it. 'You don't need to leave for another ten.'

'It's on the top shelf behind the sponges,' Alicia said. The non-bio was always in the same place. How many times did she have to say the same thing before he listened to her? 'I need to pack the car up.'

'You have one bag.' Hugh frowned at her, detergent now in hand.

'Will you stop?'

'Stop what? I'm just stating facts.'

'Being a know-it-all.'

'What are you, five?' Hugh chuckled but the laugh didn't reach his eyes. 'I'll help you to the car?'

'It's not heavy. Thanks though. See you tomorrow.' Alicia pecked Hugh on the cheek as he poured the detergent into the slot and slammed it shut.

'Bye.'

Alicia had offered to drive both herself and Hannah to the Airbnb, and insisted on picking Hannah up from the station. It made sense logistically and she couldn't face the awkwardness of having Hugh and Hannah making polite conversation in her hallway. He'd not seen her since Bali and he'd also deleted her number – his idea in a desperate attempt to appease Alicia. Despite #BaliGate having blown over, it wasn't worth risking opening up old wounds.

Alicia looked at the clock on the dashboard. Hannah was late, and she wasn't sure how much longer she could sit idling at the bus stop. Alicia was just about to send a sarcastic text – *I thought you were getting the 3:01* – when Hannah appeared, striding out of the automatic doors in her sunglasses and wheeling a nude-coloured Herschel suitcase. *That would be at least a few hundred quid,* Alicia thought. Should she get out of the car and hug her? Help her put her suitcase in the boot? Or was that too formal?

Hannah waved as she caught a glimpse of the car and before Alicia could make her mind up, Hannah pulled open the back seat door and threw her suitcase in.

'There's space in the boot—'

Hannah had already settled herself into the passenger seat. 'Huh?'

'Nothing.'

The sound of a loud horn startled Alicia. She glanced in her rear-view mirror and saw a red-faced bus driver flapping at her.

'Crap.' She indicated and pulled off, narrowly missing being hit by another car that had to brake hard and subsequently beeped her for a second time.

'I'll put my seatbelt on,' Hannah chuckled.

'Ha,' Alicia said, although her heart was hammering and her adrenaline pumping. She felt the familiar flush of her cheeks and had to take four deep breaths to ground herself.

For a few minutes, neither of them spoke. Alicia was grateful as she liked to concentrate on what lane to get in on the roundabout, and she wasn't keen on getting hooted at again.

When they'd successfully joined the motorway and Alicia's focus was back on the atmosphere in the car, she yet again became aware of the thick, weighty silence. It would be a long drive if they didn't find something to say to each other.

'Good journey?' she asked.

'Fine. Got a seat and everything.'

'Surprise you didn't take an Uber.'

'Debated it but it's no quicker.'

'Fair.'

More silence. Hannah turned to look out the window. 'How have you been?'

'Fine. Nothing new.' God, she was boring. How could she have nothing to update her on? 'You?'

'Yeah good. Busy, as always.'

'Life, eh?' More silence followed.

'Can I put some music on?' Hannah fumbled in her handbag and pulled out a phone lead. 'You have somewhere to plug this in, right?'

'Er, I think so?' Alicia wasn't one to listen to music while driving. When she did put something on it was usually just whatever popped up on the radio. 'I might need you to help navigate when we come off the motorway.' Despite having virtually done the drive on Google Maps to make doubly sure she knew where she was going, the end part of the drive was down lots of windy lanes that all looked the same.

'I can do that.' Hannah plugged her phone into a USB slot that Alicia hadn't noticed before and with a few taps Sabrina Carpenter was playing.

'I love this song.' Alicia couldn't help but drum her fingers on the steering wheel to the catchy beat.

'Me too.'

Alicia took her eyes off the road for a split second to share a smile with Hannah. Perhaps this wouldn't be quite so bad, after all.

They sailed down the motorway and much to both of their amazement, the traffic was non-existent. By an M25 miracle and some stellar navigating by Hannah (despite one wrong turn), they pulled into the driveway of a rather large cottage, having made excellent time.

'This looks right. Although, that's weird. Why are there so many cars?' Alongside Marnie's red Fiat 500, there were three other cars that Alicia didn't recognise.

Hannah looked just as baffled. 'No idea. Are we sure we're at the right place?'

Alicia looked again. 'There's Marnie's car and I recognise the sign from the photos she sent. It's definitely The Old Mill.'

'Weird.'

A twinge in Alicia's gut told her something was off. 'What's going on?' she said, suspicion clear in her voice.

Hannah shrugged. 'There's only one way to find out.' She threw open the door and climbed out of the car. She strode towards the front door.

Thank God they'd come together. Alicia wouldn't have the guts to go in on her own.

'Wait, shall I just call Marnie and check we're at the right place.'

Hannah stopped and peered into the Fiat. 'It's definitely the right place. Look, it's got her stickers on the back.'

Alicia shuffled over and surveyed the stickers. *Bestie let me merge or I'll cry* and *Hot Girls Hit Curbs*. Definitely Marnie's.

Before Alicia could get her phone out, Hannah rapped the big brass knocker three times.

As they waited, Alicia placed herself a good few feet behind Hannah, who stood with her hands on her hips, tapping her foot on the ground.

Finally, the door opened and a woman who looked to be in her fifties answered the door. She had a full face of makeup and wore a glitzy red party dress.

'Hi, I'm Andrea.' Did she look somewhat familiar? 'Are you here for the hen?'

'The hen?' Hannah said, hands still on hips. 'No, we're here to see Marnie.'

Andrea frowned.

'Who is it?' Marnie's voice called from inside. She appeared behind Andrea, frowning at first before her face cracked into a massive grin when she spotted them. 'Oh my God, Hannah and Alicia! My best friends.'

'Ah, the famous two.' Andrea smiled now and stepped aside as Marnie pulled Alicia and Hannah into a hug.

'Surprise!' She stepped back, throwing jazz hands and doing a little spin – Alicia had flashbacks to when Marnie surprised them after moving into Steven's. She wasn't going to tell them this was her new house, was she?

'What the—' It was only now that Alicia clocked what Marnie was wearing. A white lace dress. A sash that said Bride To Be. A tacky glittery crown that said Bride.

'Welcome to my hen do!' she beamed. 'Come in.'

Chapter Thirty-One

13th February, 2025

Alicia

Marnie led them into a room at the front of the house – a living room with a grand fireplace, navy curtains and a rich-coloured jungle wallpaper and shut the door behind them. Even with the door closed, the sound of music, laughter and chatter was audible. Alicia didn't realise Marnie had so many other friends, and she was not at all prepared to be social with a bunch of people she didn't know.

They settled onto two navy-blue velvet sofas and looked at each other.

'Lovely surprise! Wow,' Alicia said, as convincingly as she could muster.

Marnie grinned. 'Give over, you hate surprises.'

'Well, er—'

'It's fine, I expect you to be somewhat pissed off with me. I'd feel equally hard done by if the toe was on the other sock.'

'*Shoe* was on the other foot,' Hannah interjected.

'No one said we were feeling hard done by.' Alicia rearranged her face into a smile. 'Just shocked.'

'Your faces never lie.' Marnie shook her head, but she was still smiling. 'Look, honestly? I didn't tell you about . . . this,' she gestured to her outfit, 'because of how you reacted when I said Daniel and I were going to move in together. I didn't want the high of the engagement ruined by doubt. Also, it's a bit of a spontaneous decision so I thought why not surprise you both! It will make a good story in decades to come.'

Were Alicia's thoughts doubt or realistic concerns? Also, was that really the reason or was it actually payback for Alicia doing the same? If it was a competition, Marnie had won. They were at her hen party, for Christ's sake.

'When's the wedding?' Hannah asked, her voice calm. Alicia wondered how she felt about all this or did she just not care in the same way as her? It seemed no one ever took anything as seriously as Alicia did.

'This Saturday.' Marnie bit her lip and scrunched her face up. 'Surprise!' she said again, this time her voice wavering.

'This Saturday?!' Alicia and Hannah cried in unison.

Marnie nodded and picked up the embroidered cushion next to her. She traced the pattern with her finger, not looking at them 'It's just a quiet affair. Registry office, no white dress. No bridesmaids or evening ceremony. We might have a party at some point in the future, but for now it's just about committing to each other.'

Alicia's heart hammered. They weren't invited?

'I'm busy on Saturday,' Hannah said flatly, seemingly not grasping the very real possibility that they might not be on the guest list.

'That's okay, I wouldn't expect you to drop everything to be there.'

Alicia couldn't hold it in any longer. 'Are we actually invited?' It was her turn to avoid eye contact, instead she

316

looked at the rug on the floor, as ornate as the tropical cushion Marnie was fiddling with.

'Of course,' Marnie said as if it was obvious. 'And Hugh, too.'

'Oh.' What were they doing this Saturday? The usual, a trip to Sainsbury's, maybe the town centre. Marking. 'We're free. I don't have anything to wear, though.'

'Wear jeans for all I care. It will just mean the world to me that you'll be there.'

But clearly not enough to have invited us with more than forty-eight hours' notice.

'I'll see if I can move my meeting,' Hannah said. 'I can't miss your wedding.'

'I wouldn't hold it against you, but I would love for you to be there.'

Again, if she would love for them to be there, why was she telling them now, as an afterthought?

'God, so you're getting married.' Hannah blew air through her nose and shook her head. 'That's two out of three. No surprise I'll be the last, if I ever get married full stop. Is this the order you would have guessed? Alicia, Marnie, Me?'

Marnie finally dropped the pillow and looked at them, face more relaxed. Were they just going to move on now, then? 'I think so,' she said. 'Definitely Alicia first, but I'm torn as to whether it would have been you or me second. I didn't have myself down as the marrying type.'

'In your defence, you're doing it your own way. No white wedding for you, just a casual, last-minute affair.'

'True. I'm so glad you're both here and you're not angry with me. I hope you don't mind me co-opting Galentine's Day.' Marnie pulled her guilty face, but Hannah just laughed. 'I can't wait to introduce you to the others. Only four other girls.'

'From work?'

'Yeah! Three from my current place and good ole Andrea from the first place. She makes sure to fart in Steven's coffee mug at least once a week for me.' That's why Alicia recognised her – she must have seen her in photos. 'We've got games to play, crafts to do, wine to drink and matching PJs to wear.'

'How about the sleeping arrangements?' Alicia asked. Hopefully she wouldn't have to share with someone she didn't know.

'Three bedrooms. Two doubles and a twin plus a sofabed. Andrea and Paola are in one, Lucy and Millie in another, and I figured we'd move the two single mattresses into the main room along with the sofabed for us three.'

Alicia's shoulders relaxed. They would get some time with Marnie to themselves and have some semblance of the Galentine's Day sleepover tradition.

'Love it,' said Hannah. 'I know we're adults now, but it wouldn't be a proper sleepover if we weren't in the same room.'

'Absolutely,' Alicia added.

'Perfect. Now, how about we crack out the PJs and get this very demure, very chill party started.' Marnie stood and reached her hands out towards both Hannah and Alicia. 'You ready to rock 'n' roll? Up first, a game of Mr and Mrs!'

Alicia allowed herself to be pulled to her feet. She'd be crap at Mr and Mrs – she hadn't spent much time with the soon-to-be-married couple – but she'd give it her best shot.

The thought of Hannah and Hugh in the same room at the wedding flickered across her mind. No way of avoiding it this time. Her heart began to skip as her mind raced through images of awkward silences, misinterpreted lingering looks, what Hannah would wear . . .

Slow down. Breathe.

There's no need to stress about it. You're past that now. Hugh loves you and you love him. Hannah loves you too. There are no threats here.

Her heartbeat slowed. Thank God that voice was there, reassuring her this time, rather than torturing her.

Gosh, she'd come a long way, big thanks to the therapy and meds. Yes, it might still be a painfully awkward experience, but awkwardness wouldn't kill her. It was much better than the previous crippling insecurity and paranoia from before. And also, it could just be absolutely fine.

You've got this.

She patted herself on the back for how far she'd come.

Well done me. Everything's going to be just fine. The only thing worth panicking about right now is what to bloody wear!

Chapter Thirty-Two

13th February, 2025

Marnie

Everyone else had retired to their bedrooms, leaving Alicia, Hannah and Marnie sitting in the open-plan kitchen-diner around the table. Marnie was as horizontal as it was humanly possible to be on a dining chair, with her feet up on the table, and Hannah and Alicia weren't far off the same. It had been a long day, and they were all knackered. Their mascara was smudged and they were all yawning loudly every few minutes, but a sense of contentment hung in the air.

Marnie wiggled her toes, admiring her white socks with Bride embroidered on the ankle in gold thread. It had been weird to see her other friends mixing with Alicia and Hannah. Although she considered the latter her best friends, she actually spent way more time with Andrea, Paola, Lucy and Millie and it was odd to realise that they knew her and Daniel as a couple more than Alicia and Hannah did. It didn't matter, but it was a moment of realisation that made it starkly clear how much things changed as life marched forward.

'What do you reckon, then? You think this one's a keeper?'

Marnie uncrossed her arms and looked at her ring finger. She loved her ring – emerald and gold with a diamond halo – and everyone had made all the right noises when she showed it to them, although she wasn't convinced that Hannah liked it . . .

'I bloody hope so, you're marrying him.' Hannah cupped her mug of tea in her hand and grinned.

'I'm joking. I have no doubt he's my soulmate.'

'Thought you didn't believe in soulmates.' Alicia smiled sleepily, chin resting in her hands.

'I've changed my mind.' It was hard not to believe in something when you'd experienced it first-hand.

'What's your definition of soulmate, then?' said Hannah. 'How would I know if Marcus was mine or not? I always thought it would be obvious.'

'Hmmm.' Marnie thought for a second. 'Well, Daniel came to me at the exact right time, not when I was a complete mess. He literally just appeared even though I wasn't looking for a partner. I'd done my therapy, I'd worked out who I was and I had space in my life for someone who would enhance it, rather than fill the cracks I felt I had.'

'Bloody hell, you sound like you're the therapist.'

'And?'

'No, it's amazing. I'm impressed,' Hannah said earnestly.

Marnie looked from her to Alicia then back to her feet. 'So do I finally have the seal of approval from you both?'

Alicia sat up straighter, suddenly looking more awake. 'We've never disapproved of you.'

'Really? So when I moved in with a narcissistic twat after six weeks – my colleague at that – you approved, then? Or when I had unprotected sex with a man I've never spoken about and fell pregnant at nineteen, you thought, yes Marns, well done!' Marnie laughed, but there was a fierceness to the words that marched out of her with such intensity it made her shake.

'When you put it like that . . .' Hannah glanced at Alicia, whose wide eyes spoke volumes.

'Sorry, I'm going off on one now,' Marnie continued, although she wasn't yet finished. 'What I'm saying is maybe it's time you stop questioning everything I do and accept that I'm finally an adult. It's taken me a while to get here, but I'm fucking here now and I'm so proud of myself.' The prosecco she'd been drinking had unlocked a part of her that needed to be voiced. That wanted to say *look at me, see me for who I am now, not who I was*, and judging by Alicia and Hannah's reaction, she had finally been seen.

'Why are my eyes watering?' Hannah said, blinking madly.

'Non-existent mascara in your eye?' Marnie smiled, eyes pricking with hot tears also. 'Don't, you'll set me off.'

'Too late over here,' Alicia said through multiple sniffs.

'Aw, come here, girls. Group hug.' Marnie stood up and held her arms open, beckoning them closer. Her heartbeat slowed and her shoulders lowered. They got it. 'Thank you for sticking by me throughout all these years, and for loving all versions of me. I wouldn't want to have done any of it without having you both by my side.'

Marnie wiped the tears of happiness and gratitude that fell down her cheeks as she pulled her best friends into one of her death grip hugs.

Yes, they'd been through their ups and their downs, but here they were, still standing side by side. Ready, yet again, to take on the world.

Hot Mess Express 🚂 🤪

16th February, 2025

Marnie: Send me the photos you took at the wedding pretty plz. Daniel and I are going to make a little scrapbook!

Alicia: Will do. Hope you had a lovely day. It was a beautiful ceremony.

Marnie: Who knew the registry office in Watford had such a nice little garden?

Hannah: It was lovely. Decent weather too. You looked lovely <3

Marnie: Thanks, girls. It meant the world that you could join us on our special day.

Alicia: Pleasure <3

Hannah: Ditto xxxx

15th April, 2025

Hannah: How's married life treating you @Marns? Two months married now, right? Sorry for the radio silence, life continues to be mad.

Marnie: Don't apologise, I've been just as bad. Married life is great. No dramas.

Hannah: Love to hear it. Sometimes it's nice to be boring and drama free!

Marnie: Ya! Have you heard from @Alicia recently?

Hannah: No. @Alicia are you still alive?

Alicia: I am indeed. Don't know how. I totally understand why life insurance for teachers is so high. Summer holidays are the only thing keeping me going.

Marnie: Still tough at work?

Alicia: Yeah, but I'm getting used to it now. Just rolling with the punches.

5th May, 2025

Alicia: Are you two around at all this Saturday?

Marnie: I can be. Why?

Alicia: Hannah?

Hannah: Potentially.

Marnie: ??

Alicia: Could just do with some girl time

Marnie: Sign me up x

Hannah: Can we take a rain check?

Alicia: Sure x

16th May, 2025

Alicia: Any more thoughts on tomorrow @Hannah?

Hannah: OMG so sorry I typed a message but it didn't send. I'm currently in Ibiza on a last-minute brand trip. Will get a date in ASAP.

Marnie: Shit is that tomorrow? I'm so sorry I don't think I'm going to make it. Dan, Soph and I are going to London Zoo for the day! Everything okay your end?

Alicia: Yeah. All good x

Chapter Thirty-Three

17th May, 2025

Alicia

Alicia and Hugh were back at Brenda's, sitting in their car on her driveway waiting for their couples therapy session. How were they here, yet again? Things had seemed to have blown over after the whole *you tricked me* accusation, with life going back to semi-normality. Hugh hadn't brought it back up again, much to Alicia's relief, so she hadn't made the call to Brenda. But then slowly and insidiously, it had crept back in – the loaded comments that sprung up when another friend announced a pregnancy, the festering resentment manifesting in short tempers and cold shoulders.

After a particularly painful standoff, Alicia knew it was time to use their last resort. Therapy had always been in her back pocket – an option she kept in reserve. She just didn't want to play that card too soon and be left with nothing else if it failed.

So here they were.

It would have been nice to have the girls join her later after the session for some wine, a chat, and a debrief, but clearly they had better things to do. She hadn't mentioned her and Hugh in her message, but she thought they'd have clocked something was up when she mentioned needing some *girl time*.

Over the years she'd fought tooth and nail against family obligations, school trips and the pressures of daily life to keep them as a priority, but it seemed they didn't deem her worth quite so much effort.

Hannah was in Ibiza on a *once-in-a-lifetime* brand trip with SaltWaves and wasn't going to turn down an offer like that, although *once-in-a-lifetime* felt like an exaggeration considering she was jetting off to all sorts of events multiple times a year.

Alicia thought better of Marnie, though, who'd let her down last minute because she'd got a better offer. But Alicia had no time to dwell on it.

Hugh cleared his throat and looked at his watch. 'Shall we go in?'

'Yeah, I make it 4pm on the dot.'

They got out of the car and Hugh slammed the door a little heavily for Alicia's liking.

'Could you make any more noise?' She tried to laugh but it sounded more like a heavy sigh than anything else. She had no energy for pretending.

Hugh said nothing, shook his head and rolled his eyes.

'Sorry, I'm feeling anxious.' She was sick of hearing herself say the words – a staple in her vocabulary at this point. A personality trait. The only way she felt like she could exist.

'No worries.' Hugh rang the Ring doorbell on the side gate and stepped back, crossing his arms and frowning as he looked at the sky. God, what must they look like on that three-second recording? The perfect miserable couple, no doubt.

The door opened and Brenda appeared, smiling serenely and wearing her therapist staple – black trousers and cardigan. Alicia wondered whether she wore the same exact pieces every day or if she had an entire wardrobe with multiples – she'd never seen her wear anything else.

'Nice to see you again,' she said.

'And you,' Alicia replied like a moron. Of course it wasn't nice to be here, and it was unlikely that Brenda would take any delight in sitting with them for the next hour and a half as they berated each other and cried a lot – unless she was a masochist.

Alicia and Hugh followed Brenda down the side of her large, detached house and down the winding pathway to her counselling room – a fancy summer house painted in buttercup yellow with photos of serene seascapes adorning the walls. It couldn't be more therapy if it tried.

They settled themselves on the cream sofa in their spots, Alicia on the left, Hugh on the right while Brenda sat on her leather throne opposite them, smiling but not saying anything.

Despite having been here multiple times in 2022, Alicia was unable to relax, instead perching herself stiffly and unable to yield to the comfort of the plush cushions behind her. Hugh looked equally uncomfortable, and Alicia was certain that Brenda had already noticed they weren't touching each other.

The torturous silence continued.

Finally, Brenda broke it. 'So what has brought you back here, then? Last time we talked, things seemed to be going in the right direction.'

A sharp twist of grief stabbed in Alicia's gut. Yes, they had been in a bad place back then – working through her insecurities about Hugh and Hannah had been the darkest period of her life – but somehow, they had clawed their way back, piecing together a fragile sense of normality. She'd give anything to return to that time, as mad as it sounded. At least then, they still believed they could make it through. Hindsight made it clear – they had both been willing to fight, to hold on, to commit to finding a way forward. There had been hope. Right now, that hope felt impossibly distant.

Alicia and Hugh looked at each other. Who was going to attempt to find the words to explain what had gone wrong between then and now?

'Umm,' Alicia added helpfully. The words didn't come. She wasn't sure they even existed.

'We've been having some . . . disagreements lately. Work has been hard for Alicia also, which I don't think is helping.' Hugh didn't look at her.

'Work's been hard, but I don't think that's relevant.' She wouldn't allow herself to be blamed entirely for this. Work was the obvious scapegoat, but it couldn't be held responsible.

'Disagreements?'

Brenda had a way of saying one or two choice words that would then force them to share further details.

Hugh continued. 'Small things, like how to fill the dishwasher—'

God, how clichéd.

'Or snapping at each other for no reason.'

'No reason?'

Hugh ignored Brenda and carried on talking.

'And bigger things.'

He stopped and finally looked at Alicia. She opened her mouth and then closed it again.

Brenda nodded. 'Okay, thank you, Hugh. It's quite normal to have some small disagreements here and there in a relationship – I'm always suspicious of couples who tell me they never argue – however, it sounds like your arguments are having a largely detrimental effect on your marriage.'

'Yes. Absolutely.' Hugh's emphasis on the word *absolutely* was yet another stab to the gut. But it was true.

'We did a lot of work on resentment last time, if I remember rightly. Alicia, you were struggling with Hugh's past, and Hugh felt that you were holding it against him frequently. Do you think these small grievances you speak of are resentment manifesting itself again?'

'It's not just on me.' She sounded like an insolent teenager, but Brenda was a woman, why was she taking Hugh's side?

'No one's saying it is, Alicia. I'm just trying to work out what might be going on.'

Alicia pinched her brow and stared at her feet. *God, have I been to work every day this week with that scuff on my shoe?*

Brenda took a deep breath. 'Perhaps we should park that and come back. Please tell me more about the bigger disagreements you've been having. Alicia?'

Great, so Hugh had the easy bit.

'We're, er, struggling to see eye to eye on . . .'

'Starting a family,' Hugh interjected.

'Are we not already a family? Do we need kids to qualify for that?'

'See, every time I bring it up you get defensive.' Hugh turned to Brenda. 'This is exactly how she acts every time.'

Brenda nodded. 'That must be hard to feel unable to have a conversation, Hugh. However, I'd like to check in with Alicia. Her strong reaction is telling me that it's a very difficult conversation for her to have.'

Alicia picked at her fingernails. Why did she feel like crying?

'Am I reading that correctly, Alicia? Is this a tricky subject?'

Alicia nodded and blinked away the tears that pricked her eyes. Hugh grabbed the tissue box on the table beside him and thrust it towards her.

'And now I feel awful for upsetting her,' he said.

'Alicia is upset, yes. That doesn't mean it's your fault. It's a hard topic to navigate when two people who love each other very much don't align on how they feel about it.'

Alicia took a handful of tissues and dabbed at her eyes.

'I feel so . . . shit. Guilty. Like a failure, when I hear Hugh talking about how he wants to be a dad and wants us to have a baby, and soon at that.'

'So you feel shit and guilty. Why's that?'

Wasn't it obvious? 'Because I'm not sure I . . .'

'Not sure you . . .'

'. . . am ready right now.'

'It's not that.' Hugh huffed and shook his head.

Fury rose in Alicia's chest. 'What do you mean it's not that? Don't tell me how I feel.'

'You're acting as if it's because you don't want one *right now*, when you've told me before that you aren't sure you want to *ever* have one!' Hugh's voice was raised now, and all Alicia wanted to do was curl up into a ball and be swallowed by the worn leather cushion beneath her. 'We've been having this discussion for years now. Years! I don't want to wait another five to then find out you don't want to have babies at all.'

'I can't promise I'll ever give you what you want.' Her voice cracked as shame and sadness engulfed her. She gave in to the sobs that were pushing at her throat; trying to hold them back was like trying to construct a dam on Niagara Falls.

Hugh patted her on the back but she was frozen, unable to do anything other than cry.

No matter how many times they'd managed to bury it over the years, it resurrected itself like the bad guy from a horror movie. It wasn't going away. Hugh wanted to have children and Alicia didn't. They'd come to Brenda's because there was a deluded part of them that thought Brenda would wave her magic wand, say her magic words, and somehow, by some miracle, everything would work out.

But not even Brenda could fix it, and now they were totally and utterly out of options.

Hot Mess Express 🚂 😃

1st June, 2025

Marnie: Han, are you in Spain? I saw on your Insta!!

Hannah: Mallorca for the next month.

Marnie: Wow, what's that for?

Hannah: Secret *Love Island* stuff.

Alicia: You're not going into the villa, are you?

Hannah: I wish 😄 No, strictly business.

Marnie: Shame xxx

Alicia: We still haven't got a date in the diary x

Hannah: Soon!!

Chapter Thirty-Four

4th July, 2025

Marnie

Despite promising to be her best year yet, 2025 was shaping up to be suitably shite.

The worst had happened. The tell-tale feeling of cramps. The red stain in her knickers and on the tissue as she wiped. The midwife helpline had offered her limited reassurance – *it might just be implantation bleeding* – but ultimately had told her to expect the worst.

And the worst had happened. The cramps had ramped up and the bleeding worsened. Then there was the negative pregnancy test, and finally a scan to confirm her womb was empty.

They'd returned from the hospital an hour ago. Daniel had settled Marnie on the sofa with a cup of tea and promised he'd be as quick as he could dropping some extra clothes off to his parents' house so Sophie could stay an extra night.

Gosh, Sophie. How would Marnie tell her that she was not going to be a big sister? They waited as long as they could before telling her, knowing how precarious the first trimester was, but they couldn't hide it from her for the full twelve weeks with Marnie throwing up every five minutes. They'd told Sophie just as they hit eight weeks. She had been ecstatic. Thank God they hadn't announced it to anyone else.

She'd chosen not to tell Hannah or Alicia when they found out they were expecting, partly worried about their judgement, partly waiting until the safety of week twelve.

The front door slammed marking Daniel's return. The sound of fumbling keys and a trainer clanging off the radiator followed and then he appeared at the living room door clutching flowers and a Tesco bag.

He smiled a solemn smile and waved the flowers in the air. 'Shall I put these in a vase for you?'

Marnie heaved herself off the sofa. 'I'll do it. I'm not incapable.'

'Ouch,' Daniel said, but he chuckled. 'You may be interested in the contents of this bag.' He now waved the bag in the air and it rustled with promise.

'Better be the entire chocolate section.'

Daniel grinned knowingly. 'Nailed it. And also two tubes of Pringles, some cheese, crackers, and olives.'

'Girl dinner.'

'Girl dinner indeed. I know you might not fancy eating much but it's there if you fancy some picky bits.'

'Thanks.' She took the bag from him and placed the flowers – lilies, her favourite – on the coffee table. She pinched her brow. 'Headache.'

'Not surprised after the week we've had.'

'I didn't think it was possible to cry so much.' Marnie wasn't a crier, not really. She might cry at silly things like that scene in *Up*, or that time Paola had turned up to work with just one eyebrow on by mistake, but the big stuff? Not often. But this last week had broken her.

She knew the stats. That one in four pregnancies ended in miscarriage in the early stages, but she didn't give it much thought when she and Daniel found out she was pregnant. He was at work and Marnie had felt that telltale feeling of nausea roll over her one morning as she waved Sophie off to the bus stop. She'd pulled out her phone and counted the days since her last period. She was a week late. She did a test the minute she got home; it was positive.

It was a mix of emotions. The expected fear – oh my God, what am I doing? Do I really want to do this all over again? – mixed with the most euphoric, limbs-shaking joy she'd only ever felt when she'd given birth to Sophie. It was funny to think she was shocked by the news when they'd both made the decision to not *not* try. She'd stopped any sort of birth control and when the condoms ran out, they weren't replaced.

She'd had to sit on the news all day until Daniel had come home from work to a near hysterical Marnie clutching the test and a pair of booties she'd picked up at Morrisons. He was as pleased as she was.

She'd never felt a grief like it: a crushing emptiness, a feeling of failure, responsibility and blame at her body for not doing what it should have done to protect the little life growing inside her. Alongside the grief, there was the desperately overwhelming desire to try again. To right the wrong. To fill that space in her heart and her womb with another.

Another wave of grief crashed over her and she dropped the bag on the floor. She cradled her face in her shaking hands. She hated looking so weak.

'Oh Marns. Come here.' Daniel sat on the sofa beside her and pulled her into a hug. He was gentle but at the same time knew how to hold her in just the right way that she felt securely anchored and safe.

'It's my fault. All of it,' she sniffed, wiping her nose with her sleeve.

'Don't you dare say that. It's nothing you've done,' Daniel said into her hair. He kissed her head and squeezed her again. 'These things can't be helped.'

But still, the guilt consumed her.

'I'm being punished.'

'Why?'

'Because of how I was the first time. With Sophie.'

'And how were you the first time? Scared? Confused? Young? It's understandable you weren't sure.'

Marnie was transported back there, to her nineteen-year-old self in the week after she'd found out. She'd looked at miscarriage rates, even googled what caused them in case there was a chance she'd done something accidentally that would make the decision for her. She'd practically wished it, willed it to happen.

'It's karma.'

Daniel pulled back and gripped her shoulders beneath his hands, looking her directly in the eye. 'That's bullshit. You are the best mum in the world to Sophie. You've given her the best life imaginable. If there was a bigger force out there deciding our fates – which I'm not convinced by – they'd look down at you, at us, and see that we're fucking ace people and ace parents.' He took a breath. 'But sadly, it doesn't work like that. Life isn't fair and sometimes life can be shit. But we'll get through this together. I promise you.'

She hoped he was right. She needed him to be right. Allowing herself one more sniff, she then wiped away her tears. 'Love you,' she squeaked.

'Love you too.' Daniel let go of her shoulders and shuffled himself back on the sofa. 'Are you sure you don't want to hang out with Alicia tonight? Even just for a couple of hours? Some girl time might help.'

Alicia wouldn't get it. She had her own shit going on, and despite being empathetic and kind, she would never understand the level of Marnie's loss. How could you unless you'd been there yourself? 'No. I just want to lie here all night eating girl dinner and being looked after.' Marnie grabbed the bunched-up blanket from the arm of the sofa and threw it over herself.

Daniel leaned to tuck himself in beside her and pull her into little spoon position. 'That can be arranged,' he said.

Marnie snuggled herself back into him, feeling his breath on her neck and the warmth of his body on her still aching back. She wouldn't want to be anywhere else.

Alicia and Marnie
12th July, 2025

Marnie: This might come as a shock to you but Daniel and I miscarried a baby last week.

Alicia: No! I'm so, so sorry. I know there's nothing I can say to make it better, but please know I'm always here if you need me. Life is so unfair sometimes. ☹

Marnie: Thank you 🖤x

Alicia: Have you told anyone else?

Marnie: Just Andrea and also Paola because of all the time off I've had.

Alicia: Not Hannah?

Marnie: Not yet. I will do when the time is right. I don't want to send her a message when she's away. Don't want to ruin her vibe.

Alicia: I understand. I don't think she would look at it like that but you need to do what feels most comfortable for you.

Marnie: 😎ok

18th July, 2025

Marnie: Thank you for dropping over. What would I do without you?

Alicia: Always here for you xx

Hot Mess Express 🚂 🤪

22nd July, 2025

Alicia: Happy birthday @Han! Hope you've been spoilt.

Hannah: I have. Trip to Bath for the rooftop spa and posh dinner tonight! Hope life is treating you well xx

Alicia: Perfect.

Marnie: Happy birthday lovely xx

Alicia: Shame we haven't managed to get a date in to meet the famous Marcus.

Marnie: Shit yeah! You said if he made it to your birthday last year, you'd introduce us. Don't make it a hat-trick now.

Hannah: It's on the to-do list!

Alicia: Let's try and get a date in for a coffee and catch up soon.

Marnie: I'm busy every weekend in August apart from the last one. Feels like every one of Dan's school friends are either getting married or christening their kids.

Hannah: I'm away for the whole of August.

Alicia: All of it 😫? Booooo.

Marnie: September is also mad for me because Daniel's family have loads of birthdays in that month. Lots of festive shagging in that family, clearly.

Marnie: I'm going to throw some dates out, let me know if you can do them.

Marnie: October 4th, October 19th, November 1st, November 15th.

Hannah: I can do November the 1st.

Alicia: I'm going to see *Clueless* the musical that day. I can do both October dates?

Hannah: Hallelujah. I can do the morning of the 19th October!! Coffee?!

Alicia: Yesssss!!

Marnie: Excellent. It's in the diary. Perhaps we'll put a date in for next year while we're at it. Seems to be the only way we'll have a day we're all free lol.

Marnie: Galentines Day, duh.

Hannah and Marnie
31st August, 2025

Marnie: Hi Han, just letting you know. Me and Daniel lost a baby via miscarriage a few months ago. Sorry to put it in a message but it's easier for me to type it and also didn't want to wait until we'd have the opportunity to talk in person. I'm okay now, and don't really want to talk about it but just wanted you to know xx

Hannah: I'm so sorry :(Totally understand you don't want to talk about it so I won't push you. Just know I'm thinking of you x

Hot Mess Express 🚂 😜

29th September, 2025

Hannah: I'm so sorry I'm going to have to bail on the October date! Something's come up.

Alicia: Oh no! It took us ages to find a date that worked.

Hannah: I know I'm so sorry.

Alicia: Marnie are you still around?

Marnie: I need to take a rain check too. Daniel's sister's baby might be coming that week and we need to be around.

Chapter Thirty-Five

19th October, 2025

Hannah

Hannah was filming a 'get ready with me' TikTok when her phone – which was propped up on its trusty tripod – started to ring. Marcus. She *could* let it ring out. She was nearly finished with her makeup, only lipstick and mascara left to do and if she moved her phone now it would mess up her video transitions. It was already taking way longer than she hoped it would – her eyeliner just wasn't going right and she'd come to the awful realisation that she was now at the age where putting on any sort of eye makeup came with a challenge akin to applying it to a ballsack. *Am I too young for an eyelid lift?*

'What?' she said the minute she accepted the call. 'Sorry, you okay? I'm just in the middle of something.'

'Love you too. Did you see my message?' Marcus was walking outside as he spoke to her, silhouetted against the miserable grey sky of gloomy England.

'Which message?' He was a very enthusiastic messager – the type to send multiple messages when it could be just one. Hannah leaned into the camera and wiped away the creases that had already settled into her undereye concealer. God, and now she was getting wrinkles. Time for a Botox top-up.

'The one about Friday. Mum's birthday.' Marcus frowned.

'Errrrrr. Don't think so.' Truth be told, she'd not opened any of the messages he'd sent that day, and it was 5:30pm. But she'd been busy at a networking brunch this morning and now she was trying to get herself ready for the taxi that was picking her up at 7pm sharp.

'Me and the girls are taking Mum to The Grove this Friday for High Chai. Shall I book you a seat or not? I'd love to have you there.'

She found it endearing the way he referred to his sisters as *the girls*, and High Chai sounded fun.

'Can I check my diary and let you know?' She didn't know her arse from her elbow most weeks – Christ, she didn't even know what she was doing one minute to the next.

'Can't you check now? It's on your phone, right?' Marcus was now in his car, propping Hannah up on the dashboard as he pulled on his seatbelt.

'I just said I'm in the middle of something.'

Marcus bit his lip and ran his hands through his ruffled, copper hair. 'You're always in the middle of something.'

'Please let's not do this now. I don't have time for this.'

He sighed. 'Just let me know, okay?'

'I will. Of course I will.' She didn't know why she was being so snappy. He never asked for much, always patient, always waiting for her to do whatever she needed to. Maybe it was guilt as if pushing him away would make things easier. He deserved better.

'You know what, don't worry about it. I thought it would

be nice, but I can see you're busy. Just text me when you're home safe, okay?'

'Baby, don't be like that.'

'I'm not being like anything, I just don't know what you want me to say?'

'I don't know either.'

Hannah forced herself to pause. Slow down a minute. Relax. Marcus chewed his bottom lip as he drummed his fingers on the dashboard. She couldn't let him down.

'Book me a seat. I'll be there no matter what. This is important,' she said. 'Of course I want to be there, I was just feeling a bit overwhelmed in that moment. Lots going on.'

'Sure?'

'Sure.'

He hung up. Hannah took a deep breath. *Relationships are all about compromise. It's not just you that you have to think about these days,* she reminded herself. Even now, over a year in, having a long-term boyfriend still felt like uncharted territory. The obligations had multiplied, juggling his needs alongside her own. She'd never done this before, not properly. Meeting the parents, the siblings, the friends. God, that was terrifying. Sitting in meetings with brand managers at big labels was one thing, but nothing compared to the nerves she'd felt when Marcus took her to Topgolf to meet his old school friends. It was all lovely. But it had also been *a lot*.

The early days had been easier, the honeymoon phase making him her priority. She'd wanted to spend every free moment with him. But reality had crept back in and she realised that if she wanted to keep up with the business, she had to pull her head out of his arse and focus. Now, they were figuring out how to navigate a three-way relationship: her, him and Nala Swim.

Hannah grabbed her lipstick – this was a Charlotte Tilbury Pillow Talk occasion – and popped off the cap, but as she slicked it on her newly plumped lips, Hannah felt displaced. She'd almost upset Marcus, and she'd also bailed on the girls. It had been ages since she'd seen Alicia and Marnie properly, and she felt especially shitty considering everything Marnie had been through. But she had other things to do. Did that make her a terrible person? She wasn't sure. Things changed. Life happened. But she couldn't shake the feeling that something important was slipping away, and she wasn't sure she had the energy, time or space to stop it.

Alicia and Marnie
11th February, 2026

Alicia: Have you told Hannah why you aren't able to make Galentine's? I don't know how much she knows x

Marnie: Going to just give her the Sparknotes summary – being in hospital feels like a fair excuse. What more is there to say?

Alicia: Okay, just checking x Going to be weird without you.

Marnie: I'm surprised you didn't cancel.

Alicia: Me too! She was pretty keen and it's been so long I am intrigued to catch up. Won't be the same though.

Marnie: I look forward to hearing about it after. Don't have too much fun without me!

Alicia: Unlikely, you are the life and soul of the party! Also, it's been so long since I last saw her, and one to one at that, I fear it's going to be incredibly awkward.

Marnie: Good luck with that! Joking, you'll be fine. It's only Hannah, she's not that scary.

Alicia: She is a bit scary lol. Anyway, you feeling alright?

Marnie: Been better. Obv.

Alicia: 🙄

Marnie: It is what it is. I'll live. Hopefully.

Alicia: Don't joke about that!

Marnie: I'm okay. Plz don't worry x

Chapter Thirty-Six

13th February, 2026

Alicia

Alicia looked at Hannah, who leaned against the breakfast bar as if it hadn't been years since she'd last been in her house. Their stifled conversation since she arrived was as painful as expected. Why had Hannah been so insistent on still doing this, especially considering the whole Marnie thing? She'd not been bothered to slot them in for a speedy coffee when she was back from her various travel destinations, and Alicia knew she'd not spoken much to Marnie separately either.

She hadn't been there like Alicia had. She hadn't been on the end of the phone all hours of the night when Daniel was working away. She hadn't turned up on Marnie's doorstep at 10:30pm that Monday night fearing the worst when Marnie sent her a cryptic message about *not being able to do this anymore* and then all her messages went undelivered. She knew why Marnie wasn't here, but beyond the practical facts, she had no idea just how much of a hard time she'd been through this past year.

Alicia picked at a crisp and nibbled it. She wasn't hungry but it was something to do. She was speedily running out of topics to talk about and questions to ask – they'd already spoken about Nala Swim, their families, and in part, Marnie. Perhaps Alicia should have a drink, although she was currently attempting to extend Dry January into a Dry Year. She'd scared herself at her reliance on a glass of wine every night to 'relax' and so this year's resolution was to prove to herself it wasn't an addiction, but a choice, an act of self-care.

'Shall we go and sit in the living room?' A change of scene might help them warm up. She could put some music on the speakers in there, too.

'Sounds like a plan.'

Alicia led the way, sombrero-shaped bowl of Doritos in one hand and cup of tea in the other. She set them both down on the coffee table next to Hugh's stacks of landscape photography books and sat on the leather armchair beside the bookcase. Hannah perched herself on the sofa. It was weird to see her in the house after all these years. Alicia wondered if she was silently judging her choice of decor or spying the photos on the wall of her and Hugh on their wedding day. She tried not to look at those these days.

Alicia was pleased that he wasn't there, partly because it was still awkward when the three of them were together, and partly because Hannah looked as immaculate as ever. Her hair was in her statement loose beachy waves, face-framing curtain bangs perfectly positioned. She was in a well-fitting pair of wide-leg jeans and a simple white tee. Y2K meets Gen Z coded – she looked like one of Alicia's Sixth Form students. She'd definitely had more work done, too. It looked good, natural, although Alicia could never pull it off.

Despite the room change, the heavy silence continued, and

so Alicia busied herself with putting on a smooth jazz playlist for some background noise.

Hannah leaned back on the sofa and kicked her feet up on the footrest. Relaxing or just for show? 'So what's new with you? It's been a while.'

Understatement of the century. Over a year since they'd seen each other in person and – before their brief exchange to arrange this meet-up – Alicia couldn't remember the last time Hannah had messaged her directly; she hadn't even wished her a happy birthday this year, despite Alicia never forgetting hers.

Alicia finally allowed herself to settle on the armchair, leaning forward to grab her tea from its coaster. 'I've been promoted to head of English, well, been offered it anyway.'

'No way! That's amazing.'

It was unlikely Hannah thought it was amazing but Alicia appreciated her stellar performance of pretending she was impressed. They were no longer at the point where they could question each other with the familiarity and security that comes with a close friendship. After Marnie's surprise hen do and shotgun wedding, everything seemed like it was going to go back to how it had once been – frequent check-ins via text, coffee and catch-up dates as often as their schedules might allow, but very quickly, their enthusiasm had petered out.

Alicia couldn't quite pinpoint why things had changed. It appeared to have less to do with a big, life-changing fallout, instead being something quieter, more stealthy. A slow decay rather than a dramatic break.

Alicia sipped her tea, despite it being hot enough to burn her tongue. 'Thanks,' was all she could say.

'Will you take it?'

'Probably.' It would be mad for Alicia not to take the job.

It was a significant pay rise, although it was also a significant rise in responsibility and workload, too. But she'd made her bed and now she needed to lie in it. She had no other option. 'How are things with Marcus?'

'Yeah, great,' Hannah said a little too quickly.

'Are you living together now?'

'Not yet. He's keen but we're not sure where to put roots down. I want to stay in London and he's more of a country bumpkin.'

'How about around here? Green fields but only a twenty-minute train to London.'

'God no.' Hannah's features twisted into a grimace. 'I mean, it's just not for us.' She smiled then, but offence had already been taken.

'What about St Albans?' Alicia said. No one could scoff at St Albans, with its beautiful cathedral, Saturday market and house prices fourteen times the average annual income.

'Maybe.' Hannah shuffled in her seat and fiddled with her hair. 'So you said you hadn't heard any more details from Marnie?'

Alicia knew she wouldn't leave it at just asking the once. 'Nothing significant.' It was true. She was still in the hospital, which Hannah knew, and Alicia was working on the assumption of *no news is good news*.

Hannah frowned, the first expression of sincerity Alicia had seen since she'd arrived. 'Are you worried about her?'

Alicia sighed, feeling her own walls begin to lower. 'A bit. But she's in the best place.' Alicia knew Marnie would disagree with that. 'You?'

Hannah nodded. 'Yeah. Same. It's shit, isn't it?'

Now that was something they could agree on. 'Very.' Alicia wanted to say more but the words didn't come.

She was saved from having to conjure up any more topics of conversation by her phone pinging with multiple notifications all at once.

She looked at her screen. Daniel. She opened the chat hurriedly, eyes scanning his flurry of words.

'Shit,' she said.

'What?' Hannah's brow creased.

Alicia stood, heart pounding, adrenaline surging. 'Get your shoes on. We need to get to the hospital.'

Chapter Thirty-Seven

13th February, 2026

Hannah

Why did they make hospital waiting rooms so damn uncomfortable? Hannah had lost track of how long they'd been sitting there, but her arse was certainly keeping score against the hard plastic chair. She shuffled to try and gain some relief, to no avail.

The awkwardness between her and Alicia had alleviated somewhat, the pressure to make conversation lighter in a waiting room where others were sitting in silence too. Alicia had brought in a book she kept in the car, and Hannah kept herself busy scrolling her various socials, though she wasn't taking much in.

'Coffee?' She needed to stand up and move her legs. The adrenaline coursing through her body was too much to bear.

'Please,' Alicia said. 'I'm knackered. It's way past my bedtime.'

Hannah made her way along the corridor, the hospital smell in her nose, and head pounding from the combination of bright lights, heating on max and stark decor. She didn't spend much time in hospitals, but whenever she was in one, she couldn't help but recall the few horrible times she'd been there before. She remembered the time she and Alicia came to see Marnie when Sophie was small because she was poorly with bronchiolitis. They'd turned up with loads of goodies, but this time neither of them even thought to grab the essentials like chargers or coats. Not that Marnie would be in any state for goodies. Hannah was also pulled back to the time she'd last been in a hospital to visit her granddad. When she left the ward that day, she knew in her gut it would be the last time she'd see him and made a conscious effort to take a photo in her mind of him smiling at her as he gripped her hand and said he loved her.

Hannah distracted herself from the growing sadness in her chest by getting her and Alicia a weak-looking cup of coffee. She also bought two bags of Mini Cheddars from the vending machine. It wouldn't have been her first choice, but Hannah's stomach was so empty she was happy to fill it with anything even the slightest bit edible.

Her phone vibrated in her pocket as she snatched up the packets of crackers from the machine's grasp. She knew who it would be.

Marcus: Call me when you can. Hope everything is okay xxx

He'd messaged her multiple times today, but she'd only sent one – a vague, rushed placeholder of 'Marnie hospital, talk later.' Hannah wasn't even sure if she'd written a kiss.

She sighed and put the phone back in her pocket. She'd call him soon. She weaved her way back to Alicia, wanting to go slowly to avoid the oppressiveness of the waiting room, but unable to do so in case Daniel appeared with news.

'What's taking so long?' she said as she handed Alicia the goods and settled back down on her chair with a wince. 'They ran out of lids and sugar.'

Alicia shook her head. 'Dunno. Thanks. That's okay.'

Surely the longer it took, the worse it was . . .

Hannah's focus was pulled to the double doors at the other end of the room flinging open. A rush of scrubbed-up people whizzed past them, urgency palpable in their frenzied silence.

'What if that's for her . . .' Alicia whispered. Her face crumpled as she blinked back tears.

'It's not for her.' Hannah needed to convince herself. 'Everything's going to be fine.' Instinctively, she reached for Alicia's hand and squeezed. It was trembling and clammy, but the familiar delicate touch of her slender fingers made Hannah hold on tighter; she wasn't going to let go.

Alicia squeezed back.

They sat in silence, holding onto each other with one hand and sipping their drinks with the other. They didn't need to fill the space between them with words this time. The silence spoke for them, of their shared concern and unspoken solidarity.

After finishing off her coffee and chucking the last Mini Cheddar in her mouth, Hannah felt compelled to say something that had been building inside her for the past fifteen minutes.

'Don't take the job,' she said.

Alicia frowned. 'Why not?'

'You clearly hate it, unless something miraculous has happened over the past year that I'm not aware of.'

'I don't *hate* it.'

'Really?'

'Okay, so I might hate it. But that's just life, isn't it?' Alicia's words lacked her usual conviction.

'It doesn't have to be.'

Alicia stared into her cup. 'What would I do?'

'What do you want to do?'

'Travel? Write a book?'

'So do it.'

'I have a mortgage to pay.'

'Okay, so don't pack in the teaching just yet, but you can take a step towards the life you actually want to live. Start writing? Sign up to a course?' She was being pushy, but that familiar sense of protectiveness, of wanting to champion the people she cared about, fought its way out.

'I'll think about it,' Alicia offered. She nodded slowly, biting down on her lip, eyes still shiny. 'How about you?'

Hannah was taken aback. 'What about me?'

'Are you where you want to be? Not here obviously, I mean in life.'

'Hmm.' Hannah stared at the floor. Her immaculate nude Balenciaga trainers contrasted against the scuffed hospital floor. 'I've got money, my own business, I have what I've always wanted, and it's amazing. I love it, I'm so grateful and I wouldn't change any of it for the world.'

'But?'

Hannah paused. Was there a but? How *could* there be a but? It wasn't like it was for Alicia – thinking she wanted one thing and then realising maybe it wasn't all it was cracked up to be. Her life *did* live up to how she expected it to be; in fact, it was even better than she could have ever imagined.

Alicia continued. 'Maybe everything is perfect and I'm just pessimistic.'

Hannah paused again. Her life was exciting and thrilling and comfortable and busy and amazing, but it wasn't perfect. 'Nothing's ever *perfect*.'

'Tell me more.' Alicia put down her paper cup and leaned in close.

'Are you therapising me?'

'Maybe.'

'Okay, so I sometimes wish I had a time machine – not so I can go back and change anything – but so I can have more time. I don't have the time to do everything I want. I don't see my family anywhere near enough, especially with Gaia growing up so fast. My parents are getting older and don't even get me started on how little time I have for my friends or relationship.'

Hannah caught a look flash across Alicia's face. 'Life happens.'

'I know. But I choose what I do with my time, and I've chosen to put it all into the business.'

'It's your job, like teaching is mine.'

'Yeah.' Hannah twisted a strand of her hair, twirling it round and round her delicate finger. 'I do wonder sometimes if I've lost sight of why I wanted this lifestyle in the first place, though. I wanted it so I could have freedom from the corporate world, do my own thing, on my own time. But it certainly doesn't feel like that. I'm tearing around like a blue-arse fly most days. I feel guilty a lot because I have to choose between this event-slash-meeting-slash-party or spending time with friends, family or Marcus.' Marcus's name caught in her throat.

'Marcus is supportive though, right?' Alicia's brow furrowed with concern.

Hannah forced a smile. 'Super supportive. But I do wish

I could give him more of my time. Not because I think I owe him that but because I want to. I love the time I spend with him, it's just not enough. Even when we have a weekend away or a holiday, I'm working.'

'He knew how your life was before he chose to be with you.'

'Yeah, I guess, but we were both under the impression it would slow down a bit. That it would stop being quite so manic, and here we are, years later, and it hasn't.'

'You're being really harsh on yourself. He must be super busy with his job. It takes two to make a relationship work.'

'Maybe.' That was true to a degree. Marcus was busy, sometimes working night shifts, other times weekends, but Hannah always felt like one of his priorities. When they were together, whether it was a thirty-second phone call or an entire evening, he'd give her his full attention. Poor Marcus often only got a fraction of her focus even in those moments it was just the two of them there.

Hannah sighed. 'In one way, I really pushed against my mum when she tried to force me to be this corporate, ladder-climbing workaholic. I mean you know just as much as me how I really didn't want to become this person who put work and status above things like family and living life. But I'm coming to realise that I've still lived by that motto, just in a different way. I've still felt that pressure to do something amazing with my life, constantly going after the next thing and never feeling like it's enough. I'm starting to realise that maybe the next thing I need to pursue is balance.'

'Yeah?' Alicia's eyes were welling up again. 'You're amazing. I couldn't do half of what you do without having a breakdown.'

Hannah suddenly felt exposed. God, what had she just

said? The words had tumbled out of her mouth with very little censorship, but it felt good. It felt freeing. Hannah looked away from Alicia. 'I think the lack of sleep and this dodgy coffee has got to my brain. I'm feeling a bit delirious,' she chuckled. 'To summarise, the last thing I want to do is lose perspective on what's actually important.'

Alicia reached out and squeezed Hannah's hand. 'The fact you're saying this tells me you're far from that.'

Hannah looked up. Alicia smiled warmly at her; her cheeks flushed, mascara smudged and smile lines lit by the harsh lighting above them. Hannah's earlier feeling of vulnerability ebbed. 'Do you mind if I give Marcus a quick ring? Not very Galentine's I know, but none of this is.' Hannah motioned around them.

Alicia laughed. 'I'll make an exception. In fact, I insist.'

'Thanks. Call me if there's any news, I'll just stand out the front.' Hannah grabbed her handbag and hurried down the hall.

The chill of the cold air smacked Hannah's face as she stepped out of the automatic doors, a relief from the suffocating heat of the hospital. Marcus picked up in two rings.

'Hey, are you okay? I've been so worried about you.'

Despite the cold, Hannah's body flooded with warmth. 'It's so good to hear your voice.'

Marcus chuckled. 'Really?'

'Really.' Hannah paced as she carried on talking. She needed to keep moving or she'd turn into an ice cube. 'I'm okay. We're still waiting for news.'

'What a worry. She'll be okay. The doctors know what they're doing.'

'Yeah?'

'Yeah. Do you want me to come? My shift starts in two hours but I can be there for a bit?'

'It's okay, I've got Alicia. Thanks though. Let's hang out tomorrow after your shift though?'

'I thought Sundays were your admin days?'

'Fuck admin. I want to see you. I miss you.'

'Have they given you something at the hospital?' Marcus laughed. 'Don't get me wrong, I love it.'

'Maybe there was something in the coffee.' Hannah laughed too. 'Na, I've just had some realisations here about priorities. I want you to know I love you just as much as Nala Swim. Maybe even an incy bit more.'

'I don't need more, but I wouldn't say no to the same standing.'

'That can be arranged.' Hannah paused to switch her phone to her other hand. Her fingers were going numb. 'Right, I need to get back in there in case there's some news. Also it's freezing and I don't have a coat.'

'God yeah, get back in. We don't want you to catch a chill now. I'll see you tomorrow. I love you. Never forget it.'

Never. 'I love you too.'

Hannah made her way back to Alicia, rubbing her hands together like mad to try and bring some feeling back into them. Despite this, her heart was full.

'Did it go okay?' Alicia asked when Hannah sat back next to her.

'Yeah. I—'

'Girls.' Daniel's voice cut in as he appeared from around a corner, eyes red and cheeks wet with tears. Happy tears? They better be happy tears . . . or . . . or . . .

'He's here.'

Chapter Thirty-Eight

13th February, 2026

Marnie

Marnie took a deep breath and allowed herself to take a moment. She looked to the bassinet beside her, and there he was. A tuft of fair, almost white-blonde hair, pink skin, utter perfection. *He's actually here*. She couldn't quite believe it.

'Thank fuck that's over with,' Daniel grinned, eyes red from tears and tiredness.

'Understatement of the century.' It hadn't just been the angst of the last few days, but the previous months, that was now finally over. This little person, lying there asleep without any care in the world, had no knowledge of the toil, anxiety, joy, sadness, and at times terror, he had inadvertently caused.

The initial high of the positive pregnancy test had quickly faded into crippling anxiety as Marnie danced between excitement and total fear. Every time she went to the toilet in the first trimester, she'd take a deep breath before pulling her knickers down, and any flutter from her womb caused panic. As time progressed and they made it into the second trimester and then the third, she allowed herself to relax a little more, although the thought that it could all be snatched away was never far from her mind.

And just when they seemed to be on the home-stretch, it all started to go wrong again. High blood pressure, headaches. The diagnosis of pre-eclampsia that progressed from frequent monitoring to bed rest to being admitted to the hospital for constant observation. At thirty-six weeks exactly, baby boy decided he didn't want to wait, and they were both rushed in for an emergency C-section. Both mother and baby had gone downhill, and it was touch and go.

Marnie had been utterly terrified.

She pushed away the rising emotion in her throat and brought herself back to the present moment. They were okay. She was battered and bruised and fed up with being prodded and poked, but she was alive, and so was her baby boy.

Of course, she knew that this was just the start of a new chapter, the hard work was only beginning, but Marnie was so incredibly grateful to know that this time, she wasn't doing it alone. The night feeds, the school runs, the good times and the bad, the load would be lighter because it would be shared.

'I love you so much.' Daniel reached out to stroke her arm, being careful to avoid her cannula and bruises from having her bloods taken. He'd been there every step of the way, picking her up both physically and emotionally when things had got too much. He'd encouraged her to go back to therapy again, took care of Sophie in the early days when she was recovering from the miscarriage, and pushed her to spend time with Andrea or Paola for a coffee and a cry. In the more recent weeks when Marnie had been hospital bound, he held her hand during every scan and just now, every minute of the C-section. Even when Noah had been born, Daniel's first concern was how Marnie was doing. She'd made a lot of mistakes in her life, but marrying Daniel wasn't one of them.

Whatever the next few months, weeks and years would bring, she knew she'd be okay. Things were different this time. Not only because of him, but her, too. She was different.

She had a stronger understanding of who she was, what she wanted, and how important it was not to lose sight of that. She'd be easy on herself as she felt her way into this new world, taking the time she needed to settle into what life would look like now. But she'd also prioritise herself, picking the volunteering back up as soon as she felt ready, even if it was just once a month. If it felt right, she wanted to go back to work sometime within the next year. Crucially, she'd keep checking in with herself, seeing what she needed and wanted, not just doing what she felt like she *should* be doing. She also knew that when Noah was in nursery, she'd do her Level 3 at college. She remembered something Hannah had said back when Sophie was tiny – that this stage of life was just one of many chapters. Her time wasn't lost, just paused. She knew from experience it would come back around.

Daniel stood from the chair beside Marnie's bed. 'Shall I go and get the girls? They are dying to come in and see you.'

'Yes!' Despite being utterly exhausted, Marnie couldn't wait to see her girls and introduce them to the newest member of the crew.

'Back in two.' Daniel leaned down to kiss her on the head, his lips warm against her clammy forehead.

A few minutes later, he reappeared, followed closely by Hannah and Alicia, who both looked like they'd done two rounds with Anthony Joshua – dark circles under their eyes, unbrushed hair: the picture of exhaustion. Marnie's heart swelled with warmth and gratitude at the thought of them having sat there for God knows how long, supporting her from afar.

'Trust you to have a baby boy on the sacred day of Galentine's.' Hannah grinned at Marnie as she and Alicia shuffled into the ward.

'I know, what the hell! Noah is very sorry he caused so much drama.'

'Noah! I love that name. One of the few names I've not dated, so no ill feelings towards it,' Hannah laughed.

'I daren't ask Alicia if she's taught any naughty Noahs.' Daniel wiped at his brow, cheeks still flushed from the madness of the last twenty-four hours.

'I've taught a few Noahs in my time. Only one was a bit of a . . . challenge.' Alicia made her way around the bed and towards the bassinet. She peered in, eyes watery. 'He's perfect, Marns.'

'Thanks.' Marnie shuffled the bedsheet up over her chest, suddenly self-conscious. She didn't have time to get changed into the pretty new nightie she'd planned to wear during birth, instead she was stuck in her old granny one that her boob frequently fell out of. 'Sorry, I must look like utter shit.'

'Since when did you care?' Hannah perched on the end of the bed. 'Also, we'll let you off seeing as you've just given birth. How are you feeling?'

'Amazing, the epidural hasn't worn off yet. Ask me again in a few hours.'

'Did you know it was going to be a boy?' Alicia was still peering at Noah, totally transfixed. Marnie got it. She couldn't stop staring at him herself.

'We had no idea. Wanted it to be a surprise. I got rid of all of Sophie's baby bits years ago so it's not like I was hoping for a girl because we had all the stuff.'

'I didn't care either way as long as they were healthy,' said Daniel. He stood from the chair he was sat on and glanced yet again at his son and then to Marnie. 'Shall I leave you girls to it? I can grab coffee. Marns, do you want any more water or juice?'

'Go on then, you do spoil me.' Marnie smiled, and he smiled back. In that moment, she felt it – her chest light, her breath steady, her heart full. Pride. Relief. Joy. *We did it.*

Alicia finally pulled her gaze from Noah and locked eyes with Marnie. 'I'm so glad he's here and you're both safe. I was really worried.'

'Me too. It's been pretty shitty.' Marnie took a deep, steadying breath. 'He wanted to be here for Galentine's Day.'

Hannah chuckled. 'He did. Mad to think that, even now when Marnie's literally in labour, we're still here celebrating.'

'We've had a good run. Especially given everything that's happened over the years.'

Alicia winced and shook her head. 'Let's not talk about that,' she chuckled but crossed her arms in front of her chest and looked at the floor.

'Water under the bridge.' It was Hannah's turn to shake her head as she flapped at Alicia. Was that a genuine look of fondness that Marnie had just observed between the two of them? 'How's Soph?'

Marnie's chest physically ached when she thought about her now not-so-little girl. She missed her *so* much – three weeks was the longest she'd ever been away from her. Daniel had brought her in to visit every day after school, but it wasn't the same as being at home with her little family.

'She's so excited. I hope she's not going to throw a hissy

that she's got a brother, not a sister, though. I'm sure she'll still insist on dressing him up and doing his nails.' Marnie couldn't stop herself from imagining the future, fleeting vignettes of their life to come – Sophie and Noah's first Christmas, Sophie pushing Noah on the swings, their first easter egg hunt, both of them as teens/adults at her future graduation. 'I can't wait for her to meet him. She's going to be the best big sister. Can you believe she's a teenager this year?'

'God, don't. How has that happened?' Hannah squeezed Marnie's knee over the thin hospital bedsheet. It still felt weird from the epidural. 'Noah's a lucky lad. With a mum like you, a dad like Daniel and a sister like Sophie, he's sorted for life.'

'You'll make me cry.' Marnie stuck her bottom lip out. 'Don't forget his aunties.'

'Auntie Alicia will protect him at all costs.' Alicia moved again to be beside the bassinet and rested her hand on its edge.

'Do you want to hold him?' Marnie could tell Alicia was itching for a baby snuggle.

'Desperate to. I don't want to disturb him, though.'

'He's okay, he loves cuddles. Who's first?'

Hannah stepped aside and gestured to Alicia. 'I'll let Alicia do the honours this time. It's only fair.'

There it was again, a smile swapped between them. A signal of the ceasefire.

Chapter Thirty-Nine

13th February, 2026

Alicia

Alicia leaned down gently to scoop up Noah. He was so small and despite having more practice with babies now, there was still something scary about picking up someone so new and fragile. She was careful to support his head as she lifted him from the bassinet and slid him into the crook of her arm.

'He's tiny!' she exclaimed, as she tried to acclimatise to his feather-light weight.

'Four pounds eleven. Not bad considering.'

'I love him so much already.' Alicia settled down in the armchair beside Marnie and stared down at the baby in her arms. He was utter perfection. Such a cliché, but it was true. His skin was perfect. His white wisps of eyebrow were perfect. His nose, round and cherubic, was perfect. The way he felt warm even through his white Winnie-the-Pooh print baby grow was the perfect antidote to all the stress and anxiety Alicia's had felt over the past few hours.

She could see why people got broody, as an innate part of her chimed in: *maybe it wouldn't be that bad to have one*. Thankfully, she was able to catch the thought before it spiralled. *Just be in the moment and enjoy it for exactly what it is without overthinking and ruining it for a change.*

She couldn't take her eyes off him as she watched his chest move up and down, the picture of utter innocence. *Who will he become? What will he be like? What will he do? Will he be happy?* The last thing was most important, and as her mind raced through all of these thoughts, something shifted within her.

Life was too short to be miserable. It seemed obvious in this moment, ludicrous even to consider that she hadn't realised it sooner. But it was better late than never.

'I'm not going to take the job.' The words tumbled from her lips but she meant them with every fibre of her being. Was she totally mad? Maybe. But everyone was allowed to have a mad moment or two in their lifetime. Hers was well overdue.

'Is this the promotion?' Marnie asked.

Alicia nodded.

'Are you sure?' Hannah's eyes widened.

'No. But I'm going to try my best to follow my heart for a change.' Alicia looked back down at Noah and stroked his hand. She could never get over how soft baby skin was, especially the backs of their hands and feet. It was like stroking a cloud.

Hannah stood from the bed and made her way to Alicia and Noah. She caressed Noah's head delicately with perfectly manicured nails. 'Trying your best is all you can do,' she said.

'You know we'll support you no matter what,' said Marnie. 'What do you think Hugh would say?'

Alicia shook her head. She didn't want to talk about Hugh – not now, not while she was part of something so precious – but as always, her emotions betrayed her. Before she could stop it, a tear slipped down her cheek. With her hands full, she couldn't wipe it away. She blinked rapidly, trying to shake it off, then awkwardly brushed her cheek against her shoulder before it could fall onto Noah.

'Alicia?' Marnie sat forward.

'What?'

'Are you okay?'

'Yeah, just overwhelmed. He's perfect.'

'I totally understand that you're overwhelmed by my son's beauty, but I'm not a fool. What's up?'

Alicia felt Marnie's eyes on her but she didn't look up from Noah. 'I don't want to ruin the moment.'

'You couldn't. Babies are the perfect remedy. We can all just sniff his head and feel better.'

Alicia chuckled through her tears. She'd say it quickly and get it out of the way. Then they could all move on. Perhaps her ending wouldn't feel quite so painful against the backdrop of such a special beginning.

'Hugh and I are separating. I'm sad but I'm fine. I've cried a lot about it and it's for the best.' It sounded so blunt and curt – totally the opposite to how she was feeling – but she needed to keep it that way or she'd crumble.

'Fuck.' Marnie shook her head. 'Why didn't you say?'

'You knew we were discussing it.'

Hannah moved to perch back on the bed. 'I didn't.'

Alicia didn't know what to say, so instead offered Hannah an apologetic smile before looking back at Marnie. 'You had a lot on, Marns. I didn't want to stress you out more.'

'I wouldn't have minded.'

'Well, I did. Honestly, I'm okay. Or at least I know I will be.' Alicia had to believe that or else, what the hell was she doing?

'How did you decide that this is what you both want? God. It is what you both want, right?' Marnie winced.

Alicia nodded. Thankfully, it was a mutual decision, although that didn't make it any less painful. 'Therapy. Lots of it. Actually talking to each other.'

It was the hardest thing she'd ever done, sitting in Brenda's little summerhouse that session when they decided they'd reached the end of their journey together. As Alicia recounted the moment to the girls, she was back there, in her seat on the worn sofa.

'I can see you love each other very, very much. That is so incredibly clear to me,' Brenda had said in her usual gentle tone. 'However, I'm also hearing that you want very different things from the future. Would that be true to say?'

Alicia and Hugh looked at each other and nodded.

'And would you say you're both willing to compromise on your futures? Or is that too much of a big thing to compromise on? It's okay if it is.'

A wave of something Alicia couldn't name rolled over her and she snatched a breath. 'Is it okay, though? I feel like it shouldn't be. We should do anything for love. Love conquers all, right?' she'd said through tears.

'Have we given up? Should we be trying harder to fix this?' Hugh pinched his brow, sorrow plain to see on his furrowed face.

Brenda's eyes were kind as she spoke. 'There are no shoulds about it. I've seen you both fight so hard for this. But giving up hope that each other will change and setting the other free of that expectation could be the kindest thing you can do for one another. You can choose your relationship, but it's okay not to at the cost of yourselves.'

It was the permission they'd both needed. Relief and grief

intermingled in that moment as Alicia's carefully curated life crumbled leaving nothing but sadness and loss in its place.

Back in the hospital, Marnie and Hannah's faces shared the same sentiment.

'That's so sad.' Hannah blinked manically, eyes rolling back in an attempt to stop her tears. Alicia had always envied people who could hold back their emotions. How did anyone have control over such powerful things? Unless Alicia's were just more ferocious than others.

'It is very sad,' Marnie said in a wobbly voice, her own eyes shiny. 'Sniff the baby, quick.'

Alicia leaned forward and sniffed Noah's head. God, it did smell good. They all chuckled.

Hannah stood up again from the bed and knelt down in front of Alicia and Noah. She took a whiff of his head too and sighed. 'It's like crack.' She stood back up. 'I don't know what to say.'

'Don't say anything. I know the next few months are going to be hard. I'm going to have to give up everything I know and start again, but there's also something really exciting in that.' Alicia couldn't quite believe she was saying it, but the slight hope of something new and better was glimmering amongst all of the grief and loss.

'I'm loving this new rebellious Alicia.' Marnie wiggled her shoulders excitedly.

'I wouldn't go that far.' Alicia chuckled. 'It's a miracle if I get through an entire day without crying, but at least I'm starting to believe things will get better.'

'She's having her *Eat, Pray, Love* moment.' Hannah punched the air enthusiastically. 'Go get it!'

'I am! Better late than never.' The knot in Alicia's stomach began to unfurl.

Hannah stood, placing her hands on her hips. She always meant business with this pose. 'I have an idea, something to get you started.'

'And what's that?' Alicia eyed her suspiciously. *Intriguing*.

'Why don't you join me on my trip to Rome in the summer?'

'Yessssss!' Marnie squealed. 'Do it. Do it.'

'Really?' Alicia's heart quickened, not anxiety this time. Excitement? 'You'd take me abroad again after last time. I'm a liability!'

'I have insurance.' Hannah laughed.

'Can I tentatively say yes?' There was nothing to stop her this time apart from herself, and she'd stood in her own way enough times to not want to do it again . . . ever. Or at least stumble at the first hurdle.

'Locked in. Can't wait.' Hannah rubbed her hands together. 'And you're sure you're okay, yeah?'

Alicia paused before responding. She nodded. 'I am. Don't get me wrong, I've been having all sorts of feelings alongside the sadness. There's something really . . . shameful about the thought of getting divorced so young. Telling people, especially our families, has been *tough*. It may be a weird word to use but it feels so embarrassing, like I've failed in some way. I was so careful who I chose as my life partner, and I got it wrong. And don't even get me started on the bloody expensive wedding.'

'You didn't get anything wrong.' Marnie reached over from her spot on the bed and gently stroked Noah's cheek. 'I've had my fair share of "failed" relationships. But would I actually call them failures? No. I've learned so much from them. They've all pushed me to look inward, to really ask myself: Who am I? What do I want?' Marnie lifted her gaze from Noah to Alicia, her eyes glistening with sincerity. 'And now look. I wouldn't be here, the person I am today, without those heartbreaks and those tears. Without recognising the times I made myself smaller or changed who I was just to fit into what those past relationships expected me to be. God, imagine what my life would look like if I was still with Steven. I dread to think!'

Hannah moved herself to the edge of the bed near Marnie. 'Spot on.' She nodded enthusiastically. 'I feel like only the "lucky ones" stay with their first love and get it "right" first time. Some people are only ever meant to be a chapter in our lives. Doesn't mean we've failed, it just means we've grown.'

Tears pricked the backs of Alicia's eyes again; this time, the energy behind them was gratitude. Relief. She wasn't on her own in all this and it was unlikely she ever would be with her girls by her side. Which got her thinking . . .

'Do you think the same goes for friendships?'

Hannah tilted her head, lips pursed in contemplation. 'Some,' she said, nodding slowly.

'Ours?'

'Hmm.' Hannah continued to frown. 'I can't speak for the future but we've weathered an awful lot of change over the years. We've literally gone from teenagers to fully fledged adults.'

'And we're still here together,' Marnie added. 'Perhaps it's more about accepting that our friendship looks different now to when we were eighteen.'

'Yep. And choosing to reconnect with each other again and again, even after bust-ups, drifting away and busy lives.' Hannah reached her hand out and squeezed the crook of Alicia's elbow, being careful of Noah in her arms.

'I wanna be a part of this, but I can't bloody move,' Marnie laughed.

'We'll come to you. Here, Han, take the baby.' Alicia held Noah towards Hannah.

'Still don't know what I'm doing so I'll put him in the cot until I'm sitting properly.' Hannah placed Noah tentatively in the bassinet and stroked his head gently. She moved to perch beside Marnie on the bed and laid her head in the crook of her neck. Alicia joined them on the other side, perched at a funny angle so as to not fall off or hurt an obviously fragile Marnie. She looped her arm through Marnie's gently.

'I wonder what the next fifteen years will look like and if it will go as quick as the last fifteen.' Alicia shook her head. Her eighteen-year-old self felt like a million miles away from who she was now, but at the same time, it felt like it was only yesterday that they'd sat in her room making their Galentine's promise.

Alicia thought back to that first sleepover – the three of them on the cusp of adulthood, staring into the total unknown. All they'd had was each other, the illusion of a plan, and the fragile promise of a dream. None of them knew what was ahead of them.

What heartbreak, joys and wisdom would their next chapter reveal?

'We'll be almost fifty. Soph will be nearly thirty.' Marnie mimed gagging. 'Maybe let's not think about that. One day at a time.' She sighed. 'The only thing I know for certain is that, come hell or highwater, I'm going to show up for you both, and myself, every bloody year, no matter what. Even if I'm dead I'll come back to haunt you. Deal?'

'Don't say that! But yes, deal.' Hannah snuggled herself closer to Marnie.

Alicia did the same, shuffling over so Marnie's hair tickled her cheek. 'Sounds like a plan,' she said. *Maybe not the right word*. 'Scrap that, screw plans. Sounds like a promise. To Galentine's, no matter what.'

'To Galentine's, forever and always!'

Acknowledgements

Acknowledgements are always so hard to write because no words could ever do justice to how grateful I am to everyone, both directly and indirectly involved in the creation of this book. But here I am, giving it a go. Bonus drinking game: Take a shot every time I say thanks/champion/support. . .

The biggest of thanks to the best agent in the world, Sara O'Keeffe, who is the most enthusiastic, kind and tenacious cheerleader one could possibly want. Thank you for being with me every step of my writing journey and keeping me sane and optimistic. To many more book deals we go!

To the bestest of best friends, Heather, how lucky am I to have a twin and inbuilt best friend? You are my favourite ♡ Every day is *Galentine's Day* with you.

To Mum, Dad, Sheila, my Leicester and my Twickenham family – I am beyond grateful to have such a wonderful, loving, and normal (lol) family.

To Liam, my soulmate, my biggest supporter and champion. No words could ever do justice to how much I love you and how blessed I feel to be your Bean. I couldn't do half of what I do without your support and your encouraging words, my favourite of which: "It's not worth farting your balls over it."

Bhav, thank you for sharing your insights on what it's like to be a second-generation immigrant. Your PowerPoint presentation (and charming wit) should be shared with the world. Crack out those chinos again – second book launch incoming.

To Amy Mae Baxter – where do I begin? Firstly, huge thanks for seeing potential in me and my writing and giving me this opportunity. Secondly, *Galentine's Day* would simply not exist in the way it does right now without your wonderfully creative brain and stellar editing skills. You are a joy to work with, lightning quick, kind, funny, and an all-around good egg. Ten out of ten, no notes.

To the team at Avon, who have been AMAZING at every stage of this book's development. Every one of you is fantastic, and I am forever indebted to you.

Of course, I must mention My Gals – Emily, Katherine, Ellie, Bryony, Harriet, and Victoria, and my writing besties Gina, Daisy, Zoe, and Sophie Jo. A shoutout must also go to my school friends (The Kings Langley Lot) for supporting me at my first launch.

Lastly, Maria and Cordelia. I have never met you, but you have been an incredibly instrumental part of the Galentine's Day story. Huge thanks from Amy and from me xx